Henry Rogers

The Life and Character of John Howe

Henry Rogers

The Life and Character of John Howe

ISBN/EAN: 9783337400248

Printed in Europe, USA, Canada, Australia, Japan

Cover: Foto ©Raphael Reischuk / pixelio.de

More available books at **www.hansebooks.com**

THE
LIFE AND CHARACTER

OF

JOHN HOWE, M.A.

WITH AN

ANALYSIS OF HIS WRITINGS.

BY

HENRY ROGERS.

A NEW EDITION.

LONDON:

THE RELIGIOUS TRACT SOCIETY,

56, PATERNOSTER ROW; 65, ST. PAUL'S CHURCHYARD;
AND 164, PICCADILLY.

Butler & Tanner,
The Selwood Printing Works,
Frome, and London.

TO THE

MEMORY

OF THE BELOVED FRIEND

TO WHOM

THE FORMER EDITION OF THIS WORK

WAS INSCRIBED.

PREFACE.

The preface to the first edition of this work contained an apology for some too probable negligences and inaccuracies, which, from the unavoidable rapidity with which the work was written—though the subject and materials had been long meditated—might be found in the composition. The work has now received a careful revision, and it is hoped that many, if not all, such blemishes are removed. For the most part, however, the work is left as it was. It is true that twenty-five years cannot pass with any man, who in any measure "lives to learn," without producing changes of judgment and of taste; and possibly some of the passages in this work might have been expressed more concisely if they had been written now. I have indulged myself, however, in little more than verbal alterations, as it is easier to rebuild from the foundation than to alter a fabric in detail; such attempts seldom end in anything else than spoiling both the old and the new.

Omitting, for the reasons above assigned, the introductory paragraphs of the former preface, I retain only such portions as must be equally appropriate to every edition. I said,

a

"In the course of the work, I have, of course, been compelled to touch on many points which have often excited the utmost bitterness of party-spirit. In these cases, I can sincerely say, I have endeavoured to maintain a tone of historic impartiality. I should have felt myself utterly unworthy of being the biographer of Howe, had I not been emulous of imitating, in some humble measure, that calm, candid, dispassionate temper of mind for which he was so justly eminent.

"Howe was a nonconformist; I have endeavoured faithfully to represent his reasons for his nonconformity : but it has been infinitely far from my purpose to employ his name in subserviency to party purposes. To enlist *him*,—whose temper and spirit were so transcendently catholic; whose whole life was devoted to the cause of our common Christianity; and who abhorred all excess of party feeling, whether displayed by those with whom he agreed, or by those from whom he differed;— to enlist *him*, I say, in the mere strife of party, would, in my estimation, be a flagrant insult to his memory.

"I have not therefore made Howe's nonconformity a topic disproportionately prominent, or more so than the impartial history of his life demanded. I could not help feeling that the name and memory of such a man are the property, not of one denomination, but of the whole Christian church; and that, however strong the reasons which endear him to any one party, the reasons are still stronger which should endear him to all.

"To write the life of Howe with any mean, sectarian feeling, would, in my estimation, be as unutterably absurd, as to write the life of Cromwell merely to show that he was an

Independent, or that of Milton, to prove that he was a Baptist.

"I have only further to add, that no source of information to which I could possibly obtain access, whether in the shape of MSS. or printed books, has been neglected. The reader will see that research has not been in vain; many letters of Howe, and one or two other documents, have been recovered, as well as a considerable number of facts, not mentioned in Calamy's 'Life.'

"My cordial acknowledgments are due to the several gentlemen who have kindly answered inquiries, and contributed to my materials; more especially to Joshua Wilson, Esq., of the Inner Temple, justly distinguished for his minute and extensive knowledge of literary antiquities; to Jeremiah Wiffen, Esq., Librarian to the Duke of Bedford; to Dr. Williams, of Shrewsbury; to the Rev. Thomas Milner, of Northampton; to the Rev. R. Slate, of Preston; and to the trustees of Dr. Williams' Library, for the access they afforded me to the Baxter MSS."

It only remains to add, that I have omitted some irrelevant pages in the third chapter, the reasons for which will be found stated in the Appendix; that I have lightened some of the other chapters by omitting or abridging some of the extracts from the prefaces to Howe's various works, retaining only such portions as, like his letters and other documents, throw light upon his life and character. On the other hand, the critical remarks on his writings in Chapter XII. have been largely augmented and illustrated by brief extracts.

For a not uninteresting addition to the Appendix, containing letters of Howe hitherto unpublished, I am indebted to the courtesy of Mr. H. O. Coxe, Librarian of the Bodleian, and to the kindness of the Rev. James Turner, of Knutsford.

I am also indebted for friendly communications on some minute points in the memoir, received many years ago, from John Dove, Esq., of Leeds, and Frederick Brough, Esq., of London.

CONTENTS.

INTRODUCTORY CHAPTER.

The materials for Howe's Biography comparatively scanty—Causes of
this—Destruction of his MSS.—Probable reasons of his conduct—Chief
design of the present volume—Principal aspects under which Howe's
character is to be contemplated—Value of a certain species of biography
—This mode of presenting important truth illustrated by the structure
of the Scriptures   1

CHAPTER II.

FROM 1630 TO 1656.

Howe's family and connexions—Expulsion of his father from Loughborough, by Archbishop Laud—Causes of it—Retreats to Ireland, and
returns in consequence of the Rebellion—Account of young Howe's
studies at Oxford and Cambridge—Remarks on systematic Theology
—His catholic spirit early displayed—Account of his Ordination—
Settlement at Great Torrington—His ministerial success—State of his
opinions respecting Church Polity and Discipline—His marriage—
Account of his Fast-day services—Remarks   12

CHAPTER III.

FROM 1656 TO 1658.

Howe's first interview with Cromwell—Preaches at Whitehall—Cromwell
proposes that he should become his Chaplain—Howe's reluctance—
Scruples overcome—Motives which actuated Cromwell in the selection
of Howe—Remarks on the Protector's religious character—State of
religious parties—Letters of Howe to Baxter, published from the Baxter
MSS.—Howe's reluctance to continue at Whitehall—Grounds of it—
Manner in which he conducted himself during his connexion with Cromwell—Instances of his disinterestedness, integrity, and benevolence—
Reflections   27

CHAPTER IV.

FROM 1658 TO 1668.

Death of Cromwell—Howe still remains at Whitehall — Character of
Richard Cromwell—His deposition—Letter of Howe to Baxter on that
event—Howe returns to Torrington—Is informed against—Defends
himself successfully—Is ejected by the Act of Uniformity—Howe's interview with Dr. Wilkins—Reflections—A Citation against him — His
interview with Bishop Ward—Oxford oath—Howe's conduct on that
occasion—Letter to his brother-in-law—Reflections on Protestant persecution—Publishes " The Blessedness of the Righteous "   .   .   .   66

CHAPTER V.

FROM 1669 TO 1677.

Howe invited to become Chaplain to Lord Massarene, of Antrim Castle—
Accepts the situation—Removes with his family to Ireland—Probably
the happiest period of his life—Nature of his employments—Universal
respect he conciliated—Publishes his " Vanity of Man as Mortal "—
Circumstances in which it originated—Publishes his " Delighting in
God "—Reflections—Composes the first part of his " Living Temple "—
Is invited to the pastoral charge of a congregation in London—Self-
examination previous to leaving Antrim—Reflections—Removes his
family to London—King Charles's Indulgence—Remarks—Howe publishes the first part of his " Living Temple "   94

CHAPTER VI.

FROM 1677 TO 1678.

Andrew Marvell's defence of Howe against Thomas Danson's attack on
the treatise of " Divine Prescience "   117

CHAPTER VII.

FROM 1677 TO 1680.

Severities exercised upon the Nonconformists during this period— Howe's
earnest desire for an adjustment of the differences between the Church
and the Dissenters—The Popish Plot—Curious Interview with a certain
Nobleman—Howe's reply to Stillingfleet—Extracts—His expostulation
with Tillotson on account of his Sermon before the King—Another
attempt at Comprehension—Bill of Exclusion—Proceedings of the Parliament of 1680   133

PAGE

CHAPTER VIII.
FROM 1681 TO 1684.

Condition of the Nonconformists during this period—Howe's Meeting-house disturbed—Account of his Publications in 1681, 1682, and 1683—Preaches his Sermon on the Union of Protestants—Account of it—Letter of Consolation to Lady Russell—Reflections—Expostulatory Letter to Bishop Barlow 146

CHAPTER IX.
FROM 1685 TO 1690.

Conduct of Howe in Persecution—Is invited by Lord Wharton to accompany him in his Travels on the Continent—His Letter of Farewell to his Flock—Reflections—Settles at Utrecht—Mode of Life there—Correspondence with Lady Russell—Interview with Burnet—Is introduced to the Prince of Orange—Indulgence of James II.—Howe returns home—Conduct of the Nonconformists with respect to the designs of the Court—Howe's Interview with the King—Curious scene at Dr. Sherlock's—The Revolution of 1688—Howe's Address to the Prince of Orange—His Letter on behalf of the French Protestants—He publishes his "Case of the Dissenters Represented and Argued"—Act of Toleration passed—Howe's Address to the Conformists and Non-conformists on that event 167

CHAPTER X.
FROM 1690 TO 1703.

Disputes among the Nonconformists—Attempt to unite the Presbyterians and Congregationalists—"Heads of Agreement"—Agitation of the Antinomian Controversy—Circumstances which led to it—Dr. Crisp's Sermons—Howe's Sermons on the Carnality of Religious Contention—Letter to Mr. Spilsbury—Letters from the MSS. in Woburn Abbey—Letters from the Ayscough MSS. in the British Museum—Letters to Sir Charles and Lady Hoghton, and others—Controversy on "Occasional Conformity"—Principles on which Howe defended that practice . 206

CHAPTER XI.
FROM 1704 TO 1705.

Howe's last Illness—State of Mind—Death—Extract from his Will—His Person—Analysis of his Character 239

CHAPTER XII.

ANALYSIS OF HOWE'S WRITINGS.

Introductory Remarks—Howe's Posthumous Works —The Living Temple
—The Treatise on Delighting in God—The Blessedness of the Right-
eous—The Vanity of Man as Mortal—The Tractate on the Divine
Prescience—The Calm and Sober Inquiry into the Possibility of a
Trinity in the Godhead—The Redeemer's Tears wept over Lost Souls
—The Redeemer's Dominion over the Invisible World—Howe's Funeral
Sermons, and others occasional Discourses 273

APPENDIX.

I. A few particulars respecting Howe's Family and Descendants—II.
Calamy's account of the treatment of John Howe's father by Archbishop Laud — III. Extract from the Register at Cambridge — IV.
Remarks on Cromwell's Character—V. Outline of a Sermon preached
before Cromwell—VI. Letter to the Rev. Thomas Whitaker, of Leeds,
and extracts from a letter to Baxter—VII. Three hitherto unpublished
letters of Howe—VIII. Preface to John Chorlton's Funeral Sermon
for Henry Newcome—Dedication to the Third volume of Dr. Manton's
works 329

LIFE OF JOHN HOWE, M.A.

INTRODUCTORY CHAPTER.

THE MATERIALS FOR HOWE'S BIOGRAPHY COMPARATIVELY SCANTY—CAUSES OF THIS—
DESTRUCTION OF HIS MSS.—PROBABLE REASONS OF HIS CONDUCT—CHIEF DESIGN OF
THE PRESENT VOLUME—PRINCIPAL ASPECTS UNDER WHICH HOWE'S CHARACTER IS
TO BE CONTEMPLATED—VALUE OF A CERTAIN SPECIES OF BIOGRAPHY—THIS MODE
OF PRESENTING IMPORTANT TRUTH ILLUSTRATED BY THE STRUCTURE OF THE
SCRIPTURES.

I AM ambitious, I must confess, of rendering this book something more than a bare collection of facts and dates. Indeed, if a simple narrative had been my only object, so large a volume would have been quite unnecessary, since all that has reached us of the personal history of John Howe, might have been comprised within less than half the compass. The materials for his biography are far more scanty than is usual in the case of men, who have occupied stations so prominent, and taken a part in scenes so interesting.

That the world knows no more of him is, it is true, to be attributed to himself. If he had not in his last moments laid sacrilegious hands on the voluminous manuscripts which contained the history of his public and private life, there would have been nothing to lament and nothing to desire on this point. We should have possessed a work as delightfully minute as that of Baxter or Burnet, characterized by a freedom from prejudice which did not belong to the former of these writers, and a depth of reflection which could not be expected in the latter. If these manuscripts had been preserved, we should probably have known more of the history of religion in

B

Howe's time,—especially during the Protectorate of Cromwell,* the very interior of whose court he could have laid bare to us, —than can be obtained from any existing source. Intrinsically valuable as such information would have been, it would have derived an additional charm from the manner in which, we may fairly presume, it would have been conveyed to us; we should have had it from one who was never even suspected of partiality or prejudice; who was free alike from the meanness of the time-server, and the blind zeal of the partisan.

But these regrets are vain. The manuscripts in question were destroyed on his death-bed, by Howe's express desire. The account of this singular circumstance is still preserved in a letter from his son, Dr. George Howe, to his brother-in-law, the Rev. Obadiah Hughes, who had written to ask what manuscripts Howe had left behind him. The document announcing the mortifying fact, is here presented to the reader.

"Sir,—I am extremely concerned that some time before my honoured father's decease, I was utterly disabled to reap the advantage myself, and communicate it to his friends, of the large memorials he had collected of the material passages of his own life, and of the times wherein he lived, which he most industriously concealed till his last illness, when, having lost his speech, which I thought he would not recover, he surprisingly called me to him, and gave me a key, and ordered me to bring all the papers, (*which were stitched up in a multitude of small volumes,*) and made me solemnly promise him, notwithstanding all my reluctance, immediately to destroy them, which accordingly I did; and have left me no other of his writings but his short sermon notes, excepting some passages in the frontispiece of the Bible he used in his study, which I here transmit to you, and know it will be very acceptable. I am sorry I can give no further account, but that is a ' magnum in parvo,' etc. I am,

"Your sincerely affectionate Kinsman,
and humble Servant,
"George Howe."

---

* See at a subsequent page, some very curious letters of Howe, throwing considerable light on this subject, and first published in the former edition of the present work. The author was fortunate enough to discover them amongst the "Baxter MSS.," deposited in Dr. Williams's Library, Red Cross Street.

One feels almost tempted to regret that Howe should have recovered his speech at all, since he could find no better use for it.—His commands, however, were but too punctually obeyed, and it may be safely affirmed, that seldom has filial obedience been more exemplary, or cost a struggle more severe. Not a few would have been vehemently tempted to play the casuist on this occasion; and, if it did not imply some participation in the guilt of such conduct, I should heartily wish that Dr. George Howe had been of the number.

What might be Howe's motives for thus defrauding posterity of these important documents, it is vain to inquire. Perhaps it was charity; for he might think, that the reputation of some of the persons mentioned in his narrative would suffer more from his honesty than the world could be benefited by it. Perhaps it was modesty; for he might possibly suspect himself of some touch of vanity, in permitting such a voluminous account of himself to go forth to the world. Most men are content so long as they do not know but that they have a good motive for their conduct; it was sufficient to disquiet the sensitive conscience of Howe, if he only suspected there might be a bad one.

But though the materials for the biography of Howe are necessarily scanty; though it must be deficient in that minute particularity, which, in the estimation of triflers, is the great charm of this species of composition, and which, in the estimation of those who are not triflers, tends to relieve and enliven matter of a more grave and important character, there is still sufficient to render his life well worth writing. Many letters and two or three other documents have been reclaimed by the researches of the present writer, and are now presented to the public for the first time; * while almost every incident of his life that *has* come down to us is pregnant with instruction, because illustrative of character.

This being the case, enough is left for the main object of the present volume, which is rather to give a minute analysis of Howe's character and writings, than to furnish what, in fact, it would be hopeless to attempt,—a circumstantial account of

---

* 1836.

his life. His character, as reflected in his conduct and in his works, is, and must ever be to the Christian, but above all to the Christian minister,—a STUDY; a subject worthy of profound contemplation.

I cannot but avow my opinion,—an opinion formed after no very limited acquaintance with the lives and writings of eminent Christians,—that of the many whose memoirs are before the public, there is scarcely one characterized by excellence so various, or so great in its several kinds, as the subject of these pages; scarcely one who presents such an harmonious combination of all that is great, noble, and lovely in human character. I am well aware, indeed, that the several elements of excellence which entered into the composition of this extraordinary man, may, taken separately, be found in other men in equal, if not much larger measure; but the distinctive beauty of his character is that of combination and symmetrical relation of parts: so much so, that it is no paradox to affirm, that the very fullest development of which any single intellectual or moral quality might have been susceptible, and which in some other men, distinguished by marked inequality of character, might have been justly considered an excellence, would in his case have been a defect, because it would have impaired that rare harmony which now pervades the whole.

Without anticipating that more minute analysis of his character, which is reserved for a subsequent page, it may be allowed in this place to indicate the more important aspects under which it may be contemplated. It is true, that his intellectual qualities were of the highest order, and perhaps his aptitudes for abstract speculation have very seldom been much surpassed. It may be safely said, however, that there are other points of his character far more worthy of notice. It is the singular diversity and not less singular combination of *moral* excellence that chiefly renders him an object of such engaging interest. To use the scarcely hyperbolical language of his friend and coadjutor, who preached his funeral sermon, "it seemed as though he was intended by Heaven to be an inviting example of universal goodness."

None can peruse his writings without feeling that his mind was habitually filled with the contemplation of that peculiar but truly Divine character, that comprehensive and all-pervading excellence, the ultimate development of which, in those who embrace Christianity, is the design of all the doctrines it reveals, and of all the powerful motives by which it prompts to action. This *character* consists in the complete restoration of harmony between all the faculties of the soul; such a distribution and mutual subserviency of all the constituent principles of our nature, as shall secure the highest perfection of them all, and enable us uniformly and equably to sustain the various relations in which we stand to God, to ourselves, and to one another.

This *character*, an approximation to which is all that can be expected on earth, can be fully matured only under the influences of a far other clime; still it was the subject of Howe's habitual and intense contemplation. Plato himself never kindled with so intense a rapture over his beautiful visions of ideal virtue, as Howe, with a mind enlarged and purified by the gospel, dwelt on the lineaments of that image into which the Christian is gradually transformed as he gazes, "by the Spirit of the Lord." *

I have said that none can study his character, as reflected in his writings, without perceiving that he was enamoured of universal excellence; I add, that none can study it as illustrated by his *life*, without perceiving that he pursued it with all the strength and constancy of a predominant passion; in fact, with the same ardour with which others struggle for the realization of the darling schemes of a less noble ambition. His was no merely speculative admiration of holiness and virtue; it exerted, as all his conduct shows, an all-controlling practical influence over his whole life. His actions and motives were habitually determined by a reference to this standard. So much was this the case, that with him, most evidently, the various events of life, and its rapidly changing states of thought

---

* See his Treatise entitled, "The Blessedness of the Righteous," and on "Delighting in God," *passim*.

and feeling, were not *ends*, but only *means* to an end. Its joys and sorrows, its hopes and fears, its passions and pursuits, were but so many occasions for expanding and strengthening, in one or other respect, that *character*, which, when duly exercised by discipline and confirmed by habit, he knew, and exulted to know, should be perfected in heaven, and there receive the stamp of immortality. In a word, he was what so few Christians are, but what all ought to be, simply and habitually desirous of subjecting his whole nature to the dominion of the gospel. Time, with him, derived all its importance from a reference to eternity, and earth from its being a scene of discipline for heaven.

The progress, which a man so deeply imbued with a knowledge of Christian excellence and so deeply inspired with the love of it, would make, may be readily conceived, since he was constantly alive to what he *ought* to be, and as constantly on the watch to reduce that knowledge to practice. Between such a man and the generality of Christians, there must necessarily be as great a difference as there is between the well-instructed mechanician, who reflects on art the lights of science, and in whom theory and practice mutually aid and illustrate one another, and the rude artisan, who applies in a desultory manner, principles, of the comprehensiveness and beauty of which he knows little. The comparatively inexperienced seaman, and the dexterous pilot, may both reach the port; but the one will trim his sails to every variation of wind, and make his advantage of every breath that blows, while the other will often be driven from his course, and feel that when he reaches the haven at last, it has been without his energetic concurrence. There are many Christians, who, under the conduct of that gracious Spirit which influences the minds of *all* who are truly such, and under that various discipline of life which Divine Providence subordinates to the same great end, have made no mean attainments in holiness, and no slight approximation towards that character which is to be fully perfected in heaven; but who, nevertheless, have not been distinctly aware of the various stages of that transformation through which they have passed. As they look back upon considerable tracts of time, they can perceive a change; but they also perceive that while it was being effected, they were almost wholly passive: with them, the various exigencies of life, its trials and its temptations, unconsciously suggest, at the very time of their occurrence, the principles on which they are to act: but they cannot say that those principles are distinctly and habitually present to the mind, or that they live under a conscious readiness to employ them before the exigency which demands their exercise arrives. The consequence is, that many opportunities of this heavenly and spiritual discipline are lost altogether,—or worse than lost. This is especially the case with respect to those petty occurrences of life, which are erroneously supposed to be too insignificant to form a part of a grand course of moral discipline: though it is obvious that by their perpetual recurrence, and the subtle influence which their supposed insignificance gives them, they often exert a more powerful control over the formation of character, than events of far greater moment. On these trifling occasions, as they are absurdly thought, want of forethought and wakefulness of spirit often robs the Christian of the profit he might derive from them. There is many a man who is not ashamed to lose his temper or his patience, because his servant has been negligent, who, upon being visited by some great calamity, would probably display the resignation of a Christian.

Now John Howe evidently regarded all the events of life, great and little, as affording opportunities of discipline and self-improvement. He did not permit the occasion to suggest or not, as might happen, the principles on which he was to act, but held his principles in constant readiness to meet the occasion. If we may judge from the whole tenor of his life and writings, it is not more evident that the sculptor intends those little strokes and delicate touches by which his chisel operates on the marble, to contribute to the complete development of that image of beauty, which as yet only exists in his conception, than it is that Howe intended to subordinate to the purposes of moral discipline and improvement, all the occurrences of human life. Other characters often exhibit, though it may be in a different degree, the same results; it is to the difference in point of *design* and *systematic effort* between him and others, that we wish particularly to point the attention of the reader.

By thus habitually estimating the value and importance of present interests solely or principally from their relation to the things that are unseen and eternal, and by their ultimate bearing on Christian character, he attained that superiority to passion and prejudice, that elevation of mind, that disinterestedness and magnanimity, which were manifested throughout his life, and which so often and so deservedly excited the admiration of all parties.

Such, it appears to the present writer, is the principal aspect from which the character of this great man ought to be contemplated. He was one of the very few who, with a truly enlarged and sublime conception of that various excellence, that moral and spiritual beauty which the gospel of Jesus Christ is designed to form within us, devoted his whole powers and faculties, steadily and systematically, to the attainment of it.

A more full analysis of Howe's character will, as already intimated, be attempted after the biographical sketch of his life.

If any reader, who may be ignorant of Howe's character and writings, should think that I am dealing in indiscriminate and extravagant eulogy, I would simply ask him in what terms *he* would speak of one, of whom the following *facts* could be truly affirmed? Let it be supposed, for example, that it could be said of some individual, that throughout life he had friends in all parties, and enemies in none; that those who agreed in little else, concurred in loving and admiring him; that he conciliated the fullest esteem of those from whom he differed, without alienating the affection of those with whom he agreed; that he knew so well how to reconcile the claims of truth with the claims of charity, that he was firm without bigotry, and moderate without meanness; that in *his* hands even controversy wore an amiable spirit, and that while he never offended against his conscience by concealing his sentiments, he never offended against charity by expressing them: that this strange union of zeal and discretion, integrity and prudence, wisdom and love, was maintained throughout a long and eventful life, in an age of bitter faction, amidst scenes of civil tumult, and in situations the most difficult and perplexing;—what, I ask, would the reader say of such an individual? Would he not say that the panegyric which he had deemed extravagant, was no more than due to excellence so rare? An appeal to every record of the life of Howe, will show that all this, and more than this, can safely be affirmed of him.* If, indeed, I could forget to what all this variety of excellence was owing, or had represented it as the native growth of unaided human reason, then the language I have used might justly appear unwarrantably strong; but the light in which I regard him, is that of a signal trophy of the transforming power of the gospel,—an illustrious example of what it is, and of what it can effect. Thus viewed, his character well deserves the attentive contemplation of every Christian; and we may cease to wonder at the declaration of Robert Hall, which I once heard him make when conversing with him,—"that as a *minister*, he

---

* Even that splenetic party-writer, Anthony Wood, who seldom bestows a syllable of praise on those who differ from him, and not unfrequently traduces them in the grossest manner; who, if he had any charge to make, can hardly be suspected of suppressing it from an excess of charity, and least of all, *in favour of one of Oliver Cromwell's chaplains*, divests himself, when speaking of Howe, of all his customary bitterness. " He is a person of neat and polite parts, and not of that sour and unpleasant converse as most of his persuasion are : so moderate also and calm in those smaller matters under debate between the Church and his party, (which have been fiercely discussed by some very passionate among them,) that he hath not so much as once in writing (as I know of) interested himself in any busy and too fruitless quarrels of this kind, but hath applied himself wholly to more beneficial and useful publications on practical subjects; in which undertaking he hath acquitted himself so well, his books being penned in a fine, smooth, and natural style, (!) that they are much commended and read by very many conformists, who generally have him in good esteem." The commendation of his style is an excess of politeness, which certainly could not have been expected; and as far as truth is concerned, might have been dispensed with. For once, however, let it be said, that Anthony Wood erred on the side of candour. Such is the respect which distinguished excellence can sometimes extort even from that most hateful spirit,—equally hateful wheresoever displayed,—the spirit of party;

"——— illis carminibus stupens
Demittit atras bellua centiceps
Aures, et intorti capillis
Eumenidum recreantur angues."

had derived more benefit from John Howe, than from all other divines put together." *

The effect produced on the mind by the frequent and stedfast contemplation of rare excellence, embodied in real character, is familiar to all, and need not be insisted on. That it should produce such an effect, is a necessary result of the very structure of the human mind, which delights to contemplate abstract truths and principles, not in their naked form, but as exhibited in action, and, as Jeremy Taylor would say, "clothed in a body of circumstances." When thus presented to us, they are not only understood, but seen; not only coldly acknowledged to be true, but vividly felt to be so. The imagination aids the reason, and gives form, colouring, and substance, to what would otherwise be airy and unimpressive abstractions.

Amongst the manifold proofs which the Scripture affords of the superhuman wisdom which has presided over its composition, and which has adapted it in its very form and structure to the intellectual constitution of man, perhaps none is more striking than the *mode* in which it has exhibited its truths and doctrines. It is not after the method of a severe logic or a too solicitous philosophy. As a spirit of magnanimous wisdom will induce every true orator to sacrifice his peculiar habits and tastes of mind, if by so doing he can convey what he deems important truth, in a form more likely to impress the minds of his audience; so the Divine Author of the Scripture has condescended to impart its truths and doctrines, not in the form that might have been most worthy of His own infinite nature, but in that best suited to our limited capacities. They are developed in the course of a various and deeply interesting narrative, or embodied in the actions of those who taught them; especially in the life of HIM who was the "GREAT

---

* I was then quite a young man, and I have since, when pondering the seeming extravagance of the expression, thought whether the words might not be "more benefit than from any other divine." But I think the expression was as I have given it; and the words "as a minister" explain them. But, like many other utterances of fervid admiration which fall from the lips in conversation, the words need not be pressed to their full literal import. They do express, however, an intense sense of obligation.

EXAMPLE." Thus that very peculiarity, which a flippant and superficial philosophy has sometimes charged upon the Scriptures as a blemish, is in reality, and in the estimation of true wisdom, a Divine excellence. In any other form, the volume of revelation would have been absolutely unintelligible to the mass of mankind, and comparatively unprofitable to all.

Excellence thus exhibited is more clearly seen, more deeply remembered, more steadily fixed in the mind, simply because it is associated with the narrative in which it is unfolded, and the persons in whom it is developed. It resembles history, as told, not in the dry form of chronicle, but in the life-like forms of the painter or the sculptor.

As the mind dwells on such models day by day, it is led on from admiration to love, from love to imitation. The persons in whom such qualities reside, are familiarized and endeared to us : as we continue to gaze, a silent resemblance passes on our spirits. It is thus that the EXAMPLE OF CHRIST Himself operates on His disciples; His people are transformed into " the same image from glory to glory," though still " by the Spirit of the Lord;" and a similar influence, in a far inferior degree, results from the contemplation of the characters of those, who have diligently, though at the best most imperfectly, imitated HIM.

CHAPTER II.

FROM 1630 TO 1656.

HOWE'S FAMILY AND CONNEXIONS—EXPULSION OF HIS FATHER FROM LOUGHBOROUGH, BY ARCHBISHOP LAUD—CAUSES OF IT—RETREATS TO IRELAND, AND RETURNS IN CONSEQUENCE OF THE REBELLION—ACCOUNT OF YOUNG HOWE'S STUDIES AT OXFORD AND CAMBRIDGE — REMARKS ON SYSTEMATIC THEOLOGY — HIS CATHOLIC SPIRIT EARLY DISPLAYED—ACCOUNT OF HIS ORDINATION—SETTLEMENT AT GREAT TORRINGTON—HIS MINISTERIAL SUCCESS—STATE OF HIS OPINIONS RESPECTING CHURCH POLITY AND DISCIPLINE—HIS MARRIAGE—ACCOUNT OF HIS FAST-DAY SERVICES—REMARKS.

OF Howe's family little is known. When it has been said that his father was a clergyman, and a man of acknowledged piety and worth; that his mother was a woman of very uncommon abilities; and that his uncle, Obadiah Howe, was vicar of Boston, in Lincolnshire; almost all that is certainly known of his connexions is already told.*

Such matters, however, are of very little moment. The fame of John Howe is the fame of exalted genius and distinguished worth, and could receive but little augmentation from the proudest pedigree or the most illustrious parentage.

Of Howe's childhood as little is known as of his family. The character of his parents, however, fully justifies the belief that he was educated with care; that he must have been early im-

---

* A few particulars, some of them curious, will be found in the Appendix, No. I.

Mr. Brook, in his "Lives," tells us that the elder Howe was one of the "eminent ministers," who in their youth were pupils of Francis Higginson, of Leicester. Higginson left England for America in 1629.—*Lives of the Puritans,* vol. ii. p. 372.

Obadiah Howe was M.A., and in 1654, Minister of Horncastle; where he published "The Pagan Preacher Silenced," in answer to John Goodwin's work, entitled "The Pagan's Debt and Dowry." He died February 27, 1683.—*Nonconformist Memorial,* vol. ii. p. 443. An account of him will be found in Wood's "Athenæ Oxonienses."

bued with a reverence for religion, and nurtured in the strictest principles of morality.

He was born May 17, 1630, at Loughborough, Leicestershire; of which place his father was minister.

This excellent man had been appointed to this parish by Archbishop Laud, but was not destined to remain there long. His arrogant patron attached little less importance to the most insignificant ceremonies than to the weightiest articles of the decalogue. He could see no impropriety in sanctioning the Book of Sports, while he was ready to visit the omission of the most trifling ecclesiastical punctilios with relentless severity. As Howe's father, it seems, could not conscientiously comply with those ceremonies, which the zealous Archbishop persisted in introducing into public worship, and by which, whether he intended it or not, he was fast assimilating the Church of England to the Church of Rome, it was soon discovered that he was not the man for Loughborough, and he was consequently ejected. This can excite no surprise; for the Archbishop's whole little soul was immersed in pomp and ceremonial; he seemed to think the restoration of broken crucifixes and damaged paintings, amongst the most sacred cares of his high office, and busied himself as earnestly as if salvation depended on it, in adjusting the position of altars, in prescribing obeisances and grimaces, in regulating the attire of his clergy and in adding to it some of the frippery of the Romish ecclesiastical wardrobe, which had lain neglected ever since the Reformation.* Had the relentless spirit of persecution by which this man was animated been directed, however erroneously, against the gigantic abuses in the Church, he would at least have escaped our contempt, though not our abhorrence. But to see great power abused to such mean purposes, to see a

---

* As an example of the mummeries and antics Laud himself could enact in his public devotion, see particularly the account, in Rushworth, of the consecration of the church of St. Catherine's Creed. His diary is full of amusing traits of his superstitious character. His death alone redeems his memory from contempt. That he had considerable learning and no inconsiderable logical acuteness, is true; but they go but a little way to compensate for his abject superstition and his odious temper. Even Clarendon admits, while apologising for him as well as he can, that "men of all qualities and conditions, who agreed in nothing else," concurred somehow in their abhorrence of Laud.

tyrant with the soul of a deputy-master of ceremonies, is surely one of the most ridiculous as well as humiliating of spectacles.

On being expelled from Loughborough, Mr. Howe and his son sought a refuge in Ireland. After staying there for some time, the rebellion drove them home again. It is not known in what city or town they took up their residence; but it appears by no means to have proved a safe asylum. "It was besieged by the rebels," says Calamy, "several weeks together, though without success." *

On May 19, 1647, when seventeen years of age, young Howe was admitted as a sizar into Christ College, Cambridge. † Here he became acquainted with the celebrated Cudworth, and the not less celebrated Henry More, both of whom he admired and loved. With More he formed a close and most endeared friendship, which continued till the death of that great, though unequal and eccentric genius. To his intimacy with these men, Calamy attributes what he aptly calls that "platonic tincture," which "so remarkably runs through the writings which Howe drew up and published in his advanced years." But in all probability, he imbibed this "tincture," in a far greater degree, from the justly celebrated John Smith, of Queen's College, Cambridge, who was, at that time, in the height of his deserved reputation, and whom, in many points, Howe strongly resembled. ‡ This "platonic" taste, however, is not to be attributed solely, or even principally, to his intimacy with the admirers of "the great pagan theologue," as Howe himself styles him. Though he drank often at the streams, he drank still more frequently at the fountain. None can peruse his writings, without seeing in almost every page,

---

* Calamy, p. 7. See Appendix, No. II.

† Calamy does not mention the year, but it has been ascertained by a friend of the author, from an examination of the register at Cambridge. See the extract in the Appendix, No. II.

‡ "A mind which displays at once such vast intellectual powers, and such exalted spiritual endowments, may well excite our admiration; and leave us at a loss which most to wonder at,—that a man at thirty-five should have made such gigantic strides in literature; or that, having done so, he should at the same time have made such rapid attainments in the Divine life."—*Rev. John King, M.A., Preface to his Abridgment of the Select Discourses*, pp. 29, 30.

traces of his ardent admiration of Plato, and proofs that it was the admiration of a kindred mind. Though without the slightest pretensions to the eloquence of the renowned Greek, he bore no mean resemblance to him in loftiness of mind, sublimity of conception, and, above all, in intense admiration of all moral excellence.

Howe remained at Cambridge till 1648, when he took his degree of B.A.; after which he repaired to Oxford, where he took the same degree, January 18, 1649. He was at this time not quite nineteen years of age. *

Here he continued to prosecute his studies with unwearied industry. His extensive attainments, in conjunction with his exemplary piety, soon acquired him reputation in the University, and in due time he became Fellow of Magdalen College. On July 9, 1652, when only twenty-two years of age, he took the degree of M.A. By this time he had not only made great attainments in general knowledge, but had "conversed closely with the heathen moralists and philosophers; had perused many of the writings of the schoolmen, and several systems and commonplaces of the Reformers." Above all, he had compiled for himself a system of theology, from the sacred Scriptures alone: "a system which," as he was afterwards heard to say, "he had seldom seen occasion to alter."

It would be well if every theological student would, in this as in many other respects, imitate Howe's conduct. Systematic theology, as it has been too often compiled, has, it is true, been of questionable benefit. It has sometimes meant no more than an exposition of a certain set of dogmas, to the defence of which Scripture is by all means to be made sub-

---

* While at Cambridge his "most inward friend," as he forcibly, but quaintly expresses it, was Mr. Thomas Wadsworth, a student of Christ's College.—*Howe's Funeral Sermon for Mr. Richard Adams.*

At Oxford his most "inward friend" seems to have been Mr. Spilsbury, a truly excellent man; with whom, says Calamy, Howe "kept up a most intimate and endearing correspondence by letter, to his dying day." Two of his contemporaries at College, Theophilus Gale and Thomas Danson, attacked his admirable little treatise on the "Divine Prescience;" the former, in his great work, the "Court of the Gentiles;" the latter, in a most absurd and virulent little book, for which he received from the caustic Andrew Marvell a severe castigation.

servient, at whatever expense of honesty and sound criticism. Where Scripture speaks, or seems to speak, in consonance with the opinions of the system-maker, well and good; where it does not, various arts of critical discipline and violence have been employed to break its refractory spirit, or bend it to compliance. Forced and unnatural meanings of words, wildly conjectural emendations of the text, improbable readings, slender authorities, have in many cases been all eagerly resorted to for this unhallowed purpose; and the Bible has been made the most ridiculous book in the world, just to maintain systems inviolate, and to render theologians self-consistent. And even where the faults of systematizers have not been so glaring, they have not seldom incongruously blended Divine Truth and purely human speculation; the "head of gold" is to be supported with the "feet of clay." A thousand curious questions have been discussed, on which Scripture is silent, and to which it furnishes no solution; while the mysteries which it does reveal, instead of being received simply on the faith of the inspired testimony which has delivered them, have been defended and explained by the most presumptuous reasonings. In such pernicious systems, the boundaries between what is *certain*, because Divinely revealed, and what is *uncertain*, because merely deduced by the processes of a fallible logic, are obliterated; truth is disguised by its union with error, and error rendered plausible by its union with truth.

These faults, not seldom found in systems of theology, have been in course of correction as more just and comprehensive views of sacred criticism have diffused themselves. Having established the general truth of the inspired volume on its appropriate evidences, theologians saw that it would be more rational to suffer it to explain itself by the help of the grammar and lexicon, than to let their prejudices determine *a priori* to what doctrines it *must* be conformable; in a word, to seek, not some one system, out of the thousand which human ingenuity or folly might construct, with which it might be found to harmonize, but that system, whether apparently consistent or not, which develops itself by a fair and candid interpretation of the inspired page.

But though it is now generally admitted, that the meaning of Scripture is to be ascertained by a sound system of critical exposition, applied to it as a *whole,* and without any reference to the *apparent* (we are sure they cannot be *real*) discrepancies which may be discovered in the results, it by no means follows, that an attempt, to classify and arrange those results in a logical form, in a system of mutual connexion and dependence, may not be eminently beneficial to the professed theologian. The Bible, it is true, was not delivered to us in any such form, and for this might be assigned many satisfactory reasons, if this were the place for them. Amongst others, however, is this obvious one—that professed theologians were not the parties for whom the Bible was exclusively, or even principally intended. Nevertheless, it may be very useful for such men to attempt to reduce its contents to a scientific form. To adduce an obvious illustration : the human body is a most intricate machine, made up of a wondrous collection of organs, differing by every conceivable variety of form, texture, and structure. Now, the great *general* purposes for which this complicated mechanism was constructed, can be fulfilled only so long as the relations between its several parts remain unbroken; take it to pieces, dissolve intertexture of part with part, and the beauty and utility of the whole are gone. Still it may be very necessary for those whose direct office and professed object it is to study this wondrous piece of mechanism and to explore its manifold mysteries,—to contemplate its several parts in detail ; to consider separately, for instance, the systems of bones and muscles, of arteries and nerves. Much the same value attaches to that species of systematic theology for which we are here pleading ; that is, a coherent system of truth, elicited by an accurate analysis of the contents of revelation. The Bible, just as it is, is best adapted for the general *practical* purposes for which it was constructed : in other words, is most likely to be instructive and interesting to the generality of mankind, in that form in which Divine wisdom has presented it to us; but it may be useful to specific classes of men reverently and cautiously to analyse and classify its contents.

Nor let it be hastily supposed, that the compilation of such a system would be a very trifling matter; that it would merely require industry, or exclude the exercise of reason or judgment. It is much the contrary. Such a system would be not only valuable for its *results;* the mental discipline, the exercise of thought which it would involve, would form no inconsiderable benefit. Such a system, to be all that it ought to be, instead of consisting of a few extracts hastily made from the common version, would include a judicious selection of the several passages of the original Scriptures; statements of the authorities on which the text is sustained, where doubt is felt respecting it; a vindication of the translation adopted, on the principles of enlightened criticism; a distribution of topics in a logical and mutually dependent order; and, where it can be effected, the reconciliation of seeming discrepancies and inconsistencies. I cannot but repeat my conviction, that it would be well for every student in theology to imitate, in this matter, so far as leisure might permit, the conduct of John Howe.

Even at this early period of his life, Howe gave a striking proof, at once of his jealous regard for liberty, and of his exemption from the petty prejudices which disgraced the age. Those prejudices too often prevented Christian communion, even between those who agreed in every essential point of faith and practice. His conduct on the occasion referred to, shows that he had already adopted those just and comprehensive principles which continued throughout life to animate him, and which exhibit, in beautiful and impressive harmony, scrupulous conscientiousness in the maintenance of his own opinions, simply because *he* believed them to be true, with the most tender indulgence towards those who differed from him. While he would hold communion with none who would insist on his adopting opinions, however unimportant, in which he could not acquiesce, he was willing to extend it to all, whatever the diversity of their sentiments on minor matters, who recognised the cardinal principles of Christianity. No religious opinion or practice can be matter of indifference to the *individual,* because he is compelled to adopt or reject it as he conscientiously believes it to be true or false; but so long as all mutually claim and allow this liberty, no opinion which does not obviously strike at the vital truths of Christianity, should prevent *such communion between the members, and such interchange of offices between the ministers, of different religious parties,* as should serve to indicate their essential unity ; and show that though they are, in some respects, many, they are still, in higher and more important respects, one. If any party be unwilling to open its jealous pale, or to admit us to such catholic communion, that is not our fault. All that is demanded of each Christian is, that he should be found willing to reciprocate such communion with all who " love our Lord Jesus Christ in sincerity and in truth."

We are not, it is true, to disguise truth, or even connive at what we deem error, in order to attain this great object; but this point once secured, there is no barrier to inter-communion as is here contended for, which the genuine spirit of charity will not spurn down. These are the true principles of Christian toleration ; as *Christians*, it is not enough that we allow others to form their own opinions; we must seek to manifest our essential unity amidst circumstantial differences, by freely holding inter-communion with all, who do not demand as the condition, a surrender of our liberty or an abandonment of our principles. *

Such was the conduct of Howe on the occasion to which I now refer. It appears that Dr. Thomas Goodwin was the President of the College of which Howe was a Fellow, and had invited the scholars of his house to meet for Christian worship and fellowship. It excited some astonishment, that Howe, whose reputation was already great, both for talent and piety sought no admission into their society. After a time, the Doctor took an opportunity of expressing his surprise, that a

---

* These conclusions (although it is admitted that the work was not written precisely with this design) inevitably follow from Jeremy Taylor's theory of Toleration, as expounded in his beautiful treatise, entitled " The Liberty of Prophesying." It is true that he has not fully followed out his principles, but they clearly involve the consequences above stated. The *latitude* which he allowed to the *ministers*, none would deny to the other members of the Church of Christ.

person so universally " esteemed in the College, should not
avail himself of such a means of spiritual improvement." Upon
this, Howe frankly declared, "that the true and only reason
of his conduct was, that he understood they laid considerable
stress among them on some peculiarities which he loved not,
though he could give others their liberty to take their own
way, without censuring them or having unkind thoughts of
them; but that if they would admit him into their society upon
catholic terms, he would readily become one of them." To
this proposal Dr. Goodwin readily consented.

Howe could not at this time have been more than twenty-
two, or at most twenty-three years of age. At a period of life
thus early, did he show that a jealous self-respect and the most
scrupulous regard to liberty were by no means incompatible
with a magnanimous disregard of minor differences. He had
already attained the difficult medium between an excessive zeal
and a too compliant charity.

Very soon after taking his degree of M.A., he was ordained
at Winwick, in Lancashire, by Mr. Charles Herle, who was
chosen, at Dr. Twisse's death, Prolocutor of the Westminster
Assembly. In the parish of Winwick, there were several
chapelries, the officiating Ministers of which assisted at Howe's
ordination. It was with reference to this, that Howe used to
say, "there were few men whose ordination had been so truly
primitive as his, having been devoted to the sacred office by a
primitive Bishop and his officiating presbytery." Of Mr.
Herle, he uniformly spoke in terms of the highest respect. *

Some time after this, he was 'led by "an unexpected conduct of Divine Providence," as Calamy informs us, (though he
does not mention what it was,) to Great Torrington,† in Devon.
With this place, he seems to have ever after had associations
of the strongest and most delightful kind. Here some of the
happiest years of his life were spent; here his labours were

---

* Calamy, p. 13.
† Theophilus Powell was ejected from this place in 1646, by the Presbyterians.
He was succeeded by Lewis Stukely, an Independent; after whom came Howe.
—*Calamy,* p. 13. Mr. Stukely, it appears, removed to Exeter about 1650.—
Non. Con. Memorial. Vol. ii. p. 31.

rendered signally useful; and here he preached those discourses, the substance of which was afterwards embodied in
two of his most useful and impressive treatises,—his "Delighting in God," and his "Blessedness of the Righteous." Though
when he first went to Great Torrington, he could have been
little more than twenty-four years of age, his persuasive style
of preaching, and his still more persuasive example, soon secured him the esteem and affection of his people. A striking
proof of his influence over them, is afforded in the fact, (inci-
dentally mentioned in one of the letters I have extracted from
the Baxter MSS.,) that though, "at his first coming to Torrington," he found the church divided into two parties, he
succeeded, "through God's blessing on his endeavours," in
restoring union. The strong impression which he must have
produced in this place, is not less strikingly evinced in another
fact, recorded by Calamy. It appears that several inhabitants
of Torrington,* who had previously been members of the congregational church at Bideford, under the pastoral care of an
old College friend of Howe,† sought and obtained "their dis-
mission" from the church at Bideford, and returned to the
bosom of that which, for some unknown reason, they had left.

Various circumstances have led to the supposition, that
Howe was at this time a "congregationalist," in the ordinary
sense of that term. Indeed, Dr. Increase Mather, with whom
he became acquainted after his removal to London, and whom
he persuaded to supply his place at Torrington for some months
previous to his own return thither, expressly calls Howe
"Pastor of a congregational church at Great Torrington."
But I cannot think that, either at this or any other time,
Howe exactly symbolized with the congregationalists, or indeed with any other party. That his own opinions and practices, *especially in all matters of discipline,* more nearly coincided with those of·the congregationalists, than with those of
any other denomination, is most true; all this, however, is by

---

* It is not improbable that these formed one of the two parties into which
Howe tells us, in the above-mentioned letter, the church at Torrington was
divided.
† Mr. William Bartlett. *Calamy*, p. 14.

no means inconsistent with the supposition, (justified by many passages in his writings,) that on some of those minor points which were fiercely agitated in his day, he had no fixed opinion, and that even on some others, in which he had his *preferences*, he was willing (spiritual discipline, on which he always laid great stress, being duly enforced) to sacrifice his own inclinations, * if by so doing, he could promote the union of true Christians, and the welfare of the universal church; provided always, that the concessions required of him were not of such a *nature*, nor demanded in such a *manner*, as to trench upon the rights of conscience, which, with all his latitude, no man guarded with a stricter jealousy than he.

For example; though his ejectment is conclusive evidence that he could not belong to the Church of England, as actually established, I do not think that he would have objected to some such modified episcopacy, as would have contented Baxter or Archbishop Usher. That he was not, in several important points, *a presbyterian*, is plain, though Calamy, who was himself one, would apparently leave us to infer that he was. I do not think, however, that he would have objected to some slight modification of that form of church government, if he could thereby have promoted the union and prosperity of the Church.

As it was, the unyielding rigour with which uniformity was enforced, demanded far greater concessions than any with which even his catholicity of temper and latitude of sentiment could comply. Left, therefore, to follow his own judgment and inclinations, he became, *in fact*, much more of a congregationalist than anything else; indeed, as it respects his views of spiritual discipline, he was strictly so.

None but such a catholic and magnanimous spirit as his, could have carried into effect, (which he appears to have done

---

* See particularly some parts of his incomparable letter to a "Person of Quality," on Stillingfleet's sermon, in which, pleading for his more scrupulous brethren, he speaks of his own comparative "latitude" of opinion. See also the prefaces to his "Blessedness of the Righteous," and his "Delighting in God," as well as several other portions of his writings. Nor can the reader fail to perceive some curious instances of his latitude of opinion, or at least of his undecided state of mind on some minor points, in the subsequent letters (pp. 39–56).

most successfully,) the noble plan mentioned in one of the letters now for the first time published from the Baxter Manuscripts. This was no less than a "settled meeting of the neighbouring ministers of *different persuasions*," for mutual edification and fellowship. Great Torrington was the place at which they met. It seems to have been a miniature of that much more extensive scheme, which Baxter was throughout his life toiling in vain to carry into execution, and in which, as the subsequent letters will show, he more than once called Howe, unavailingly, to his aid.

While at Great Torrington, Howe formed a most endeared intimacy with Mr. George Hughes, of Plymouth, a minister distinguished no less by his piety and worth than by his learning and talents. The connexion between them was further cemented by Howe's marrying the daughter of his friend. This event took place March 1st, 1654.

The two friends maintained a weekly correspondence in Latin. A curious incident, connected with this correspondence, deserves mention. One day a fire broke out in Howe's house, which was providentially extinguished by a heavy shower of rain. On that very day Howe received a letter from his father-in-law, concluding with this remarkable expression, "Sit ros cœli super habitaculum vestrum;" "May the dew of heaven be upon your dwelling."

Of his indefatigable labours at Torrington, some idea may be formed from the singular account which Calamy received from Howe's own lips, of the services ordinarily held on the public fast-days, which in those times were by no means infrequent. "He told me," says his biographer, "it was upon those occasions his common way, to begin about nine in the morning, with a prayer for about a quarter of an hour, in which he begged a blessing on the work of the day; and afterwards read and expounded a chapter or psalm, in which he spent about three quarters of an hour; then prayed for about an hour, preached for another hour, and prayed for about half an hour. After this, he retired and took some little refreshment for about a quarter of an hour more, (the people singing all the while,) and then came again into the pulpit and prayed for another hour, and gave them another sermon of about an hour's length; and so concluded the service of the day, at about four of the clock in the evening, with about half an hour or more in prayer."

This extraordinary passage suggests two or three reflections.

On the supposition—a supposition which the whole history of the period amply justifies—that such long services were not peculiar to Torrington, but were the common practice of the day, religious enthusiasm must have been at least as prevalent as sober piety. Nothing but this will account for the outrage on common sense implied in the above-mentioned services, as well as in other practices of the age, not less extravagant. Considering the constitution of the human mind, and the average degree of attention which men are willing to pay, or even *capable* of paying, not merely to religious duties, but to *any* duties, we may rest assured that such prolonged devotions could not be generally beneficial. It may perhaps be said, that some few might possess minds so strenuous and piety so exalted, as to enable them to attend to such exercises without distraction. This will be admitted; but it will be replied, that the duration of public services should be regulated, not by the capacities of the *few*, but of the *many*; for whom, indeed, they are instituted. Nor is it to be forgotten, that to thousands they must have been not simply unprofitable, but prejudicial. The young, whose unwilling attendance could have been enforced only by parental authority—not to mention other classes whose compliance with the spirit of the age must have been wofully reluctant—could hardly retire from such scenes without feeling a strong repugnance to a style of religion which condemned them to such wearisome formalities: and to *such* it is certain they could have been nothing more.

Indeed, in this point of view, not only the practice now under consideration, but many other extravagances which marked the religious spirit of the age, must have been eminently injurious, as indeed everything must ultimately be which violates the dictates of nature and common sense, or which at best is adapted only to a transient and preternaturally excited condition of the human mind. It is true that when the mind *is* thus stimulated, it will often display an energy of character, which we shall in vain seek in its more ordinary and healthy state; it will not only submit to any constraints, but dare any dangers. It was thus with our Puritan ancestors; but that depth and energy of character could not last, any more than the unnatural fervour which burned in the bosom of the Crusaders: it became extinct in a single generation. If we would have institutions to be lasting, or to exert a permanent influence on human character, we must adapt them to human nature, not as it is found under exceptional conditions or circumstances, but as it exists in every country and in every age.

Ardent as was the piety of thousands of those times, there can be no doubt that to the severe, uninviting, and exaggerated forms of devotion to which it gave rise, is to be attributed not a little of the licentiousness and irreligion of the succeeding reign. The youth, be it recollected, of the Commonwealth, were men in the reign of the second Charles, and were but too likely to take revenge for the constrained austerity in which their childhood was passed, by a proportionate licence when they became their own masters.

We may rest assured that many a little Puritan, who had been tutored into precocious gravity and unnatural decorum under the grim discipline of his austere elders, was loudest in laugh and song, and wildest in folly and dissipation, when the violent constraint under which he had acted was removed. The transformation which passed on his outward man, when the closely-cropped hair expanded into fashionable luxuriance, and the plain, stiff, and closely fitted dress was exchanged for ruffles and embroidery, was not more striking than that transformation of mind, of which indeed it was the expression and the index.

But to return to the subject which immediately elicited these remarks. Is it at all probable that, except in very rare instances, the ministers (however well disposed the audiences might be) *could* render such services any other than most wearisome? It is just conceivable, indeed, that a man like Howe, distinguished by such exalted piety, by such rare qualifications as a preacher, and by a mind so singularly fertile and original, might sustain the attention of the more intelligent amongst his auditors,—making allowance, it may be, for a few oblivious moments; but it is quite appalling to think of the tedium of such a service conducted by men (and there must have been many such) of no more than ordinary piety, and less than ordinary abilities. If, under such circumstances, their congregations *did* maintain their attention, all that can be said is, that there was at least one text of Scripture on which it would have been superfluous for the ministers to expatiate,— " Patience " must already have had its " perfect work."

Even Calamy, a man of the very next generation, confesses that the above service was one "which few could have gone through without inexpressible weariness, both to themselves and their auditors." Well might the preachers of that day be called "painful" preachers; and surely their auditors were hardly less entitled to be called so too.

If it were desirable to spend so large a portion of any one day in public services, how easy was it to obviate all inconvenience! Why not divide the service into two or three? But here are seven unbroken hours of " preaching, prayer, and exposition," with the exception of one brief fifteen minutes. That little pause, moreover, was allowed only to the minister; the congregation, it appears, were *" singing all the while!"*

CHAPTER III.

HOWE'S FIRST INTERVIEW WITH CROMWELL—PREACHES AT WHITEHALL—CROMWELL
PROPOSES THAT HE SHOULD BECOME HIS CHAPLAIN—HOWE'S RELUCTANCE—SCRUPLES
OVERCOME—MOTIVES WHICH ACTUATED CROMWELL IN THE SELECTION OF HOWE—
REMARKS ON THE PROTECTOR'S PROBABLE MOTIVES—STATE OF RELIGIOUS PARTIES
—LETTERS OF HOWE TO BAXTER, PUBLISHED FROM THE BAXTER MSS.—HOWE'S
RELUCTANCE TO CONTINUE AT WHITEHALL—GROUNDS OF IT—MANNER IN WHICH HE
CONDUCTED HIMSELF DURING HIS CONNEXION WITH CROMWELL—INSTANCES OF HIS
DISINTERESTEDNESS, INTEGRITY, AND BENEVOLENCE—REFLECTIONS.

HOWE was no longer to remain the pastor of an obscure country town. One of those *trifling* incidents, as men are wont to consider them, but on which Divine Providence seems to delight in suspending the most important events, changed the whole tenor of his life, and placed him in a situation of peculiar difficulty and delicacy. At the close of 1656, or in the beginning of 1657,* some important business brought him to London. On the last sabbath of his stay there, (and it is worthy of remark that he had been already detained beyond the period he had assigned for his return,) curiosity led him to the Chapel at Whitehall. The name of the preacher who attracted him thither is unknown. Cromwell was present; and as "he generally had his eyes everywhere," (to use an expression of Calamy's, not very complimentary to Oliver's devotion,) the noble and expressive physiognomy of Howe soon fell under his notice. Nor was this to be wondered at; an observer of human nature, far less sagacious than Oliver Cromwell, might have discerned in the lineaments of Howe's face, the indications of no common character.

---

* The exact period cannot be ascertained. The first of the letters of Howe to Baxter, which will be found in this chapter, is dated March 12, 1657; it shows that he was then Cromwell's chaplain.

As soon as service was concluded, a messenger was despatched, to inform Howe that the Protector desired to speak with him. If surprised at such an extraordinary summons, he must have been still more surprised to hear the Protector (who had already concluded from his appearance that he was a minister) request him to "preach at Whitehall Chapel on the following Lord's day." Howe, whose modesty recoiled from a proposal, which other and more ambitious men would have exulted to embrace, endeavoured to excuse himself. Cromwell, with that peremptoriness which ever characterized him, told him "that it was in vain to think of excusing himself, for that he would take no denial." Howe, who did not know much of the arts of a courtier, and probably would have disdained to practise them, pleaded with much simplicity, that "he had despatched all the matters which had brought him to London, that he was now anxious to return home, and that he could not be detained longer without serious inconvenience." "Why," rejoined the pertinacious Oliver, "what great injury are you likely to sustain by tarrying a little longer?" To this Howe—who, in the spirit of a true pastor, considered the welfare of his flock far more important than the favour of the Protector, their esteem as his highest honour, and their love as his most grateful reward—replied, "that his people were very kind to him; that they would be uneasy at his protracted absence; that they would think he neglected them, and that he but little valued their esteem and affection." "Well," said Cromwell, "I will write to them myself, and will undertake the task of procuring them a suitable substitute." This he actually did; and Howe, being thus relieved from his scruples, or rather not knowing how to persist in opposing the wishes of one, whose requests, like those of kings, were little less than commands, consented to the Protector's proposal. But after he had preached once, Cromwell in the same manner insisted upon a second and a third sermon, and prevailed by the same pertinacity as before; and at length, after much private conversation, told him, that "nothing would serve him but Howe must remove to London and become his domestic chaplain, and that he would take care that the people at Torrington should be supplied to their satisfaction." Howe exerted himself to the utmost to escape such an unwelcome honour; but Cromwell, who, as Calamy truly observes, "could not bear to be contradicted after he had once got the power into his hands," would listen to no denial. * At length, therefore, Howe, who (as appears from a hitherto unpublished letter, which will be found in the following pages) was assured that he would have the means of doing great service to religion in the Protector's household, the whole arrangements of which were to be submitted to himself and a reverend colleague, † was induced to consent. He accordingly removed with his family to Whitehall, where some of his children were born.

We might conclude, *a priori*, that if Howe had been at liberty to shape his own destiny, such a situation would not have been precisely the one he would have selected; and the curious correspondence to which reference is made above, proves it. Indeed, such a post, even under far more inviting circumstances, would never have been his *choice;* for though he had practical talents, which eminently fitted him for important public functions, all the strongest tendencies of his nature were in favour of contemplative retirement and quiet usefulness. Such a situation, however, as that in which he now found himself, must for special reasons have been distasteful to him. The fanaticism which so strongly pervaded

---

* Palmer, in his "Nonconformist's Memorial," differs somewhat from Calamy in the account he gives of the *manner* of Howe's first introduction to the Protector. He says that his name had been already mentioned to Cromwell, when he appeared at Whitehall Chapel, and that he came there by appointment. But the account in other respects bears on its front marks of improbability, which render it very questionable. Thus it represents Howe, and the gentleman who mentioned his name to Cromwell, *as at that time* dividing the suffrages of the congregation at St. Saviour's, Dartmouth. If so, one would think that Howe must have been at least in a condition to accept such a situation, since he would hardly have been proposed candidate against his known wishes. Yet at this period, so far as any evidence can be obtained, nothing could be farther from his thoughts than removing from Torrington, where he had been recently settled, and where he was exceedingly happy. On what authority Palmer's account rests, I know not. Some parts of the account Palmer had received were so improbable, that I see he himself has suppressed them in his later editions. Calamy, from habits of personal intimacy with Howe, was more likely to know the truth.

† Who this colleague was I know not.

Oliver's court and household, must, as his conduct and his letters both testify, have been to the last degree repulsive to a mind so remarkably free from every tinge of enthusiasm, and so habitually under the dominion of judgment. Even the extravagances and eccentricities of *manner*, which marked so many of the religionists in the court of the Protector, must have excited strong disgust in one whose judgment was too sound and healthy not to dislike oddities of all kinds, but religious oddities above all others; these last being not only offensive to taste, but injurious to piety. Little knowledge of human nature is requisite to convince us, that the severe sense of propriety, the dignity, the almost majesty of manner, which all who knew Howe have concurred in attributing to him, must have been grievously offended at some of the scenes enacted in Oliver's household, and even in the Chapel at Whitehall.

But this is not all. The office to which he was thus reluctantly promoted, must, for other and still more important reasons, have soon become, as his letters show, intolerably irksome, because it must have been eminently difficult to discharge it at once with that discretion which was requisite to secure his own safety, and that integrity which alone would satisfy his conscience. If Howe had been a blind and unscrupulous partisan, who was prepared to concur with obsequious acquiescence in all that his patron and his patron's adherents might approve, and to purchase a character of devoted loyalty to one party, by a hatred and abuse of every other, his course, however degrading, would have been comparatively plain. But so far from this, there is incontrovertible historic evidence (which will be immediately laid before the reader) that he never concealed his opinions, however adverse to those of his best friends; that when he did not agree with Cromwell himself, he did not scruple to say so, and (if he thought the occasion of sufficient importance to warrant it) to say so even in public; and, lastly, that he never missed an opportunity of using his influence with the Protector and his government, in behalf of those who were opposed to both. That he did all this is well known; but that he should have been able to do it, without compromising principle or incurring censure, without giving irretrievable offence by his honesty or exciting suspicions by his moderation, argues an extraordinary union of integrity and discretion. His success, however, seems to have been complete; for not the faintest whisper of calumny has been breathed against him by any party.

All further remarks on the manner in which Howe conducted himself in this arduous situation, will be postponed, until the curious letters, which he addressed to Baxter during the period he remained at Whitehall, shall have been submitted to the reader. In the mean time, some observations on the motives which might have induced Cromwell to select such a man as Howe for his chaplain, may not be thought irrelevant; especially as they may enable the reader to form a more just idea of the peculiar arduousness and difficulty of the post Howe was now called to occupy.

For Cromwell's selection of a man like Howe it may appear, at first, difficult to account.

Of the character of the Protector it would be difficult, even under the most favourable circumstances, to form a just estimate. The special pleading of party-writers, who, by disguising or exaggerating facts, have obscured the very evidence on which a dispassionate opinion might be founded, has rendered it still more so. If we could believe the contradictory accounts of his admirers and enemies, we should alternately revere him as adorned with every virtue, and execrate him as disgraced with every crime. So singular has been his destiny, that his worst actions have found apologists; his best, traducers. *

What, it may be asked, may have been Cromwell's motives in so pertinaciously insisting that Howe should be his chaplain?

There is one solution, indeed, of the mystery, which, if admitted, must be satisfactory enough; it has been contended that Cromwell was a man of genuine piety. Those who adopt this opinion can, of course, have no difficulty in assigning

---

* See Appendix, No. IV.

adequate motives for his conduct on the present occasion. In
their estimation, he would have been led purely, or, at all
events, principally, by his spiritual sympathies ; he coveted
the solace and edification which the conversation and discourses of such a man as Howe could not but afford him. This
view, Howe's letters to Baxter, inserted in this chapter,
though not inconsistent with it, will hardly tend to confirm.

But whatever side men may take on this subject, we are not
without a sufficient clue to the motives which might lead the
Protector to select such a chaplain as John Howe.

Not to mention the admiration which the noble intellectual
and moral qualities of the man were calculated to inspire,—
and very many of them Cromwell was capable of fully appreciating,—the position in which the Protector stood to the
religious parties of the age, especially in the latter period of
his life, demanded that he should have at least some such
individuals in his court and household; and if he had found
twenty of equal piety, prudence, and reputation, he might have
rendered them all subservient, not only to the stability of his
government, but to the welfare of the country. Precisely the
same motives which impelled him to make the inflexible
Hale one of his judges, and Milton one of his secretaries,
would lead him to make such a man as Howe one of his
chaplains. Of the many proofs of astonishing sagacity which
Cromwell displayed, none is more striking than his happy
selection of public functionaries. "In nothing," justly observes Bishop Burnet, "was his good understanding better
discovered than in seeking out able and worthy men for all
employments." Whatever latitude and licence he might
occasionally allow himself, he was far too sagacious not to
perceive that the more upright, impartial, and discreet, were
the instruments by which he carried on his administration, and
the greater the reputation for piety, for integrity, or for
talents, they enjoyed,—the more stable would be his government and the more imperishable his renown, because both
would so far be identified with the prosperity and glory of a
grateful and exulting nation. The event has justified his
sagacity. The general splendour of his administration has

half obliterated, in ten thousand minds, the remembrance of his more questionable deeds. But his reasons for the choice of such a man as Howe, will more fully appear, if we consider the peculiar position in which the Protector stood to the religious factions of the age.

In the great convulsions which preceded the establishment of the Commonwealth, and in which the whole social and religious system seemed resolved back into its original elements, it required no great sagacity to "prognosticate" what Milton calls "an era of sects and schisms." The tremendous excitement which those stupendous events produced would alone account for such a result. We might from the history of all such periods be assured, that there would be no lack of system-mongers and theorists of every kind. The usual enthusiasm, too, which distinguishes periods of revolution, was the deeper and more extravagant, that it sprang immediately from religion —of all impulses the most powerful.

Nor was this the only cause of this strange fecundity of "sects and schisms:" the principles of toleration were now for the first time in extensive operation.

The liberty of opinion, like every other privilege, might of course be expected to be most abused when first enjoyed.* Accordingly, in the age of Cromwell, there were to be found religious parties of every conceivable variety of opinion. Not only were there those great and powerful bodies, constituting the bulk of the people, which still worshipped, as ardently as ever, their idol of "uniformity," and were only waiting for an opportunity of re-imposing the yoke which the nation had shaken off; but numberless others which (though it might be inconsistent with their principles or impossible from their insignificance and numerical weakness, to cherish any such ambitious designs) eyed each other with mutual jealousy, and struggled for precedence at court or for influence in the army. It was said of Athens, that you might walk through her streets,

---

* It is an axiom now with Englishmen, that whatever the wild forms of error to which freedom of opinion may give rise, it is a privilege, the advantages of which no such evils can ever countervail.

D

and more readily find gods than men: it might be said of the latter years of the Commonwealth, that there were almost as many sects as worshippers. There were those who were separated by the widest extremes, and those who differed only by the most invisible shades of opinion; those who stood "far as the poles asunder," and those who disputed with a still fiercer animosity about some inconsiderable point of ceremonial. From the Papists, who clung to every particle of ancient error, to the Seekers, who, relinquishing Scripture itself, wandered about, like the ancient Jews, "without ephod and without teraphim, without altar and without temple," having, as their name imported, all to *find;*—from those who brought their illuminations fresh every day from the seventh heavens, to those who still paid the most credulous and timid deference to tradition and antiquity;—from those who had been inspired with such plenary light as to dispense with all morality, and with whom, as they perversely expressed it, "all things were pure," to those who practised the most rigid austerities, there might be found every variety and gradation of religious opinion. Some would hear of nothing but an "inward light;" others clung, with all the tenacity of the ancient Jews, to "carnal ordinances and a worldly sanctuary;" here were sects all rapture and ecstasy, and there others all austerity and decorum; while some, just rising into notice, united, by a peculiar affinity for absurdities, the profound nonsense of the mystic with the solemn precision of the Pharisee. Here was one pouring out unintelligible rhapsodies; and there another waiting in more grateful silence the illapses of inspiration. There were some so *spiritual,* that the fine essence of their piety remained intact amidst the grossest immoralities; and there were others, to whom cheerful looks and an innocent jest were as any of the deadly sins. I say nothing of the still more astounding, though, happily, more rare species of religious extravagance; of Behmenists snuffing after "angels," and fighting with "fiery dragons;" or of naked prophets running through the streets, and most truly representing themselves as "signs and wonders."

Nor were the controversies on the subject of church government and discipline less various or edifying, than those which respected doctrine and practice. While some would have "all the Lord's people prophets," others would have no ministry at all: here was a party who would divest religion of everything external, and there another, who would make it entirely a matter of ceremony. Religion in one was à disembodied spirit, so purified and defecated, as no longer to need the aids of external worship; and in another, so gross and sensual, as to live only amidst outward observances.

Some, again, would intrust the magistrate with the "power of the keys," and others would clothe the priesthood with secular authority. While many were for stripping Cæsar even of his rightful purple, others were for throwing over it the sacerdotal vest. In not a few instances, the most opposite parties arrived at an edifying unanimity in errors; and, as if to prove that extremes meet, fifth-monarchy men proclaimed that "all dominion is founded in grace," as vehemently as Papists demanded for the Archpontiff the homage of the world. *

It is quite true that many of these sects were inconsiderable in point of numbers; while some of the wilder religious obliquities which characterized the day, were confined to a few individuals, and even expired with their authors. Nor is it improbable that, if we were to make due search in holes and corners, we might even now hunt out as many sects, and tatters of sects, as could be found at any period of the Commonwealth. But the difference between those times and our own is this; that the religious extravagancies, which at the formei period stalked abroad at mid-day and in the open streets, now, for the most part, dwell in obscurity and silence; and that while, in modern times, one monstrous folly suffices for one generation, † they sprang up in that age like mushrooms. Nor, if enthusiasm had not taken a far deeper and more general hold on the public mind that at any other period of our his-

---

* An amusing account of the principal sects of the age, though in some points, doubtless, exaggerated, will be found in Baxter's Life and Times. The inferior sects would, it seems, defy all classification.

† For example; the heresies of Regent's Square (1831).

tory, would even individual extravagancies have manifested themselves in the same *way*. It will be long, it is to be hoped, in the present day, before we shall see naked prophets running about the streets, or inspired women breaking trenchers in the face of parliament, "as a sign and testimony."

Though the various religious parties of the day must, in some measure, have neutralized each other's influence; their mutual jealousies, fierce disputes, and in many instances extravagant pretensions, must have given the Protector no little trouble. Indeed it may be safely said, that none but himself could have controlled and managed them; especially when we take into consideration the fact already stated, that there were large and powerful parties waiting only for an opportunity to re-assert their supremacy. Nor is it to be forgotten, that there were amongst these sects designing hypocrites, who, caring for no form of religion, and making their advantage of all, were not scrupulous by what means they promoted the objects of their ambition; while others, no better than heathens in their hearts, and smiling in secret contempt at all the religious extravagancies of the age, * sighed after a republic on the old Roman model, and consequently exulted in any discontents which might increase the perplexities or shake the government of the great usurper. As long as Cromwell retained the supreme power, he, they well knew, would frustrate every attempt to realize their visionary schemes.

Such was the conflict of opinion and interest amidst which the proud structure of the Commonwealth was reared; and we may well wonder that its builders, like those of Babel, were not compelled to abandon their design long before its completion; and to abandon it from the same cause—the confusion of tongues.

When we reflect on the discordant elements which Cromwell was compelled to render, not only consistent with his safety, but subservient to his power, exiled royalty itself need not have envied the Protector of England his unstable throne. Of

---

* See a remarkable passage in a letter of Howe to Baxter, inserted in the next chapter.

his empire, that of Æolus itself was only an expressive type. The *manner* in which he controlled those tempestuous elements, and even when almost universally distrusted and hated, maintained his supremacy unimpaired, strikes us with awe and wonder. Such achievements, though less dazzling to the eye, afford a far more conclusive proof of the vigour of his intellect, than the most renowned exploits of his arms. To poise and balance himself amidst so many disturbing forces, to make anarchy itself do fealty and homage at his throne, required a sagacity and dexterity to which history scarcely presents a parallel.

The main object of Cromwell's policy was to allow ascendancy to none of the many religious parties by which he was surrounded; but, at the same time, the amplest liberty—compatible with the maintenance of his power—to all. This was evidently his best policy, even if he had not been inclined to pursue it: to do him justice, however, (and this, indeed, constitutes the glory of his government,) his wishes in this respect fully coincided with his interests. He was, as Baxter himself admits, in a letter first published in this volume, a man "noted for a catholic spirit, desirous of the peace and unity of all the servants of Christ." *   To maintain this difficult policy of conciliation, his sagacity would instantly perceive, that he must not only have a variety of instruments, but select those instruments with the utmost care. In his transactions with such men as those who composed Baxter's party, for instance, he would naturally feel that those whom he employed must be men above suspicion. Distrusted himself, *they*, at all events, must be capable of inspiring confidence; and, as they would have to do with so many discordant parties, it was requisite that they should often be men distinguished no less by moderation than by integrity.

Could it escape the penetration of Cromwell, that considerable advantages might be derived from a man of Howe's integrity, temper, discretion, and, above all, unsullied reputation

---

* See the same sentiments still more strongly expressed in Baxter's Life and Times, in his last and revised judgment of Cromwell's character.

amongst all parties? That he was frequently employed in important missions by Cromwell, is mentioned by Calamy;* and that men like Baxter gladly availed themselves of such a means of communicating to the Protector their thoughts on public measures connected with religion, is evident from the documents inserted in this chapter.

Before proceeding to give any further account of Howe's conduct during the period of his residence at Whitehall, I shall lay before the reader the letters he addressed to Baxter from that place; as well as one from Baxter to him. The originals may be seen among the Baxter MSS., at the library in Red-cross-street.†

The passages on which some of the previous remarks have been founded, and which may call for further observation at a subsequent page, will, in order to prevent the necessity of repeated citation, be printed in italics.

The first of these letters is dated, "Whitehall, March 12, 57," and must have been written a very few months, perhaps weeks, after Howe's arrival there. It is full of the modesty and courtesy which were characteristic of him. It also shows the high estimation in which he held the character of Baxter, to whom such an epistle, from such a man, must have been not a little gratifying.

---

* "Whilst he continued in Cromwell's family he was often put upon secret services; but they were always honourable, and such as, according to the best of his judgment, might be to the benefit either of the public, or of particular persons. And when he was once engaged, he used all the diligence, and secrecy, and despatch he was able. Once, particularly, I have been informed, he was sent by Oliver in haste, upon a certain occasion, to Oxford, to a meeting of ministers there; and he made such despatch, that though he rode by St. Giles's church at twelve o'clock, he arrived at Oxford by a quarter after five. In short, he so behaved himself in this station, that he had the ill-will of as few as any man, and the particular friendship of the great Dr. Wilkins, who was afterwards Bishop of Chester, and several others, who were great supports of real piety and goodness in those times, and afterwards eminent under the legal establishment." —Calamy, p. 24, 25.

† As my distance from London prevented my collating the proofs of these letters in the former edition, with the original MSS., a few verbal errors of the copy (which had been hastily made) were retained. These a recent inspection of the MSS. has enabled me to correct. Here and there I have found it difficult to decipher a word, and I have been obliged to give it conjecturally. In the present edition I have adopted the modern orthography, and for perspicuity's sake have printed the contracted forms of certain words in full.

"*Reverend and worthily honoured Sir,*

"I should have been at some uncertainty, whether it were not more proper for me to make an apology for my forbearing the civility of such a paper salutation to you all this while, or [for] giving you the trouble of it now, had I not suffered myself to be determined by the direction of my honoured friend, the bearer. I have been often prompted to what I am now doing, by a deep sense of obligation, and an almost passionate desire of some communication with you; but my resolutions (even after I have put pen to paper and drawn out my mind into many lines) have been checked by a fear, lest I should be troublesome whilst I would appear thankful, and lest my desire of advantage to myself might seduce me into an attempt, either in itself unseemly, (as the affectation of so unequal an acquaintance might well be thought,) or ungrateful to you, whose constant employments I can easily think to be such as will not allow you to hold a correspondence with any one whose interest it may be to desire and seek it. Only that which with me made the balance more fairly to turn that way 'tis now cast, was the experience I had (and my obligation thereby, as well as encouragement) of your great friendship some years since, when, upon a journey, the providence of God afforded the opportunity of seeing you at Kidderminster, which, though I might well suppose you not to remember it, I ought not to forget.

"And truly, Sir, if that had not been, yet such advantage have your public labours (as I must ever acknowledge) afforded me, both in directing my thoughts in some important doctrines of the gospel, when I was much fluctuating, and not able with any satisfaction to acquiesce in the common dictates of modern writers, as also, through the mercy of God, in further awakening and quickening my heart in minding the concernments of another world; and such have your endearments been to me thereby, that I could not, without offering violence to myself, (as in a measure I have for some years,) have forborne to tell you how much I owe you upon that account.

"And, Sir, my heart's desire and prayer is, that your Lord would long continue and succeed your labours to the good of his church, and that the great acceptance they have found, and the visible blessing that hath attended them, may so far outweigh the discouragements you may have received from the opposition of prejudiced minds, that they may not prevail with you to desert any cause of God you have undertaken to plead for. And, indeed, Sir, it is my strong persuasion, that if your long expected new edition of your 'Aphorisms' may at length see the light, with what you have prepared about universal redemption, the entertainment they will find with this next generation, when they shall meet with unforestalled judgments, at liberty to receive things according to their evidence; and the influence those principles will have into preaching of the gospel,—which, according to the divinity that hath of late generally obtained, I know not how any could preach consistently, and without hesitance and regret, which cannot also, as we know by experience, but be derived into the minds of hearers, and so make at last but halting and unsettled Christians, and divert many from ever being such in truth,—will be such as will greatly overbalance the evil that may be occasioned by some men's present impatient reception of them. And however about *redemption*, Davenant and Amyrald may have spoken many of your thoughts, yet their books do not so commonly fall into the hands of young scholars (whose minds, while such, are least prepossessed, almost 'rasa tabula') as yours are like to do. I rejoice to hear what you are doing about confirmation; I doubt not but it will be a welcome endeavour to many that easily see the convenience, but understand not the warrant of such a course; and am much confident that if that practice shall appear to have as clearly a *necessitas præcepti* as *medii** to enforce it, the latter is so clear that we may hope it to obtain generally in a short time.

"Sir, I presume upon your pardon for this trouble. I shall only add to it thus much. I perceive you have understood, by my uncle,† where my present station is. ‡ If you can think it

---

* This, I apprehend, is explained in the foregoing sentence. I presume he means, that if confirmation could be as clearly shown to be a *duty enjoined* in the word of God, as he deemed it to be *useful and convenient*, the practice would soon become general. Further light is thrown upon this passage by the reasons which Baxter himself assigns for writing the work. "Many," says he, "called on me to try whether some more Scripture proofs might not be brought for it, that the *preceptive* as well as the *mediate* necessity might appear." It is proper to add, that this work is not intended to be, as many readers of the title would imagine, a defence of any *special* mode of confirmation, but of the *principle* on which some such rite is professedly founded; that all who are baptized in infancy should make a public profession of religion when they arrive at years of discretion, and that unless such profession be deemed satisfactory, they should not be admitted to the privileges of church membership.

† Mr. Upton, mentioned in Baxter's reply.   ‡ At Whitehall.

worth your while, I should be exceeding desirous to hear from you, what you apprehend to be the main evils.* of the nation that you judge capable of redress by the present Government ? —*what you conceive one in my station obliged to urge upon them as matter of duty in reference to the present state of the nation ? —and how far you conceive such a one obliged to bear a public testimony, against their neglects, in preaching,*† after use of private endeavours; supposing that either they be not convinced that the things persuaded to are duties to them, or else, if they be, that it be from time to time pretended that other affairs of greater moment are before them for the present; which being secret to themselves, as I cannot certainly know that they are so, so nor can I deny but they may be. Sir, the Lord knows I desire to understand my duty in matters of this nature; I hope he will then give me a heart not to decline it :‡ and if you will* please to contribute your help hereto, it may possibly be of public use; and will certainly (though that signify little) be exceeding acceptable and obliging to him, who must profess and subscribe himself,

"Rev. Sir,
"An affectionate honourer of you,
and your labours,
"JOHN HOWE.

"*Whitehall, March 12, 57.*"

The reply to this, the only letter of Baxter's in this correspondence which I have been able to recover, is dated April 3, 1658; seemingly, more than a year after the receipt of Howe's letter, unless, indeed, we may suppose the discrepancy accounted for by a reference to the *old style* of dating letters. § The contents, however, show that it was really a *reply*, and that no letter had passed in the mean time, whether the interval be

---

* With respect, of course, to the state of religion.

† Howe, no doubt, soon began to find, that the office of chaplain to Oliver and his household would be no sinecure to a conscientious man, who, like himself, could not wink at what he deemed inconsistencies of conduct or omissions of duty. *He*, at least, was in earnest—more so, probably, than his patron could wish. Had he simply lent his talents and his character to aid Cromwell's designs, and, while supporting his public influence, shut his eyes to the state of things at home, the Protector would probably have been quite satisfied.

‡ This part of Howe's letter is highly creditable to him. It is a noble exhibition of conscientiousness and integrity.

§ Nor does there seem any reason to doubt, that this is the true way of accounting for the apparently long interval between Howe's first letter and Baxter's

longer or shorter.   Baxter, at the commencement of the letter, admits, and apologizes for, his long silence.   When we consider the multiplicity and magnitude of his labours, the wonder is, that he should have found time for any epistolary correspondence at all. *

This letter—which is, in many respects, very characteristic of the writer—is now subjoined :

" TO THE REV. JOHN HOWE.

"*Dear Brother,*

"Upon this first opportunity, (though long after,) I return you thanks for your visit at Kidderminster, and another thanks for your kind and acceptable letters. You'll pardon me the omission of all compliments. Your famed worth, with your advantageous station for a serviceableness to these churches, doth make me very ready and glad of a correspondence with you. As to the subject of your letters, 1°, The cause of the delay of the (appearance) of my 'Aphorisms' hath been, that I thought totally to suppress them, and publish a small body of Theology in its stead; but multitudes of pressing businesses have so oft and long diverted me from so great a work, (begun,) that I am changing my thoughts, upon a despair of leisure. My pages of 'Redemption' have long lain by me; but I suppress them for Peace. †   2°, I would have you very tender and

---

reply. At this period, and up to 1753, there were two methods of computing the commencement of the year. The *historical* year began 1st of January; the *civil, ecclesiastical,* and *legal* year on the 25th of March. Supposing Howe and Baxter to use the latter method, as they very probably would, Howe's first letter, dated March 12, would have been written in 1657, and Baxter's reply, dated April 3, 1658, as truly in 1658, though little more than three weeks, instead of somewhat more than a twelvemonth, had elapsed between them.

* Yet, from the immense mass of letters (and but a small portion of his correspondence can have been preserved after all) in the Baxter MSS.—most of them, by the by, on controversial subjects, and many of them as large as a *modern pamphlet*—one would think that letter-writing was this great man's sole employment. That he could manage, amidst it all, to compose his eight score and eight publications, many of them quartos, besides prefaces and commendatory introductions innumerable, is a miracle of industry, which might well astonish even his voluminous contemporaries, and which will continue to puzzle a degenerate posterity.

† Printed Pearse in the former edition. I imagined it might refer to some expected piece of Dr. Thomas Pierce, or Peirce, (for the name is spelt in various ways,) one of the most vigorous of the innumerable opponents, with one or other of whom this Ishmael amongst controvertists was perpetually engaged. But on looking more carefully at the MS., I think the present is the most probable reading.

cautelous * in publishing any of the neglects of governors. A time there is for open plain dealing; but as long as the case is not palpable, desperate, and notorious, and you have leave to speak privately, that may suffice you. The welfare of the church, and peace of the nations, lies much on the public reputation of good magistrates, which, therefore, we should not diminish, but promote. 3°, *I would awaken your jealousy to a careful (but very secret and silent) observance of the infidels and Papists, who are very high and busy, under several garbs, especially of Seekers, Vanists, Behmenists.* Should they infest our vitals, or get into the saddle, where are we then ——? 4°, The Lord Protector is noted as a man of a catholic spirit, desirous of the unity and peace of all the servants of Christ. We desire nothing in the world (at home) so much as the exercise and success of such a disposition: but more is to be done for union and peace. Would he but, 1°, take some healing principles into his own consideration; 2°, and, when he is satisfied in them, expose them to one or two leading men of each party, (Episcopalian, Presbyterian, Congregational, Erastian, Anabaptist,) and privately feel them, and get them to a consent; † 3°, and then let · them be printed, to see how they will relish, (with the reasons annexed;) 4°, and then let a free-chosen assembly be called to agree upon them,—he would exceedingly oblige, and endear all the nations to him; and I am confident as I live, that, (by God's blessing,) he may happily accomplish so much of this work, if he be willing, as shall settle us in much peace, and prevent and heal abundance of our distempers: for, 1°, I dare undertake to produce such principles as may do it; 2°, and his interest (supposing our general preparation, by a weariness of divisions) may well bring them (as far as aforesaid) into association.

"Because Mr. Upton told me that you desired a correspondence with me, in order to this business, (and nothing in the world belonging to these nations sits nearer my heart,) I have adventured to inclose these three pages, ‡ which will acquaint

---

* This illustrates the old adage, that "those who look on see better than those who are engaged in the game;" for Baxter was not always quite so "cautelous" as he here recommends his friend to be.

† "Comprehension," was Baxter's favourite and long-cherished project. His temperament, we know, was sanguine. If we had no other proof, however, the above passage would be sufficient. What else could sustain the hope, that, in the then circumstances of the nation, these heterogeneous parties could be made to coalesce? by what spiritual alchemy did he expect to effect it?

‡ This was one of several proposals for a " comprehension," which Baxter, at different periods, laid before the Protector's chaplains. Some remarks on these,

you with the healing principles, though a more exact digesting
and wording of them is necessary. One was intended for some
Parliament men, for their satisfaction, but never showed them.
Another was in answer to a reverend brother near you, who,
being asked by me to write down all that he judged of necessity for the Presbyterians to grant to the Congregational party
for unity sake, did write down only the words mentioned in
Micah vi. 8. So that we are fully agreed if men be willing;
(and yet more may be done.) The third is a form of agreement to be subscribed by associations of godly men, of different
judgments; containing so few things and plain, as all may
agree in that are fit for our communion. Somewhat more I
shall venture to say to the rulers in my treatise of confirmation,
if God will, which is about a fortnight ago finished. It's a
fearful case, that godly ministers should be so bad that all this
ado should be necessary to our healing, and all will not do
without the magistrate. The Lord require not this at our
hands. I have proposed nothing but what I am confident all
parties may yield to, without crossing their principles, if they
will. Sir, I commit these things to your consideration, remaining

" Your unworthy Brother,

"*April 3, 1658.*"   " RI. BAXTER.

" I pray you persuade men not to despise those they call
Royalists and Episcopalians, either because they are now under
them, or because of contrariety of worldly interests; for these
things signify less than carnal hearts imagine : and who knows
what a day (and a righteous God) may bring forth ? " *

The next letter of Howe's is dated Whitehall, April 13,
1658, and is almost wholly taken up with the proposed plan
for " comprehension," mentioned at the close of Baxter's
letter.

" TO THE REV. RICHARD BAXTER.

" *Reverend Sir,*

"I have with much gladness and satisfaction received
and perused your treatise, with the inclosed papers. I dare not

---

his praiseworthy, though, under the circumstances, futile efforts, will be found
at a subsequent page.

* This postscript indicates the high opinion Baxter entertained of the
moderation and liberality of his correspondent. To what other member of Oliver's
household would he have thought it worth while to prefer such a request as this ?

further press the first thing I mentioned in my former.* And do most heartily thank you for your advice as to the second. †
That which you next mention hath been much in my *fears,* ‡
and the next to that (which your papers have referred to) as much in my *desires,* § since I came to have any understanding and consideration of the public affairs of the church of Christ. As to this last, but a few days before yours came to my hands (upon occasion of the presentation of the articles of the Essex association to his Highness, in order to the obtaining an approbation from him,) and his committing yours to my perusal, I made such a motion to him that he would please once for all to invite by some public declaration, the godly ministers of the several counties and of several parties, to the work of associating upon such common principles as might be found tending to general good, and not cross to the private opinions of the several parties; which was a thing the Essex articles pretended to, but, to my apprehension, did not attain. He expressed a great willingness thereto, might he but see anything in writing, that upon consideration he could judge likely to serve such a purpose. Your papers I reckon came very seasonably upon that account. Only before I offer any of them to his view, I thought it meet to advise with you. 1°, whether it may not be a more hopeful course to attempt first the reconciling only of the two middle parties, Presbyterian and Congregational? inasmuch as the extreme parties would be so much startled at the mention of an union with one another (as Anabaptists with Episcopalians, yea, or with Presbyterians) that it might possibly blast the design in its very beginning: but if those two other parties could be brought together first, endeavours might afterwards be used for drawing in the rest (probably with more success); and therefore whether accordingly it were not best to present to his Highness only what might serve that end? ‖ 2°, Whether it were not very ex-

---

* The reader will recollect that Howe had urged on Baxter a republication of his "Aphorisms."

† That is, as to the conduct he should pursue with respect to the before-mentioned "neglects of governors."

‡ The movements of the several religious parties, which Baxter in the preceding letter advises him so narrowly to watch.

§ He alludes to the last topic of Baxter's letter, "comprehension."

‖ This letter strikingly exhibits certain points of difference between Howe and Baxter. Both possessed a large and catholic spirit; both pursued with equal ardour the welfare of the Christian church: but Howe united with all this a coolness of judgment, a discreet and cautious spirit, which could not

pedient that you did (ere anything be further done) drive the business to an issue with that reverend person you have been treating with, that, if he be satisfied, his concurrence herein may be obtained, and help in presenting and explicating things to his Highness for his satisfaction; because if he be a person of interest with his Highness, (as I guess him to be,) it is likely he will .be consulted with, at least will hear something about the business before it comes into act, and so might possibly (being unsatisfied) hinder what otherwise he might greatly help. *   Sir, out of a real fear, lest so excellent a work should be spoiled in the managing, I shall wait to hear further from you about these things, and in the meantime, remain,

" Sir,

" Yours in sincere affection and observance,

" JOHN HOWE.

" *Whitehall, April* 13, 1658.

" Sir, be pleased to underwrite to your subscription of future letters thus :—To be left with Mr. Edward Raddon, at the letter-office, in the Poultry, to be conveyed," &c. †

In the next letter, dated May 8, 1658, we find Howe still on the same subject.

" TO THE REVEREND RICHARD BAXTER.

" *Reverend and dear Sir,*

"The occasion of my so long silence hath been the difficulty of Mr. Nye's and my meeting together; he having been at sometimes out of town, and myself at others, ever since

---

consist with the sanguine temperament of Baxter, and which are indeed rarely conjoined with so much integrity and so much benevolence as Howe possessed. He saw at once the hopelessness of the scheme as proposed by Baxter, but had the object too sincerely at heart to abandon the attempt altogether.

* In this part of his letter Howe shows not only his discretion, but his superiority to mean and petty jealousies. The "reverend person" to whom he alludes, was, as it appears by the subsequent letters, Mr. Nye. Howe was willing to relinquish the honour of being the sole or even the principal party intrusted with the management of this affair. So that the thing were done, he cared not by whom.

† What might be Howe's motives for requesting his correspondent (whose previous letters were directed to Whitehall) to send his communications by this circuitous route, it is in vain to inquire. One might conjecture that possibly some persons, jealous of his correspondence with Baxter, and thinking that it might be as well to learn what was its import, had been tampering with the seal of former letters.

yours came to my hands, until Monday last, when I had the opportunity of some discourse with him, which I purposed to have given you an account of by the Thursday's post, but the (to me) sudden news of a fast to be kept here next day, diverted me.

"I judged it necessary to treat with him about what we have in hand, as easily foreseeing so public a business of that nature was not likely to be brought to pass but he would either be consulted with (which I thought most probable) or at least would some way hear of it, and if he disliked, hinder it. Two of your papers he perused, that you sent up last, and that which is drawn into the form of an agreement. In your letter he disliked what you lay down, or rather what he thinks you intend, as descriptive of visible believers, namely, a credible profession of faith and holiness ; and said he was confident you intended by profession, something in *opposition* to such a deeper discovery as he should think necessary, and that there would never be an agreement about that matter. Also he expressed a dislike (much according to what you intimated in your last) of an association so formed by a covenant or engagement to such and such practices ; for he said, such things as you therein engage to practise, were either duties before or not ; if they were, 'tis unnecessary ; if not, he was born free, and why should he come under bonds ? fearing (as he said) a reproachful ejection out of such communion, if there should not be a compliance in all things. To which my thoughts were that it was no unnecessary thing to engage to what was duty before, except all renewing of our covenant with God were unnecessary ; and for his fear, etc., I propounded that this might be put into the agreement, that no person should be liable to ejection for any such principles or practices, as he or any were known to be of at their admission. In fine, he professed a willingness to promote an Association, to be founded only on the fourth article of your practical agreement, and that all differences and further overtures for agreement be left unto debate after such an association should be entered, and that he could yield so far, in order to accommodation, as was expressed in a paper presented to the committee for accommodation of Lords and Commons. Which paper he said you knew, and desired me to inquire of your thoughts concerning it. The paper you will find at the thirtieth page of the last part of that book, entitled "The Grand Debate," if you have it by you. I desired him to give his sense of the whole business in writing, lest I should misrepresent him, but that I could not obtain.　But I think this is a true sum of what I had from him.

"Sir, I shall wait for your further directions, only my present thoughts are, that if his offered help be accepted for procuring of such a general association as was before mentioned, the other practicals in your paper will be found (as to the main of each) of so evident necessity, that they will, by recommendation, easily obtain throughout the whole.　More I have not to add but that I am, Sir,

"Yours most affectionately,

"*May 5th*, 58.　　　　　　　　　　　　　"JOHN HOWE.

"*To my reverend friend,*
　"*Mr. Richard Baxter,*
　　"*Minister of the Gospel, Kidderminster.*"

On the two last letters, I have to make a few remarks.　If the representation given in a preceding page, of the state of religious parties be correct, it seems wonderful that men like Baxter and Howe should have laboured in the hopeless attempt at uniting even the principal of them.　But "comprehension," as it was called, or an union of all the considerable parties of the church, based on the admission of the fundamental doctrines of Christianity, had been, for many years, a darling scheme of Baxter's.　Though this great man loved his prejudices much, it is but just to say, that he loved charity and peace still more. Howe was a man of a spirit yet more catholic.　Provided liberty of conscience in indifferent matters were insured to each party, he would have freely held communion with all who did not deny the essential doctrines of the gospel.

Such a "comprehension," or rather "inter-communion," between both ministers and people of different denominations, is what the church of Christ sighs for.　It would prove her members to be truly one, far more conclusively than could the exactest external uniformity; for such an union would carry the evidence of its reality with it.　Unlike those kinds of union which have hitherto contented the Christian church, it would not *depend* on party-prejudices, but exist *in defiance* of them. To feel ourselves one with those who differ from us, requires and proves the existence of an ardent charity: to be one with our own party, demonstrates, at best, only our participation in the opinions of others, and frequently no more than a participation in their prejudices.

Such an union as that for which Baxter and Howe panted, awaits the gradual growth of a more expansive spirit of charity throughout the Christian church : it must be the *effect* of love, but cannot *precede* it. In the time of the Commonwealth, the animosities between religious parties were evidently far too strong to admit any hope of attaining this object; nor is the period yet arrived at which any such sublime theory can be realized.

The present letters, however, serve to show, with what single-minded purpose, with what exalted charity, these great men laboured in this thankless office. *

---

* I do not know any part of the volume in which I can more appropriately introduce the following document of Howe which I found, in his own hand-writing, amongst the Baxter MSS. It appears to have been the copy of some paper, drawn up by him at the command of the Protector, during his residence at Whitehall. The latter part of it is deeply interesting, and shows that he had lost nothing of that healing and peaceful spirit which induced him, when at Torrington, to form a " settled meeting " of the ministers of different persuasions, and which animates the preceding letters on the subject of a " comprehension."

" That it must be acknowledged, God hath blessed this nation with great plenty and liberty of gospel preaching beyond what it hath enjoyed in former times.

" That it is yet to be observed and lamented, that the gospel hath not a success proportionable thereto.

" That a more general conversion of souls throughout the land cannot but be a thing most desirable to every upright and honest heart, both as a pledge of God's continued presence among us, and as the great end (as it is to be hoped) of all the salvations he hath wrought for us.

" That however the Spirit of God is acknowledged most free in all its operations upon the souls of men, as ' the wind that bloweth where it listeth ; ' yet, since it is its wonted course to work by means, it cannot but be much the concernment of them who, by their calling, are more especially obliged to intend the conversion of souls, to take heed lest they be wanting in any such endeavours as the Lord may probably bless and prosper to that end.

" That the public preaching of the gospel is to be confessed an ordinance of God of great necessity and usefulness in order thereunto.

" That it is yet to be hoped, it might prove a great furtherance to the success of the gospel, if they who are appointed to the work of public preaching, did also (within their respective precincts) use other more private endeavours with their hearers, (such as shall admit thereof,) instructing them in the things of God they are ignorant of ; pressing upon them what they know ; inquiring into the state of their souls ; and applying themselves to them accordingly.

" That it cannot but seem probable, that many ignorant hearers, not so well capable of understanding a continued [continuous] and transient discourse, might yet, by a way of private and familiar interlocution, be brought to some

E

But to return to the correspondence.

The next letter of Howe, dated Whitehall, May 25, is inscribed by an unknown hand, to Mr. Vines. If really addressed to that person, it is impossible to tell what was the subject of

---

knowledge of the doctrines of the gospel they are yet unacquainted with ; and that many inattentive hearers (who regard not often what is spoken to them from the pulpit, though of weightiest concernment to their souls) would yet be obliged to attention unto such a discourse wherein themselves are to bear a part.

" That, upon the account of the public maintenance such persons in the ministry enjoy for their work's sake, they are necessarily obliged, in justice and equity, to make it their business to seek the good of souls, and spend their time and strength herein ; having an universal care (as much as in them lies) of the people among whom they are placed.

" That, however this infer not an obligation upon them of dispensing unto *any*, such privileges or ordinances as they are not in a present capacity for: yet it cannot but be obliging [on] them not to neglect any necessary endeavours for the good of their souls, and by which they may be instrumental to help them into that capacity for more peculiar ordinances they are yet short of.

" That, therefore, the ministers of the gospel within this nation, as they would approve themselves persons seriously intending the honour of God and saving of souls, be exhorted to give all diligence for the fulfilling of their ministry. And that besides their constant work in public preaching, they design some time from week to week, for visiting of families within their several charges, or otherwise conferring with particular persons (to whom their labours in this kind shall be acceptable,) about the state of their souls, and the concernments of another world ; and that, (where either the numerousness or averseness of their people do not render it impossible to them,) they labour to be acquainted with the spiritual states of all under their charge, and accordingly to instruct, warn, exhort, or comfort them, as the case shall require. Futhermore,

" That the people be exhorted to accept and improve their offered help and assistance herein.

" And that, whereas the present differences in judgment and practice among the professors and preachers of the gospel, about some circumstantial matters relating to church order and discipline, together with their too visible distances and estrangements from each other upon that account, are so apparently obstructive to the progress of religion and conversion of souls, (through the scandal and offence that arises hereby unto many :) the godly ministers be invited to maintain (as far as possible) a Christian and brotherly communion with each other. And to that end, that they hold frequent meetings together, within convenient circuits, for the amicable debating of all the things wherein they differ, and the strengthening one another's hands in the things wherein they agree ; the repressing the growing errors of the times, and carrying on (with as much unanimity and consent as may be) the great work they are engaged in. And finally,

" That all lawful protection and encouragement be promised them, while they are thus faithfully active (within their spheres and in the things that concern their calling,) for the honour of God and the good of souls.

" JOHN HOWE."

I need not add, that this document fully shows that the principles of toleration were extensively understood, and must have been, also, extensively recognised and acted on by the Protector's government.

the conversation with Mr. Nye referred to in the commencement of the letter; but if, as seems most probable, the letter
was addressed to Baxter, the passage in question is explained
by the preceding letter. The writer, however, soon hastens to
another, and to us, more interesting matter—his repugnance
to the thought of remaining any longer at Whitehall. The
whole is worthy of an attentive perusal.

" Reverend Sir,

"I cannot yet meet with an opportunity for further
discourse with Mr. Nye, nor do I hope for much success in any
further treaty with him; I perceive so steady a resolution to
measure all endeavours of this kind by their subservience to
the advantage of one party. I resolve, therefore, to make
trial what his Highness will do, as speedily as I can. *My time
will not serve me long; for I think I shall be constrained in
conscience (all things considered) to return, ere long, to my former station. I left it, I think, upon very fair terms. For, first,
when I settled there, I expressly reserved to myself a liberty of
removing, if the providence of God should invite me to a condition of more serviceableness anywhere else,—which liberty I
reckon I could not have parted with if I would, unless I could
have exempted myself from God's dominion. My call hither,
was a work I thought very considerable;—the setting up of the
worship and discipline of Christ in this family, wherein I was
to have joined with another, called upon the same account;—
I had made, as I supposed, a competent provision for the place
I left. But now at once I see the designed work here hopelessly
laid aside. We affect here to live in so loose a way,* that a
man cannot fix upon any certain charge to carry towards them*

---

* This passage is explained by a sentence at the close of the letter. He there
cautions his correspondent not to disclose too freely "the disorderliness of
Cromwell's household, as to the matters of religion and God's worship." This
makes it evident that the above words, "so loose a way," were not intended to
imply, as they ordinarily would in our times, any licentiousness or immorality.
The gravity and almost austerity of Cromwell's manners, and the severe propriety which ever characterized his court, are well known; nor have any but
his most unprincipled traducers, ventured to say anything to the contrary. Had
he kept the more subtle and spiritual vices of the human heart, such as ambition and pride, in the same severe subjection as those of animal nature, history
would have had little but what was grateful to say of him.
It is a conclusive proof of the propriety of manners which must have pervaded
Cromwell's court, that such men as Howe could stay there. Had it been like
that of the second Charles, he would not have applied to his friend Baxter to
know whether he should remove or not?

as a minister of Christ should : so that it were as hopeful a course to preach in a market, or in any assembly met by chance, as here. In the meantime, the people I left are breaking into parties; cannot meet in any one person as they profess they could in me; and are now wholly destitute; and, having heard of some inclinations on my part towards them, invite my return. I cannot meet with any argument against it, except fleshly ones, which I hope God will help me to slight. If you will please to afford me your thoughts about it, I shall be thankful; being desirous (so far as I understand myself) to spend my little time in the world to the best advantage of the glory of God. I am through haste constrained abruptly to subscribe,

" Sir,

" Yours to honour and love you,

" John Howe.

" Whitehall, May 25th."

Postscript to the preceding letter.

" *Sir,*

" *The affected disorderliness of this family as to the matters of God's worship, (whence arises my despair of doing good here,) I desire as much as is possible to conceal,* and therefore resolve, to others, to insist upon the necessitous condition of the place I left as the reason of my removal, (if I do remove;) to yourself I state my case more fully, as expecting some direction and help from you about it; but I desire you to be very sparing in making it known as 'tis here represented." *

The next letter is still on the same subject. It is evident that his friend Baxter was opposed to his leaving Whitehall, and had been endeavouring to dissuade him from that step.

" TO THE REV. RICHARD BAXTER.

" *Dear and honoured Brother,*

" 'Tis my unhappiness that I cannot give so clear a state of my case, as may make way for a grounded judgment. 'Tis

---

* The concluding paragraph of this letter would justly expose Howe to the charge of insincerity, had not the "lamentable condition" of the people at Torrington, been a real and very powerful reason of his leaving Whitehall. Provided we state a real reason for our conduct, it is agreed by all casuists, that we are not bound to state *every* reason.

a hard matter to describe the state of the place I have left, (as now it is.) I left it in a hopeful way of being happily supplied; but one party rejected the person I recommended, another party (for I found the best there, at my first coming, two parties, which were, through God's blessing on endeavours, brought into one body, and are now breaking into two parties again) have since rejected another; who yet all profess a readiness to meet in me as before. Also, (which I should not speak did not the matter require it,) some overtures made by me were the occasion of a settled meeting of the neighbouring ministers of different persuasions, (kept up for some time, not without hopes of good success,) which hath been discontinued and forsaken by one party, and 'tis represented to me, by some of them, as a matter of ill consequence to those parts. Torrington was the place of meeting, and the only convenient place for that purpose; which, if not supplied by a person inclined to peace, (of which my frustrated endeavours have made me despair,) will not draw in both parties thither. My ministry there was not (thro' God's grace) altogether in vain; and the advantage I may hope from the increase of their affections by absence, seems to promise it may be more prosperous, should I return.

"Here, my influence is not like to be much, (as it is not to be expected a raw young man should be much considerable among grandees ;) my work little ; my success hitherto little ; my hopes, considering the temper of this place, very small ; especially coupling it with the temper of my spirit, which, did you know it, alone would, I think, greatly alter your judgment of this case. I am naturally bashful, pusillanimous, easily brow-beaten, solicitous about the fitness and unfitness of speech or silence in most cases, afraid (especially having to do with those who are constant in the ' arcana imperii ') of being accounted uncivil, etc. : and the distemper being natural (most intrinsically) is less curable. You can easily guess how little considerations are like to do in such a case. I did not, I confess, know myself so well as, since my coming up, occasion and reflection have taught me to do. I find*

---

* Howe's estimate of himself is, of course, what might be expected from his modesty; but it is one, in which few who have studied his life or writings will be disposed to acquiesce. When we consider the uncommon prudence with which he conducted himself in this difficult situation, the supposition of his being "a *raw* young man " is out of the question; and when we reflect on the signal courage and firmness which he manifested at the call of duty, (some striking proofs of which will be given in a subsequent page,) the description of his bashfulness and pusillanimity is perfectly ludicrous.

*now my hopes of doing good, will be among people where I shall
not be so liable to be overawed. I might have known this sooner,
and have prevented the trouble I am now in. Though the case of
my coming up hither, and continuance, differ much, so as that I
can't condemn the former, yet I more incline to do that than justify
the latter.* Your intimations (now renewed) of the danger of,*
etc., are sad; but what can I do for prevention? or (if I might
hope my persuasions would signify anything) what course should
I persuade to? Besides, there are store of good men about
the city who have as free access, and probably more regard
than I. What I may do in befriending good causes, will be
according to my calling.

"I have devoted myself to serve God in the work of the
ministry, and how can I want the pleasure of hearing their
cryings and complaints, who have come to me under conviction, etc.? I shall beseech you to weigh my case over again.†

"Pardon this importune trouble from,
"Sir,
"Yours in affection and observance,
"JOHN HOWE.

"*Whitehall, June 1, 58.*

"For the Rev. Mr. Richard Baxter, Minister of the Gospel
at Kidderminster, Worcestershire."

The next letter, which is dated May 8, 1658, is the last on
this subject. It appears that Howe stayed at Whitehall until
after the Protector's death, which took place in the following
September. This, together with other circumstances, to which
I shall presently advert, proves that some such arrangement
as that mentioned in the following letter had been approved
by Cromwell. On the deposition of Richard Cromwell, Howe
returned to his flock at Torrington.

---

* Alluding, I imagine, to the designs of the "infidels and Papists," mentioned
in a former letter.

† It is evident from this, as well as from some other passages of the letter,
that Baxter was extremely unwilling that his friend should leave the Protector's
court. He probably felt that there was no one else who was likely to fill the
same arduous post, with an equal measure of integrity and discretion, or with
such a conscientious regard to the public good.

" Reverend Sir,

"Since my last, something has come into my thoughts, which may be a medium betwixt my deserting my present station, etc.; *i.e.* to retain a relation still to Torrington, (which hitherto, for want of a successor, I could not divest myself of,) and get leave to be with them a quarter of a year, or as much time as I may be allowed in the year, procuring another *who shall enjoy the profits of the place, to be constantly resident.** This, if it may be done, will be a double satisfaction to me. 1. That while I am with them, (as I shall much desire to be sometimes,) it will give me the advantage of dealing with them as their minister, which will both procure me more liberty in my own spirit in my applications to them, when I shall not fear to be looked upon as an encroacher, and an uninterested person, and probably more regard from them.† 2. That by this means a door will be kept open for my return to them, if hereafter it should be more apparently my duty so to do; which will be a great relief to me against what may possibly prove otherwise very afflictive, namely, the fear lest I should have irrecoverably thrown away the best opportunity of doing God service, that may ever be offered me while I live. My only doubt is about the lawfulness of such a course; namely, of continuing related to a people with whom we can so little

---

* We may rest assured that it was only on such terms that a man like Howe could ever have resorted to such a course. As it was, the latter part of this letter shows, that he had doubts about its propriety, and he therefore requests Baxter's judgment upon it. If all pluralists were of the same stamp, if they were characterized by the same disinterestedness and benevolence of intention, the church of Christ would have small quarrel with them.

As it appears that he alone could hold the people at Torrington together, and as he could not at present reside with them, the course he proposed seemed to be the only one open to him. It is, however, a striking proof, that general principles are not always to be strained to their extreme consequences; that in the infinite complications of human affairs, such principles cannot be applied with absolute precision; and that if we will not consent to modify our theories to meet peculiar cases, we shall be likely sometimes to lose the fairest opportunities of doing good. And in fact, what party is it whose ecclesiastical system does not exemplify, in its practical working, many deviations from the letter of its principles?

† This letter powerfully demonstrates the intense interest this faithful pastor took in his flock at Torrington. Indeed, his feelings of attachment towards them never seem to have suffered the slightest diminution; witness the affecting appeal which, after a lapse of nearly twenty years, he addressed to them from Ireland, on the occasion of his publishing his treatise on "Delighting in God."

reside. I know not whether the not common occasion of my absence may plead anything for it. I shall entreat your judgment in this case, and that you will please to afford it speedily, because I shall forbear till then to propound it to,* etc.

"I am, Sir,

"Yours, much obliged,

"J. Howe.

"*Whitehall, June 3, '58.*

"For the Rev. Mr. Richard Baxter, Minister of the Gospel at Kidderminster, Worcestershire."

The principal motives which induced Howe to accept the situation at Whitehall have been already adverted to in the course of the narrative, and are more fully disclosed in the preceding letters. We cannot be surprised, that a man like Howe, a man whose whole life was dedicated to the service of religion, should think the situation Cromwell offered him † one not to be at once refused. It was, as he himself declares, "a very considerable work to which he was called." In such a position, and with the opportunities which that position could not fail to give him, he might reasonably hope, not only to do good within the limits of the Protector's court and household, but to exert a beneficial influence on the interests of religion at large. And though those hopes were, as he himself sadly admits, disappointed, the incidental opportunities of doing good were so numerous, and he was disposed to make such good use ‡ of them, that Baxter, as we have seen, was altogether averse to his quitting his post, even when Howe had so strongly expressed his reluctance to continue in it.

---

* To the Protector.

† Or rather, the situation which Cromwell *thrust* upon him; for, as we have seen, he could scarcely be said to have any choice in the matter.

‡ Some instances of his kind offices on behalf of individuals of the opposite party, will be mentioned in the course of the narrative. And who can tell how many others were the fruit of that confidence with which the Protector never ceased to honour him? who can tell but that the same generous mediation which induced Cromwell to act so noble a part to Dr. Ward, might also have prompted him to some other of those truly splendid actions, which though they cannot justify his usurpations, yet shed a redeeming lustre on his name?

As he had been induced to accept the office only from the purest motives, he immediately wished to abandon it, when he found that the main objects he contemplated in accepting it could not be realized; when he discovered that he could not "carry it," as a "minister of Christ," to such an extraordinary "charge," and that he might as well preach in a "market," or to the most tumultuous assembly, as to an audience which "affected" such "a license" of opinion and practice.

That he did not immediately resign, none, after reading the preceding letters, can hesitate to ascribe to the advice of Baxter. His friend rightly thought that the personal influence he could still exert with the Protector, was considerable, and ought not to be lightly thrown away. That Howe remained, in compliance with this friendly advice, is much to his credit; for a more difficult or irksome situation to one of his character and habits can hardly be conceived. It has been already observed, that almost under any circumstances Howe would have preferred retirement to publicity; studious solitude to the pursuits of active life; humble usefulness as a minister of Christ, to the proudest honours that ever waited on successful ambition. But the situation, in which he was now placed, must have been distasteful in the last degree. Compelled to live amidst those with whom he had no sympathy, to witness exhibitions of fanaticism and extravagance, which he could not control,—how must he have sighed for the quiet of Great Torrington!

Still he was right in not hastily abandoning Whitehall. His personal character stood high with all parties, but especially with the Protector: he was sometimes able to mitigate the evils he could not prevent, and to exert, in the cause of charity and moderation, the influence which, had he abandoned his station, might have been employed by others only to gratify religious rancour or promote the objects of selfish rapacity.

"Never," says Calamy, "can I find him so much as charged, even by those who have been most forward to inveigh against a number of his contemporaries, with improving his interest in those who then had the management of affairs in their hands, either to the enriching himself, or the doing ill offices to others, though of known differing sentiments. He readily embraced every occasion that offered, of serving the interest of religion and learning, and opposing the errors and designs which at that time threatened both."

These traits of character seem to have been properly appreciated by his great patron, who on one occasion paid him the following noble compliment: "You have obtained," said Cromwell, "many favours for others; I wonder when the time is to come that you will solicit anything for yourself, or your family."

Of the disinterestedness, integrity, and generosity, with which he filled this difficult situation, the following may suffice as examples.

Amongst many other Episcopalians whom he befriended in distress was the celebrated Seth Ward, afterward Bishop of Exeter, who always retained a grateful sense of Howe's kindness. It appears that Dr. Ward, who had been sometime Professor of Astronomy at Oxford, became a candidate for the principalship of Jesus College in that University, on the resignation of Dr. Michael Roberts. A gentleman of Exeter College, Mr. Francis Howel, was another candidate. Dr. Ward, it seems, had the suffrages of a majority of the Fellows in his favour; but, on the other hand, his opponent had obtained from the Protector a positive promise of the appointment. Dr. Ward, ignorant of this, was anxious to secure the same all-powerful interest. For this purpose he applied to Howe, who, without promising much, promised to do all he could, and readily procured him an audience. When Dr. Ward had been introduced to the Protector, Howe proceeded to speak, in terms of the strongest admiration, of his worth and learning; and intimated, that it would be no very creditable thing, if a man of such rare attainments, and who, moreover, was supported by a majority of the Fellows, should fail in obtaining the principalship. Cromwell answered, that Dr. Roberts had resigned his office into his hands; that he had been told that it was his right to fill up the vacancy; and lastly, that as he had promised the situation to Mr. Howel, he could not in honour retract. At the same time he took Howe aside, and began to question him more closely about Dr. Ward. Howe "assured him that it would be much for his honour" to befriend the Doctor. Cromwell, turning to Dr. Ward, told him, that he found "Mr. Howe to be very much his friend, and was, on such recommendation, disposed to give him some tokens of his regard." He then "pleasantly asked him, what he thought the principalship of Jesus College might be worth?" The Doctor told him what it was generally *computed* to be worth. Upon this, the Protector promised that he would allow him an annual sum to that amount.

Of the estimation in which Howe was held by the Episcopalians, some striking proofs were given at the time that extraordinary conclave was sitting, commonly known by the name of the "Triers." It was the duty of these men to ascertain the qualifications of all candidates for the ministerial office : * many of the Episcopalians, having no unreasonable apprehension of this ordeal, applied to Howe for advice. Amongst others was the worthy humorist, Dr. Thomas Fuller. "You may observe, Sir," said that facetious person, "that I am a somewhat corpulent man, and I am to go through a very strait passage : I beg you would be so good as to give me a shove, and help me through." Howe willingly gave him his best counsel. When he appeared before the examiners, and they proposed the usual question, "Whether he had ever had any experience of a work of grace on his heart?" he answered, that "he could appeal to the Searcher of hearts, that he made a conscience of his very thoughts :" implying, that it was not

---

* It was the candid admission of Baxter, who, be it recollected, was by no means favourable to the "Triers," who thought their tribunal constituted by no just authority, and who refused to participate in their proceedings, that, *on the whole*, they had discharged their duties with great impartiality and discretion, and with signal benefit to the church and the nation. Still it is very possible, notwithstanding the generally beneficial results of their labours, that many pious and excellent men may have been much perplexed by the needless minuteness of their inquiries. If not deeply versed in the abstruse controversies, and thoroughly familiarized to the religious phraseology of the age, simple-minded piety might be easily wrecked on some of the subtle interrogatories with which Mr. Nye, and some of his colleagues, might attempt to elicit "those deeper discoveries," to which reference is made in one of Howe's letters to Baxter.

without the strictest strutiny into his motives that he had ventured on the ministerial office. "With this answer," says Calamy, "they were satisfied, as indeed they might well be." There can be little doubt that Howe suggested it. While it was sufficient to answer the general purpose for which the question was put, it was not so particular as to involve any of those perplexing discussions which were the delight of the men and of the age. If honest Thomas Fuller had attempted a more specific answer, it is by no means improbable that in spite of all his excellence, he would not have satisfied the subtle and "distinguishing" spirit which animated many of his examiners. He might, but for Howe's timely "shove," have stuck in the dreaded passage after all.

Of the conscientiousness and integrity, with which Howe fulfilled his duties as Cromwell's domestic chaplain, an impressive example was given in his sermon, "On a particular Faith in Prayer." As many readers may not understand this mysterious phrase, a word of explanation may be desirable. It was a very prevalent opinion in Cromwell's court, and, as will appear in the sequel, seems to have been entertained by Cromwell himself, that whenever eminently religious persons offered up their supplications for themselves or others, secret intimations were conveyed to the mind, that the particular blessings they implored would be certainly bestowed, and even indications afforded of the particular way in which their wishes would be accomplished. Howe himself confessed to Calamy, in a private conversation on this subject, that the prevalence of the notion at Whitehall, at the time he lived there, was too notorious to be denied; that great pains were taken to cherish and diffuse it, and that he himself had heard "a person of note" preach a sermon with the avowed design of maintaining and defending it. To point out the pernicious consequences of such an opinion would be superfluous; of course there could be no lack of such intimations in an age and court like those of Cromwell; and all the dangerous illusions which a fanatical imagination might inspire, and all the consequent horrors to which a fanatical zeal could prompt, might plead the sanction of an express revelation.

Howe, regarding this notion with the abhorrence which it must inspire in every man of sound judgment and sincere piety, thought himself bound, when next called to preach before Cromwell, to expose the fallacies on which it rested, and the pernicious consequences to which it led. This accordingly he did, doubtless to the no small surprise and chagrin of his audience. During his discourse, Cromwell was observed to pay marked attention; but, as his custom was when displeased, frequently knit his brows, and manifested other symptoms of uneasiness. Even the terrors of Cromwell's eye, however, could not make Howe quail in the performance of an undoubted duty; and he proceeded, in a strain of calm and cogent reasoning, to fulfil his difficult but honourable task.* When he had finished, a person of distinction came up, and asked him "whether he knew what he had done?" at the same time expressing his apprehension that he had irretrievably lost the Protector's favour. Howe coolly replied, "that he had discharged what he considered a duty, and could trust the issue with God." He told Calamy, "that he observed that Cromwell was cooler in his carriage to him than before, and sometimes seemed as if he would have spoken to him on the subject, but that he never did." †

There are not many men who would have had the moral courage requisite for the above task; fewer still who would have accomplished it in such a manner, as, if not to convince, to silence and abash the gainsayer; while almost any one but Howe would have drawn down upon himself the utmost indignation of such an audience. Properly to administer reproof, even in private, is difficult; to expose public errors, and in a public assembly, abundantly more so. To do this, when the errors in question are cherished by the great and the powerful,

---

* For the outline of this sermon, which is all that Calamy could recover, see Appendix No. III.

† "He added, that he had a great deal of satisfaction in what he did in this case, both in the time of doing it, and ever afterwards, to the time of our conversing together upon this subject."—*Calamy*, p. 23.

and by those whose base interest it is to flatter their pride by echoing their sentiments, is more difficult still; while the task, already thus formidable, is rendered almost hopeless, when the errors which call for rebuke, are, as in this case, the offspring of the rankest fanaticism. As the propriety of administering reproof at all, presupposes that those who are the objects of it, will admit at least the *possibility* of error, how slender is the hope of success, when the feeble arguments of reason and common sense may be met by an appeal to infallible inspiration! Yet almost hopeless as the task of Howe was, he did not shrink from it, simply because it was enjoined by the voice of duty.

It is wonderful that this bold step should not have been attended with the total forfeiture of Cromwell's favour and esteem. That this was not the case, is to be accounted for, only by supposing that Howe's rare integrity was conjoined with as rare discretion. To undertake such a task, with any hope of success, it is not simply necessary to possess the requisite boldness; there must be proportionate prudence. So perverse is human nature, that the very confidence which conscious integrity inspires, will often give a man, in the performance of a difficult duty, an arrogant and over-weening air, which diminishes, and sometimes totally neutralizes, the just influence of all that he says and does. In such duties as Howe was, on this occasion, called to perform, men almost always do too little or too much; they want courage, or they want discretion.

While Howe was Cromwell's chaplain, Calamy informs us that he was often employed in important services, which required secrecy and despatch; but he adds, "they were always honourable." Indeed, we may be assured, that when Cromwell knew the character of the man—and he would not be long in discovering it—he would not propose to him any service that was otherwise. Such is the value of a character for integrity, when once established. Not only are temptations resisted with less difficulty when they assail at all, but the occasions of temptation become less frequent. So true, in this respect, as well as in many others, is that sentiment of Simonides, as expounded in the lively comment of Socrates, "It is not difficult *to be*, but *to become*, virtuous." *

I have said more than once, that the native tendencies of Howe's mind would probably have induced him, under almost any circumstances, to prefer a contemplative to an active life; yet, upon a review of his conduct during his residence at Whitehall, it is obvious that his practical talents must have been of no mean order. Great sagacity and prudence alone could have enabled him, in a situation so difficult, not merely to evade the censure, but to secure the admiration of all parties. Incapable of artifice or disguise, and noted for inflexible rectitude of purpose, he yet managed to conciliate the esteem of the most opposite factions: constantly teaching and as constantly practising charity and moderation, he yet happily escaped the hostility of the eager partisans, who were hungering and thirsting for the annihilation of every party but their own: without the slightest sympathy with fanaticism, he somehow disarmed the wrath and malice of the enthusiasts, whose extravagancies and follies he rebuked, sometimes by his discourse and always by his actions. To exist in the midst of such a strife of tempestuous elements, without yielding to them or being destroyed by them, is a mystery of circumspection not easily unravelled. In many respects, indeed, that mystery would be equally difficult of solution, even if we were to suppose that he was in the constant habit of compromising principle, and that his life was a series of unscrupulous adaptations of opinion to the company into which he was thrown; for hypocrisy so various and versatile, could not long escape detection. The many and violent changes to which, on such an hypothesis, he must have subjected himself, would have confounded Proteus himself, since there is not a party that does not venerate the name of Howe.—But I need not pursue this subject; all the records of his life leave his character altogether unimpeached.

Some might perhaps think that the supposition of disinterestedness and integrity is alone sufficient to solve the question.

---

* Plato. Protag.

Such a solution would be far from satisfactory. In general, indeed, such qualities will eventually secure a man's reputation, but they will not ordinarily protect him from calumny or malice during the actual discharge of difficult duties. On the contrary, there are never wanting those whose malignity is only inflamed by that goodness which they know not how to emulate, and who consider excellence in others as a libel on themselves.

The foregoing letters serve to show in a very striking and affecting point of view, Howe's devoted character as a PASTOR. It is evident that, to preach the gospel, and to train the immortal spirits of men for heaven, were, in his estimation, unspeakably the most honourable and delightful of all employments. In comparison with his office as minister to the humble flock at Torrington, his chaplaincy at Whitehall—offering as it would, to any ambitious man of equal talents, such tempting opportunities of promoting selfish interests—possessed no attractions. Nor, if we would do him full justice, must we forget that, in those days, and in such a court as Cromwell's, the situation which Howe held, was not such as the name "chaplain" would ordinarily suggest. In that age of religious enthusiasm, and in the peculiar position of public affairs, almost all questions of state were strangely complicated with those of religion. How many a fanatic, unconscious that his ruling motive was ambition, and how many a hypocrite, who knew it but too well, would have exulted to obtain Howe's place in Oliver's confidence—his intimate knowledge of state intrigues, and his share in secret and important negotiations. He would have known how to turn to his own selfish advantage, that power which was never employed by Howe, except for the benefit of others, and which he would, at any time, have been heartily glad to relinquish.

During the time Howe was in Cromwell's household, he appears to have officiated frequently, if not regularly, at St. Margaret's Church, Westminster. Wood says he was Lecturer there.

He appears also to have preached once before Parliament, though on what occasion is not certainly known. The sermon, as is shown by an advertisement of 1659, was entitled, " Man's Duty in Magnifying God's Work." I presume it was published on occasion of one or other of those brilliant successes, which attended the arms of England abroad, during the latter period of the protectorate. In these advertisements he is described as " Preacher at Westminster." *

---

* This was the earliest of Howe's productions, and as such, if for no other reason, would have been an object of curious interest. One would have liked, moreover, to see how such a man as Howe acquitted himself on such an occasion. For this sermon, however, I have searched in vain. I have met with no traces of it in any public or private collections to which I have been able to obtain access. Amongst other places, I have searched the British Museum, and Dr. Williams' library, (where, if anywhere, it might be expected to be found;) as also the catalogues of the Bodleian, Sion College, and Lambeth libraries. Whether it was advertised, but never published ; or, if published at all, issued to such a limited extent, that not a single copy has survived the wastes of accident and time, I cannot pretend to decide.

CHAPTER IV.

FROM 1658 TO 1668.

DEATH OF CROMWELL—HOWE STILL REMAINS AT WHITEHALL—CHARACTER OF RICHARD CROMWELL—HIS DEPOSITION—LETTER OF HOWE TO BAXTER ON THAT EVENT—HOWE RETURNS TO TORRINGTON—IS INFORMED AGAINST—DEFENDS HIMSELF SUCCESSFULLY—IS EJECTED BY THE ACT OF UNIFORMITY—HOWE'S INTERVIEW WITH DR. WILKINS—REFLECTIONS—A CITATION AGAINST HIM—HIS INTERVIEW WITH BISHOP WARD—OXFORD OATH—HOWE'S CONDUCT ON THAT OCCASION—LETTER TO HIS BROTHER-IN-LAW—REFLECTIONS ON PROTESTANT PERSECUTION—PUBLISHES "THE BLESSEDNESS OF THE RIGHTEOUS."

WHEN Cromwell died,* Howe did not, as might have been expected from the preceding letters, relinquish his situation at Whitehall. It is by no means improbable that, in addition to those general reasons, which had already induced him to sacrifice his own inclination to what his friend Baxter represented as a duty, the personal character of the new Protector had a considerable share in reconciling him to his office. It is certain, at all events, that the principal reason for relinquishing that office, must have ceased with the life of Oliver. To Richard Cromwell, he could have had no personal objections; on the contrary, he uniformly expressed the highest opinion of his worth and integrity.

His situation was rendered still more tolerable, from his having effected those arrangements with regard to Torrington, to which a reference has been already made. This is confirmed by a letter to Baxter, inserted in this chapter. From that letter, it appears, that the first visit which he paid to Torrington, in consequence of those arrangements, was almost immediately after the Protector's death. He remained in the

---

* September 3, 1658.

west for some months, and consequently could have resumed his duties at Whitehall only a very short time before Richard's deposition.*

Richard Cromwell was utterly incapable of governing that distracted empire, which tasked to the full even the sagacious and powerful intellect of his father. His deposition, therefore, soon became inevitable. He was not destitute of abilities, but they were such as fitted him rather for private than for public life; least of all for wielding such a sceptre as his predecessor had bequeathed him. Nor did he want merely the energy and ambition of the old Protector: he could not employ—what the situation would have required—the exertion of arbitrary power or an unscrupulous policy. He was a man, not indeed of genius, but of honour and humanity; one of the few, who would have preferred the humblest obscurity to the most splendid diadem, if power was to be purchased or retained by a course of violence or treachery.

Immediately after Richard Cromwell's deposition, Howe, at the request of a relative, addressed the subjoined letter to Baxter, in explanation of the recent changes. It is now published for the first time, and will be read, I feel confident, with considerable interest.

In this letter the conduct of Richard Cromwell, which all historians admit to have indicated as much of disinterestedness and patriotism as it betrayed of timidity and irresolution, is represented by Howe—and no man was more likely to be acquainted with the truth than himself—in a light still more favourable, than that in which it has been generally regarded. It appears, that even that fatal dissolution of the Parliament, which was the death-warrant of his power, was a deliberate sacrifice of his own interests to patriotism. He saw, from the first, the full effects of this measure,—but, as it was inevitable, resolved to venture upon it himself, rather than suffer it to be

---

* In a little more than three weeks after Cromwell's death, the congregational brethren met at the Savoy, (Sept. 29,) and drew up that "confession of faith," etc., still known by the name of the "Savoy Confession." Howe, it appears, was present at their deliberations. It was, in all probability, within a very few days after this, that he departed on his visit to Torrington.

taken, with more hazard to the country, by others. The letter also shows, that both Richard and his father, the one from principle, the other in obedience to a sagacious policy, had long desired the diminution of the military power, and the "civil settlement" of the nation. Cromwell, at the close of life, had learned, for good reasons, to dread the predominate influence of that very army, which, at an earlier period, had been the great instrument of his successful ambition. In this instance, as in many others, it was found more easy to set the elements of political power at liberty, than to reclaim or control them.

"TO THE REV. RICHARD BAXTER.

"*Rev. and dear Brother,*

"Since my return from the West, (where I suppose you may have heard I spent some months of late,*) I have often been putting pen to paper to write to you; but have deferred, —being still held in expectation of some further issue,—that I might know what to write that might be a ground of some action or treaty for the church's good. Such expectations are now at an end. I know not to what purpose it will now be to fill a letter with complaints of man's iniquity, and our present and approaching miseries. My kinsman, Mr. Upton (now in town), showed me a letter of yours, wherein you express your wonder at our late turns, as well you may. He hath made it my task to give what account I can. It cannot be new to you that the council in the old Protector's time was divided into two parties; the one was for a settlement on such terms as might please the nation, as he himself also was; those, except one of late, had no present relation to the army; the other, who were (the chief of them) army men, were not much pleased with, nor did study any such thing; but thought it their duty, in order to the safety of religion and liberty of conscience, to keep up the power of the army as much as they could, and thereby to curb and repress the spirit of the nation, as they use

---

* This letter is dated May 21, that is (evidently) of the year 1659, immediately after Richard Cromwell's deposition. Soon after the death of Oliver, Howe, as already mentioned, had paid a visit to Torrington, where he remained till the spring of the following year. He had now, it would appear, returned to London, where, it is plain, this letter was written. He could not, therefore, have officiated at Whitehall more than a month or two, during the short period of the younger Cromwell's protectorate.

to phrase it. The young Protector—following (in this) his father's steps, I mean in the study and endeavour of a civil settlement, whereby a just provision might be made also for religious liberty by a law, without having the nation under a force, and that things might run in their natural channel—is looked upon with a jealous eye by the military part of the council; lest he should mingle interests with the nation, and master theirs, and so the army, wherein their *places* of power and profit lay, by degrees become insignificant. To obviate this, after his entrance into the government, they attempt to vote the army independent of him, etc. A parliament being called, they find his interests to be prevailing there against the Commonwealth's-men, (as they are called;) so that the *other* house * is owned and agreed to be transacted with. They find that this other house will be no balance to the Commons, as being much of their temper; for though it be true the old Protector called several swordsmen into that house to please the army, yet he wisely contrived it, that they should not be so many as to hurt the nation; the judges and several gentle-men of the country, and quite of another temper, being the major part; and easily perceive that whatever shall be done by the Commons, in order to the restraining of religious liberty,† and the subjugating of the army to the civil govern-ment, is likely to meet with no great opposition in the other house. Therefore they (the army) think it necessary to have the Parliament *gospelled* or dissolved; and because they can-not procure this by persuasion, they embody and resolve upon force; which the Protector perceiving, and understanding, if the work must be done by them, they intended only gospelling, and to leave a remnant that should do their work, and put a pretext of legality upon whatever they should have a mind to ; for prevention of this, choosing rather to dissolve them, not dreaming, as one would think no man could, of such a thing as this rag of ——, etc. This action of the army, which pro-cured the Parliament's dissolution, occasioned a mighty acces-sion and confluence to them of wild-headed persons of all sorts,

---

* The House of Lords ; to which that part of the Council, which favoured the ascendency of the army, were willing to appeal, when they found the Commons too strong for them.

† In the army, the doctrine of religious liberty has been employed, to justify every species of extravagance. With whatever *real* fears for " religious liberty," some few of the " army-men " may have regarded " a civil settlement," it is evident, as Howe shows in the sequel of this letter, that the most selfish ambi-tion was the prime motive of all their proceedings.

whom they refuse not, as fearing they might have need of them: these infuse into the inferior officers a disaffection to government by a single person;* the stream runs so strong this way, that the chief officers cannot withstand it; and they *endeavour* faintly enough, some of them at least; hence rather than undertake the modelling of a new government, they think it advisable rather to work the nation with the price of the

"Sir, such persons as are now at the head of affairs, will blast religion,† if God prevent not. The design you writ me of, some time since, to introduce Infidelity or Popery, they have opportunity enough to effect. I know some leading men are not *Christians*. *Religion is lost out of England, farther than as it can creep into corners.* Those in power who are friends to it, will no more suspect these persons, than their ownselves. I am returning to my old station, being now at liberty beyond dispute.

"I am,

"Sir,

"Your much obliged,

"*May 21.*"   "JOHN HOWE.

No sooner was Howe at liberty, than he availed himself of the opportunity of resuming his labours amongst his beloved people at Great Torrington. He had been reluctantly separated from them, and he now joyfully returned.

He returned unchanged. His spirituality and simplicity of mind had not been impaired, or even touched, by the secular spirit or the subtle temptations of the scenes in which he had lately moved. Ambitious only of doing good, he was still as

---

* That is, they excite clamour for their long-cherished scheme of a pure republic.

† This letter was written during that unsettled year which intervened between Richard Cromwell's resignation and the restoration of the King. The "army-men," who had so successfully conspired the downfall of the young Protector, were now at the "head of affairs." They pretended to be anxious to govern by a parliament, (without a Protector or a House of Peers,) which should be called "Keeper of the liberty of England." But, as Howe truly says in this letter, it was to be a parliament meanly and hopelessly subservient to their designs; and on the first symptom of independence, they were contemptuously dismissed. Sovereign power was then *openly assumed* by the small junta, who had already really possessed it ever since Oliver's death, under the name of the "Council of Officers."

firmly convinced as ever, that the humble office of the Christian minister is the most illustrious which can be coveted by man.

But he was not long to enjoy unmolested the tranquillity and retirement for which he had pined. That spirit of persecution, which more fully disclosed its malignity in the Act of Uniformity, began to manifest itself in acts of petty malice, almost immediately after the Restoration. Such was the intoxication of delight with which the whole nation greeted the King's return, that even common sobriety of mind was almost enough to subject a man to the charge of disaffection. It can hardly be a matter of surprise, therefore, that those who had in any way been connected with Cromwell's government, should become the special objects of suspicion; especially, if they were ministers. In many congregations, the vilest informers lay in ambush, waiting for some incautious or ambiguous expression, which they might turn to the speaker's disadvantage. Even John Howe did not altogether escape their calumnies. At the close of the year 1660, (about eighteen months after his return to Torrington, (two men, named John Evans and William Morgan, charged him with having uttered seditious and even treasonable matter in two sermons, preached from Gal. v. 1, 7, 8.* The information was laid before the Mayor, a Mr. Wellington, who bound Howe, and several others on his behalf, to appear at the next sessions.

This charge against a man like Howe, whose characteristic prudence and quiet spirit afforded a double security for his innocence, was to the last degree ridiculous; and it might be predicted in what way it would terminate.

Before the sessions came on, some of the Deputy Lieutenants of the County, " not willing," according to Calamy, " that the magistrates of the several corporations should be too powerful," informed the Mayor, " that they could not be present at the

---

* The sermons were preached on September 30th, and October 14th, 1660. The words were, " Be not deceived; God is not mocked : for what a man soweth, that shall he also reap. For he that soweth to the flesh, shall of the flesh reap corruption : but he that soweth to the Spirit, shall of the Spirit reap life everlasting." It would have required more than ordinary ingenuity, or a special genius for rambling beyond the limits of the subject, to preach sedition and treason from such words as these.

Sessions, but desired to hear the matter at some other time, and appointed a day for that purpose." In this arrangement the Mayor acquiesced.

When the affair came on, Howe demanded the benefit of the statute,* "to purge himself by more evidence than that of the informers." The Mayor accordingly administered oath to one and twenty witnesses, "judicious men," and "enjoined them, on his Majesty's behalf, to declare the truth of the matter." Their testimony was unanimous in Howe's favour, and he was accordingly discharged.

But the affair did not rest here. The above transaction took place November the 14th. On the 24th of that month, one of the constables summoned the Mayor to appear before the Deputy Lieutenants, by a warrant dated exactly ten days back. To the warrant were attached five signatures; those of four gentlemen who had been at Torrington on the day of Howe's examination, and that of the Sheriff, then at a considerable distance. Not knowing by whom the warrant had been made out, the Mayor wrote to the Sheriff to know the truth; at the same time declaring, that if his appearance was insisted on, he would prepare for it, "as far as would consist with his office and place;" an expression which would tend to prove the truth of Calamy's representation, as to the existence of some petty jealousies between the Corporation Magistrates and the Deputy Lieutenants.

As the messenger did not return soon enough, (there being only an interval of three days between serving the warrant and the time fixed for his appearance,) the Mayor sent another letter to the Deputy Lieutenants. They summarily decided the matter by sending a party of horse to bring him to Exeter. Having told him he had acted unwarrantably in the case of Howe, they committed him to the Marshalsea; compelled him to pay three pounds for fees; and bound him over to appear at the next assizes. When the assizes came on, the charge against Howe was argued at large before the Judge, who, having heard the short-hand notes taken on the former occasion, said,

* I. of Edward VI. and I. of Elizabeth.

"the charge was wholly founded on a *mistake*, and cleared him." Whether the Deputy Lieutenants acted in this extraordinary manner merely to humble "a Magistrate of the Corporation," or, which is not improbable, with the hope of proving Howe guilty, or from both these motives, cannot be ascertained. "One of the accusers," says Calamy, "soon left the town, and was seen no more; and the other cut his own throat, and was buried in the cross-road."

But the spirit of persecution did not long content itself with such petty exhibitions of spite as these. Such methods were always tardy, and at best uncertain; the charges, moreover, were limited to political disaffection, were generally difficult of proof, and, as in the present instance, often ended in the discomfiture of the accusers.

They were speedily abandoned, therefore, for a more comprehensive scheme of persecution; a scheme by which not only those who were supposed to be disaffected to the government, but those who might find it impossible to comply with the requirements of the most rigid ecclesiastical uniformity, would be infallibly ejected from the church; or rather be compelled, unless they could first silence their consciences, to eject themselves. This object was effected by the Act of Uniformity; which passed both Houses of Parliament, (though by a very small majority in the House of Commons,) in May, 1662, and most appropriately took effect on Bartholomew-day, August 24th, of the same year.

An attempt has sometimes been made to defend this oppressive act, by representing it as merely a righteous retribution for the severities practised on the Episcopalian clergy by the Presbyterians. To those, who undertake to justify those severities,—if, indeed, in this day there are any such persons to be found,—such an argument may, for aught I know, be conclusive. To those who, with the present writer, disdain to be the apologists of the excesses of any party, and who refuse to admit recrimination to be argument, such considerations are of no force whatever. Tyranny and oppression will never want an adequate excuse, if *precedent* can furnish it.

When shall we cease to act in this blind spirit of partisanship, and no longer absurdly burden ourselves with the defence of the crimes and follies of our forefathers? When shall we learn to call injustice and wrong by their right names, by whatsoever party they may be committed?

But though it is not for me to decide on the point of precedence in cruelty between the Episcopalians and Presbyterians, or to determine whether the pages of Walker or of Calamy authentically record the largest portion of human suffering, it can hardly be denied, that several circumstances stamp on the Act of Uniformity a peculiar character of bigotry and folly. It was passed at a comparatively late period; when history had already recorded some of her most impressive lessons on the wickedness and inutility of persecution; when the principles of toleration were, in some measure, understood; and, what is still more important, had been to a considerable extent acted on. Many of the points to which assent and consent were so rigidly demanded, were acknowledged by the imposers to be in themselves indifferent. It did not come into operation gradually, but at once, leaving its victims no time to seek shelter from the storm; with such absurd and indecent haste, indeed, that multitudes could not have had time even to read, much less calmly investigate, the matters to which their solemn assent was demanded.* And lastly, the execution of the law was *timed* with such ingenious malice, as to deprive the unhappy men who found compliance with it impossible, of a whole year's income; thus in very many cases, not only securing their expulsion from the church, but involving them in absolute beggary. This circumstance alone would prove, that the gratification of party feeling, not a conscientious regard for the welfare of the church, was uppermost in the minds of the framers of the Act. Had the latter been their motive, they would have commiserated the sufferings which they erroneously thought themselves compelled to inflict, and would have earnestly sought every expedient of diminishing and alleviating them.

Happily, in our day, there is something approaching unani-

---

* Locke's Works, vol. x. p. 203, 204.

mity in the view generally taken of the spirit which framed and enforced the Act of Uniformity. "It is a passage of history," says the writer of a candid review of the first edition of the present work, inserted in a high-church organ,—"it is a passage of history, we must honestly confess, which we love not to dwell upon;" he truly adds, "such times can never return." The churchman who can conscientiously subscribe, feels the impolicy of that rigorous demand of conformity in things admitted to be "indifferent," by which so many were prevented from subscribing, and are still prevented; and if the thing were to be done over again, he would, in general, plead strongly for a relaxation of the rigidity and minute exactions of the Act, even though he needed it not himself. Such, in truth, is the very generally prevailing feeling of the present day. The contemplation of the history of that period excites the less acrimony, that it is felt—whether the change be right or wrong—that the whole position of the controversy between the churchman and the nonconformist has shifted its ground since that day. The argument for and against State-establishments,—an argument we are happily exempt from discussing here,—was, in the days of Howe, utterly unknown. It is but candid to say, that probably scarcely one (if one) of the two thousand ejected ministers would have scrupled to officiate in the Establishment as such, supposing some indulgence and latitude in minor matters had been extended to them: on the other hand, it is equally true, that multitudes of the nonconformists of our day would never have laid any stress upon some of the scruples which so needlessly troubled the consciences of our forefathers. Still, the subject is a very instructive one; it shows the danger and folly of multiplying beyond confessed necessity the terms of subscription or communion; of forgetting that nothing ought absolutely to bar the way into any church, but what will, in the estimate of its founders and members, bar the way to heaven also.

The decision of Howe is well known. With all his catholicity of spirit and his magnanimous disregard of minor differences; with all his disposition even to forget many of those differences for the sake of unity and peace, and to comply with the

practices of various parties, (so long as it was mutually admitted, that such compliance was a compliance of charity only,)
he could not prevail on himself to conform, though never ques-
tioning that multitudes honestly could. He felt that it was
one thing to admit that certain propositions might be embraced
or rejected according to each man's opinion respecting them,
and another solemnly to subscribe that he believed *that* to be
true, (however trivial in itself,) which he nevertheless believed
to be false; one thing to declare a certain practice of no
importance, and another to renounce that liberty of adopting
it or not, which ought to be the very consequence of its alleged
insignificance.

It is evident, indeed, from a conversation which Howe held
with his liberal-minded and amiable friend, Dr. Wilkins, and
which will be presently narrated, that even apart from conscientious scruples with respect to some of the terms of the
Act of Uniformity, his catholicity of temper and liberality of
opinion (which, at first sight, would appear to render conformity
so easy) were amongst the very things which made him hesitate. It was precisely because he was of so catholic a spirit,
that he objected to a system of ecclesiastical policy built on
an unnecessarily restricted basis; it was because he was so
superior to minor differences, that he condemned the prejudices
which magnified their importance; it was because he really
believed many opinions and practices indifferent in themselves,
that he could not bear to see them treated as though they were
not indifferent; it was because he was so anxious for the communion of all true Christians, of whatsoever party, that he
mourned to see the limits of church fellowship determined, not
by broad, well-defined lines which should separate vital truth
from destructive error, but in effect by the least significant
matters the Act of Uniformity enjoined. We say the least
significant, because though it is most true that the Act of
Uniformity enjoined many things of grave importance; still,
as ejectment was the consequence of anything short of "unfeigned assent and consent to the whole Book of Common
Prayer," etc., and as the most harmless scruple was as fatal as
the most weighty objection, it is evident that the bigoted and

exclusive spirit of the Act is to be determined by the *most insignificant* of the matters which it rendered imperative. If a man were willing to comply with everything except the use of the cross in baptism, his ejectment was still inevitable.

On these grounds, therefore, it is not improbable, that even if the Act of Uniformity had demanded subscription to no proposition which he did not believe true, and compliance with no practice at which he would have scrupled, he would still have hesitated to conform.

On the day on which the Act took effect, Howe preached two pathetic farewell sermons, at which, says Calamy, his audience "were all in tears." Having told his audience that "he had consulted his conscience, and could not be satisfied with the terms of conformity fixed by law," he proceeded to give an account of the principal reasons of his refusal to subscribe.

Shortly after his ejectment, occurred the conversation to which I have already adverted, between Howe and Dr. Wilkins, afterwards Bishop of Chester. This excellent man still continued to be a friend of Howe, whose ejectment, indeed, made no difference whatever in his private intimacies. Amongst other things, the Doctor said, that the "Act of Uniformity had had such consequences as a little surprised him; in that while some, that he should have thought much too stiff and rigid ever to have fallen in with the establishment, had complied and conformed; others, that he thought had a sufficient *latitude* to have conformed, had stood out, and continued non-conformists." He then hinted to Howe, that "he took *him* for one of the latter sort, and should be glad to know the reasons of his conduct." Howe at once declared, "that he had weighed that matter with all the impartiality he was able; that he had not so slender a concern for his own usefulness and comfort, as not to have been willing and desirous to have been under the Establishment, could he but have compassed it with satisfaction to his conscience; that to give a particular account of all the reasons of his conduct, (which he was free to do without any reserve, when a convenient opportunity offered,) would take up much more time than they had to spend together; that so many things were necessarily to be touched upon in a discourse on that subject, that it was not possible for it to be crowded into a transient conversation; and therefore he should reserve it to a season when, having more time, he might have more scope. *But one thing he could tell him with assurance,*—that that *latitude* of his, which he (Dr. W.) was pleased to take notice of, was so far from inducing him to conformity, that it was the very thing that made and kept him a nonconformist." The Doctor then asked him, whether it was the *discipline* of the church to which he chiefly objected. Howe replied, "that he could not by any means be fond of a church, that in reality had no discipline at all, and that he thought that a very considerable objection against the establishment." The Doctor then said, that though he was sensible there was no time for lengthened discourse on the subject, he should be glad of some general mention of his principal objections.

On this Howe intimated, "that he could not recognise, in the present constitution, those noble and generous principles of *communion*, which he thought must, sooner or later, characterize every Church of Christ; that consequently, when that flourishing state of religion should arrive, which he thought he had sufficient warrant from the Word of God to expect, a constitution which rested on such an exclusive basis must fall: that, believing this to be the case, he was no more willing to exercise his ministry under such a system, than he would be to dwell in a house built on an insecure foundation." *

---

* Of Dr. Wilkins, Calamy has preserved the following amusing anecdote:—

"This Dr. Wilkins was ever a great enemy to rigour and severity. When he was made a Bishop by King Charles II., (which was not compassed without considerable difficulty,) I have been credibly informed, he waited on the famous Dr. Cosins, Bishop of Durham, among other spiritual lords, and desired his company at his consecration dinner. Upon this occasion Bishop Cosins entered into a free discourse with him, about moderation on the one hand, and a vigorous supporting the ecclesiastical constitution on the other. Bishop Wilkins frankly told his lordship, that for his part, it was his apprehension, that he who was by many (with ill nature enough) reflected on for his moderation, was in reality a better friend to the church than his lordship, who was for rigorously supporting the constitution. Bishop Cosins seeming surprised, Bishop Wilkins added this as the reason of his assertion: For while you, my lord, said he, are for setting the top on the piqued end downwards, you won't be able to keep it up any longer than you continue whipping and scourging; whereas I, says he, am for setting the broad end downward, and so it will stand of itself. 'Tis a pity this good Bishop died so soon as 1672, and did not live till the revolution in 1688."

The surprise of this estimable prelate, at finding that a man of Howe's *latitude and catholicity* should have scrupled at the terms of conformity, has probably been felt by many others. Yet to dismiss for a moment the fact, already insisted on, that it was this very "latitude and catholicity," which, on general grounds, made Howe reluctant,—what can be more obvious, than that the most magnanimous contempt for petty scruples, and the utmost liberality of temper, could not preserve the *conscientious* man from ejection, if he really did not concur in propositions (let the subject-matter of those propositions be ever so insignificant) to which "an unfeigned assent" is demanded ? To lay little stress on things of comparatively little importance, is the mark of an enlarged mind; but to "declare" a solemn "assent," and to back that assent by an equivalent subscription, to propositions, which, whether in themselves important or not, we believe to be *false*, would be the grossest violation of the law of conscience.

Thus the apparent paradox which perplexed the worthy Bishop is susceptible of a very easy solution. Many of the most pertinacious and quarrelsome might readily conform, if they possessed a pliable conscience; and many of the most liberal-minded would infallibly be ejected, if they possessed a scrupulous one. There are many things enjoined in the Book of Common Prayer, for example, which a man might think of little moment, and the consequence of such latitude of opinion would be, that he would allow every one to form his own judgment of them ; but it by no means follows, that he could solemnly declare and subscribe "an unfeigned assent" to them.

It is well known, that the ejected ministers justified their nonconformity on widely different grounds; the obstacles which appeared insurmountable to one, occasioned no difficulty at all to another ; and, as might be expected from their diversities of intellect and education, of habit and prejudice, the reasons they alleged for their conduct varied in force and importance, from scruples* the most narrow-minded and child-

---

* It is never to be forgotten, however, in treating this subject, that even *such* scruples, if really conscientious, deserve compassion rather than ridicule ; or at

ish, to objections well worthy of the most candid and serious consideration. The points on which the comprehensive mind of Howe principally fastened, have been already mentioned. It would have been interesting to possess a full account of his objections. Unfortunately, of the two sermons preached on the day of his ejectment, not a syllable remains; but, from his still extant writings, it is clear what they chiefly were.

It has been sometimes represented, that the plea of conscience in the case of the ejected ministers was absurd and ridiculous, inasmuch as the very things at which conscience hesitated, were "indifferent" or "unimportant." But, supposing this true, could this relieve in the slightest degree the difficulties of those, who, like Howe, did *not* believe all the points on which they hesitated "indifferent" or "unimportant;" or prove that any other course was open to them, than that which they actually took? Let us just for a moment, and for the sake of argument, suppose them so:—are those who so frequently urge this view of the case, prepared to affirm,—and unless they go this length, their reasoning is altogether illogical,—that all conscientious objections, respecting matters which *others* pronounce indifferent—for of course, by supposition, the parties themselves do not think them so— are at once to be abandoned? Suppose, for example, an edict had been issued in the early ages of the Church, that no Christian should henceforth scruple to eat meat offered to idols— which the Apostle Paul declares *indifferent* enough—ought the scruples of those who still conscientiously demurred, to be at once renounced? The Apostle has satisfactorily settled the question by saying,—in accordance with the dictates of nature and of common sense, as well as the conclusions of all the soundest moralists,—that to him who *thinks* it sinful, it is sin. A really conscientious objection, though it should be about the most insignificant thing that ever divided the opinions of mankind, cannot be dismissed in this summary way. We may pity the man's fond prejudices—we may, if we will, laugh at his

---

least, that if the scrupulosity, which transforms evident trifles into matters of importance, be ridiculous at all, the pertinacity which makes compliance necessary, in matters so trifling, cannot be less so.

imbecility; but, while the objection still retains its force, he has only one path of conduct honourably open to him.

If it be replied, it is not because the men were conscientious, but because, out of a factious spirit, they *pretended* to be so when they were not,—that is another thing. But none who have charity will accuse them of this, unless they can claim to be "discerners of spirits." Meantime, if it were true, we must wonder at the pertinacious folly of the accused, who could embrace poverty, degradation, and ruin, for no advantage whatever! Even if we could imagine some few to have been idiots enough to act thus; still, to suppose that the great bulk of the ejected ministers were not impelled by a sense of duty which, even to preserve their dearest interests, they dared not disregard, is to suppose a total subversion of all the principles of action which ordinarily regulate human conduct, on a scale seldom exhibited before or since.

Some are willing to admit that if the ejected ministers *really* had conscientious objections to the oaths and subscriptions required of them, they could not with honour conform; but at the same time profess pity for understandings which could be fettered by prejudices so weak and scruples so frivolous. Compassion for the imbecility of such men as Howe and Baxter, would at all events be a novel exhibition of the sentiment, and entitle him who professed to feel it, to be compassionated in his turn, for his ignorance and presumption. This, however, leads to a brief re-consideration of the point, which, as already stated, was conceded only for the sake of argument. Surely, it may justly be argued, matter to which *such* men objected,— men possessing minds so enlarged, and knowledge so ample,— could not be so utterly indifferent as they have been often represented. I have already said, that if they had been in themselves indifferent, it would little matter as far as the question of *conscience* and *duty* is concerned; what I further insist on is, that, considering the character of the men, it is eminently improbable that they should have been indifferent.

When it is urged that the ejected ministers were needlessly scrupulous about things "indifferent or insignificant," it is often forgotten that the oaths, subscriptions, and unfeigned assent and consent demanded of them extended to a great variety of matters, which differed by every conceivable degree of importance. Some of them, it is true, were "indifferent" enough, and the scruples they excited may perhaps surprise us : but others involved considerations of such magnitude, that they might well exercise the most enlarged understanding and perplex the most enlightened conscience. There were not only cobwebs to catch insects, but nets, in the meshes of which even noble animals might struggle in vain.

This led, as already stated and as might be expected, to a corresponding difference in the grounds on which the ejected ministers justified their nonconformity. The sufficiency or insufficiency of those grounds could not be determined merely by the *fact* of nonconformity; since the Act of Uniformity made "him who was guilty in *one* point guilty in *all*." A separate examination of the reasons alleged by the several parties can alone decide this question; and to represent the men in general as needlessly and frivolously scrupulous, because some were so, is grossly unfair.

Whether it was reasonable to demand rigorous compliance with all—even the most minute—requisitions of the Act of Uniformity, Churchmen, no less than Dissenters, have pretty well decided in our day; and that many of them respected no "insignificant" or "trifling" matters, can hardly be denied.

But even supposing an individual to have no *specific* objections to any of the above requisitions; supposing he merely took his ground on some matters of ceremonial, which he himself acknowledged to be in their own nature "indifferent," still it does not follow that he might not plead objections which, whether really sound or unsound, cannot at all events be deemed frivolous.

If any believed, for instance, (as Howe and many did,) that rites and ceremonies of purely human origin, for which, by the *confession of all parties*, there was no inevitable necessity,*

---

* This was the case, be it recollected, with some of the matters of ceremonial which were objected to.—Nevertheless, the bulk of the ejected ministers did not wish that such things should be *prohibited* in the service of the Church, but that their observance should not be made *compulsory*. They would have been satis-

ought not to be introduced into public worship, or, that things, which are in their own nature "indifferent," should be left to every man's judgment and conscience,—to them it was not a matter of "indifference" whether they proceeded to sanction a principle which might serve to justify far more extensive innovations in matters of ceremonial, on the ground that they were "indifferent," or were left undetermined by Scripture. Many things may be confessedly "indifferent" in their own nature, which can no longer be considered so, the moment it is demanded that we should *act* as though they were not.. In this case, it is not the value of the concession that determines the controversy, but the *principle* involved in it.

Once more : even if the ejected ministers had conceded all the matters to which they objected, in the Common Prayer, to be in themselves "indifferent," yet, as public functionaries, they might not think it "indifferent," (as was Howe's case,) whether they had the power of *accommodating themselves to the scruples* of those among their audience who had not arrived at the same latitude of opinion, or were compelled to restrict the benefit of their labours to those only who on such matters thought with themselves. For example, a minister might think it very "indifferent" whether he used the sign of the cross in baptism or not, but he might *not* think it indifferent whether he was to exclude those from that rite altogether, who had conscientious objections to the accompanying ceremonial.

If any one will candidly weigh the preceding observations, I cannot but think he will be disposed to admit that neither were all the matters imposed on the ejected ministers, indifferent or unimportant in themselves ; nor, if they had all been so, was it "indifferent," whether they conformed or not ; that, on the contrary, there was abundantly sufficient to justify hesitation without supposing the recusants to be either over-scrupulous fools or factious hypocrites.

---

fied, if every man had been allowed to use his own liberty in such matters. Whether the men who pleaded for such reasonable latitude, or the then rulers of the Church, (who, even to prevent a great schism, refused to surrender one of the ceremonies which they themselves in the same breath confessed were not absolutely necessary,) were the more unwisely pertinacious, let posterity judge.

But, lastly, if the matters about which the ejected ministers scrupled were, indeed, so "indifferent," (and it is those who imposed them, who most loudly declared they were so,) there can hardly be a doubt that it would have been more wise and more Christian, not to demand compliance in these instances at all. Their "indifference" is an argument which tells both ways, or rather, which tells much more powerfully one way than the other; since it was much more easy for the one party to refrain from imposing a condition which they proclaimed to be indifferent, or, at all events, which they could not say they were *conscientiously obliged* to impose, than for those to comply with it, who declared they *conscientiously* believed it *not* to be "indifferent;" or who, if they believed it in its own nature indifferent, had, on other and more general grounds, *conscientious* objections to compliance. If, indeed, the framers of the Act of Uniformity had declared that they were *conscientiously* obliged to impose those terms with which the ejected ministers could not *conscientiously* comply, the argument would have been equal on both sides. Under such circumstances, and so long as it remains true that "an erroneous conscience obliges," none could blame, however all might lament, the conduct of the authors of the Act of Uniformity. But until such a plea (never yet heard of) be advanced, it is hardly worth while to consider it. To be told that the licentious Charles, and his profligate advisers, or even that Lord Chancellor Hyde and Archbishop Sheldon were, like the ejected ministers, troubled with scruples of conscience in this matter; and that these were so strong as to *compel* them to render the cross in baptism, kneeling at the sacrament, and the use of the ring in marriage, obligatory, would be enough to discompose the gravity of the gravest historian. Yet this alone would be an adequate defence. If both parties had been equally infected with the same troublesome disease of conscience, nothing could be said, but that the one was compelled to impose conditions which the other must continue to reject. Until such a plea is admitted, however, or at least pretended, it will be reasonably maintained, that the more plainly "indifferent" the matters which the Church imposed, the more imperative was the duty not to impose them. To relax needless rigour on the one side, was, in the actual circumstances, easy; compliance on the other, impossible.

It is often said, indeed, that all churches must have *some* terms of communion. True; but if it really wishes to render its pale as wide as possible, in other words to exclude the smallest number of sincere Christians, it will insist, if it be possible, on nothing as necessary to admission, but what the Scripture declares to be so; or if it deem itself obliged to decide on some lesser matters, which Scripture leaves undetermined, it will take care that these shall be as few as possible. ·The question is, were these the principles by which the framers of the Act of Uniformity were actuated? If not, and it seems nearer the truth to suppose that their object was the very reverse,* it is no argument to say, that every church must have *some* terms of admission and communion; because, though this is true, it does not follow that a church is justified in multiplying them confessedly beyond necessity; in imposing any which itself is compelled to admit it is not conscientiously *obliged* to impose, on those who, at the same time, are conscientiously obliged to reject them.

But though Howe was an *ejected* minister, he could not consent to be a *silenced* one. He still continued in Devonshire, availing himself of every opportunity of preaching in private houses those truths, which he was no longer permitted to proclaim in public. Such conduct, as may be supposed, soon brought him into trouble.

Having preached at the house of a gentleman whom he had been visiting for a few days, he found on returning home that

---

* There seems abundant reason to believe that the main object of some of the authors of the Act of Uniformity, was the exclusion of the Presbyterian clergy, and that this was the reason of the strictness with which it was framed. The language of Sheldon, of whom Burnet says, that he seemed not to have any clear sense of religion, if any at all, and that he spoke of it most commonly, as of an "engine of government and a matter of policy," is well known. When Lord Manchester remarked to the King, that he was afraid the terms of uniformity were so rigid that the ministers would not comply with them, Sheldon replied, "I am afraid they will."

Thus to gratify party-spirit, the Church lost nearly two thousand ministers, many of whom ranked amongst the most pious, diligent, and exemplary of her clergy.

an officer from the Bishop's court had been to apprehend him, and not finding him, had given notice that citations were out against both Howe and his friend.*

With characteristic promptitude, Howe, the next morning, went to Exeter. While standing before the gate of the inn at which he had put up his horse, and anxiously pondering the course which it would be best for him to pursue, a dignitary of the Church, to whom he was known, came past, and recognising Howe, asked him, "what he did there?" "Pray, Sir," replied Howe, "what have I done that I may *not* be here?" His friend informed him that a process was out against him, and that being so well known, he would find the utmost vigilance necessary to secure himself from being apprehended. He then asked Howe, "whether he would not wait on the Bishop?" Howe, who wished not to appear too solicitous about the matter, and yet to have an opportunity of meeting the charges of the court without seeming to have sought it, replied, "that he had no intention of doing so, unless his lordship, *hearing* of his being in the city, should invite him." His good-natured friend took the hint, and engaged, if Howe would wait in the mean time at the inn, to let his lordship *hear* of his being in the city. In a short time he returned with the intelligence that the Bishop would be glad to see him.

When Howe was introduced, his lordship received him with much politeness, and treated him as an old acquaintance. He soon, however, began to use the freedom of an old acquaintance, by expostulating with him on his nonconformity. Like Bishop Wilkins, he asked him his *reasons*. Howe replied, that without taxing his lordship's patience beyond all decency, he could not give such an account of his objections as justice to himself required. The Bishop then requested him to mention any one of the points at which he scrupled. On this Howe specified re-ordination. "Pray, Sir," said the Bishop, " what

---

* The Bishop of Exeter at this time was no other than Dr. Seth Ward, whose cause Howe had so effectually pleaded before Cromwell. Though Dr. Ward afterwards unrelentingly enforced the severe laws against the nonconformists, it is pleasing to reflect that he manifested on this occasion a grateful sense of Howe's former kindness.

hurt is there in being twice ordained?" "*Hurt*, my Lord," rejoined Howe, "it *hurts* my understanding; the thought is shocking; it is an absurdity; since nothing can have two beginnings. I am sure I am a minister of Christ, and am ready to debate that matter with your lordship, if your lordship pleases; but I cannot begin again to be a minister." The Bishop dismissed him with strong expressions of regard, assuring him that if he would conform, he might have considerable preferments. Howe then took his leave; and as the Bishop said nothing of the process that was out against him, his visitor, in conformity with the plan he had laid down, also abstained from all allusion to the subject; wisely concluding, that if the Bishop intended to proceed against him, he would hardly have failed, on such an occasion, to mention it. The event justified his inference; as neither he nor his friend heard anything more about the matter.

In 1665, the Parliament assembled at Oxford passed an act, by which nonconformist ministers were called upon to swear that it was not lawful, upon any pretence whatsoever, to take arms against the King; that they abhorred the traitorous position of taking arms by his authority against his person, or against those commissioned by him, in pursuance of such commission; and that they would not at any time endeavour any alteration of the government, either in Church or State.*

The nonconformist ministers, as might be expected, were much divided in their opinions about the propriety of taking this oath. At length about twenty, amongst whom was Dr. Bates, took it in London;† about twelve, amongst whom was Howe, in Devonshire;‡ and a few in Dorsetshire.

---

* The hard penalty attached to a refusal to take this oath was, "not being allowed, except on the high road, to come within five miles of any city, or corporation, or any place that sent burgesses to Parliament, or any place where they had been ministers, or had preached, since the Act of Oblivion."

† The principal thing which satisfied those of the nonconformist ministers who took the oath, was the declaration of the Lord Keeper Bridgman, that by *endeavours* to change the government was meant *unlawful endeavours*. The pressure of the Act was so severe, that its victims were naturally glad to avail themselves of any honourable method of gaining exemption from the severe penalties attached to a refusal to take the oath.

‡ The names of those who took the oath in Devonshire, (as Calamy ascertained from a manuscript of a Mr. Quick,) were John Howe, Humphrey Saunders,

On this occasion, Howe made the following candid and explicit declaration of the principles on which he took the oath in question. Nothing could be more abhorrent from his nature, than to avail himself of any ambiguity in the terms of the oath, or of any evasive interpretation of its meaning. In his estimation such conduct would have been fraud of the most iniquitous description. The sophistical casuistry, by which such practices have sometimes been defended, is with great brevity, but great clearness, exposed in this declaration; and, indeed, as Calamy truly observes, "it states the matter of oaths in general, as judiciously and fully as can well be supposed or imagined in so narrow a compass."

"1. My swearing is my act. 2. The obligation I hereby contract is voluntary. 3. Swearing in a form of words prescribed by another, I adopt those words, and make them my own. 4. Being now so adopted, their first use is to express the true sense of my heart, touching the matter about which I swear. 5. Their next use, as they have now the form of an oath, is to assure him or them who duly require it from me, that what I express by them is the true sense of my heart. 6. 'Tis repugnant to both those ends, that they should be construed (as now used by me) to signify another thing than what I sincerely intend to make known by them. 7. If the words be of dubious signification, capable of more senses than one, I ought not to hide the sense in which I take them, but declare it, lest I deceive them whom I should satisfy. 8. That declaration I ought to make, if I have opportunity, to them whose satisfaction is primarily intended by the oath; if not, to them whom they entrust and employ. 9. This declared sense must be such as the words will fairly bear, without force or violence."

When Howe and the others appeared in court, for the purpose of taking the oath, one of their number made the following declaration of what they *conceived* its tenor and import :—

" I confess I have had some doubts concerning this oath; but understanding, partly by discourse about it with some who

---

Gunnery, Mortimer, Parre, Francis Whiddon, Fairant, Wilkins, Binmore, Barry, Cleveland, and Baily. The last two took it before the Act came into force; the others, subsequently, at the county sessions.

concurred in making of the law, and partly by consideration of the law itself, and other laws, that the oath hath no other meaning or end, than to secure the person of the King's Majesty, and his authority, whether in his person or commissioners, and the government in Church and State, from being shaken or subverted, by any unpeaceable or seditious endeavours, out of our place and calling, I am abundantly satisfied to tender myself to this honourable court, for the taking of it."

To this declaration, which prevented all possibility of pretence that the oath had been evasively dealt with, the court made no objection. Under these circumstances the oath was administered.*

Calamy says, he had been told that in this year (1665) "Howe was imprisoned for two months, in the Isle of St. Nicholas."† That his father-in-law, George Hughes, and his brother-in-law, Obadiah Hughes, had recently been imprisoned there, and for a much longer period, is certain. On what grounds he supposes Howe himself to have been thus hardly dealt with, I know not. The name of his informant, and the reason for which he gave credit to the information, he has neglected to mention. As he admits, however, that he knew " nothing of the occasion of this imprisonment, or of what was alleged to justify it, or in what way Howe obtained deliverance ; " it may be doubted whether his information was correct.

That Howe, about this time, had been called to sustain some severe affliction is indeed evident from an affecting letter, which he wrote to his brother-in-law, Obadiah Hughes, shortly after that gentleman and his aged father had been set at liberty. Part of it is as follows :—

"Blessed be God, that we can have, and hear of, each other's occasions of thanksgiving, that we may join praises as well as prayers,—which I hope is done daily for one another. Nearer approaches and constant adherence to God, with the improve-

---

* Two of them, Fairant and Wilkins, took it with this limitation : " so far as the laws of man are agreeable to the word of God ; " a limitation which does not seem to have awakened any suspicions in those who imposed it. But much stranger things were thought " agreeable to the laws of God " in those days.

† Near Plymouth.

ment of our interest in each other's heart, must compensate
(and I hope will abundantly) the unkindness and instability of
a surly treacherous world, that we see still retains its wayward
temper, and grows more peevish as it grows older, and more
ingenious in inventing ways to torment whom it disaffects. It
was, it seems, not enough to kill by one single death, but when
that was almost done, to give leave and time to respire, to live
again, at least in hope, that it might have the renewed pleasure
of putting us to a further pain and torture in dying once more.
Spite is natural to her. All her kindness is an artificial disguise; a device to promote and serve the design of the former
with the more efficacious and piercing malignity. But patience
will elude the design, and blunt its sharpest edge. It is
perfectly defeated when nothing is expected from it but mischief; for then the worst it can threaten finds us provided, and
the best it can promise, incredulous, and not apt to be imposed
upon. This will make it at last despair and grow hopeless,
when it finds that the more it goes about to mock and vex
us, the more it teaches and instructs us; and that as it is
wickeder, we are wiser. If we cannot, God will outwit it, and
carry us, I trust, safe through, to a better world, upon which
we may terminate hopes that will never make us ashamed."

The expressions in this letter, however, by no means warrant
us to conclude, that Howe had been subjected to the same
rough treatment as the relatives with whom he thus condoles.
Unhappily, the afflictions of an ejected minister were too
various, sprang from too many sources, to sanction such a hasty
inference. Degrading and painful as imprisonment might be,
it was not the worst that could befall him. He was often called
to endure trials far more severe; trials, compared to which the
most protracted imprisonment was light and trivial. To wander
forth with his family, (as was the lot of many of them,) without
a home, or to sit over a desolate hearth, and listen to the cry
of his famishing children,—these were the severest trials of an
" ejected minister."

Indeed, in reading the history of the persecutions with
which the various parties of Protestants have, at different
periods, assailed each other, a very painful reflection can hardly
fail to suggest itself. Though the spirit of persecution has
been less bloodthirsty and unsparing amongst those parties

than under the papal domination, and therefore less detestable, its comparative lenience, and moderation of purpose, must often have occasioned (quite undesignedly it is admitted) more suffering than would have resulted from a more summary and less scrupulous cruelty. The brief horrors of the stake—the momentary pang which at once dismissed the weary spirit to its everlasting rest, would often have been gladly preferred to that slow, protracted torture, which was inflicted on many of the sufferers for religion during the seventeenth century.

The privations and sorrows of those who were more dear to them than their own lives, the sordid wants by which they were oppressed, the contempt with which they were treated, the intense solicitude, the perpetual suspicion which robbed them of peace by day, and haunted their sleep by night, must have wruug with anguish maay a heart which would not have faltered at the stake. Martyrdom might have been borne, nay, in many instances, would have been most welcome; but long years of penury and destitution, with the maddening spectacle of a starving family,—these must have been worse than many martyrdoms.

Whatever the sorrows or sufferings to which Howe alludes in the above letter, it is plain he had well learned how to bear them; or rather, to convert them into sources of instruction and improvement. Every line of it breathes the serenest resignation, the loftiest and most unbroken spirit of hope, patience, and superiority to the world.

For several years Howe continued to lead the life of a fugitive and wanderer; staying now with one friend, now with another; literally "preaching from house to house," and procuring a precarious and slender subsistence by performing any service, however humble, of which he was capable. His bitter recollections of this period of his life, seem to have suggested that brief but vivid description which he gave of the condition of the ejected ministers, in a document published nearly forty years after. "Many of them," said he, "live upon charity; some of them with difficulty getting, and others (educated to modesty) *with greater difficulty* begging, their bread."

At length, impelled perhaps by necessity, he published his justly admired treatise, entitled, "The Blessedness of the Righteous." It was published in 1668, and seems to have met with all the success it so well deserved.* It was the substance of sermons preached during his residence at Great Torrington.—Some time during this year, it appears that Howe was at Bath for the benefit of his health.†

All remarks of a critical nature upon Howe's works will be reserved for the close of the volume; but the preface to "The Blessedness of the Righteous" is so characteristic of the author—breathes such a noble and catholic spirit—evinces a mind so deeply intent on the great realities of religion—and displays such magnanimity and elevation of feeling, that I cannot pass on without commending it to the special attention of the reader. It conveys to us, indeed, a more accurate, as well as more impressive idea of the author, than the most elaborate description of the ablest biographer. Nor is this "Preface" destitute of other, though, it will be admitted, inferior claims to attention. Viewed simply as a piece of composition, its merits are of no mean order. The masculine thought which pervades it, the striking illustrations with which it is enlivened, and even its occasional felicities of expression and of style, (not often met with in the writings of our author,) render it well worthy of perusal. We may find room for a sentence or two:

"I am not at all solicitous, that the world should know the history of the conception of this treatise. . . . If there be anything that shall recompense the pains of such as may think fit to give themselves the trouble of perusing it, in the work itself, I should yet think it too much an undervaluing of them, if I did reckon the minuter circumstances relating thereto fit matter for their entertainment. . . . Nor am I more concerned to have it known what were the inducements to the publication of it. Earnest protestations and remonstrances of our good intentions in such undertakings, as they leave men

---

* This, it appears, was not his earliest production; in 1660 he published the sermon entitled "Man's Creation in a Holy but Mutable State." It was inserted in the "Morning Exercises Methodized."

† Life of Rev. Joseph Alleine, page 96.

still at liberty to believe or doubt at their pleasure, so they gain us little if they be believed. It is no easy matter to carry one, even, constant tenor of spirit through a work of time. Nor is it more easy to pass a settled, invariable judgment concerning so variable a subject; when a heart that may seem wholly framed and set for God this hour, shall look so quite like another thing the next, and change figures and postures almost as often as it doth thoughts. And if a man should be mistaken in judging himself, it would little mend the matter to have deceived others also into a good opinion of him. But if he can approve himself to God in the simplicity of an honest and undeceived heart, the peace that ensues is a secret between God and him. 'They are theatre enough to one another,'* as one said to his friend. It is an enclosed pleasure ; a joy which the stranger cannot intermeddle with.

"It is therefore any man's concernment herein rather to satisfy himself than the world; and the world's, rather to understand the design of the work than the author; and whither it tends, rather than whereto he meant it. And it is obvious enough, to what good purposes discourses of this nature may serve. This is, in the design of it, wholly practical ; hath little or nothing to do with disputation. If there be any whose business it is to promote a private, divided interest, or who place the sum of their religion in an inconsiderable and doubtful opinion, it doth not unhallow their altars, nor offer any affront to their idol."

---

* Seneca.

CHAPTER V.

FROM 1669 TO 1677.

HOWE INVITED TO BECOME CHAPLAIN TO LORD MASSARENE, OF ANTRIM CASTLE—ACCEPTS THE SITUATION—REMOVES WITH HIS FAMILY TO IRELAND—PROBABLY THE HAPPIEST PERIOD OF HIS LIFE—NATURE OF HIS EMPLOYMENT—UNIVERSAL RESPECT HE CONCILIATED—PUBLISHES HIS "VANITY OF MAN AS MORTAL"—CIRCUMSTANCES IN WHICH IT ORIGINATED—PUBLISHES HIS "DELIGHTING IN GOD"—THE PREFATORY LETTER—REFLECTIONS—COMPOSES THE FIRST PART OF HIS "LIVING TEMPLE"—IS INVITED TO THE PASTORAL CHARGE OF A CONGREGATION IN LONDON—SELF-EXAMINATION PREVIOUS TO LEAVING ANTRIM—REFLECTIONS—REMOVES HIS FAMILY TO LONDON—KING CHARLES'S INDULGENCE—REMARKS—HOWE PUBLISHES THE FIRST PART OF HIS "LIVING TEMPLE."

ABOUT a year, or a little more, after the publication of "The Blessedness of the Righteous," and perhaps in consequence of the deserved reputation which he acquired by it, Howe was invited to become domestic chaplain to Lord Massarene,* of Antrim Castle, Ireland; and the invitation, flattering in itself, was accompanied by very advantageous offers. The proposal, even if it had been less tempting, would have been backed by an argument perfectly resistless:—he was by this time in necessitous circumstances. How, indeed, could it be otherwise? He had now been ejected six years, and during this period had subsisted on an income, which, even if it had been less precarious, was miserably insufficient, and, unhappily, was as precarious as it was scanty. Poverty brought with it the deeper anguish and solicitude, that it found him with a young and numerous family.

---

* Originally Sir John Skeffington, of Fisherwick, Staffordshire (fifth Baronet). He became Viscount Massarene in right of his wife, Mary, the only daughter of Sir John Clotworthy, who, having been very active in the restoration of Charles II., was rewarded with the title of Lord Massarene. Howe's patron, therefore, was *second* Lord Massarene. He was active in the revolution of 1688. He died June 21st, 1695.

Under these circumstances he did not hesitate long. Gratefully embracing the offer of Lord Massarene, he set sail for Dublin early in the year 1671.* He embarked at some port in Wales, which Calamy conjectures to be Holyhead.

While waiting at this place for a fair wind, a circumstance occurred which showed both his anxiety to avail himself of every opportunity of doing good, and the impressive character of his preaching.

It appears that he was detained at the port for more than a week. On the Sunday, he was of course anxious, if not to preach, at least to hear the gospel; but though there was a large parish church, there was no preaching, it being the practice of the clergyman only to read prayers.

As there were many who, like Howe, were waiting for a fair wind, they were anxious to find some secluded spot in which he might preach to them. While they were seeking some such place on the sea-shore, they met two persons on horseback riding towards the town, "who proved to be parson and clerk." One of the party accosted the latter, and asked him, whether his master would preach that day? "My master," replied the clerk, " is only accustomed to read prayers." He then asked whether the clergyman would have any objection to allow a minister who was tarrying in the town, waiting to embark for Ireland, to occupy his pulpit for that day. He replied, that he believed that his master would willingly comply with such request. Upon this the proposal was made, and the clergyman instantly acceded to it. Howe accordingly preached twice in the parish church that day. In the afternoon, the congregation was very large, attentive, and apparently much affected.

The wind continued contrary all the next week; and the people having heard of Howe's destination, and observing that the vessel had not left the port, thronged the church on the Sabbath morning in expectation of again hearing the stranger, who had preached in a style so impressive, and to them so

---

* Calamy says in *April;* but, for reasons hereafter to be assigned, it would appear to have been somewhat earlier.

novel. The clergyman, who had quite forgotten the whole matter, and had doubtless expected only the usual quiet audience, was confounded at this prodigious concourse of people. Totally unprovided himself to meet the exigency, he hastily despatched his clerk to implore Howe's assistance : declaring, that "if he would not come he knew not what to do, for that the country had come in from several miles round, in the hope of hearing him." The messenger found Howe, who had been much indisposed, in bed. On being told the cause of this strange summons, he was at first in doubt whether he ought to venture; but reflecting that he knew not how much good might be done by his efforts, amongst a people who seemed eager to hear the word of God in proportion to the rarity of their opportunities of hearing it, he resolved to risk it. He afterwards declared that he had seldom preached with more fervour and energy, and never saw a congregation more attentive or devout. He at the same time added, "If my ministry was ever of any use, I think it must be then." A few days after, he set sail for Ireland.

After remaining a short time at Lord Massarene's, his whole family joined him.

The years Howe spent in Ireland were probably the happiest in his life. Under the protection of a powerful patron, and in the enjoyment of a competent income, he quietly pursued his two most cherished employments,—the ministry of the gospel and the study of divinity.

Antrim Castle, even then a noble structure, though it has gradually reached its present scale of grandeur by successive enlargements since that period, is situated in the midst of the most magnificent scenery. The spacious and fertile domain is watered by a beautiful lake, called Lough Neagh, from which the Lords Massarene took one of their titles.*

It was here that Howe revised and published his sermon

* "Antrim Castle adjoins the town from whence it takes its name; a view up the principal street of which is commanded from the parapet of an adjoining terrace-garden, ascended from the castle-yard by a handsome flight of stone steps. It is enclosed from the town by a gateway, and stands on a walled terrace, overhanging the river Ovenoeen, or Six Mile Water, which flows into the

entitled "The Vanity of Man as Mortal," and his valuable
little treatise on "Delighting in God." It was here also that
he prepared for the press, the first part of his greatest work,
"The Living Temple." The deep solitude and the romantic
beauty of the scenes in which he now dwelt, well harmonized
with the tendencies of a mind so contemplative and so fond of
abstraction. To the opportunities of prolonged and solitary
meditation which such scenes afforded, we are perhaps, in some
degree, indebted for the sustained sublimity, the noble sentiments, and the subtle trains of abstract reasoning, with which
the works he produced at this period of his life abound.

It is not a little singular, that not many years before, in the
same part of Ireland, and under circumstances very similar,
was produced the larger part of another of the many great
works which adorn the theology of our country. I allude to
the "Ductor Dubitantium" of Jeremy Taylor. When the
Episcopal party was under a cloud like that which in its turn
overshadowed the "ejected ministers," Taylor found, in the
patronage of the Earl of Conway, the protection which Howe

---

vast waters of Lough Neagh, within sight of the castle, at about the distance of
a quarter of a mile.

"This castle is among the few found to be preserved in Ireland, of those
erected in pursuance of the injunctions of the grant made by James I., for the
protection of the colonies or plantations then about to be established. The
building was raised, as appears by an inscription on a large carved mantel of
stone, covering the centre of the principal front, in the year 1613, by Sir Hugh
Clotworthy, and has been subsequently altered, according to the different tastes
of its successive proprietors.

"The front of the castle is also decorated with the armorial bearings of the
family, and those of their alliances, surmounted by the royal arms of England,
and a carved head, in relief, of Charles I.

"The suite of rooms is extensive and modern, the entire castle having undergone a thorough repair in the time of the last Earl of Massarene. The exterior
towards the court has been restored, by the present possessor, to the character
of the period in which it was originally erected.

"Few places in Ireland command greater power of beauty, or extent of drive.
Its demesne and deer-park stretch along the shore of Lough Neagh for above
two miles, ornamented with fine old timber and copse wood, covering every
headland, down to the water's edge, with various plantations, calculated to
blend in the scenery of as rich and highly cultivated a country as any to be
found in Ireland. The view over the lake towards the south is bounded only
by the horizon, while towards the west it rests on the distant Tyrone and Derry
mountains, and the nearer woods of Shane's Castle, the ancient seat of Earl
O'Neile, whose towers project into the lake itself. These two fine domains,
indeed, embrace, with their woods and pleasure grounds, the whole bay of
Antrim, an extent of six or seven miles."—*Neal's Seats.*

now enjoyed in that of Lord Massarene; and amidst the magnificent and romantic scenery which encircled the seat of his noble patron, composed the greatest part of his comprehensive treatise on casuistry. The work which Howe produced at Antrim Castle, though on a subject totally different, deserves equal celebrity. Both works indicate intellect of the highest order, though of character as different as the subjects of which they respectively treat.

Nothing can more strongly evince the rare conjunction of excellence that must have met in Howe—his catholic temper, his consummate prudence, his unaffected modesty, his insinuating manners—than the fact, quite unprecedented, that the Bishop of the diocese, in concurrence with the wishes of his Metropolitan, permitted him, without any demand of conformity, to preach at Antrim church every week. The Archbishop is even reported to have publicly told his clergy, that he could wish every pulpit in his province to be open to the distinguished nonconformist.

Within a very short time after his arrival in Ireland, certainly within a month or two, he published the first of the three works above mentioned, " The Vanity of Man as Mortal." Of all his smaller pieces, this, perhaps, has been most read, and most admired. It was written on one of the most affecting occasions that can well be conceived; an occasion calculated to stir the deepest emotions of a mind, which, indeed, scarcely needed any such extraordinary admonitions of Providence to enforce—what it habitually felt—the vanity of mortality and of time. The event to which reference is now made, was the death of Mr. Anthony Upton, the son of John Upton, Esq., of Lupton, in the county of Devon, a relative of Howe's. This son had been absent in Spain for more than twenty years, and had at length, at the earnest entreaties of his friends, consented to return home. His family having received intimation of the probable period of his arrival, it was arranged that there should be a meeting of his brothers and sisters, and all his other near relations, at his father's house, to celebrate the joyous occasion of his return. They assembled accordingly; but what was their consternation, when the vessel which was to have brought their long-lost friend, brought him in his shroud ! It appears that, immediately after he had made ar- rangements for embarkation, he had been attacked with some violent disease, which in a few days terminated his life; so that the first notice his friends had of this sad event, (to use the language of Howe in his Dedicatory Epistle,) " was the arrival of that vessel clad in mourning attire, which, according to his own desire in his sickness, brought over the deserted body to its native place." The family who had arranged their meeting under such far happier auspices, instead of assembling, as they had expected, to greet him after his long absence from his country, met only to " celebrate the mournful solemnity of his interment."

All remarks of a critical nature on this sublime discourse, will, as usual, be reserved for the proper place. I may here make special mention, however, of the Dedicatory Epistle, both because it is in itself a striking composition, and because it serves to determine some few points respecting the time and circumstances of Howe's removal to Ireland. It is dated from Antrim, April 12th, 1671. The date alone, coupled with the fact that he " had suspended his consent to the publication of this discourse " (composed before he left England) " till a copy had been transmitted for his inspection," would be a sufficient proof that the time* Calamy has assigned for his removal to Ireland cannot be correct. This " Epistle," however, mentions a circumstance which at once removes all doubt on the subject. In one part of it Howe adverts to a letter, which, " in conse- quence of his removal to Ireland, had not come, till long after" its date, " to his hands." These words certainly imply, that when he wrote this prefatory letter he had been at Antrim at least some weeks.—This letter also shows that Howe had been in London a short time previous to his taking up his abode at Antrim Castle.

One noble passage, in which he laments the spread of that infidelity which naturally flourished in the profligate age of the

---

* April, 1671.

second Charles, and to which the "Mortality" of man was the most welcome doctrine, is worth citing :

"If he that, amidst the hazards of a dubious war, betrays the interest and honour of his country, be justly infamous, and thought worthy severest punishments, I see not why a debauched sensualist, that lives as if he were created only to indulge his appetite ; that so vilifies the notion of man, as if he were made but to eat, and drink, and sport, to please only his sense and fancy ; that in this time and state of conflict between the powers of this present world, and those of the world to come, quits his party, bids open defiance to humanity, abjures the noble principles and ends, forsakes the laws and society of all that are worthy to be esteemed men, abandons the common and rational hope of mankind concerning a future immortality, and herds himself among brute creatures : I say, I see not why such a one should not be scorned and abhorred as a traitor to the whole race and nation of reasonable creatures, as a fugitive from the tents and deserter of the common interest of men ; and that, both for the vileness of his practice and the danger of his example. . . .

"One would think whosoever have remaining in them any conscience of obligation and duty to the common Parent and Author of our beings, any remembrance of our divine original, any breathings of our ancient hope, any sense of human honour, any resentments of so vile an indignity to the nature of man, any spark of a just and generous indignation for so opprobrious a contumely to their own kind and order in the creation, should oppose themselves with an heroic vigour to this treacherous and unnatural combination. And let us, my worthy friends, be provoked, in our several capacities, to do our parts herein ; and, at least, so to live and converse in this world, that the course and tenor of our lives may import an open asserting of our hopes in another ; and may let men see we are not ashamed to own the belief of a life to come. Let us, by a patient continuance in well-doing, (how low designs soever others content themselves to pursue,) seek honour, glory, and immortality to ourselves ; and by our avowed, warrantable ambition in this pursuit, justify our great and bountiful Creator, who hath made us not in vain, but for so high and great things ; and glorify our blessed Redeemer, who, amidst the gloomy and disconsolate darkness of this wretched world, when it was overspread with the shadow of death, hath brought life and immortality to light in the gospel. Let us labour both to feel and express the power of that religion which hath the inchoation of the participated divine life for its principle, and the perfection and eternal perpetuation thereof for its scope and end."

It has been mentioned that Howe published his treatise on "Delighting in God," during his stay at Antrim Castle. It first appeared in London, in 1674. It purports to be the *substance* of a series of sermons, preached many years before at Great Torrington, and is prefaced by a most affectionate letter to his friends there.

For the same reasons which induced me to offer a remark or two on the preface to the "Blessedness of the Righteous," I shall not dismiss the introductory letter just mentioned without observation. It displays, in common with all the author's writings, a spirit supremely intent on those great truths in which Christians are agreed, and consequently disposed to form a very moderate estimate of the points in which they differ. Not that he would represent these last as matters of no importance at all ; or content himself with the exercise of that spurious charity, which consists simply in laxity of opinion; a charity which disposes its possessors to agree with all parties, simply because they belong to none. *His* charity is of a very different complexion. He declares that he "is not indifferent about those matters which he cannot discern to be in their own nature so ; " he pretends not " to be without his opinions about those smaller things ; " he is simply anxious to unite an open and honest avowal of those opinions, with a mild and forbearing spirit: he will not surrender his own judgment out of a regard for charity; but he endeavours—and this is the real difficulty—to vindicate truth in the spirit of love. There is a beautiful passage in which, while he contends that on those points which divide Christians, he must adopt the opinions which, after mature deliberation, he believes to be right, he at the same time admits, that even where he is most *confident* of being in the right, the possibility of error should still teach caution and humility ; and that even on the supposition that he *is* in the right, there can be no ground for

any overweening conceit of superiority, since " of every differing party, he knows some by whom he finds himself much excelled in far greater things, than is the matter of their difference." How rare was such a spirit as this in that day! How
rare even in our own!

The whole composition displays an elevation of mind and an
amplitude of charity, to be found only in one who already
dwelt on the confines of heaven. Nothing but this could have
so defecated the judgment from all vulgar prejudices, and
composed the spirit to so serene a temper. From the lofty
elevation he had attained, he daily looked out on the solemn
and tranquil scenes of the eternal world, and as he gazed on
them, the turbulent passions of his fellow-men, and the noisy
controversies of the age, disturbed him as little as the hum
of a distant village might be supposed to interfere with the
musings of some contemplative spirit, eyeing a far-spread and
glorious prospect in the last fading and solemn splendours of a
summer sunset.

Nor does this letter exhibit in a less striking point of view,
Howe's truly *pastoral* character. The ties which bound him
to his early and humble flock, were not like those which too
often subsist between a minister and his people,—slight, and
easily severed. They resembled those which subsist between
a parent and his children,—ties, the strength of which, neither
time, nor even neglect and ingratitude, can impair. Those to
whom he had once been a spiritual father and guide, seem to
have been for ever graven on his memory; and in the spirit
of an apostle, he never " bowed his knees before the God and
Father of his Lord," without " making mention " of them.
No lapse of time, no change of circumstances, could banish the
scene of his early labours, or abate his interest in his flock;
and now, after a lapse of twenty years, he again addresses
to them his paternal rebukes and his paternal benedictions.
With what solemnity, with what fidelity, with what passionate
earnestness, does he apply himself to this task! Is it possible
that any of them could read the expostulations with which it
closes,—expostulations conceived in such a spirit of exquisite
pathos and melting tenderness,—without being softened into
tears ?

The following passages are very characteristic :

" Great reason I have to repent, that I have not with greater earnestness pressed upon you the known and important things wherein serious Christians do generally agree. But I repent not I have been so little engaged in the hot contests of our age, about the things wherein they differ. For, as I pretend to little light in these things; (whence I could not have much confidence to fortify me unto such an undertaking;) so I must profess to have little inclination to contend about matters of that kind. Nor yet am I indifferent as to those smaller things, that I cannot discern to be in their own nature so. But though I cannot avoid to think that course right which I have deliberately chosen therein, I do yet esteem that but a small thing upon which to ground an opinion of my excelling them that think otherwise, as if I knew more than they. For I have often recounted thus seriously with myself; that of every differing party in those circumstantial matters, I do particularly know some persons by whom I find myself much excelled in far greater things than is the matter of that difference. I cannot, it is true, thereupon say and think everything that they do; which is impossible, since they differ from one another as well as me. And I understand well, there are other measures of truth than this or that excellent person's opinion. But I thereupon reckon I have little reason to be conceited of any advantage I have of such in point of knowledge, (even as little as he should have, that can sing or play well on a lute, of him that knows how to command armies or govern a kingdom,) and can with less confidence differ from them, or contend with them; being thereby, though I cannot find I err in these matters, constrained to have some suspicion lest I do; and to admit it possible enough that some of them who differ from me, having much more light in greater matters, may have so in these also. Besides, that I most seriously think humility, charity, and patience, would more contribute to the composing of these lesser differences, or to the good estate of the Christian interest under them, than the most fervent disputes and contestations." . . .

He thus concludes :

" I bow my knees for you all, that a living, delightful religion may flourish in your hearts and families, instead of those dry, withered things, worldliness, formality, and strife about trifles: which will make Torrington an Hephzibah, a place to be delighted in; your country a pleasant region; and (if he may but hear of it) add no little to the satisfaction and delight of

> "Your affectionate servant in Christ,
> "Who most seriously desires your true prosperity,
> "JOHN HOWE.

"*Antrim, Sep.* 1, 1674."

Howe remained in Lord Massarene's family about five years. In 1675, he was invited to London, to take the charge of the congregation recently under the pastoral care of Dr. Lazarus Seaman, just deceased. Dr. S. was one of the most able, learned, and influential of the metropolitan ministers. He was a strict Presbyterian, and an advocate of the *jus divinum* of that form of church polity. He died September 9, 1675. For some time before his death he had shared the pastoral charge with Dr. Thomas Jacomb, who continued for some years to hold the same relation to his successor.*

As there was some division of opinion amongst the congrégation, (many of whom were anxious to secure the services of the well-known Stephen Charnock,) and as it was impossible to obtain by letter a full knowledge of all the circumstances on which his decision must depend, Howe resolved on a voyage to England before he replied to the application. Previous to his departure from Ireland on this important object, he subjected his motives and feelings to a most conscientious and rigid examination. His thoughts on this occasion he minuted down, under the title of—

"*Considerations and Communings with myself concerning my present Journey. Dec.* 20, 75, *by Night, on my Bed.*

"I. Quære—*Have I not an undue design or self-respect in it?*

"1. I know well I ought not to have any design for myself, which admits not of subordination to the interest and honour of the great God, and my Redeemer, and which is not actually so subordinated.

---

* See the Appendix to Howe's Sermon on "Patience in Expectation of Future Blessedness."

"2. I understand the fearful evil and sinfulness of having such an undue design; that it is idolatry, the taking another god, and making myself that god.

"3. I find (through God's mercy) some sensible stirrings of hatred and detestation, in my breast, of that wickedness, and a great apprehension of the loveliness and beauty of a state of pure, entire devotedness to God in Christ, and of acting accordingly.

"4. I have insisted on this chiefly in prayer to God, in reference to this business, ever since it was set on foot, that I might be sincere in it; and though I have earnestly begged light to guide me therein, so as that I might do that herein which in the substance of the thing is agreeable to the holy will of God, yet I have much more importunately prayed that I might be sincere in what I do; not only because I know God will pardon ignorance (unremedied by utmost endeavours) where he beholds sincerity, whereas he will never accept the knowledge of our duty, nor the doing what is in substance our duty, if that right manner of doing it, or principle whence it is done, be wanting; but, also, from the higher esteem I have of sincerity, above all light and knowledge without it, and the greater excellence of the thing itself.

"5. I have carefully examined what selfish respects I can have in this matter. Is it worldly emolument? In this my heart acquits me in the sight of God. Is it that I affect to be upon a public stage, to be popular and applauded by men? To this I say, 1. That I do verily believe, that I shall be lower in the eye and esteem of the people in London, when I come under their nearer view. I know myself incapable of pleasing their genius. I cannot contrive nor endure to preach with elaborate artifice. They will soon be weary, when they hear nothing but plain discourses of such matters as are not new to them. Yea, and ministers that now judge of me by what I have written, (when matter and words were in some measure weighed,) will find me, when I converse with them, slow to apprehend things, slow to express my own apprehensions, unready, entangled, and obscure in my apprehensions and expressions: so that all will soon say, 'This is not the man we took him for.' 2. It displeases me not, that they should find and say this. I hope I should digest it well. 3. I have found (blessed be God) that the applauses some have imprudently given me in letters, (as I have received many of that strain, very many long before this business, and that had no relation unto any such, that no eye hath ever since seen but my own,) an occasion and means to me of deep humiliation, when my own heart hath witnessed to me my miserable penury, and that I am thought to be what I am not. 4. So far as I can find, I do not deliberately covet or desire esteem but for my work's sake, and the success of my work. Of applause I have often found an inward abhorrence. I both know I have nothing but what I have received, and that I have received a great deal less than many think I have: which I say with reflection on myself; not to diminish the bounty of the Free-giver, from whom I know I might have received much more, if I had sought and used his gifts aright. All the design I can more vehemently suspect myself of that looks like self-interest any way, is, 1. The improvement of my own knowledge, which I know there may be great opportunities for, if this journey should issue in my settlement at London. 2. The disposal of my children. Yet I hope these things are eyed in subordination, and indifferently, so as not to sway with me against my duty.

" II. Quære—*Have I not a previous resolution of settling at London before I go up?*

" 1. I have a resolution to do what I shall conceive shall make most to the usefulness of the rest of my life, which resolution I ought never to be without.

" 2. I am seriously yet at a loss as to judging this case, whether in this country or there.

" 3. If I can find clearly it is my duty to return in order to continuance at Antrim, I shall do it with high complacency.

"III. Quære—*Am I not afraid of miscarrying in this under-taken voyage, by shipwreck, &c.?*

" 1. I find little of that fear, I bless God.

" 2. Nor is it that I think I have attained any eminent degree of grace, that I am not afflicted with that fear: nay, more than that, I acknowledge, to be delivered from such fear is itself a great mercy, and gracious vouchsafement.

" 3. I hope I am in a state of favour and acceptance with God, which I apprehend I owe to infinite rich mercy in the Redeemer's blood. Great forgiveness I need, for I am a miserable sinful wretch: this I trust I have upon gospel terms.

" 4. It is pleasant to me hereupon to think of going into eternity; of laying down the body of flesh, and sin, and death, together; and of being perfectly holy, and associated with them that are so, in holy work and enjoyment.

"5. To put off this tabernacle so easily, I reckon would to me be a merciful dispensation, who am more afraid of sharp pains than of death. I think I should joyfully embrace those waves that should cast me on an undesigned shore, and, when I intended Liverpool, should land me in heaven. .

"6. Yet I bless God I have no weariness of life, nor of his work, in this world, if he shall yet please further to employ me here.

"IV. Quære—*But am I not solicitous, lest if this should prove the event, it will be judged a testimony against me, as to this present undertaking?*

"1. It is an honest design I go upon. I have, as I said, no selfish design that oversways me in it. I have no design to prejudice Mr. Charnock. I believe I shall do him no actual prejudice. Wherein I can justly befriend him, I go resolved to do it. If I can do anything for the holding of the remainder together, without the neglect of greater work, I do apprehend I shall do a just and needful thing; but should do nothing if I had opportunity, till I knew more. But,

"2. To judge of the justice of a cause by the success, is a most unjust way of judging. Many a just business has miscarried. If I get well into the other world, such censures will be a small matter in my eye; and they are not great now.

"3. God will accept my sincere intentions, though I effect nothing.

"4. My journey was to me absolutely necessary, who could without it neither grant nor deny.

"*Consolations to my wife and other relations, supposing they hear of my death.*

"1. Whom or what have you lost? A poor creature that could never be of much use to you.

"2. You are to consider me, not as lost in my prime, but as now I am, sensibly under great decays, and not likely to continue long, except some means hitherto not thought on should have been tried. What a summer had I of the last! seldom able to walk the streets; and not only often disabled by pain, but weakness. And what great advantage to you

would it have been to see me die? I know not when I have
had so much ease and health as in this journey.

"3. God not only hath determined the thing, we must die,
but all circumstances, when and where, and after what manner,
and all wisely and well. Why should you be grieved, that he
hath done well? not only well in itself, but well for you, if
you love him?

"4. You must ere long follow, and shall not be always in
this world without me.

"5. What there is of evil in this case, admits of remedy.
Draw so much nearer to God, and cease from man: mind
heaven more, and your loss is made up.

"6. I have, through the grace of God, preached immortal
truth, which will survive, and may be to your advantage.

"7. As to you who have dependence upon me for worldly
concernments: I was never a good projector for the world; so
the loss is not great. How many, dear to God, make a shift,
in a worse condition! Forget not the motto, 'God will pro-
vide.' He that feeds ravens, and takes care of sparrows, will
he not take care of you? Are you of his family, and will he
not take care of his own? Instead of distrust and repining,
give thanks. Oh bless him with all your soul, that he hath
revealed and given himself to you for an everlasting portion;
and whose covenant is to be your God, and the God of yours.

"8. Let it be some satisfaction to you, that I go willingly,
under no dread, with no regret, but with some comfortable
knowledge of my way and end."

Who can read these musings of an upright and conscientious
mind without the deepest admiration? It is true that in the
minuteness of this self-examination, and the precision and
formality with which it is prosecuted, we are reminded of the
excessive scrupulosity of the times, and of the too systematic
method in which the spiritual casuist was in the habit of treating "cases of conscience," as they were called. In the present
instance, it may, perhaps, be admitted that Howe need not
have inquired so industriously, whether he was likely to be
swayed in a transaction so important by the fear of shipwreck,*
or by the uncharitable judgments which others might form of
him, if he *should* be shipwrecked.† It might be justly con-

---

* As in Query III.   † As in Query IV.

tended, that considerations such as these could not have had much influence on his final decision; or that, if they operated as motives at all, it was in a degree so very slight as not to entitle them to a formal investigation.* Yet, though there may be in these passages a little too much of the superfluous minuteness and self-suspicion, which were so characteristic of the age, who could wish to blot them out? What an enviable state of mind do they manifest! How especially beautiful is that sentence: "I think I should joyfully embrace those waves that should cast me on an undesigned shore, and when I intended Liverpool, should land me in heaven."

As a whole, none can read this soliloquy of a sensitive conscience, without feeling convinced that to Howe (as stated in the introductory chapter), duty was a study. To ascertain conscientiously in every case *what* duty was, and to perform it from the *right* motives, were evidently the great objects of his life; and rapid, indeed, is the progress in holiness and virtue likely to be, when, in every important step in life, motives and conduct are subjected to such a severe and rigid scrutiny.

Nor is it less to the purpose to remark that there is nothing in the above self-examination, scrupulous as it is, which betrays the slightest taint of a fanatical spirit. There is no pretence to superhuman purity of motive—no fond disclaimer of human feelings and passions: if these last be but innocent, Howe seeks not their extinction, nor even that they should not be duly gratified; he is only anxious that they should be in their proper place; strongly subordinated to higher and more important principles of action.†

The fourth and fifth paragraphs (Query IV.) are very beautiful; the modesty they display, the humility, the purity of

---

* Still something may be said in his defence even with reference to these. points. With regard to the first, it is not to be forgotten that a voyage from Ireland was not in those days the trifle it would be considered now; and with regard to the second, proof is but too abundant, that in defiance alike of common sense, daily experience, and Christian charity, the ordinary calamities of life were, in those times, too often considered *special* judicial marks of the Divine displeasure.

† See close of observations on Query I.

feeling, the superiority to every form of petty vanity, the secret dissatisfaction at human applause (arising from the exalted conceptions he had formed of absolute excellence, combined with his consciousness that he was still so very far from having reached that standard,) are calculated to inspire the liveliest admiration. The confessions of his own unworthiness which are contained in these passages, entirely free, as they are, from every symptom of affectation, and evidently never intended for any eye but his own, only endear him to us the more; and, as we read them, we feel that in this, as in other and more important respects, those words of Christ are true, " He that humbleth himself shall be exalted."

After staying some time in London, and giving the whole subject mature deliberation, he resolved on accepting the invitation which he had received from Dr. Seaman's congregation. He, in consequence, shortly after removed with his family from Antrim Castle, deeply grateful for the protection its noble owner had afforded him. With Lord and Lady Massarene, he maintained a friendly intercourse till their death in 1695. In 1676, the year after his departure, their daughter Mary was married · to Sir Charles Hoghton, of Hoghton Tower, in the county of Lancaster; on which occasion, Howe addressed the newly wedded pair in the following characteristic letters, written on the same sheet of paper. They bear no date, but the marriage itself determines it.

" Most honoured Sir,

" I thankfully acknowledge the favour of your welcome lines, which ought to be most entirely so, both upon the account of the author and the matter of them. For though my opportunity for so desirable an acquaintance hath been but little as to the circumstance, it hath been much as to the substance of what I know of you, in ways that gave me greatest assurance, before I had the happiness of oral converse with you. Nor could anything be more grateful to me, than to read you from your own hand so related, and so well pleased (as I doubt not you will be daily more and more) with your relation, and the other accessory correlates, with whom God hath cast your lot.

"I believe you have much reason to bless God (who orders all things to the best advantage to such as sincerely give themselves up to his conduct,) that he led you not into such a condition and state of life as he now at length hath brought you into, before you were well acquainted with the rules and duties of it, better than to need help from such a one as I. But among the many other precepts that concern that case, I dare adventure to recommend those of 1 Cor. vii. 29, 30, 31, and pursuantly thereto, to offer to your thoughts, that this can be but a partial temporary felicity, and so far only so at all, as it is enjoyed only as mediate and subservient to the full and final felicity, which we are professedly seeking and waiting for ; so far ought it to be, to oppose it, or let it be an obstruction thereto : which is the nature of all good things that have only the goodness of the means, and not of the end, that their goodness is variable, and by misapplication may degenerate into a hurtful evil. Within the compass of such things is the truth of those words to be confined: *Nil prodest quod non lædere possit idem.* It is beyond the measure of any created good to be universally so. That therefore which in its own place is a real good, applied to the particular purpose which it is capable of serving,—out of that place, and being trusted, valued, and delighted in beyond the measure which God and the nature of the thing have stated and set, may become a hurt to us.

"But there can be no greater or more endearing obligation to use any mercy for God, than an habitual fixed sense of its having been received from him, and a deeply radicated and often repeated agnition of his sovereign hand in ordering it to be our lot, with all the circumstances that have had any reference thereto. For what ingenuous heart can endure to oppose to him, or employ against him, the (apprehended) fruit of his own favour and kindness ? a pledge of his paternal love and care so understood ? And therefore the greater the gift is (still considered under that strict notion) the stronger is the inducement to honour and serve the giver with it, and to enjoy according to his prescription, what we enjoy not but by his vouchsafement.

"If to all this I should add a request to you to be exceeding kind to my most dear and honoured friend, it were the greatest impertinence in all the world. For she, having such a temper to work upon, will make you so whether you will or no : and I might as well use arguments to persuade a fragrant flower to

send forth its grateful odours, when a most benign orient sun
is plying it with its cherishing morning beams. Such may
you long be, both of you mutually (sun and flower) to each
other, shining and flourishing with all the influence, and under
the continual blessing of Heaven. So shall you communicate
a part of that joy, which I most entirely wish you, to

" Sir,

" Your very faithful and affectionate humble Servant,

" J. Howe."

" Whatsoever leisure, most dear and honoured Madam, you
may suppose me to have, I had little reason to suppose Sir
Charles and yourself to have much, from the reading of one
another, to cast your eyes upon anything I could write. But
if after this paper shall have lain one quarter of a year somewhere near your dressing-box, you find it not unseasonable to
bestow a glance upon it, you will then at length find your
disappointment. For it will tell you nothing but what you
well knew, or might easily guess before; that having a constant most affectionate respect and honour for you, I cannot
but be highly pleased that you are so [happy].

" And methinks it should not much surprise you, if I further
say, I would have you somewhat to alter (or make your exception to) your own rule, and not show the less kindness to
Sir Charles for that he is a married man. This will not be
strange to you, if you remember some of your last winter lines.

" After this hath made you smile a little, as that of yours
did me, then think that this novelty in your condition will
neither make nor allow you to smile always, though I hope it
will add a great deal to the comfort and pleasantness of your
days.——And you may sometimes have occasion to think
seriously together, of the sense of those words, Luke xiv. 26.
And always remember the subordination that all creature-
love must be in, to that of the supreme object of our love.
How pleasant a thing will it be to have hearts united and
consenting in the resolution of loving him perpetually above
all, to whom we owe our all, and who is altogether lovely !
to consult and conspire together, how most to promote his
interest, and improve in acquaintance with him, and conformity to him. This I believe your heart to be much formed
to beforehand. The great care must be, that such resolutions
do not gradually languish. We find many are apt by un-
observed degrees to starve the good affections and inclinations

which they would abhor to assassinate by a sudden violence.   I
write securely, that such an intimation will by so great a kindness as yours, be very well taken, from

> "Your Ladyship's
>> "Most affectionate humble Servant,
>>> "J. Howe."

During the time Howe was in Ireland, King Charles had
published his celebrated "Declaration of Indulgence."*   Calamy says, that upon his return to London, he "made a quiet
and peaceable use of this indulgence."   This, however, must
be an error, for the Declaration was revoked in the spring of
1673 ; that is, as soon as Charles wanted his next *subsidy*.
For such a cause, he would have been willing to repeal the
whole decalogue.

It is quite true, however, that it still served in some measure
to protect the nonconformists, as it tended to diminish the
hostility of those who had more reverence for the royal prerogative than for the two Houses of Parliament.   Amongst these
persons (as Baxter assures us) might be reckoned a large
number of the magistrates, whose loyalty for once was happily
at variance with their bigotry.   Although, therefore, the recall
of the Indulgence left the nonconformists in fact exposed to
all the severe laws which had been enacted against them, their
condition was upon the whole somewhat ameliorated.   If we
may believe Calamy,† the liberty which Charles's Indulgence
gave them, was not entirely lost, though constantly diminishing, till the year 1681.

The reasons which prompted Charles to put forth this Indulgence, as well as the history of its recall, are well known.

As to the first, suffice it to say, that the whole history of
Charles's reign, and especially his conduct in 1675, preclude
the charitable suspicion that he was actuated by the slightest
regard to the principles of toleration, or that he was visited by
any foolish feelings of remorse on account of his past severities.
In all such respects Charles II. was one of the most consistent
of mankind.

---

* 1672.   † Life and Times, vol. i. p. 72.

I

His true reason seems to have been the same which, a few years after, led to a similar measure on the part of that miserable dotard, James II. It was an anxiety to exempt the *Papists* from persecution.

The Indulgence was no sooner published, than it was vehemently opposed by both Houses of Parliament, on the just ground that to dispense with any existing laws on the sole authority of the Crown, was an invasion of the rights of the legislature, and an unwarrantable and dangerous stretch of the royal prerogative. Accordingly, when Charles stood in need of his next *subsidy*, it was revoked.

While the Indulgence was in force, however, one would think that all the nonconformists might have gladly availed themselves of it. Yet, strange to say, some of them, in the excess of their scrupulosity, doubted whether they would be justified in resuming those sacred rights of which neither kings *nor* parliament could justly deprive them, in a manner so informal! Had they, indeed, been called upon to *justify* the unwarrantable extension of the prerogative, or to acknowledge that their privileges might be granted or resumed at the King's pleasure, the case would have been different. But they were called to do nothing of the kind. All that was necessary, was to avail themselves of a happy accident; to resume a natural right, which no law of man could righteously invade; leaving the King and Parliament in the meantime to settle their disputes as they best could. Their conduct was almost as absurd as that of a man who, having been most unjustly imprisoned, and finding his oppressors quarrelling about the propriety of detaining him, should consult his *conscience*, whether he could rightfully step out at the door which in their dispute they had left open, or avail himself of such an unusual method of regaining his freedom. It is such instances of perverse scrupulosity as these that give edge, because they give some plausible appearance of truth, to the bitter satire of Butler:

> "The self-same thing they will abhor
> One way, and long another for.
> Free-will they one way disavow;
> Another, nothing else allow.

> Rather than fail, they will defy
> That which they love most tenderly;
> Quarrel with minced pies, and disparage
> Their best and dearest friend, plum-porridge."*

Howe was not plagued with any of this excessive conscientiousness. He on this, and every subsequent occasion, appears to have eagerly availed himself of every fair opportunity of securing his own peace and fulfilling the great ends of his public ministry.

Such was the regard which his talents, learning, and worth conciliated, that his nonconformity did not prevent his being on the most intimate terms with many who already were, or who afterwards became, some of the most distinguished ornaments of the Establishment. Amongst others may be mentioned Stillingfleet, afterwards Bishop of Worcester; Tillotson, afterwards Archbishop of Canterbury; Sharp, afterwards Archbishop of York; Drs. Whichcot, Kidder, Fowler, and Lucas.

Very soon after his removal to London, appeared the first part of his largest and most celebrated work, " The Living Temple." It was prepared, as already mentioned, during his residence at Antrim Castle; and on this account is, with great propriety, dedicated to the " Lord Viscount Massarene, governor of the county of Londonderry, and one of the Lords of His Majesty's most honourable Privy Council in the kingdom of Ireland." The dedications of that age, in general, were conceived in the spirit of the grossest and most fulsome adulation, and it is often hard to say who were the more contemptible, the authors who could compose or the patrons who could relish them.† Those of Howe were of a more manly stamp; although it must be confessed, that even he is sometimes a little infected with the complimentary folly of the times.

---

* Hudibras, part i. canto 1.

† There is often a whimsical contrast between the dedications of that age and the works to which they are prefixed; especially when those works turn on any of the more fiercely agitated points of controversy. The spirit of the one is so bland and gentle, that it would seem as though the author could not by possibility drop a harsh or uncourteous word; that of the other so coarse and savage, that malignity and scorn would appear to be the only elements in his composition. In passing from the one to the other, the sensation is much the same as though, in taking a draught of some excessively sweet and luscious liquor, it had, by some magical process of acetation, been all at once turned into verjuice.

This Dedication, however, is so full of noble thoughts, expressed in a style so manly, that its length alone prevents me from inserting it entire, nor should any reader enter the "Temple" itself without pausing in its vestibule. One short but characteristic passage I shall extract.

"But as this temple is quite of another constitution and make, than that at Jerusalem, and (to use those words of the sacred writer) ἀχειροποίητος, τουτέστιν, οὐ ταύτης τῆς κτίσεως *'not made with hands, that is to say, not of this building,'*—so what is requisite to the interest and service of it, is much of another nature. Entire devotedness to God, sincerity, humility, charity, refinedness from the dross and baseness of the earth, strict sobriety, dominion of one's self, mastery over impotent and ignominious passions, love of justice, a steady propension to do good, delight in doing it, have contributed more to the security and beauty of God's temple on earth, conferred on it more majesty and lustre, done more to procure it room and reverence among men, than the most prosperous violence ever did."

CHAPTER VI.

ANDREW MARVELL'S DEFENCE OF HOWE, AGAINST THOMAS DANSON'S ATTACK ON THE TREATISE OF "DIVINE PRESCIENCE."

AS the following chapter will probably contain little to interest the general reader, I may apprize him that it may
be omitted without impairing the continuity of the narrative,
since it is almost wholly parenthetical.

If the reader should chance to belong to that class, who,
when they have once been induced to commence a volume,
make it a point of conscience—no matter what its bulk, or
how repulsive its contents—to read right on from the title-
page to the end, and on whom, I well know, all premonitions
of the ruggedness or inconveniences of the road would be
totally lost,—even for such there is consolation: the chapter
will be a *brief* one.

But to the curious in literary history, and to the admirers
of Andrew Marvell's genius, I feel that no apology is necessary. They will probably think a chapter which has in it so
much of Andrew Marvell, and so little of the author, by far
the most interesting in the volume.

That I may not detain them, therefore, from matter which
I know will be so much more grateful to them than any
observations of mine, I shall simply beg their attention to a
short detail of the circumstances which led to the curious
publication from which the following extracts are made, and
then dismiss them, to enjoy those extracts at their leisure.
I would merely remark further, by way of whetting their appetite, that the tract in question is extremely rare; that it is
not published in any edition of Marvell's works, and was
evidently unknown to his biographers and editors. I know

of only one copy in existence—the one from which the subjoined extracts have been transcribed.*　This I procured from
Dr. Williams' library.

In 1677, Howe, at the request of the Hon. Robert Boyle,
published his little treatise, entitled, " The Reconcilableness
of God's Prescience of the Sins of Men with the Wisdom and
Sincerity of His Counsels and Exhortations, and whatever
other means He uses to prevent them."　The motives which
induced him to write it are given in the following short prefatory letter to his illustrious friend :—

" *Sir*,

　　　" The veneration I have long had for your name,
could not permit me to apprehend less obligation than that of
a law, in your recommending to me this subject.　For within
the whole compass of intellectual employment and affairs, none
but who are so unhappy as not at all to know you, would dispute your right to prescribe, and give law.　And taking a
nearer view of the province you have assigned me, I must
esteem it alike both disingenuous and undutiful wholly to
have refused it.　For the less you could think it possible to
me to perform in it, the more I might perceive of kindness,
allaying the authority of the imposition ; and have the apprehension the more obvious to me that you rather designed
in it mine own advantage, than that you reckoned the cause
could receive any, by my undertaking it."

Admirable as the tract is, it appears the author composed
it under very disadvantageous circumstances ; and for its
supposed defects, he offers at the close the following needless
apology :—

" The disorder, Sir, of this heap rather than frame of
thoughts and discourse, as it cannot be thought more unsuitable to the subject, than suitable to the author ; and the less
displease, by how much it could less be expected to be otherwise, from him, even in the best circumstances ; so it may lay
some claim to your easier pardon, as having been, mostly,
huddled up in the intervals of a troublesome, long journey ;

---

* This rare tract has since been reprinted, together with Howe's treatise
which evoked it, by my late excellent and venerated friend, Dr. John Brown,
of Edinburgh, in a series of " Theological Tracts."　Vol. iii. pp. 75–138.
Edin. 1854.

wherein he was rather willing to take what opportunity the inconveniencies and hurry of it could allow him, than neglect any, of using the earliest endeavour to approve himself—as he is your great admirer—

"Most honoured Sir,

"Your most obedient, humble Servant."

All remarks on this treatise will be reserved for the critical estimate at the close of the volume. Its history, as serving to illustrate that of its author, is the sole subject of the present chapter.

The views which this tract contains are so sober and chastened, that Anthony Wood—who, by the way, was about as competent a judge of such a question, as a mere antiquary would be of a question of science—proclaims the author "a great and strict Arminian."

It could hardly be expected, therefore, that it would satisfy those who held extreme opinions on the subject of the Divine *predetermination*, and it was, accordingly, attacked by no less than three writers. The first was Theophilus Gale, who inserted some animadversions in the fourth and last part of his celebrated work, "The Court of the Gentiles." To these animadversions Howe himself replied, in a postscript to his treatise, in which he exposes the false logic, and, what is worse, the glaring misstatements of his adversary. A second assailant was an ejected minister, named John Troughton. His initials only are prefixed to his piece, which professes to be a reply not only to Howe's original treatise, but to the postscript also.* The third was Thomas Danson, also an ejected minister. He had been an intimate friend and fellow-collegiate of Howe's, for which reason he also affixed only his initials to the title-page.†

To neither of these latter opponents did Howe publish any

---

* It is entitled, "A Letter to a Friend, touching God's Prescience about Sinful Actions." 12mo. 1678.

† It is entitled, "De Causâ Dei; or a Vindication of the Common Doctrine of Protestant Divines concerning Predetermination, viz.—'The Interest of God, as the first Cause, in all the Actions, as such, of rational Creatures,' from the invidious Consequences with which it is burthened by Mr. John Howe, in a late Letter and Postscript of God's Prescience, by T. D." 1678.

reply. As to Danson, his little book was not only most illogical, and full of misconception and misrepresentation, but displayed much arrogance and vanity; and these considerations alone would probably have deterred Howe from breaking silence. He would have been, in the last degree, unwilling to say anything in a case in which, if he had spoken at all, he must have spoken with an unwonted, and, to him, ungrateful severity.

But though Howe himself was silent, a very sufficient champion voluntarily undertook his defence. This was no less than Andrew Marvell.

If not distinguished by any extraordinary aptitude for metaphysical speculation, this great man at least possessed a clear, sound, healthy understanding; and, in more than ordinary measure, that practical sagacity, which admirably qualified him for appreciating the character and detecting the sophistry of an over-subtle and trifling disputant.

Much subtlety of reasoning was not what the case principally required. Marvell had what was much more effective in such a controversy; the wit and sarcasm which had so often chastised ignorance, insolence, and vanity.

It is highly honourable to Marvell that his extraordinary powers of satire, (powers which are so often employed to gratify malignity of feeling, or at the best an ostentatious vanity,) were in his case never employed except in the cause of truth or oppressed innocence. He reminds one of Spenser's Talus, the attendant of Arthegal, "that yron man" whose terrible severities were meted out with the strictest justice, and never descended except on the head of flagrant crime.

> " His name was Talus, made of yron mould,
>   Immoveable, resistless, without end;
>   Who in his hand an yron flail did hold,
> With which he threshed out falsehood and did truth unfold."
>
> *Spenser's Fairy Queen.* Book V. canto i.

But though Marvell never employed his powers of wit and sarcasm for any selfish purpose, and seemed quite willing, as far as his own fame went, to let them slumber for ever in the cloud, any impudent assault on innocence and virtue, any extraordinary display of tyranny, meanness, fraud, or falsehood, never failed to provoke the bolts of this great avenger. All his principal productions owed their origin solely to his chivalrous love of truth, justice, and honour. It was thus with his greatest work, "The Rehearsal Transprosed," against Parker; with his "Defence of the Naked Truth," against the flippant and conceited Francis Turner; and with his present tract against Danson.

This tract is entitled, " Remarks on a late disingenuous Discourse, written by one T. D., under the pretence ' De Causâ Dei,' and of answering Mr. John Howe's letter and postscript of ' God's Prescience,' etc., affirming as the Protestant doctrine, ' That God doth by efficacious influence universally move and determine men to all their actions, even to those that are most wicked.' By a Protestant."*

From the more strictly argumentative parts of this tract, I shall refrain from making any extracts. They could not be fully understood without making large extracts from Danson's work; and with any considerable portion of that publication I should be sorry to try the patience of my readers.

The tract opens with the following noble reflections on the unprofitable questions which often occupy speculative theology.

---

* Wood ("Athenæ Oxonienses," Edition Bliss, vol. iv.) says, in the account of Thomas Danson, " This book," speaking of the tract against Howe, " hath only the initial letters T. D. set to it, because it was written against his intimate friend and fellow-collegiate. Afterwards came out a book entitled, ' Remarks upon a late disingenuous Discourse, writ by one T. D., London, 1678,' said to be by ' A Protestant,' but whether by John Howe, query." This sage query shows that Wood could never have seen Marvell's Tract, or he would never have been at a loss for an answer to his own interrogatory. It is avowedly written by a *layman*, with the express purpose of inducing Howe *not to engage in the controversy;* it is full of his *praises* from beginning to end; and has just all those qualities, both of thought and style, of which he was most destitute.

But though it was certainly not written by Howe, this, it may be said, does not prove it to have been written by Marvell. I grant it: that is to be determined by other evidence. That the tract was, in Marvell's day, universally and undoubtingly ascribed to him, appears from Calamy, who says without the slightest qualification, " Mr. Danson also wrote against this tract, but I know not that Mr. Howe took any notice of him ; though the ingenious Andrew Marvell, Esq., made a very witty and entertaining reply to him." The point, however, would be sufficiently clear, even if this testimony were wanting. The internal evidence alone would decide it. None who are in the slightest degree acquainted with Andrew Marvell's peculiar vein of humour, can mistake any half-dozen pages as the composition of any other author.

To the sagacious and practical mind of Andrew Marvell, a man engaged all his life in public affairs, such questions were likely to appear in all their frivolity. He thus begins :—

"Of all vocations to which men addict themselves, or are dedicated, I have always esteemed that of the ministry to be the most noble and happy employment; as being more peculiarly directed to those two great ends, the advancement of God's glory, and the promoting of man's salvation. It hath seemed to me as if they who have chosen, and are set apart for that work, did, by the continual opportunity of conversing with their Maker, enjoy a state like that of paradise; and in this superior, that they are not also, as Adam, put in, 'to dress and keep a garden;' but are, or ought to be, exempt from the necessity of all worldly avocations. Yet, upon nearer consideration, they likewise appear to partake of the common infelicities of human condition. For, although they do not, as others, eat their bread in the sweat of their brows, (which some Divines account to be, though in the pulpit, undecent,) yet the study of their brain is more than equivalent; and even the theological ground is so far under the curse, that no field runs out more in thorns and thistles, or requires more pains to disincumber it. Such I understand to be those peevish questions which have overgrown Christianity; wherewith men's minds are only rent and entangled, but from whence they can no more hope for any wholesome nourishment, than to 'gather grapes from thorns, or figs from thistles.' And (if I may so far pursue the allegory) this curse upon divinity, as that upon the earth, seems to have proceeded also from tasting that forbidden fruit, of the 'tree of knowledge of good and evil.' For, in general, many Divines, out of a vain affectation of learning, have been tempted into inquiries too curious, after those things which the wisdom of God hath left impervious to human understanding, further than they are revealed. And hence, instead of those allowed and obvious truths of faith, repentance, and the new creature, (yet these too have their proper weeds that pester them,) there have sprung up endless disputes concerning the unsearchable things of God, and which are agitated by men, for the most part, with such virulence and intricacy, as manifest the subtlety and malice of the serpent that hath seduced them. But, more particularly, that very knowledge of good and evil, the disquisition of the causes from whence, and in what manner they are derived, hath been so grateful to the

controversial *female* appetite, that even the Divines have taken
of it as ' a fruit to be desired to make them wise,' and given to
their people, and they have both eaten, at the peril of God's
displeasure and their own happiness. Whereas that second
chapter of Genesis contains the plain history of good and evil,
and (not to mention so many attestations to it of the Old and New
Testament) what other comment needs there, for what belongs to
good, than that it is from God only, 'that every good giving, and
every perfect gift descendeth ? ' And, as to evil, that also of St.
James is sufficient conviction, ' Let no man say, when he is
tempted, I was tempted of God ; God cannot be tempted with
evil, neither tempteth he any man : but every man is tempted,
when he is drawn aside by his own lusts and enticed.' Or that
of the same apostle, ' From whence come wars and fightings
among you ? ' (and even that *Logomachia*, I fear, with which
this question is vexed,) ' Come they not hence ? even from your
lusts that fight in your members.' And there is no examining
Christian but must find both these truths evidently witnessed
by his own conscience.

"Nevertheless, the theologians of former and later times,
not content with what is held forth in Scripture, have attempted
to clamber and palm up higher, by the philosophy of that
school where each of them hath first practised, and have drawn
God's prescience and predetermination, upon this occasion,
into debate ; arguing upon such points as no man, unless he
were prior and precedent to the First Cause, can have the
understanding to comprehend and judge of : and most of them
do but say and unsay ; and, while in words they all deny God
to be the author of sin, yet in effect and by the manner of their
reasoning they affirm it ; I, therefore, being both apprehensive
of the danger of such arguments, and more particularly conscious
of mine own weakness, shall not presume to interpose my
opinion in the differences about this matter, further than to
say ;—that if men, by this fancied ' opening of their eyes,'
have attained to see more clearly, and acknowledge the wickedness of their own actions, it resembles the modesty of our first
parents discerning their ' nakedness : ' but, if men shall also
assert a predeterminative concourse of God to our evil, it seems
to have too much of original perverseness, and of that fallen,
shortness of reason, whereby they would have found a nudity
in the Creator, and did implicitly reject their fault upon him,
for the ' serpent that he had made,' and the ' woman that he
had given.'

"But, if any man there be that can reconcile this controversy, and so many more that arise out of it; (for all the most important doctrines of Christianity serve on the one side, and all the fiercest questions of religion on the other, depending for truth and falsehood upon the success of this engagement;) if he can extinguish all those ill consequences, dull distinctions, and inconsistent notions, which have been levied in this quarrel, and reduce each party within the due limits of Scripture and saving knowledge; such a person indeed deserves all commendation. And such an one I thought I had met with, nor yet see reason, notwithstanding all the late attempts upon him, to alter my opinion; in a book entitled, 'The Reconcilableness of God's Prescience of the Sins of Men, with the Wisdom and Sincerity of his Counsels, Exhortations, and whatsoever other means he uses to prevent them. In a Letter to the Honourable Robert Boyle, Esquire;' and in a 'Postscript to the late Letter of the Reconcilableness of God's Prescience, by John Howe, the Author of that letter.'"

These observations are followed (for Marvell could not long maintain so grave a strain) by some good-humoured banter on Howe's apology for the *haste* with which his work had been written: after which, he suddenly drops his ironical vein, and breaks out into expressions of the most ardent admiration, both of Howe and his performance.

"Yet there was one passage in the close of his letter, which seemed, as I thought, to lie open to censure; where he asked pardon, as 'having huddled it up mostly in the intervals of a troublesome long journey.' It seemed a piece too well elaborate to have been perfected amidst the hurry of the road, the noise of inns, and the nausea of the packet-boat. And how could he hope, after saying this, in so captious an age as we live, to escape some reflection? but that at least men would inquire whether he went by stage-coach, or on horseback; both which are professed enemies to meditation and judgment? (for it is probable he had not that ancient accommodation of horse-litters, wherein, without any impediment to their thoughts, men travelled with all the privacy and equipage of a closet:) whether he had not lost his way, or fallen among thieves, and how he found himself after his journey? with all the questions that men are subject to at their arrival home, and which, even when asked in civility, yet are troublesome. He might, had it not been for the jogging, have remembered how unfortunate most writers have been in such excuses, and what advantage ill-natured men have taken to misinterpret them. So he that apologized for using a foreign tongue, was told, that no man had prohibited him his native language in his own country; others, alleging that they had at the same time a fit of the stone, gout, or other distemper, have been taxed, as lying under no obligation of publishing their infirmities, but who might, however, have cured themselves of that of writing. . . . . .

"But, in earnest, this confession of Mr. Howe's is so far from any such arrogance, that it rather argues his modesty. For, if some can even in riding name all the contrary motions, till they have by memory played out a game at chess, (which was first invented as an emblem of predetermination,) why should it be more difficult, or less allowable, to one of Mr. Howe's abilities, in the interruptions of travel, to give a mate also to that question? The worst therefore that can be said of him, in allusion either to his letter or his journey, is—'*at poterat tutior esse domi.*' Yet seeing this was the greatest fault that I remarked in reading him over, I would not pass it by without notice, lest I might have cause to suspect myself of a partiality, which I desire not that others should exercise in mine own particular.

"But for the rest, whereas the things considerable in all discourses are the subject, the end, the reasoning, the method, and the style; I must profess that, as far as I understand, I have met with few manual treatises, that do in all these respects equal it. For the subject, it appears in the title; than which there is none of greater dignity to be handled, or of greater use, if rightly explained and comprehended. And no less is that of *predetermination*, which he only treats of collaterally; and upon which therefore, in hope to find him less prepared, he hath been attacked, as in the flank, with most vigour. His end was most commendable, being to make the paths straight, and remove those stumbling-blocks which the asperity of others had laid in the way to heaven; to rectify men's apprehensions concerning God, and leave them without pretence for negligence in their duties, or despair of performance; much less for despite against the Creator. His arguing then is plain and solid, for evidence, rather than dispute; nor does he either throw the dust of antique distinctions in the eyes of his readers, to blind them; or raise the spectres of ancient authors, or conjure their venerable names, to fright men out of their senses and understanding; but declares against all the prejudice or advantage by such proceeding, as unlawful charms, and prohibited weapons in the controversy. His method thereafter is direct and coherent, his style perspicuous and elegant: so that it is, in short, a manly discourse, resembling much, and expressing, the human perfection; in the harmony of language, the symmetry of parts, the strength of reason, the excellency of its end, which is so serious, that it is no defect in the similitude with man, that the letter contains nothing in it suitable to the property of laughter."

He then proceeds to give the following ludicrous account of Danson's reply :—

"All which put together, and although it does and must everywhere partake also of human imperfection, the treatise on 'Divine Prescience' might have been hoped capable of that civility which men, and especially learned men, but most of all Divines, do usually, or should allow, one another: that it should not be made ridiculous, being writ in so good earnest; nor assaulted, being so inoffensive; much less that it should be defaced, mutilated, stabbed in so many places, and the author through it, which is even in writing a kind of felony. Yet this hath been its misfortune in a rencounter with an immodest and hectoring discourse, pretending to the title, 'De Causâ Dei; or a Vindication of the Common Doctrine of Protestant Divines concerning Predetermination; namely, the Interest of God, as the First Cause, in all the Actions, as such, of rational Creatures; from the invidious Consequences with which it is burthened by Mr. John Howe, in a late Letter and Postscript of God's Prescience; by T. D.' By which first letters, seeing it appears that he desires to pass *incognito*, I will so far observe good manners, as to interpret them only 'The Discourse,' heartily wishing that there were some way of finding *it* guilty, without reflecting upon the author; which I shall accordingly endeavour, that I may both preserve his whatsoever former reputation, and leave him a door open to ingenuity for the future. But 'The Discourse' justifies itself, as if it had been typified by Paul's withstanding Peter to his face, when he came to Antioch, (so easy is it to patronise human passions, under the pretence of the cause of God and apostolical example,). whereas it rather resembles in the bravery, though not in the occasion, that exploit of Peter's, for which our Saviour, though done in his defence, rebuked him; adding, 'They that take the sword shall perish by the sword:' and the taking the pen hath seldom better success, if handled in the same manner. I, therefore, having had the leisure to read it over, and thereby the opportunity of a second caution, how the unruly quill is to be managed, have thought that I could not at present render a better account of that time to myself or others, than by publishing these remarks; that, as Mr. Howe's Letter may serve for a pattern of what is to be imitated, so 'The Discourse' may remain as a mark (the best use it can be put to) of what ought to be avoided, in all writing of controversies, especially by Divines, in those that concern religion. The nature of this matter would admit of no better method, than that the errors observable should be distinguished under several heads, to each of which the particular instances are referred."

In accordance with the above pretended compassion towards the unknown author, he continues throughout to speak only of " The Discourse," not of the author, simply designating his adversary by the contemptuous neuter pronoun—"*it.*"

Such is the introduction to this tract. The author then proceeds to convict " The Discourse " of several different kinds of misstatement, or fallacious reasoning;—as " of its trifling and cavilling about words, when they affect not the cause; of its ignorance and confusion about the matter that is in controversy; of its falsifications and fictions of what its opponent hath *not* said; of its injurious perverting of what he *hath* said; of its odious insinuations; of its violent boasting and self-applause; of its gross absurdities, inconsistencies, self-contradictions, and unsafe expressions; and of the wrath and virulence of its spirit."

A few brief extracts will amuse the reader. The following is a ludicrous description of the manner in which his opponent manages to shift the terms of the question, as suited his convenience.

" It is a worse thing to adulterate truth than money. The terms of the question are the standard. But at this rate no man can know what is *meum* or *tuum*, which is his own hypothesis, and which his adversary's, while what he issued in current sense and weight is returned him clipped or counterfeit. But the observation of this manner of dealing hath put me upon another thought much differing, and which at first perhaps may seem something extravagant.

"The camel is a beast admirably shaped for burthen, but so lumpish withal, that nothing can be more inept for feats of activity. Yet men have therefore invented how to make it dance, that, by how much unnatural, the spectacle might appear more absurd and ridiculous. Its keeper leads it upon a pavement so thoroughly warmed, that the creature, not able to escape nor abide it, shifts first one foot, and then another, to relieve itself, and would, if possible, tread the air on all four, the ground being too hot for it to stand upon. He in the meantime traverses and trips about it at a cooler distance, striking some volunteer notes on his Egyptian kit, like a French dancing-master. But, knowing that his scholar is both in too much pain, and too dull to learn his measures, he therefore upon frequent observation accords a tune to its figure and footing, which comes to the same account. So that, after daily repeating the lesson in private, they seem both at last to be agreed upon a new Arabic saraband. Having thus far succeeded, he tries next whether what he taught by torture be not confirmed by custom, and if a cool hearth may not have the like effect. The camel no sooner hears his fiddle, but, as if its ears burned with the music, and its memory were in its feet the animal bestirs forthwith its long legs, and, with many an antic motion and ill-favoured *coupe*, gratifies the master's patience and expectation. When he finds, upon constant experiment, that it never fails him, he thenceforward makes it public, and, having compounded with the master of the revels, shows it, with great satisfaction, to the vulgar, every Bartholomew fair in Grand Cairo. I would not too much vex the similitude, but was run upon this by a resemblance it hath with some, who, not being framed at all for controversy, and finding the question too hot for them, do, by their flinching and shuffling from it, represent a disputation, till it is grown habitual to them, and they change ground as often, and have the same apprehension of the sound of an argument, as the camel of an instrument.

"And yet 'The Discourse' hath a fifth loose foot to clap on at need, as if four had not sufficed to prevaricate with."

The two next extracts exhibit in a very laughable point of

view, Danson's affectation of the logical formality and unintelligible jargon of the schools.

"This [argument of Howe] was as plain and distinctly laid out as possible, but must forsooth be cast into a logical figure, where the officiousness argues the fraud; as of those who make false plate, embezzling part of the metal, and yet make the owner pay moreover for the fashion."

* * * * * *

"Yet how much powder is spent without doing the least execution! First a categorical, then an hypothetical syllogism fired at him; then forces him to distinguish, which is among disputants next to crying quarter, but will not give it him: runs him through with three replies to his distinction, and leaves him dead upon the place. While the proposition is all this while untouched, Mr. Howe is out of gunshot, and his adversary (if one that only skirmishes with himself, deserves to be called so) is afraid to take aim, and starts merely at the report of his own musket. Thus hath 'The Discourse' five several times altered the property of the question; which is my fourth instance of its ignorance and confusion about the matter in controversy; unless it ought to be interpreted as an argument rather of a strong brain, after so many times and suddenly turning round, not to have fallen down senseless."

* * * * * *

"I shall now come to the last instance of this article. Not that I want abundance of more, or might not produce the whole book in evidence, but because it were time that I came to some period. And lest 'The Discourse' should think I avoided its main strength, I shall there examine it, where it pretends to no less than demonstration. For never was there thing so dreadfully accoutred and armed *cap-à-pie* in logic, categorical and hypothetical syllogisms, majors, minors, enthymems, antecedents, consequents, distinctions, definitions, and now at last demonstration, to pin the basket: terms that good Mr. Howe as a mere novice is presumed to be acquainted with."

* * * * * *

He apologizes for not pursuing Danson's misrepresentations and fallacies, so far as he might have done, in the following striking image:—

"But I spare my hand, 'The Discourse' all along boiling

over, foaming, frothing, and casting forth the like expressions :
which I refrain to enumerate, that I may not incur the fate of
him that stirs the Indian's poison pot, who when he falls down
dead with the steam and stench, they then throw the doors
open and dip their arrows."

*   *   *   *   *   *

The conclusion is truly eloquent, and is all I can afford space
to give. In the ludicrous remarks he makes on Howe's three
opponents, the readers of Marvell cannot fail to recognise that
felicitous readiness of repartee, and that sustained and apparently exhaustless humour, by which his wit is so especially
characterized.

"But, however, I hope that I may have done a good work, if
upon sight of these remarks, Mr. Howe, though fitted doubtless
for a much better and fuller reply, would deliberate before he
makes this adversary so considerable as to blot paper on its
occasion. Let it, in the meantime, venditate all its street
adages, its odd ends of *Latin*, its broken shreds of poets, and
its musty lumber of schoolmen. Let it enjoy the ingenuity of
having unprovoked fallen upon a person, ' whose parts it
acknowledged,' for whom it ' had such an affection,' with whom
it ' had so many years' academical society,' and so ' long friendship :' but whom it now ' must number among God's adversaries.' Let it value itself upon these things : for all these
considerations do heighten the price of an assassinate. But
may Mr. Howe still continue his sobriety, simplicity, and
equality of temper; glorifying God rather in the exercise of
practical Christian virtues, than affecting the honour of a
speculative question. But if he had a mind to be vindictive,
there is no way to despite the adversary more sensibly, than,
as clamorous women, by giving them no answer. Till men
grow into a better humour, and learn to treat of divinity more
civilly, they are unfit for conversation.

"Another, I see, who is now his third aggressor, hath
already assaulted him, though less barbarously, in ' A Letter
to a Friend,' etc. Yet even he introduces his book with Job :
' Wilt thou speak wickedly for God, and talk deceitfully for
him ?' What shall Mr. Howe do in this case ? Is the Bible
therefore to be turned into a libel ? and shall he search the
Scriptures to find out a text equally cutting ? He need not
go far, were he of that mind, to retaliate. How easy were the

parallel betwixt Job's three friends (to whom those words were spoken) and three such comfortable gentlemen! And why may not Mr. Howe nick them as well out of Job? 'But I have understanding as well as you; I am not inferior to you; yea, who knoweth not such things as these? I am as one mocked of his neighbour, who calleth upon God, and he answereth him. The just upright man is laughed to scorn.' Or, if he would be yet severer, the same book will hit them home. 'But ye are forgers of lies; ye are all physicians of no value. Oh that you would altogether hold your peace, and it should be your wisdom.' And then at last, to determine the whole dispute, he might conclude with Job: 'The Lord said to Eliphaz the Temanite, My wrath is kindled against thee, and against thy two friends; for ye have not spoken of me the thing that is right, as my servant Job hath.' After all which, what more seasonable, in order to reconciliation, than the verse following? 'Go to my servant Job, and offer up for yourselves a burnt-offering, and my servant Job shall pray for you (for him will I accept), lest I deal with you after your folly, in that you have not spoken of me the thing that is right, as my servant Job hath.' But the word of God is not so to be turned into the reproach of man, though the allusion may seem never so happy; nor have I instanced thus far, otherwise than to show the frivolousness, though too usual, of that practice.

"But therefore I would advise Mr. Howe, though not to that excusable sullenness and silence, with which some have chastised the world for having used them unworthily; nor to that tacit contempt of his adversaries, in which he were hitherto justified; yet, that, having made a laudable attempt, of which several good men are it seems not capable, he would, for peace' sake, either wholly surcease this contest, or forbear at least till they have all done. For it is more easy to deal with them all than single; and, were they once embodied, come to a consistence among themselves, or had agreed who should speak for them, they had right to his answer. But until then, Mr. Howe is no more obliged in whatsoever is called honour, reason, or conscience, than if every hair of T. D.'s that stands on end, should demand particular satisfaction. It is the same for such a divine as he, to turn common disputant, as for an architect to saw timber, or cleave logs; which, though he may sometimes do it for health or exercise, yet to be constant at it, were to debase and neglect his vocation. Mr. Howe hath work enough cut out of a nobler nature, in his 'Living

Temple,' in which, like that of Solomon, there is 'neither hammer, nor axe, nor any tool of iron to be heard,' nothing that can offend, all to edify. And this I heartily wish that he may accomplish : but therefore, as he hath not hitherto sought, so that he would avoid all contention ; lest, as David, for having been a man of blood, was forbid to build the temple, so he, as being a man of controversy.

" As for myself, I expect in this litigious age, that some or other will sue me for having trespassed thus far on theological ground : but I have this for my plea, that I stepped over on no other reason than (which any man legally may do) to hinder one divine from offering violence to another. And, if I should be molested on that account, I doubt not but some of the Protestant clergy will be ready therefore to give me the like assistance."

CHAPTER VII.

SEVERITIES EXERCISED UPON THE NONCONFORMISTS DURING THIS PERIOD—HOWE'S EARNEST DESIRE FOR AN ADJUSTMENT OF THE DIFFERENCES BETWEEN THE CHURCH AND THE DISSENTERS—THE POPISH PLOT—CURIOUS INTERVIEW WITH A CERTAIN NOBLEMAN—HIS REPLY TO STILLINGFLEET—EXTRACTS—HIS EXPOSTULATION WITH TILLOTSON ON HIS SERMON BEFORE THE KING—ANOTHER ATTEMPT AT COMPREHENSION—BILL OF EXCLUSION—PROCEEDINGS OF THE PARLIAMENT OF 1680.

DURING this period, and, indeed, till the close of Charles's infamous reign, the nonconformists were generally persecuted with great rigour; the King himself, as if in mockery of the principles of his late hollow indulgence, permitting the utmost severities. The numerous laws which had been enacted against them were all strictly enforced; their families and assemblies were infested by the vilest informers—wretches who did not scruple to assume even the mask of religion, to enable them more effectually to play the traitor; while the prisons in many cases were literally crowded with victims.

It is true that to a few, circumstances, local or temporary, often afforded partial protection. Some of the nonconformists were less obnoxious than others, some more prudent; in many cases the magistrates connived at their proceedings, or, when compelled to take notice of them, mitigated the penalties to which the accused were exposed; while a few, at their own proper risk, nobly refused to exercise their odious office, or to receive the depositions of the infamous creatures who lived upon the spoil of innocence and piety.

There were, also, brief intervals in which the whole body of the nonconformists were favoured with some mitigation of their sufferings—moments when the blast of persecution, having blown its fill, seemed for a while to have spent itself. These pauses, however, were short and of rare occurrence; the general condition of the nonconformists during the remainder of this reign, and the commencement of the next, was most deplorable.

For the intervals of comparative quiet to which I have just adverted, they were, generally, indebted to the prevalence of those alarms of Popery, which were not infrequent in the reign of the Second Charles, and which reached their height at the time of the celebrated " Popish Plot," in 1678–9. During such periods of panic, the schismatics were in some measure forgotten, and even regarded with some favour, as valuable allies in case of need; and though some of the high church bigots would have contemplated even the restoration of Popery with less displeasure than a relaxation of the terms of conformity, a majority of the clergy held very different sentiments. On more than one occasion of this kind, some overtures had already been made towards a " comprehension," especially in the memorable attempt of 1674–5,—in which the leading men on the side of the Church were Bishops Morley and Ward, and Dean Tillotson; those on that of the nonconformists, Baxter, Pool, and Bates. This occurred just before Howe returned to England. Like every other scheme of the kind, it came to nothing.

Howe had never abandoned his hopes of an adjustment between the Church and the nonconformists; and now, in the same spirit of charity which had induced him twenty years before to toil with Baxter in the fruitless schemes of "comprehension," he availed himself of every favourable opportunity of urging on persons of influence or authority in the Church, the desirableness of some attempt at accommodation. At the time of the Popish Plot especially, as well as during a considerable part of the following year, when the nation was frantic with the most absurd and fantastic terrors of Popery, he never ceased to maintain—what was, indeed, obvious to every unprejudiced understanding—that the best method of fortifying Protestantism against the designs of Rome, was to close those wide breaches through which alone the enemy could hope to assail it with success. Nor could any time for any such attempt be more auspicious than during the agitation produced by the Popish Plot, and within a year or two after.

About this period, an amusing incident occurred, which Calamy has related at the close of his volume, but which, for the sake of preserving the continuity of the narrative, I prefer relating here. He tells us, that "during Charles's reign, Howe had it signified to him, by several, that a certain nobleman, who was at that time great at court, was desirous to see him." Calamy does not tell us who this nobleman was; but there can be little doubt, after carefully weighing the whole circumstances, that it was the notorious Duke of Buckingham. This nobleman, it is well known, affected, at this period, extraordinary liberality, and employed no small efforts to conciliate the sectaries—for what purposes, I do not now inquire.* Howe took an opportunity of waiting on him. After some conversation the *soi-disant* patron hinted, that " the nonconformists were too numerous and powerful to be any longer neglected; that they deserved regard; and that. if they had a friend near the throne, and who possessed influence with the court generally, to give them advice in critical emergencies, and to convey their requests to the royal ear, they would find it much to their advantage." He was further pleased to express himself in such a manner as necessarily led his visitor to conclude, that he himself would have no objection to become their advocate and representative at court. Howe, penetrating at once the sordid and ambitious motives which prompted this modest proposal, and fully impressed with the preposterous unfitness of such a person for such an office, replied, with an air of great simplicity, " that the nonconformists being an avowedly *religious* people, it highly concerned them, should they fix on any one for the purpose mentioned, to choose some one who would not be ashamed of *them*, and of whom *they* might have no reason to be ashamed; and that to find a person in whom there was a concurrence of those two qualifications, was

---

* His conduct at this period forms an important feature in the plot of Scott's novel of " Peveril of the Peak."

exceedingly difficult." I need not say that this reply put an end to all negotiations in this quarter.

Howe seldom entered the arena of controversy. In the year 1680, a circumstance occurred which, in his opinion, justified him in doing so. Amongst others, whom the spirit of party hurried into excesses utterly unworthy of them, was the celebrated Dean Stillingfleet,* afterwards Bishop of Worcester; a man deservedly respected for his learning and talents, and hitherto distinguished by a moderate and conciliatory temper.

On the 2nd of May, 1680, he preached a sermon before the Lord Mayor and Aldermen of the city, and the Judges and Serjeants,† as uncharitable in its spirit as it was absurd in reasoning. His text was, " Nevertheless, whereto we have already attained, let us walk by the same rule; let us mind the same thing." ‡ The sermon was afterwards printed under the title of " The Mischief of Separation." In this discourse, he not only inveighs most bitterly against the nonconformists, on whom he charges the sole guilt of the great schism which had rent the Established Church in twain, but maintains the dangerous position, " that though the *really conscientious* nonconformist is justified in not worshipping after the prescribed forms of the Church of England, or rather would be *criminal* if he did so, yet he is not less criminal in setting up a *separate* assembly." Such is the pleasant dilemma to which, according to this writer, the sensitive consciences of the nonconformists

---

* In 1659 he published his book called " Irenicum," the grand object of which was to prove that no form of church government could be proved to be *jure divino* from any passages of the New Testament. This made the vehemence and violence of the " Mischief of Separation " the more glaring, and gave Howe and others, in their replies, an opportunity of using the *argumentum ad hominem* with considerable effect. Supposing his adversaries in the wrong, it was urged that more forbearance might have been expected from one who had been twenty years in amending his theory and correcting the errors of his youth.

† Calamy has virtually represented Stillingfleet as having preached this sermon *after* the " Exclusion Bill " (designed to shut out James II., then Duke of York, from the throne, on the ground of his being a papist) had been rejected by the House of Lords; and has even left the reader to infer, by the manner in which he introduces the mention of it, that it was to be attributed to the rejection of that bill. This seems to be a mistake; since the Exclusion Bill was not lost till November, 1680, whereas the sermon of Stillingfleet was preached on the 2nd of May.

‡ Phil. iii. 16.

had reduced them. An inevitable *necessity* of crime was the direct consequence of their scrupulous anxiety to avoid it. It was at their peril, if they worshipped with the Church of England; it was at their peril, if they worshipped in the conventicle; and it was certainly not less at their peril, if they abstained from worship altogether!

While other writers opposed the argumentation of the discourse in general,* Howe set himself more immediately to the refutation of this simple position. He was in the country when the discourse was printed, but received it together with an enclosed letter from a " person of quality," who had read the Dean's sermon with equal surprise and indignation. As Howe thought he perceived in his correspondent's letter somewhat of the same angry spirit which was but too evident in the discourse itself, he, in his reply,† expresses his intention, first, " of defending the cause of the nonconformists against the Dean, and then of adding something in defence of the Dean against his correspondent."

The first part, though written in haste, is full of close and powerful reasoning, and thoroughly demolishes the untenable position of his opponent. The latter part, in which he proceeds to allay the anger of his correspondent, and to apologize for the conduct of the Dean, is eminently beautiful, strikingly illustrative of the writer's character, and furnishes a perfect model of fair and gentlemanly controversy. While I earnestly entreat the reader carefully to peruse the whole composition, I cannot refrain from inserting here one or two short extracts from it; not without a faint hope, that some of the writers on the same controversy in the present day, who seem to be emulating, in virulence and uncharitableness, the spirit of their forefathers, may be impressed with the contrast between Howe's temper and their own. Such a temper is rare at any period; but in that age of fierce and savage controversy, of the tomahawk and scalping-knife, it was indeed a phenomenon.

---

* As Owen, Baxter, Alsop, and others.

† The reply was entitled, " A Letter out of the Country to a Person of quality in the City, who took offence at the late Sermon of Dr. Stillingfleet, Dean of St. Paul's, before the Lord Mayor."

The contrast, however, between such a temper and that which animated controvertists in general, more strongly displays the elevation and spirituality of mind which secured Howe against the infectious example of bigotry, and enabled him, when writing on topics so exciting and irritating, to preserve the courtesy of a gentleman and the charity of a Christian.

"I must here indeed tell you, that I cannot blame you for being in some measure offended, as I can excuse the Doctor but in part. I do dislike, as well as you, two things especially in his way of managing this business; his too great acrimony and too little seriousness." . . .

After thus admitting, and rebuking, but with most winning gentleness, the faults of the preacher, and especially the sarcastic and derisive tone in which he had indulged, Howe proceeds :—

"One would rather have thought he should have bedewed that discourse with tears, which had in itself, most manifestly, so awful and tremendous a design, as not only the devoting of so great numbers, that might possibly not be convinced and persuaded by him, to a temporal ruin ; but the depriving them of the ordinary means of their salvation : and that, if he thought it necessary for the preserving of order in the church, they should be so dealt with, he should have spoken of their case with the greatest compassion and tenderness, not with derision and contempt.

"Yet I would have you use lenitives with yourself, and calm your own spirit ; and I wish you were capable of contributing anything to the moderating and pacifying his too : that though he have been angry unprovoked, and with a sort of men that have ever respected and honoured him, as if he had been of themselves ; his anger, that hath been without cause, (as you know perhaps who in a like expression blame the exorbitancy of another passion,) may not also be without end. At least, I pray you, take heed you do not deserve the like sharp repartee, which the cynic met with from that noble philosopher, that he taxed his pride with greater pride ; that you exceed not the heats whereof you complain. . . . If he will still retain his fervour, let him be angry alone ; and his displeasure have its continuance with as little influence or concomitancy of yours, (and I could wish of any other man's,) as, for ought I know, it had its beginning. And that since he thinks of being a sacrifice, he may only burn gently in his own flame, which he may moderate as he pleases, and I hope will seasonably extinguish, before he hath suffered much harm by it.

"For the qualifying of your own too great resentment and offence; *I would have you consider how great reason you have to believe, that this blow came only from the (somewhat misgoverned) hand of a pious and good man.* Be it far from you to imagine otherwise. If you think he was to blame for intimating suspicions of *their* sincerity whom he opposes, make not yourself equally blameable, by admitting hereupon any concerning his: which would argue a mean, narrow spirit, and a most unwarrantable fondness of a party, as if all true religion and godliness were bound up in it.

"And if it look unlovely in your eyes to see one of so much avowed latitude and enlargedness of mind, and capable on that account of being the more universally serviceable to the Christian church, forsaking that comprehensive interest, so far as to be engulfed into a party upon a private and distinct basis, consider what aspect the same thing would have in yourself; and never make his difference with you in this matter, a reason to yourself of a hard judgment concerning him; who can, you must consider, differ no more from us, than we do from him.

"*Believe him, in the substance of what he said, to speak according to his present judgment.* Think how gradually and insensibly men's judgments alter, and are formed by their converse; that his circumstances had made it necessary to him to converse most, for a long time, with those who are fully of that mind which he here discovers; that his own real worth must have drawn into his acquaintance the best and most valuable of them, and such for whom he might not only have a kindness, but a reverence; and who therefore must have the more power and influence upon him, to conform his sentiments to their own.

"*We ourselves do not know, had we been by our circumstances led to associate and converse mostly with men of another judgment, what our own would have been.* And they that are wont to discover most confidence of themselves, do usually but discover most ignorance of the nature of man; and how little they consider the power of external objects and inducements to draw men's minds this way or that. Nor, indeed, as to matters of this nature, can any man be confident that the grace of God shall certainly incline him to be of this or another opinion or practice in these matters ; because we find those that we have no reason to believe have greater assistances of Divine grace are divided about them, and go not all one way.

"We may indeed be confident that had the *same* considerations occurred to us which have, we should have been of the same mind and judgment that we are. But it is very supposable that some accidental occasions might possibly have happened, that might hinder our actual taking up such considerations, though the things to be considered were not unknown to us : and not that only, but that might prevent our knowing even matters of fact, that have signified not a little to the determining our judgments that way which they now incline to. . . .

"So that for the substance of what he hath said against such meetings, we have reason to impute it to his judgment; and his judgment to such circumstances, very much as I have mentioned, that have led him the way he hath taken ; and not given him opportunity to know what might have begot a better opinion in him of the way which he opposes.

"But for the manner of treating this subject, that I impute to the prevalency of some present temptation ; and hope he did not express in that sermon his habitual temper : *and am highly confident, (notwithstanding what he hath said in it,) if it were in his power, we might even safely trust him to prescribe us terms, and should receive no hard ones from him.*

"Somewhat it is likely he was expected (and might be urged) to say to this business; and his own thoughts being set a work, fermented into an intemperate heat, which, it is to be hoped, will in time evaporate."

After stating his conviction that the spirit of unity and peace would result from earnest and universal prayer for it, he thus concludes :—

"Do you your own part herein; you will find your own present advantage by it; it will fill you with good thoughts, hopes, and expectations: the kindly benign influences whereof will pleasantly qualify and temper your spirit, and make you know how much more grateful an inhabitant that charity is, ' which thinketh no evil, beareth all things, believeth all things, hopeth all things, endureth all things,' than frowardness, discontent, vexation, and anger, at any one that thinks and speaks otherwise than you did expect or wish."

It is no wonder that Stillingfleet, charmed with the spirit of his opponent—a spirit very different, it must be admitted, from that of others who had replied to him—confessed, " that Howe had discoursed gravely and piously, more like a gentleman than a divine, without any mixture of rancour or any sharp reflections, and sometimes with a great degree of kindness towards him, for which and his prayers for him, he heartily thanked him."

Howe's gentle spirit and conciliatory temper were not less strikingly displayed in another occurrence which took place about the same time.

In the same year* in which Stillingfleet preached his strange sermon before the Lord Mayor, " On the Mischief of Separation," Tillotson (one of the most amiable of men, and in his spirit and temper worthy of being compared with Howe himself) preached a discourse, equally paradoxical, before the King. His text was, " And the people answered and said, God forbid that we should forsake the Lord to serve other gods." By what imaginable subtlety of reasoning he could extract the sentiment from such a passage, I know not; but in his sermon he maintained, " That no man is obliged to preach against the religion of his country, though a false one, unless he has the power of working miracles." The irreligious monarch, as was often the case, slept during the greater part of the sermon. As soon as the service was over, a nobleman stepped up and said, " It is a pity your Majesty slept, for we have had the rarest piece of *Hobbism* that ever you heard in your life." " Odsfish ! " exclaimed the King, with one of his usual oaths, " he shall print it then," and enjoined the Lord Chamberlain to convey his commands to the Dean. When printed, the Dean, as was usual with him, sent a copy to Howe, who, on perusing it, was filled with alarm at the dangerous position which the preacher had thought proper to maintain.

---

* 1680.

He instantly sent the Dean a long letter of expostulation, which, unhappily, has not been preserved. Calamy, however, whose information seems worthy of implicit confidence,* has mentioned the principal topics on which it insisted. Howe expressed his conviction that the sermon was "directly opposed to all the principles on which alone the Reformation could be justified;" reminded its author "that Calvin and Luther were, happily for mankind, of a very different mind; that the Christian religion being already confirmed by miracles, was not to be repealed every time a wicked governor chose to establish a *false* religion;" and "that, consequently, its ministers were bound publicly to advocate it, even though they could not work miracles." In conclusion, he expressed deep regret, that in a sermon professedly against Popery, the Dean should thus have pleaded "the Popish cause against the Fathers of the Reformation." This letter Howe carried himself, and delivered into Tillotson's own hands. After hastily glancing at its contents, the Dean told Howe that he was willing freely to discuss the matter with him; and proposed that, to insure uninterrupted privacy, they should ride together a little way into the country. Howe accepted the invitation, and they agreed to dine that day with the Lady Falconbridge at Sutton Court. As they rode together in the Dean's chariot, Howe read his letter aloud, more fully explaining and enforcing it as he went on. Tillotson, at length convinced that the doctrine he had advocated was utterly untenable, even wept over his error, and declared that "this was the unhappiest thing which had for a long time happened to him." In mitigation of his fault, however, he pleaded "that he had been unexpectedly summoned by the Lord Chamberlain to preach on that day,—the individual whose turn it was having been suddenly taken ill; that, having little time for preparation, he had fastened on the topic which was at that period uppermost in the public mind—the fear of Popery; and lastly, that immediately after he had delivered

---

* At the close of his account of this affair, Calamy says, "I am the better satisfied that there is no mistake as to the substance of this passage, because he from whom I had it, did not trust to his bare memory, but committed it to writing, presently after he received the account from Mr. Howe himself."

the sermon, he received the King's command to print it, which rendered all revision impossible."

Tillotson's conduct on this occasion places his amiable character in the fairest light. One can hardly regret that he committed a fault for which he so nobly atoned, and which has furnished us with so impressive an example of ingenuousness, candour, and humility.

At the same time, there must have been about Howe's manner of expostulation something peculiarly insinuating, since, in general, a more hopeless task can hardly be imagined than that of inducing a man to recant an error, to which he has given his *public* sanction. Pride and shame alike impel him to an obstinate defence of it.

Doubtless, on the present occasion the temper of both parties equally conspired to produce the happy result : even the expostulations of Howe might have failed, unless it had been a Tillotson to whom they were addressed; and even Tillotson might not have relented, had the reproof been administered by a spirit less gentle than that of Howe.

In this same year, the attempts at comprehension were again renewed. That the object was seriously contemplated by some of the Bishops, is evident from the following fact, related by Calamy. It appears that, at the close of 1680, Howe received an invitation from Bishop Lloyd * to dine with him. As he had no acquaintance with that prelate, he suspected that it must be some very important reason which had led to such an unusual courtesy. Being engaged to dine elsewhere on that day, Howe sent word that he would wait on his Lordship in the evening. On this, the Bishop sent again, to say, " that since Mr. Howe could not dine with him, he would not trouble him to come so far as his house, but would meet him at Dr. Tillotson's," then Dean of Canterbury. When they met, the Bishop told him, that he had sought this interview to ask him, " what would satisfy the nonconformists, if an attempt should

---

* There were two Bishops of this name living at this period—one of Norwich, the other of St. Asaph, afterwards of Worcester. Calamy does not tell us which of these two prelates it was who honoured Howe with this invitation. There can be little doubt, however, that it was the latter.

be made to adjust the differences between them and the
Church." Howe, with his usual caution, replied, that "as all
had not the same latitude, he could only answer for himself."
He was then requested to state, "what concessions, in his
opinion, would satisfy the scruples of the greater part: for,"
added the Bishop, "I would have the terms so large as to
comprehend the most of them." On this, Howe declared, that
he thought "a very considerable obstacle would be removed,
if the law were so framed as to enable ministers to attempt
parochial reformation." "For that reason," said the Bishop,
"I am for abolishing the lay chancellors, as being the great
hindrance to such reformation." They then agreed to meet
again the following evening at Dr. Stillingfleet's, Dean of St.
Paul's. Howe asked if he should bring Baxter with him?
But this the Bishop (who was doubtless well aware of that
unhappy propensity for "distinguishing," by which, with the
best intentions in the world, Baxter often managed to multiply
and aggravate the points of dispute) positively forbade. Howe
then proposed Dr. Bates; and was answered, "that no man
could be more proper." At seven, therefore, on the following
evening, Bates and Howe repaired to Dr. Stillingfleet's,
"who," says Calamy, "had provided a *handsome treat*" for
his visitors. Of this "handsome treat" the Bishop was either
disinclined or unable to partake; for ten o'clock came, and
they neither saw nor heard of him. The next morning, the
mystery was solved;—on that very evening the Bill of Exclusion * was thrown out of the House of Lords, by a majority
of thirty votes—fourteen of which came from the bench of

---

* This was the celebrated Bill for *excluding* James II., then Duke of York,
from the *succession*, on the ground of his being a Papist. A bill for this purpose had been passed more than once in the House of Commons, but had been
defeated by the dissolution or prorogation of Parliament. In order to frustrate
that measure, the King, between 1679 and 1681, dissolved not less than three
Parliaments, in the hope of more favourable elections. Those hopes, however,
were vain; the country each time returning a Parliament bent on this project.
The Parliament of 1680, especially, was determined not only to exclude the
Duke of York from the throne, but, as seen above, to effect, if possible, the
union of "his Majesty's Protestant subjects." The last of the above three Parliaments met at Oxford, and after sitting only a week, was dissolved. The King
after this *dispensed* with all such refractory assemblies to the end of his reign.

Bishops. After this, the scheme of comprehension, so far as the Church was concerned, was heard of no more.

The Parliament which met in 1680, was, like that which had been dissolved the preceding year, of a very liberal character. During the session, and soon after the Bill of Exclusion had been rejected by the Upper House, they brought in a measure for "uniting his Majesty's Protestant subjects." They were especially anxious to effect the repeal of certain persecuting laws of Elizabeth, which had been directed against Popish recusants, and which were now cruelly put in force against the nonconformists. A bill, with this object, after having passed both houses, was quietly *withdrawn* by the Clerk of the Crown, at the command of the King; who took this characteristic method of quashing a measure he dared not openly reject. The Commons, indignant at this insult, resorted to the unprecedented step of passing a vote, " That the Acts of Parliament made in the reigns of Queen Elizabeth and King James against Popish recusants, ought not to be enforced against Protestant Dissenters;" and, "That the prosecution of Protestant Dissenters, upon the penal laws, is at this time grievous to the subject, a weakening of the Protestant interest, an encouragement to Popery, and dangerous to the peace of the kingdom."

CHAPTER VIII.

FROM 1681 TO 1684.

CONDITION OF THE NONCONFORMISTS DURING THIS PERIOD—HOWE'S MEETING-HOUSE DISTURBED—ACCOUNT OF HIS PUBLICATIONS IN 1681, 1682, AND 1683—PREACHES HIS SERMON ON THE UNION OF PROTESTANTS—ACCOUNT OF IT—EXTRACTS—LETTER OF CONSOLATION TO LADY RUSSELL—REFLECTIONS—EXPOSTULATORY LETTER TO BISHOP BARLOW.

IN the year 1681, the condition of the nonconformists became yet more deplorable. The various circumstances which had sometimes mitigated the rigour of former persecutions, no longer afforded them protection; and for the next two or three years, they were exposed to the full fury of the tempest.

Not only were the harsh laws which had been expressly enacted against them, enforced with the utmost rigour, but laws which had never been intended to apply to them—laws which were made against the Papists in the reign of Elizabeth —had been recently revived, and were now vigorously acted on, in defiance of the late vote of the House of Commons. Some of the dignitaries of the Church actively seconded the designs of the government, incited the civil magistrate to greater severity, and put into motion all the crushing machinery of the ecclesiastical courts.

The inoffensive habits and great prudence of Howe seem in some measure to have secured him against the severities to which so many of his brethren were exposed; yet even he (as appears by an expression in the "Pastoral Letter," which will be found in a subsequent page) rarely ventured into the streets, during this and the two following years. It also appears that, on one occasion, about this time, his meeting was disturbed by the emissaries of persecution while he was preaching, and seven of his hearers committed to Newgate; amongst whom was the Rev. Richard Dowley, one of the ejected ministers, in the account of whose life this circumstance is preserved.*

During this gloomy year, Howe made diligent use of the solitary hours to which persecution doomed him, in preparing for the press several of his smaller publications. Amongst these were the discourses entitled, "Thoughtfulness for the Morrow," (to which was attached an appendix, "Concerning the immoderate Desire of Foreknowing Things to Come,") and "On Charity in reference to other Men's Sins." The former was dedicated to the Lady Anne Wharton,† of Upper Winchingdon, in the county of Bucks, at whose request it was written. The discourse "On Charity in reference to other Men's Sins," originated in the following circumstances.

A person who had been for some time a colleague of Howe, and whose name was Daniel Bull, having been betrayed into some grievous immorality, the irreligious, as usual, set up a shout of triumph. Howe, who was ever ready to throw the mantle of love over the failings of an erring brother, exposed from the pulpit, in a most cogent manner, the malignity and folly of such exultation. The sermon he afterwards published, by request, under the above title. The "preface" is exquisite in sentiment, and often in expression; and the close, also, is exceedingly eloquent. On such a subject Howe had a peculiar right to speak, for the principles he lays down were never more fully exemplified in any man's life than in his own.

It is proper to add, that Mr. Bull became truly penitent, and died generally esteemed for his piety and humility.

This same year, Howe published his Funeral Sermon for Margaret, the wife of Richard Baxter, from the text, "We are confident, I say, and willing rather to be absent from the

---

* Palmer's "Noncon. Memorial," vol. ii. p. 395.

† This was the wife of Philip, Lord Wharton, with whom Howe, three years after, travelled on the Continent. She appears, from Howe's language, to have been a very excellent woman. He tells her, "Your ladyship hath been called to serve religion in a family wherein it hath long flourished, and which it hath dignified beyond all the splendour that antiquity and secular greatness could confer upon it."

body, and to be present with the Lord."*　It is dedicated to Baxter.

In 1682, (public affairs continuing in the same gloomy state,) Howe seems to have employed his solitude much in the same manner as during the preceding year. Restricted in the exercise of his public ministry, he sought to extend his usefulness by means of the press. His publications this year were numerous. The first was, "The Right Use of the Argument in Prayer from the Name of God, on Behalf of a People who profess it;" the second, his well-known sermon on "Self-Dedication." It was preached "at the anniversary thanksgiving for a great deliverance vouchsafed" to the Earl of Kildare, Baron of Ophalia, to whom it is dedicated.† There is one passage in this dedication which is much after the manner of Jeremy Taylor :—

"Your lordship was pleased to allow an hour to the hearing of that discourse. What was proposed to you in it, is to be the business of your life. And what is to be done continually, is once to be thoroughly done. The impression ought to be very inward, and strong, which must be so lasting as to govern a man's life. And were it as fully done as mortality can admit, it needs be more solemnly renewed at set times for that purpose. And, indeed, that such a day should not pass you without a fall, nor that fall be without a hurt, and that hurt proceed unto a wound, and that wound not be mortal, but even next to it, looks like an artifice and contrivance of Providence, to show you how near it could go without cutting through that slender thread of life; that it might endear to you its accurate superintendency over your life; that there might here be a remarkable juncture in that thread; and that whensoever such a day should revolve in the circle of your year, it might come again and again, with a note upon it under your eye, and appear ever to you as another birth-day, or as an earlier day of resurrection."

---

* 2 Cor. v. 8.

† This was John Fitzgerald, eighteenth earl. His uncle Robert married a daughter of Colonel James Clotworthy, related to the Massarene family. This may account for Howe's acquaintance with him. The Countess of Kildare was esteemed one of the most amiable women of her time.

His third publication this year was an eloquent Funeral Sermon for the Rev. Richard Fairclough, entitled, "The Faithful Steward Applauded and Rewarded." In the same year, he also composed the Annotations on the three Epistles of St. John, forming a part of the second volume of Pool's Annotations.*

In 1683, appeared his justly-celebrated discourse on "Union among Protestants; or, An Answer to the Question, 'What may most hopefully be attempted to allay Animosities among Protestants, so that our Divisions may not be our Ruin?'" † This was a subject to which Howe was admirably qualified to do justice, and which, throughout his life, was inexpressibly dear to him. Here his enlarged and truly catholic spirit—his superiority to all the littleness of party feeling—his absorbing solicitude for the interest of *real* religion, whatever its outward forms—display themselves to the greatest advantage. His text was that sublime prayer of the apostle for the Colossians, "That their hearts might be comforted, being knit together in love, and unto all riches of the full assurance of understanding, to the acknowledgment of the mystery of God, and of the Father, and of Christ." ‡ He declares, at the commencement, that it is by no means his design to discuss "what might be attempted towards remedying the evils in question by laws and public constitutions," or to argue any of the points controverted by the several parties; but to urge on all those parties alike the great *moral means*, by which a unity might be secured far more noble than that of identity of opinion. This, he tells us, might be effected "by the maintaining sincere love among Christians, and the improving of their faith to greater measures of clearness, certainty, and efficacy, in reference to the *substantials* of Christianity." None, I would fain believe, can read the passages which occur in the discussion of the *first* of the two above-mentioned topics, without feeling, for a moment, at least,

---

* Pool died before this work was finished. It was completed by different persons after his death.

† Published in the Continuation of the Morning Exercise.

‡ Col. ii. 2.

elevated above the meanness of party spirit, and emulous of imitating the sublime charity of the author.

In this discourse he also enters into a full and very philosophical disquisition on the *causes* which often determine men's tastes and preferences in favour of this or that system of religious worship, and from thence deduces the lessons of forbearance, which, on this as well as on other and higher accounts, Christians should mutually practise.

In the second part, he urges the necessity of "attaining a deeper sense of the importance and truth of the substantials of Christianity;" and then proceeds to show how this would operate to the proposed end. It would fill the mind, he tells his hearers, with an habitual persuasion "of the infinitely greater importance of those things in which Christians agree, than of those in which they differ."

The whole discourse is adapted not only for those times, but for all, and is worthy of the serious, devout perusal of persons of all religious parties.

On the 20th of July, 1683, was beheaded the truly noble William Lord Russell, in atrocious violation of every principle of equity and justice. Lady Russell, who during the trial of her noble husband had borne up with unparalleled fortitude, drooped after his death, and for a time seemed hopelessly overwhelmed with the contemplation of her dreadful loss. Howe, touched with the melancholy accounts he had received of her, addressed to her the following anonymous letter of consolation : —

"*Madam,*

"It can avail you nothing, to let your honour know from what hand this paper comes; and my own design in it is abundantly answered if what it contains proves useful to you. Your affliction hath been great, unspeakably beyond what it is in my power or design to represent; and your supports (in the paroxysm of your affliction) have been very extraordinary; and such as wherein all that have observed or heard, could not but acknowledge a Divine hand.

"But your affliction was not limited and enclosed within

the limits of one black day, nor is like those more common ones, the sense whereof abates and wears off by time; but is continued, and probably more felt, as time runs on: which therefore makes you need continued help from Heaven every day.

"Yet there is here a great difference between what expectations we may have of Divine assistance, in the beginning or first violence of some great affliction, and in the continued course of it afterwards. At first we are apt to be astonished; a consternation seizes our thinking faculty, especially·as to that exercise of it whereby it should minister to our relief. In this case the merciful God doth more extraordinarily assist such as sincerely trust and resign themselves to him; unto these, as his more peculiar favourites, his sustaining influences are more immediate, and more efficacious, so as even (in the present exigency) to prevent and supersede any endeavour of theirs, whereof they are, then, less capable. And of the largeness and bounty of his goodness, in such a case, few have had greater experience than your-ladyship; which was eminently seen, in that magnanimity, that composure and presentness of mind, much admired by your friends, and no doubt by the special favour of Heaven afforded you in the needful season: so that while that amazing calamity was approaching, and stood in nearer view, nothing that was fit or wise or great was omitted, nothing indecent done: which is not now said, God knows, to flatter your ladyship, (whereof the progress will further vindicate me,) for I ascribe it to God, as I trust your ladyship, with unfeigned gratitude, will also do. And I mention it, as that whereby you are under obligation to endeavour, your continued temper and deportment may be agreeable to such beginnings.

"For now (which is the other thing whereof a distinct observation ought to be had) in the continuance and settled state of the affliction, when the fury of the first assault is over, and we have had leisure to recollect ourselves, and recover our dissipated spirits, though we are then more sensible of pain and smart, yet also the power of using our own thoughts is restored. And being so, although we are too apt to use them to our greater hurt and prejudice, we are really put again into a capacity of using them to our advantage, which our good God doth in much wisdom and righteousness require we should do. Whereupon, we are to expect his continual assistance for our support under continued affliction in the way of concurrence and co-operation with our due use of our own thoughts, aptly chosen, as much as in us is, and designed by ourselves, for our own comfort and support.

"Now as for thoughts suitable to your honour's case, I have reason to be conscious that what I shall write can make but little accession, I will not say to a closet, but to a mind, so well furnished, as you are owner of: yet I know it is remote from you to slight a well-intended offer and essay, that really proceeds only from a very compassionate sense of your sorrows, and unfeigned desire to contribute something (if the Father of mercies and the God of all comforts and consolations will please to favour the endeavour) to your relief.

"And the thoughts which I shall most humbly offer, will have that first and more immediate design,—to persuade your making use of your own; that is, that you would please to turn and apply them to subjects more apt to serve this purpose, the moderating your own grief, and the attaining an habitual well-tempered cheerfulness, for your remaining time in this world. For I consider how incident it is to the afflicted, to indulge to themselves an unlimited liberty in their sorrows, to give themselves up to them, to make them meat and drink, to justify them in all their excesses, as that (otherwise) good and holy man of God did his anger, and say, they 'do well to be sorrowful even to the death,' and (as another) 'to refuse to be comforted.' And I also consider that our own thoughts must and will always be the immediate ministers either of our trouble or comfort, though as to the latter, God only is the supreme Author; and we altogether insufficient to think anything that good is, as of ourselves. It is 'God that comforts those that are cast down,' but by our own thoughts employed to that purpose, not without them.

"I do not doubt, Madam, but if you once fixedly apprehend that there is sin in an over-abounding sorrow, you will soon endeavour its restraint: for I cannot think you would more earnestly set yourself to avoid anything than what you apprehend will offend God, especially the doing that in a continued course. Is there any time when joy in God is a duty? it is very plain the sorrow that excludes it is a sin. How the former may appear to be a duty, and how far, let it be considered.

"It is not to be doubted but that he that made us hath a right to rule us; he that gave us being, to give us law: nor again, that the Divine government reaches our minds, and that they are the prime and first seat of his empire.   His kingdom is within us. We are not then to exercise our thoughts, desires, love, joy, or sorrow, according to our own will, but his; not as we please, or find ourselves inclined, but suitably to his precepts and purposes, his rules and ends.

"It is evident that withal the earthly state is mixed; intermediate between the perfect felicity of heaven, and the total misery of hell: and further, that the temper of our spirits ought to have in it a mixture of joy and sorrow, proportionable to our state, or what there is in it of the just occasions or causes of both.

"Where Christianity obtains, and the gospel of our Saviour is preached, there is much greater cause of joy than elsewhere. The visible aspect of it imports a design to form men's minds to gladness, inasmuch as, wheresoever it comes, it proclaims peace to the world, and represents the offended Majesty of heaven willing to be reconciled to his offending creatures on earth.   So the angel prefaced-the gospel, when our Lord was born into the world, ' I tell you glad tidings of great joy, which shall be to all people.'   And so the multitude of accompanying angels sum it up: ' Glory be to God in the highest, peace on earth, good will towards men.'

"To them that truly receive the gospel, and with whom it hath its effect, the cause of rejoicing riseth much higher. For if the offer and hope of reconciliation be a just ground of joy, how much more actual agreement with God, upon the terms of the gospel, and reconciliation itself! 'We rejoice in God through Jesus Christ, by whom we have received the atonement.'   To such there are express precepts given to ' rejoice in the Lord always.'   And lest that should be thought to have been spoken hastily, and that it might have its full weight, that great apostle immediately adds, ' And again I say to you, Rejoice.'   And elsewhere, ' Rejoice evermore.'

"Hence, therefore, the genuine right temper and frame of a truly Christian mind and spirit may be evidently concluded to be this, (for such precepts do not signify nothing, nor can they be understood to signify less,) an habitual joyfulness, prevailing over all the temporary occasions of sorrow that occur to them. For none can be thought of that can preponderate, or be equal to the just and great causes of their joy. This is the true frame, model, and constitution of the kingdom of God, which ought to have place in us; herein it consists, in 'righteousness, and peace, and joy in the Holy Ghost.'

"Nor is this a theory only, or the idea and notion of an excellent temper of spirit, which we may contemplate indeed, but can never attain to. For we find it also to have been the attainment and usual temper of Christians heretofore, 'that being justified by faith, and having peace with God,' they have rejoiced in hope of the glory of God, unto that degree, as 'even to glory in their tribulations also.' And that in the confidence they should be 'kept by the power of God through faith unto salvation,' they have hereupon greatly rejoiced, though with some mixture of heaviness (whereof there was need) from their manifold trials. But that their joy did surmount and prevail over their heaviness is manifest; for this is spoken of with much diminution, whereas they are said to rejoice greatly, and with 'a joy unspeakable and full of glory.'

"Yea, and such care hath the great God taken for the preserving of this temper of spirit among his people more anciently, that even their sorrow for sin itself (the most justifiable of all other) hath had restraints put upon it, lest it should too long exclude or intermit the exercise of this joy. For when a great assembly of them were universally in tears, upon hearing the law read, and the sense given, they were forbidden to weep or mourn, or be sorry, 'because the joy of the Lord was their strength.' That most just sorrow had been unjust had it been continued so as to exclude the seasonable turn and alternation of this joy. For even such sorrow itself is not required, or necessary for itself. It is remote from the goodness and benignity of God's ever-blessed nature to take pleasure in the sorrows of his people, as they are such, or that they should sorrow for sorrow's sake; but only as a means and preparative to their following joy. And nothing can be more unreasonable, than that the means should exclude the end, or be used against the purpose they should serve.

"It is then upon the whole most manifest, that no temporary affliction whatsoever, upon one who stands in special relation to God, as a reconciled (and, which is consequent, an adopted) person, though attended with the most aggravating circumstances, can justify such a sorrow (so deep or so continued) as shall prevail against and shut out a religious holy joy, or hinder it from being the prevailing principle in such a one. What can make that sorrow allowable or innocent, (what event of Providence, that can, whatever it is, be no other than an accident to our Christian state,) that shall resist the most natural design and end of Christianity itself? that shall deprave and debase the truly Christian temper, and disobey and violate most express Christian precepts? subvert the constitution of Christ's kingdom among men? and turn this earth (the place of God's treaty with the inhabitants of it, in order to their reconciliation to himself; and to the reconciled, the portal and gate of heaven, yea, and where the state of the very worst and most miserable has some mixture of good in it, that makes the evil of it less than that of hell) into a mere hell to themselves, of sorrow without mixture, and wherein shall be nothing but weeping and wailing?

"The cause of your sorrow, Madam, is exceeding great. The causes of your joy are inexpressibly greater. You have infinitely more left than you have lost. Doth it need to be disputed whether God be better and greater than man? or more to be valued, loved, and delighted in? and whether an eternal relation be more considerable than a temporary one? Was it not your constant sense in your best outward state, ' Whom have I in heaven but thee, O God? and whom can I desire on earth, in comparison of thee?' Herein the state of your ladyship's case is still the same; if indeed you cannot with greater clearness and with less hesitation pronounce those latter words. The principal causes of your joy are immutable, such as no supervening thing can alter. You have lost a most pleasant, delectable, earthly relative. Doth the blessed God hereby cease to be the best and most excellent Good? Is his nature changed? his everlasting covenant reversed and annulled, ' which is ordered in all things and sure, and is to be all your salvation and all your desire, whether he make your house on earth to grow or not to grow?' That sorrow which exceeds the proportion of its cause, compared with the remaining true and real causes of rejoicing, is in that excess causeless; that is, that excess of it wants a cause, such as can justify or afford defence unto it.

"We are required, in reference to our nearest relations in this world, when we lose them, ' to weep as if we wept not,' as well as, when we enjoy them, to ' rejoice as if we rejoiced not, because our time here is short, and the fashion of this world passeth away.'

"We are finite beings, and so are they. Our passions in reference to them must not be infinite and without limit, or be limited only by the limited capacity of our nature, so as to work to the utmost extent of that, as the fire burns and the winds blow, as much as they can : but they are to be limited by the power, design, and endeavour of our reason and grace (not only by the mere impotency of our nature) in reference to all created objects. Whereas, in reference to the infinite uncreated Good, towards which there is no danger or possibility of exceeding in our affection, we are never to design to ourselves any limits at all; for that would suppose we had loved God enough, or as much as he deserved, which were not only to limit ourselves, but him too ; and were a constructive denial of his infinite immense goodness, and consequently of his very Godhead. Of so great a concernment it is to us, that in the liberty we give our affections, we observe the just difference which ought to be in their exercise, towards God, and towards creatures.

"It is also to be considered, that the great God is pleased so to condescend, as himself to bear the name and sustain the capacity of our nearest earthly relations ; which implies that what they were to us, in this or that kind, he will be in a transcendent and far more noble kind. I doubt not but your ladyship hath good right to apply to yourself those words of the prophet, 'Thy Maker is thy husband.' Whereupon, as he infinitely transcends all that is delectable in the most excellent earthly relation, it ought to be endeavoured, that the affection placed on him should proportionably excel. I cannot think any person in the world would be a more severe or impartial judge of a criminal affection than your ladyship : or that it would look worse unto any eye, if anyone should so deeply take to heart the death of an unrelated person, as never to take pleasure more in the life, presence, and conversation of one most nearly related. And you do well know that such a height (or that supremacy) of affection as is due to the ever-blessed God, cannot without great injury be placed anywhere else. As we are to have none other God before him, so him alone we are to love with all our heart and soul, and might and mind.

"And it ought further to be remembered, that whatsoever interest we have or had in any the nearest relative on earth, his interest who made both is far superior. He made us and all things primarily for himself, to serve great and important ends of his own; so that our satisfaction in any creature is but secondary and collateral to the principal design of its creation.

"Which consideration would prevent a practical error and mistake that is too usual with pious persons, afflicted with the loss of any near relation, that they think the chief intention of such a providence is their punishment. And hereupon they are apt to justify the utmost excesses of their sorrow upon such an occasion, accounting they can never be sensible enough of the Divine displeasure appearing in it; and make it their whole business (or employ their time or thoughts beyond a due proportion) to find out and fasten upon some particular sin of theirs, which they may judge God was offended with them for, and designed now to punish upon them. It is, indeed, the part of filial ingenuity deeply to apprehend the displeasure of our Father; and an argument of great sincerity, to be very inquisitive after any sin for which we may suppose him displeased with us, and apt to charge ourselves severely with it, though perhaps, upon utmost inquiry, there is nothing particularly to be reflected on, other than common infirmity incident to the best, (and it is well when at length we can make that judgment, because there really is no more, not for that we did not inquire,) and perhaps also God intended no more in such a dispensation, (as to what concerned us in it,) than only, in the general, to take off our minds and hearts more from this world, and draw them more entirely to himself. For if we were never so innocent, must therefore such a relative of ours have been immortal? But the error in practice as to this case, lies here; not that our thoughts are *much* exercised this way, but *too much*. We ought to consider in every case, principally, that which is principal. God did not create this or that excellent person, and place him for a while in the world, principally to please us; nor therefore doth he take him away, principally to displease or punish us; but for much nobler and greater ends which he hath proposed to himself concerning him. Nor are we to reckon ourselves so little interested in the great and sovereign Lord of all, whom we have taken to be our God, and to whom we have absolutely resigned and devoted ourselves, as not to be obliged to consider and satisfy ourselves, in his pleasure, purposes, and ends, more than our own apart from his.

"Such as he hath pardoned, accepted, and prepared for himself, are to serve and glorify him in a higher and more excellent capacity than they ever could in this wretched world of ours, and wherein they have themselves the highest satisfaction. When the blessed God is pleased in having attained and accomplished the end and intendments of his own boundless love, (too great to be satisfied with the conferring of only temporary favours in this imperfect state,) and they are pleased in partaking the full effects of that love; who are we, that we should be displeased? or that we should oppose our satisfaction, to that of the glorious God and his glorified creature? Therefore, madam, whereas you cannot avoid to think much on this subject, and to have the removal of that incomparable person for a great theme of your thoughts, I do only propose most humbly to your honour, that you would not confine them to the sadder and darker part of that theme. It hath also a bright side; and it equally belongs to it, to consider whither he is gone, and to whom, as whence and from whom. Let, I beseech you, your mind be more exercised in contemplating the glories of that state your blessed consort is translated unto, which will mingle pleasure and sweetness with the bitterness of your afflicting loss, by giving you a daily intellectual participation (through the exercise of faith and hope) in his enjoyments. He cannot descend to share with you in your sorrows; you may thus every day ascend, and partake with him in his joys. He is a pleasant subject to consider: a prepared spirit made meet for an inheritance with them that are sanctified, and with the saints in light, now entered into a state so connatural, and wherein it finds everything most agreeable to itself. How highly grateful is it to be united with the true centre, and come home to the Father of spirits! To consider how pleasant a welcome, how joyful an entertainment he hath met with above; how delighted an associate he is ' with the general assembly, the innumerable company of angels, and the spirits of just men made perfect;' how joyful a homage he continually pays to the throne of the celestial King!

"Will your ladyship think that a hard saying of our departing Lord to his mournful disciples, 'If ye loved me, ye would rejoice that I said, I go to the Father; for my Father is greater than I?' As if he said, he sits enthroned in higher glory than you can frame any conception of, by beholding me in so mean a condition on earth. We are as remote, and as much short in our thoughts as to the conceiving the glory of the Supreme King, as a peasant, who never saw anything better than his own cottage, from conceiving the splendour of the most glorious prince's court. But if that faith, which ' is the substance of things hoped for,' and 'the evidence of things not seen,' be much accustomed to its proper work and business, —the daily delightful visiting and viewing the glorious invisible regions; if it be often conversant in those vast and spacious tracts of pure and brightest light, and amongst the holy inhabitants that replenish them; if it frequently employ itself in contemplating their comely order, perfect harmony, sublime wisdom, unspotted purity, most fervent mutual love, delicious conversation with one another, and perpetual pleasant consent in their adoration and observance of their eternal King; who is there to whom it would not be a solace to think, 'I have such and such friends and relatives (some perhaps as dear as my own life) perfectly well pleased and happy among them?' How can your love, Madam, (so generous a love towards so deserving an object!) how can it but more fervently sparkle in joy for his sake, than dissolve in tears for your own?

"Nor should such thoughts excite over-hasty, impatient desires of following presently into heaven, but to the endeavours of serving God more cheerfully on earth for our appointed time: which I earnestly desire your ladyship would apply yourself to, as you would not displease God, who is your only hope, nor be cruel to yourself, nor dishonour the religion of Christians, as if they had no other consolations than this earth can give, and earthly power take from them. Your ladyship (if any one) would be loth to do anything unworthy your family and parentage. Your highest alliance is to that Father and family above, whose dignity and honour are, I doubt not, of highest account with you.

"I multiply words, being loth to lose my design; and shall only add that consideration, which cannot but be valuable with you, upon *his* first proposal, who had all the advantages imaginable to give it its full weight; I mean that of those dear pledges left behind: my own heart even bleeds to think of the case of those sweet babes, should they be bereaved of their other parent too. And even your continued visible dejection would be their unspeakable disadvantage. You will always naturally create in them a reverence of you; and I cannot but apprehend how the constant mien, aspect, and deportment of such a parent will insensibly influence the temper of dutiful children; and if that be sad and despondent, depress their spirits, blunt and take off the edge and quickness, upon which their future usefulness and comfort will much depend. Were it possible their now glorious father should visit and inspect you, would you not be troubled to behold a frown in that bright serene face? You are to please a more penetrating eye; which you will best do, by putting on a temper and deportment suitable to your weighty charge and duty, and to the great purposes for which God continues you in the world, by giving over unnecessary solitude and retirement, which (though it pleases) doth really prejudice you, and is more than you can bear. Nor can any rules of decency require more. Nothing that is necessary and truly Christian, ought to be reckoned unbecoming. David's example * is of too great authority to be counted a pattern of indecency. The God of heaven lift up the light of his countenance upon you, and thereby put gladness into your heart; and give you to apprehend him saying to you, 'Arise, and walk in the light of the Lord.'

"That I have used so much freedom in this paper, I make no apology for; but do, therefore, hide myself in the dark, not judging it consistent with that plainness which I thought the case might require, to give any other account of myself, than that I am one deeply sensible of your and your noble relatives' great affliction, and who scarce ever bow the knee before the mercy-seat without remembering it: and who shall ever be,

"Madam,

"Your ladyship's

"Most sincere honourer, and

"Most humble devoted servant."

Though this epistle was anonymous, the peculiarities of style and manner, as well as some other circumstances, betrayed the author. The noble lady to whom it was addressed, replied in a letter of thanks, in which she told him, that "he must not expect to be concealed." This led to further correspondence, and eventually to an intimacy with the noble family of Bedford, which continued till his death.

Who, on perusing the foregoing letter, can forbear to reflect, and to reflect with delight, on the diffusive character of that benevolence in which it originated, and which is so beautifully illustrated at its close? The illustrious lady to whom it was addressed, was an utter stranger to Howe, or was known to him, only as she was known to all the rest of the world—by

---

* 2 Sam. xii. 20.

the fame of her unutterable sorrows. Yet the deep sympathies which the gospel inspired, induced him not only to address this elaborate and most affecting letter of consolation to her, but to make specific mention of her in his private devotions. He assures her that he "seldom bowed his knees before the mercy-seat without remembering her there."

It is delightful to reflect that this is not a solitary instance,* though a most touching and impressive one, of the expansive spirit of Christian benevolence. Who can tell, indeed, how often that spirit prompts supplications in secret on behalf of those who little know the compassion their sorrows have inspired, and are personally strangers to the individuals who so benevolently plead for them? Nay, more; who can tell how often not only individuals, but communities, have been benefited by the "effectual and fervent," though secret and silent prayer of those who are in Scripture called "the salt of the earth and the light of the world?"

Is it fanciful to suppose, that in heaven, (where the methods of the Divine Providence, and the complicated system of means and instruments it has adopted, will, there is reason to believe, be more fully explained to us,) one source of delight to many, will be the grateful discovery that on earth they have had unknown friends; friends who have interceded for them in secret; friends who, in these, the highest exercises of charity, as well as in those of a more ordinary benevolence, have not suffered their "left hand to know" what "their right hand did?"

In 1684, Howe published his treatise, entitled "The Redeemer's Tears wept over Lost Souls: with an Appendix, where somewhat is occasionally discoursed concerning the Blasphemy against the Holy Ghost, and how God is said to will the salvation of them that perish."

During this year, the nonconformists were persecuted with the most unrelenting ferocity. Not only sins of "com-

---

* For an illustration of these remarks, see the affecting correspondence between Mr. Sheppard and Lord Byron, in the well-known work entitled, "Thoughts on Private Devotion," pp. 343–350.

mission," but those of "omission," were visited upon them : they were punished, not merely for frequenting the conventicle, but for *not* going to church, and for *not* taking the sacrament. In short, all those merciless laws which had been enacted a century before, and which bigotry, at much earlier and less enlightened periods, had often suffered to slumber, were now rigorously enforced against the unhappy dissidents.

To the shame of the episcopal bench, there were not wanting bishops, who hallooed on the inferior clergy and the civil magistrates, in this cruel and ignoble sport. Amongst them was Barlow, Bishop of Lincoln, of whom better things might have been expected; but who now published, (concurrently with a most cruel order of the justices of the peace in a part of his diocese,* bearing date, January 14, 1684) a most intemperate address to his clergy, on the necessity of enforcing the laws against the nonconformists.

On this, Howe sent him an anonymous letter of expostulation, of which a copy has happily been preserved. It was surely impossible for the prelate, however angry his present mood, to read it without some relentings of heart, inspired as it was by a spirit so beautifully contrasted with that which had dictated his own mischievous and cruel appeal. Howe concludes his letter with the prayer, that if the prelate "had either *misjudged,* or *misdone* against his judgment, God would rectify his error by gentler methods and by less affliction than he had designed for his brethren ;" and with the expression of his belief, that "he did not doubt after all (any more for the prelate's part than for his own) to meet him one day in that place where Luther and Zuinglius were well agreed."

"*Right Reverend,*

"As I must confess myself surprised by your late published directions to your clergy of the county of Bedford, so nor will I dissemble, that I did read them with some trouble of mind, which I sincerely profess, was more upon your lordship's account than my own, (who for myself, am little concerned,) or any other particular person's whatsoever. It was

---

* County of Bedford.

such as it had not been very difficult for me to have concealed in my own breast, or only to have expressed it to God in my prayers for you, (which, through his grace, I have not altogether omitted to do,) if I had not apprehended it not utterly impossible, (as I trust I might, without arrogating unduly to myself,) that some or other of those thoughts, which I have revolved in my own mind upon this occasion, being only hinted to your lordship, might appear to your very sagacious judgment (for which I have had long, and have still, a continuing veneration) some way capable of being cultivated by your own mature and second thoughts, so as not to be wholly unuseful to your lordship.

"My own judgment, such as it is, inclines me not to oppose anything, either, 1. To the lawfulness of the things themselves which you so much desire should obtain in the practice of the people under your lordship's pastoral inspection: or, 2. To the desirable comeliness of an uniformity in the public and solemn worship of God: or, 3. To the fitness of making laws for the effecting of such uniformity: or, 4. To the execution of such laws, upon some such persons as may possibly be found among so numerous a people as are under your lordship's care.

"But the things which I humbly conceive are to be deliberated on, are, 1. Whether *all* the laws that are in being about matters of that nature, ought now to be executed upon *all* the persons which any way transgress them, without distinction of either?　2. Whether it was so well, that your lordship should advise and press that indistinct execution, which the order (to which the subjoined directions of your lordship do succenturiate) seems to intend; supposing that designed execution were fit in itself.

"I shall not need to speak severally to these heads: your lordship will sufficiently distinguish what is applicable the one way or the other.　But I humbly offer to your lordship's further consideration, whether it be not a supposable thing, that some persons, sound in the faith, strictly orthodox in all the articles of it taught by our Lord Jesus or his apostles, resolvedly loyal, and subject to the authority of their governors in church and state, of pious, sober, peaceable, just, charitable dispositions and deportments, may yet (while they agree with your lordship in that evident principle, both by the law of nature and Scripture, that their prince and inferior rulers ought to be actively obeyed in all lawful things) have a formed fixed judgment (for what were to be done in the case of a mere doubt, that hath not arrived to a settled preponderation this way or that, is not hard to determine) of the unlawfulness of some or other of the rites and modes of worship enjoined to be observed in this church? For my own part, though, perhaps, I should not be found to differ much from your lordship in most of the things here referred unto, I do yet think that few metaphysical questions are disputed with nicer subtlety, than the matter of the ceremonies has been by Archbishop Whitgift, Cartwright, Hooker, Parker, Dr. Burgess, Dr. Ames, Gillespy, Jeanes, Calderwood, Dr. Owen, Baxter, etc. Now, is it impossible that a sincere and sober Christian may, with an honest heart, have so weak intellectuals, as not to be able to understand all the punctilios upon which a right judgment of such a matter may depend? And is it not possible there may be such a thing as a mental as well as a merely sensitive antipathy, not vincible by ordinary methods? Is there no difference to be put between things essential to our religion, and things confessed indifferent on the one hand, and on the other judged unlawful; on both hands but accidental? (though they that think them unlawful dare not allow themselves a liberty of sinning even in accidentals.) If your lordship were the ' paterfamilias' to a numerous family of children and servants, among whom one or other very dutiful child takes offence, not at the sort of food you have thought fit should be provided, but somewhat in the sauce or way of dressing, which thereupon he forbears; you try all the means which your paternal wisdom and severity think fit, to overcome that aversion, but in vain; would you finally famish this child rather than yield to his inclination in so small a thing?

"My Lord, your lordship well knows the severity of some of those laws which you press for the execution of, is such as, being executed, they must infer the utter ruin of them who observe them not, in their temporal concernments; and not that only, but their deprivation of the comfortable advantages appointed by our blessed Lord for promoting their spiritual and eternal well-being. I cannot but be well persuaded not only of the mere sincerity, but eminent sanctity of divers, upon my own knowledge and experience of them, who would sooner die at a stake, than I or any man can prevail with them (notwithstanding our rubric, or whatever can be said to facilitate the matter) to kneel before the consecrated elements at the Lord's table. Would your lordship necessitate such, *perdere substantiam propter accidentia ?* What if there be considerable numbers of such in your lordship's vastly numerous flock; will it be comfortable to you, when an account is demanded of your lordship by the great Shepherd and Bishop of souls concerning them, only to be able to say, ' Though, Lord, I did believe the provisions of thine house purchased for them, necessary and highly useful for their salvation, I drove them away as dogs and swine from thy table, and stirred up such other agents as I could influence against them, by whose means I reduced many of them to beggary, ruined many families, banished them into strange countries, where they might (for me) serve other gods; and this not for disobeying any immediate ordinance or law of thine, but because, for fear of offending thee, they did not in everything comport with my own appointments, or which I was directed to urge and impose upon them?' How well would this practice agree with that apostolical precept, ' Him that is weak in the faith receive, but not to doubtful disputations?' I know not how your lordship would relieve yourself in this case, but by saying they were not weak, nor conscientious, but wilful and humoursome. But what shall then be said to the subjoined expostulation, ' Who art thou that judgest thy brother? we shall all stand before the judgment seat of Christ.' What if they have appeared conscientious, and of a very unblamable conversation in all things else? What if better qualified for Christian communion in all other respects than thousands you admitted? If you say you know of none such under your charge so severely dealt with, it will be said, ' Why did you use such severity toward them you did not know? or urge and animate them to use it, whom you knew never likely to distinguish?' A very noted divine of the Church of England said to me in discourse, not very long ago, upon mention of the ceremonies, ' Come, come, the Christian church and religion is in a consumption; and it ought to be done as in the case of consumptive persons—shave off the hair to save the life.' Another (a dignified person) present, replied, ' I doubt not it will be so in the Philadelphian state.' I long thought few had been in the temper of their minds nearer it than your lordship; and am grieved, not that I so judged, but that I am mistaken; and to see your lordship the first public example to the rest of your order in such a course. Blessed Lord! how strange is it that so long experience will not let us see, that little and so very disputable matters can never be the terms of union so much to be desired in the Christian church;

and that, in such a case as ours is, nothing will satisfy but the destruction of them, whose union upon so nice terms we cannot obtain ; and then to call *solitudinem, pacem !* But we must, it seems, understand all this rigour your lordship shows, to proceed from love, and that you are for destroying the Dissenters only to mend their understandings, and because *afflictio dat intellectum.* I hope, indeed, God will sanctify the affliction which you give and procure them, to blessed purposes ; and, perhaps, *periissent nisi periissent :* but for the purposes your lordship seems to aim at, I wonder what you can expect. Can you, by undoing men, change the judgment of their consciences ? or if they should tell you, 'We do, indeed, in our consciences judge, we shall greatly offend God by complying with your injunctions ; but yet, to save being undone, we will do it ; ' will this qualify them for your communion ? If your lordship think still you have judged and advised well in this matter, you have the judgment of our sovereign, upon twelve years' experience, lying against you : you have, as to one of the laws you would have executed, the judgment of both Houses of Parliament against you, who passed a Bill (to which, perhaps, you consented, for taking it away. You have (as to all of them) the judgment of the last House of Commons sitting at Westminster, so far as to the season then, of executing those laws. It may be your lordship thinks it now a fitter season ; but if you have misjudged, or misdone against your judgment, I pray God to rectify your error by gentler methods, and by less affliction, than you have designed to your brethren ; and do not, for all this, doubt (any more for your part than my own) to meet you there, one day, where Luther and Zuinglius are well agreed. If I did think that would contribute anything to the honest and truly charitable design of this letter, I should freely, and at large, tell you my name ; and do, however, tell you I am,

> " A sincere honourer of your lordship,

> " And your very faithful, humble Servant."

CHAPTER IX.

CONDUCT OF HOWE IN PERSECUTION—IS INVITED BY LORD WHARTON TO ACCOMPANY HIM IN HIS TRAVELS ON THE CONTINENT—HIS LETTER OF FAREWELL TO HIS FLOCK—REFLECTIONS—SETTLES AT UTRECHT—MODE OF LIFE THERE—CORRESPONDENCE WITH LADY RUSSELL—INTERVIEW WITH BURNET—IS INTRODUCED TO THE PRINCE OF ORANGE—INDULGENCE OF JAMES II.—HOWE RETURNS HOME—CONDUCT OF THE NONCONFORMISTS WITH RESPECT TO THE DESIGNS OF THE COURT—HOWE'S INTERVIEW WITH THE KING—CURIOUS SCENE AT DR. SHERLOCK'S—THE REVOLUTION OF 1688—HOWE'S ADDRESS TO THE PRINCE OF ORANGE—HOWE'S LETTER ON BEHALF OF THE FRENCH PROTESTANTS—HE PUBLISHES HIS " CASE OF THE DISSENTERS REPRESENTED AND ARGUED "—ACT OF TOLERATION—HOWE'S ADDRESS TO THE CONFORMISTS AND NONCONFORMISTS ON THAT EVENT.

IT was remarked in the Introductory Chapter, that it seems to have been the habitual desire of Howe to render all the events of life, every combination of external circumstances in which he might be placed, subservient to the sublime purposes of spiritual discipline. Of the success with which his efforts were attended, a more signal proof can hardly be imagined than the even temper, the serene spirit of meekness and love, which he maintained amidst the severest persecution; and of the many exhibitions of excellence with which his character delights us, none inspires us with greater delight than this. As the maintenance of a truly Christian spirit is far more difficult under such circumstances than under any other, so, when it *is* maintained, it argues a proportionate energy of religious principle.

" Persecution," as the intrepid John Hicks said to Charles II., " will drive a wise man mad." Though it does not justify, it almost inevitably excites a bitter and vindictive spirit. Such feelings may be less criminal than the conduct which has provoked them, but they are still flagrantly inconsistent with the spirit of the gospel. Yet rare indeed is that command of temper—that deep and all-pervading charity—which, under the burning consciousness of wrong, can suppress the emotions of anger and impatience. This, however, was the case with Howe. Injury and oppression could not discompose his calm and stedfast spirit; or, rather, they only served to exhibit, in novel and striking aspects, the various excellence of his character. To a spirit such as his, the darkest scenes of persecution were but what the clouds of evening are to the setting sun, which, so far from obscuring, transmit and diffuse its radiance. Of this, one instance has been already furnished in the letter which concludes the preceding chapter; and the document, which I am about to lay before the reader, furnishes another still more remarkable.

In 1685, the persecution of the nonconformists had reached its height, and the prospect at home was in every respect most gloomy.* Under these circumstances, Howe gladly embraced the invitation of Philip, Lord Wharton, † to accompany him in his travels on the Continent. The interval which elapsed between the proposal and his departure (which was in August) was so short, that he could take no formal leave of his people. From the Continent, therefore, he sent them a most affecting farewell letter.

In this letter, he says little (though what he does say is deeply touching) of the sufferings he must have undergone previously to his leaving England. It was not his wout to speak much of himself.

His main solicitude is evidently for the welfare of his flock. That this might be *truly* promoted, he exhorts them to endeavour to attain à more deep, habitual, practical sense of religion; and, at the conclusion, guards them against indulging, under the pressure of persecution and suffering, in a spirit either of repining towards God, or of bitterness towards man.

---

* See Howe's own dreadful account of the sufferings of the nonconformists in the " Case of the Dissenters ; " inserted further on.

† This nobleman had taken an active part in favour of the Parliament against Charles I. He was one of the lay members of the Westminster Assembly, and a decided nonconformist. Locke gives him the character of " an old expert Parliament man, of eminent piety and abilities ; a great friend to the Protestant religion and interest of England."

He declares that one of his own chief consolations in suffering
has been his " consciousness that he had no other than kind or
benign thoughts towards those whom he has suffered by, and
that his heart tells him he desires not the least hurt to those
that would do him the greatest; that he feels within himself
an unfeigned love and high estimation of divers of them, accounting them pious, worthy persons, and hoping to meet
them in the *all-reconciling* world." The all-reconciling world!
How beautiful is that expression !

The whole document, which is strikingly characteristic of
his contempt for the distinctions of party, of his supreme
regard for the essence of religion in whatsoever party found,
and of his devotedness as a pastor, is here subjoined :—

TO SUCH IN AND ABOUT LONDON, AMONG WHOM I HAVE
LABOURED IN THE WORK OF THE GOSPEL.

*" My most dearly beloved in our blessed Lord and Saviour
Jesus Christ, grace, mercy, and peace be through him multiplied unto you.*

"That I am, at this time, at this distance from you, is, I am
persuaded, (upon the experience I have had of your great love
and value of my poor labours,) not pleasant to you, and I do
assure you it is grievous to me, though I murmur not at the
wise and holy Providence that hath ordered things thus, in
reference to you and me : but it added to my trouble, that I
could not so much as bid farewell to persons to whom I had so
great endearments, the solemnity whereof you know our circumstances would not admit. Nor could I have opportunity
to communicate to you the grounds of my taking this long
journey, being under promise, while the matter was under
consideration, not to speak of it to any one that was not concerned immediately about it : neither could I think that imprudent in itself, where acquaintance was so numerous, silence
towards dearest friends in such cases usually being designed
for an apology to all others. And, after the resolution was
taken, my motion depending on another, I had not time for
that, or any such purposes. And should I yet communicate
them, as they lie particularly in my own thoughts, it would
lose time that I may more profitably employ for both you and
myself, while I do it not. You will, I may be confident, be

more prudent and equal, than to judge of what you do not know : but so much I shall in the general say, that the providence of God gave me the prospect of a present quiet abode, with some opportunity of being serviceable ; (and I hope, as it may prove through his help and blessing, unto you, if I have life and health to finish what I have been much pressed by some of yourselves to go on with ;) which opportunity I could not hope to have nearer you, at least without being unreasonably burdensome to some, while I was designing service, as much as in me lay, to all. It much satisfies me that I have a record above, I am not designing for myself ; that he who knoweth all things, knows I love not this present world, and I covet not an abode in it, (nor have I when it was most friendly to me,) upon any other account than upon doing some service to him, and the souls of men. It therefore has been my settled habitual sense and sentiment a long time, to value and desire (with submission to sovereign good pleasure) peace and quiet, with some tolerable health, more than life. Nor have I found anything more destructive to my health, than confinement to a room a few days in the city air, which was much better and more healthful to me formerly, than since the anger and jealousies of such as I never had a disposition to offend, have of later times occasioned persons of my circumstances very seldom to walk the streets.

"But my hope is, God will in his good time incline the hearts of rulers more to favour such as cannot be satisfied with the public constitutions in the matter of God's worship, and that are innocent and peaceable in the land ; and that my absence from you will be for no long time, it being my design, with dependence upon his gracious providence and pleasure, in whose hands our times are, if I hear of any door open for service with you, to spend the health and strength which God shall vouchsafe me, (and which I find through his mercy much improved since I left you,) in his work with and among you. In the meantime, I believe it will not be unacceptable to you, that I offer you some of my thoughts and counsels, for your present help, such as are not new to me, nor as you will find to yourselves, who are my witnesses that I have often inculcated such things to you ; but they may be useful to stir you up, by putting you in remembrance.

"I. I beseech you, more earnestly endeavour to reduce the things you know (and have been by many hands instructed in out of the gospel of our Lord) to practice. Nothing can be more absurd than to content ourselves with only a notional knowledge of practical matters. We should think so in other cases. As if any man should satisfy himself to know the use of food, but famish himself by never eating any, when he hath it at hand : or that he understands the virtues of this or that cordial, but languishes away to death in the neglect of using it, when it might cheer his spirits, and save his life. And the neglect of applying the great things of the gospel to the proper uses and purposes of the Christian life, is not more foolish, (only as the concernments they serve for are more important,) but much more sinful and provoking to God. For we are to consider whence the revelation comes. They are things which the mouth of the Lord hath spoken; uttered by the breath of the eternal God, as all Scriptures are said to be. God-breathed, as that expression may be literally rendered.

"And how high a contempt and provocation is it of the great God, so totally to pervert and disappoint the whole design of that revelation he hath made to us, to know the great things contained therein, only for knowing sake, which he hath made known that we might live by them. And, oh! what holy and pleasant lives should we lead in this world, if the temper and complexion of our souls did answer and correspond to the things we know! The design of preaching has been greatly mistaken, when it has been thought it must still acquaint them who live (and especially who have long lived) under it, with some new thing. Its much greater and more important design is, the impressing of known things (but too little considered) upon the hearts of hearers, that they may be delivered up into the mould and form of the doctrine taught them ; and may so learn Christ, as more and more to be renewed in the spirit of their minds, and put off the old man and put on the new. The digesting our food is what God now eminently calls for.

"II. More particularly labour to have your apprehensions of the future state of the unseen world and eternal things, made more lively and efficacious daily, and that your faith of them may be such as may truly admit to be called the very substance and evidence of those things. Shall that glorious everlasting state of things be always as a dark shadow with us, or as the images we have of things in a dream, ineffectual and vanishing, only because we have not seen with our eyes, where God himself hath by his express word made the representations of them to us, who never deceived us, as our own eyes and treacherous senses have done? Why do we not live as just now entering into the eternal state, and as if we now beheld the glorious appearing of the great God our Saviour, when we are as much assured of them as if we beheld them? Why do we not oftener view the representation of the heavens vanishing, the elements melting, the earth flaming, the angels everywhere dispersed to gather the elect, and them ascending, caught up to meet the Redeemer in the air, ever to be with the Lord? What a trifle will the world be to us then!

"III. Let the doctrine of the Redeemer be more studied, and of his mighty undertaking, with the immediate design of it, not merely to satisfy for sin by the sacrifice he once for all made of himself, and so to procure our pardon and justification without effecting anything upon us, but to redeem us from all iniquity, to purify us to himself, and to form us after his own holy likeness, and for such purposes to give his Holy Spirit to us. Consider that our Redeemer is mighty, who hath such kind designs upon us; and that as they shall not therefore finally fail of accomplishment, so will they be carried on without interruption, and with discernible success, if we fail not as to what part (in subordination to him) belongs to us. How cheerfully should the redeemed of the Lord go on in their course, under such conduct!

"IV. Endeavour your faith may be stronger, more efficacious and practical, concerning the doctrine of providence, and that the workings and events of it lie all under the management and in the hand of the Redeemer, who is Head over all things to the church: that therefore how grievous and bitter soever be his people's lot and portion at any time, there cannot but be kindness at the bottom; and that, not only designing the best end, but taking the fittest way to it. For can love itself be unkind, so as not to design well? or wisdom itself err so as to take an improper course in order thereto? Hereupon let not your spirits be imbittered by the present dispensation of Providence you are under, whereby you are in so great a part deprived of the helps and means of your spiritual advantage, which you like and relish most. And to this purpose consider—

"1. Our wise and merciful Lord (though perhaps such means might be in some measure useful to us) doth for the present judge that his rebuking our undue use of them will be more useful; either overvaluing or undervaluing his instruments, turning his ordinances into mere formalities, preferring the means of grace (as they are fitly called) before the end, grace itself.

"2. Consider whether there be no disposition of spirit to treat others as you are treated. The inward temper of our minds and spirits is so much the more narrowly to be inspected, by how much the less there is opportunity to discover it by outward acts. As to such as differ from us about the forms and ceremonies that are now required in the worship of God, would we not be glad if they were as much restrained from using them in their worship, as we from worshipping without them? And do not we think that that would as much grieve them, as our restraint doth us? And why should we suppose that their way should not as much suit their spirits, and be as grateful to them, as ours to us? 'But we are in the right way,' some will say, 'and they in the wrong:' and why cannot any man say the same thing with as much confidence as we? Or, do we think there is no difference to be put between controversies about matter of circumstance, and about the essentials of Christianity? Undoubtedly, till those that affect the name of the Reformed, and count it more their glory to be called Protestants than to be good Christians, have learnt to mingle more justice with their religion, and how better to apply that great advice of our Lord's, 'Whatsoever ye would that men should do to you, do that to them,' and till they become studious of excelling other men, in substantial goodness, abstractedness from the world, meekness, humility, sobriety, self-denial, and charity, and to lay a greater stress hereon than on being of one or other denomination, God's controversy will not cease.

"I reckon it much to be considered, and I pray you consider it deeply, that after that great precept, 'Grieve not the Holy Spirit of God,' it immediately follows, 'Let all bitterness, and anger, and wrath, and clamour, and evil speaking, be put away from you, with all malice:' plainly implying that the Spirit of God, that Spirit of all love, goodness, sweetness, and benignity, is grieved by nothing more than by our bitterness, wrathfulness, etc. And it appears that the discernible restraint and departure of that blessed Spirit from the church of Christ in so great a measure, for many foregoing generations, in comparison of the plentiful effusion of it in the first age, hath ensued upon the growth of that wrathful contentious spirit which showed itself early in the Gnostic, but much more in the after Arian persecution, which was not in some places less bloody than the pagan persecution had been before. Oh, the gentleness, kindness, tenderness, and compassionateness of the evangelical, truly Christian spirit, as it most eminently appeared in our Lord Jesus Christ himself! And we are told, 'If any man have not the Spirit of Christ, he is none of his.' And how easy and pleasant is it to one's own self, to be void of all wrathfulness, and vindictive designs or inclinations towards any other man! For my own part, I should not have that peace and consolation in a suffering condition, (as my being so many years under restraint from that pleasant work of pleading with sinners that they might be saved, is the greatest suffering I was liable to in this world,) as through the goodness of God I have found, and do find, were I not conscious to myself of no other than kind and benign thoughts towards them I have suffered by, and that my heart tells me I desire not the least hurt to them that would do me the greatest; and that I feel within myself an unfeigned love and high estimation of divers, accounting them pious worthy persons, and hoping to meet them in the all-reconciling world, that are yet (through some mistake) too harsh towards us who dissent from them; and in things of this nature I pray that you and I may abound more and more.

"But again, as I would not have your spirits imbittered, so I would not have your spirits discouraged, or sunk in dejection. 'The Lord will not cast off his people, because it hath pleased him to make them his people;' I do not mean those of this or that party, but who fear God and work righteousness, be they of what party soever. As I often think of that saying of an ancient, Clement of Alexandria, that he counted not that philosophy, which was peculiar to this or that sect, but whatsoever of truth was to be found in any of them, so I say of Christianity; it is not that which is appropriate to this or that party, but whatsoever of sincere religion shall be found common to them all. Such will value and love his favour and presence, and shall have it; and he will yet have such a people in the world, and, I doubt not, more numerous than ever. And as the bitterness of Christians one towards another chased away his Spirit, his Spirit shall vanquish and drive away all that bitterness, and consume our other dross. And as the apostasy long ago foretold, and of so long continuance in the Christian church, hath been begun and continued by constant war against the Spirit of Christ; the restitution and recovery of the church, and the reduction of Christianity to its ancient self, and primitive state, will be by the victory of the Spirit of Christ over that so contrary spirit. Then shall all the enmity, pride, wrathfulness, and cruelty, which have rent the church of Christ and made it so little itself, be melted down; and with all their great impurities besides, earthliness, carnality, love of this present world, and prevalence of sensual lusts, be purged more generally away; and his repairing work be done in a way grievous to no one, whereby those that are most absolutely conquered will be most highly pleased: not by might or by power, but by the Spirit of the Lord.

"In the meantime let us draw nigh to God, and he will draw nigh to us. Let us more study the exercising ourselves to godliness, and take heed of turning the religion of our closets into spiritless, uncomfortable formalities. 'Their hearts shall live that seek God.'

"To that blessed, and faithful, and covenant-keeping God I commit you; and 'to the word of his grace, which is able to build you up further, and give you an inheritance among them that are sanctified.'

"And as I hope I shall without ceasing remember you in mine, so I hope you will remember too in your prayers,

"Your sincerely affectionate,
"Though too unprofitable,
"Servant in Christ,
"JOHN HOWE."

In company with Lord Wharton, Howe visited some of the most celebrated cities in Europe, and enjoyed literary intercourse with learned men of all parties.

As he received no tidings from England which could induce him to return home, he settled, in 1686, (after having spent a year in travel,) at Utrecht. Here he took a large house for the reception of English lodgers; probably at the suggestion of some of his more wealthy fellow-exiles, who felt the desirableness of such an establishment. Amongst other inmates he had the Earl and Countess of Sutherland, several English gentlemen, and his nephews, George and John Hughes.

Nor was he entirely without opportunity of exercising his ministry. Sad, indeed, would have been his circumstances had he been compelled utterly to abandon duties to which he had dedicated his life, and which to him formed the sweetest solace of adversity.

While at Utrecht, he regularly preached in turn at the English church, with the Rev. Messrs. Matthew Mead, Woodcock, and Cross; men who, like himself, had preferred exile in Holland to persecution at home. These worthy men frequently spent together days of prayer for their unhappy and degraded country. On the evening of every Lord's day, Howe performed Divine service in his own household.

Nor were these the only modes in which he endeavoured to be useful during his sojourn in Holland. As there were several English students at the University, preparing for the ministry, he kindly consented to hear their "orations and disputations," at his own house; and gave them instruction and advice as to the best method of pursuing their studies. Such a man as Howe could not be idle. He was one who, wherever he was, would either *find* opportunities of doing good, or *make* them.

Several Englishmen of rank and fortune were staying in Holland during Howe's residence there; like himself, expatriated by persecution. Amongst them were Sir John Thompson,* Sir John Guise, Sir Patience Ward, and Thomas Papillon, Esq.,† with whom he formed a close intimacy. The professors of the University uniformly treated him with the utmost respect, and afforded him the advantages of learned society.

While at Utrecht, the following curious correspondence passed between Howe and Lady Rachel Russell. The letters are extracted from the collection published some years ago from the Devonshire MSS., by the editor of Madame du Deffand's Letters.

---

* Afterwards Lord Haversham. He is often mentioned cursorily by Burnet. He was of a republican family. This recommended him to the Earl of Anglesey, a patron of the Dissenters. He married Frances, the daughter of that earl, who strongly recommended him to the good graces of Charles II. The King made him a baronet. During the reign of James II. he joined the party of the Prince of Orange, who made him a baron and lord of the admiralty. "Afterwards," says Walpole, "he seems entirely to have abandoned his first principles, and to have given himself up to the high church party, though he continued to go sometimes to meetings."

† First Commissioner of the Victualling Office in the reign of William III. De Foe gives him a very high character.

Howe's letter contains nothing less than certain overtures of "an advantageous marriage," between Frances, the widow of —— Lloyd, Esq., a lady of great fortune and accomplishments, and Mr. (afterwards Lord) Edward Russell, brother-in-law to Lady Rachel Russell. He was long member for the county of Bedford. The proposed marriage afterwards took place, "with much happiness to both parties."

This, as we shall afterwards see, was not the only occasion on which Howe's good offices were employed in negotiating marriages between persons of distinction; and his prudence and integrity well qualified him for so delicate a business.

THE REV. JOHN HOWE TO LADY RUSSELL.

"*Utrecht, February* 9, 1686-7.

"I doubt not, Madam, but you believe me sincerely willing to serve any relative of your ladyship, or of the honourable family I am about to mention; and shall therefore forbear everything of apology for the trouble I now give you. If your ladyship think it not unfit to give me a character of my Lord of Bedford's (now) eldest son, and it prove as good, on his part, (which what I already know leaves me little place to doubt of,) as I am sure it will be true on your ladyship's, supposing he have not determined still to live single, or be not otherwise pre-engaged, I might perhaps (though I can only promise faithful endeavours) improve it to his advantage with an English lady, my present neighbour, so very deserving in respect of all personal qualifications, family, and fortune, as to be capable of contributing what can be expected from such a relation, to the making a person, suitable to her, very happy in it. It would be requisite, to qualify me for attempting anything herein, that I be able to give an account, besides his strict sobriety, of his seriousness in religion, without being addicted (to the degree of bigotry) unto any the distinguishing modes of it used among sober-minded Protestants; and (which is a great essential) of that goodness of temper, wherein is a composition of prudence and kindness, that shall neither incline to a fond levity nor too morose sourness; together with his certain estate, without reference to such possibilities, as, which God forbid they should, signify anything, either in reality or expectation. I doubt not I might receive very liberal encomiums of this noble person from other hands; but if I

N

should ever mention such a thing to the lady herself, nothing could give me so great a confidence therein as I should receive from your ladyship's testimony; nor can anything (upon what I know of her just and high honour for your ladyship) signify so much with her. I apprehend it will be the less inconvenient for your ladyship to give your sense upon this subject, that there will be no need, in doing so, again to mention his name, and that mere silence will serve as to any part (if there should be any) wherein your ladyship cannot allow yourself to be positive; and it would be the more convenient, for that I doubt not your ladyship can say all that will be for the present requisite, without making any inquiries from a third person, which, as yet, would not be seasonable.

"Your ladyship so well understands how little reason there is the great and wise Lord and Ruler of all things should make the state of things perfect and unexceptionable, in a world not intended for perpetuity, and designed to be a place of discipline for the exercise and improvement of virtue and religion, not of full rewards for them; and you are so fully persuaded that the rewards of the other state will be sufficiently ample for all the sufferings and sorrows, wherewith sincerity is often attended in this, that I need wish no more for your ladyship's present continual support and consolation, than that you may have the constant living sense of what you already know; which I cease not to pray for to your ladyship, together with the fulness of all blessings upon the most hopeful plants under your care; as greatly becometh,

"Most honoured Madam,
"Your ladyship's most obliged,
"And most faithfully devoted
"Humble Servant,
"JOHN HOWE."

The following is Lady Russell's reply:—

FROM LADY RUSSELL TO REV. JOHN HOWE.

"*February*, 1687.

"Let me assure Mr. Howe I do not write this with indifference, upon several accounts. I receive your letter as a kind testimony of your remembrance, which I value very much; and yet I feel myself more engaged by your zeal to do good to that family I have known so true content in, and am entirely dedicated to. It is honourable and worthy in the whole, and every branch of it have their peculiar virtues; but every highest respect (meaning that sex we are to speak of) is placed, where my best and blessed friend placed is. This may possibly be a bar to your concluding, that what I may say should be received as impartially given; though yet I think it may, since I am sincerest in searching, where I desire to find the fewest faults. Some in this imperfect state must be found in man; but I do sincerely believe the person is highly qualified to make one happy in the nearest relation we can have upon earth. I would, for no advantage to myself, or friend, deceive any; especially by false acts, be an instrument to lead one, eminently confident, into error, and so desperate a one, out of which there is no recovery. But where there is great honour, truth, courage, and great good-nature, what supposition can there be that, when joined with a prudent and virtuous woman, they should not feel the felicity of the happiest state of life? Self-interest does not bribe me to say this, since now the drudgery of living only remains to me; but in my pleasant days, so near a relation, so very deserving, must have been gladly received, and even now must be owned a kind providence; and would undoubtedly not fail to be so by the obliged family, which, I can pronounce, is the easiest to converse or live with, that ever I have known or could observe. There is one particular that, without making inquiries from a third person, (which you are of opinion would not yet be seasonable,) I can give no report of, that is, their certain estate. I am entirely ignorant in that point; but do imagine Mr. Ashurst not quite so. I am very nice of inquiring into those particulars, of all others; but I know they have an equal and just father, and what is once promised will be punctually performed. Proceedings of this nature can move so slow at such a distance, that more than I have said I do not take to be necessary, in order to your friendly attempting to facilitate a happy union, When the lady is again in England, I shall be early in paying my respects, and with great integrity acquitting myself of any part in this affair that can fall upon me; or, if it sinks into nothing, ever retain the sense of your good-will and forwardness to dispose the lady towards it; and shall as little fail to acquaint my Lord Bedford, whose mind is ever prepared to all real acknowledgments where he feels himself obliged."

Among the distinguished men who honoured Howe by their visits while he was in Holland, was Gilbert Burnet (afterwards

Bishop of Sarum), who, when at Utrecht, scrupled not to preach at the English church, and with much liberality openly " advocated occasional communion with those of different sentiments."   Calamy relates, that in a conversation with Howe at this period, Burnet expressed his conviction, " that nonconformity could not last long ; that, after Baxter, Bates, and he (Howe) were once laid in their graves, it would die of itself." Howe replied, that in his opinion, its existence depended much more on *principles* than on *persons;* that the surest as well as speediest method of destroying nonconformity would be to abate the rigour of the terms of conformity; and that unless this were done, in other words, so long as ground was left for conscientious nonconformity, present differences must necessarily be perpetuated.   The men might die, but the principles would live.

While in Holland, Howe was honoured by several interviews with William, Prince of Orange, afterward King of England. The prince discoursed with him, says Calamy, "with great freedom, and ever after maintained a great respect for him." *

In 1687, James II., suddenly abandoning every principle of his past policy, published his "Declaration for liberty of conscience;" and Howe's congregation, who were most anxious that he should resume his labours amongst them, wrote to remind him that he had promised to do so as soon as circumstances would permit him.   With their request he immediately complied.

Though the nonconformists, under the shadow of this indulgence, were now permitted to adopt their own modes of worship without molestation, no one acquainted with the character of the bigoted James, can be in any doubt as to the motives which prompted this unexpected lenity.   How, indeed, could it be expected that one, whose whole life had been marked by the blindest bigotry, and whose darling project (pursued at all

---

* " I well remember," says Calamy, " that he himself once informed me of some very private conversation he had with that prince (then king) not long before his death.   Among other things, the King asked him a ¦great many questions about his 'old master, Oliver,' as he called him, and seemed not a little pleased with the answers that were returned to some of his questions."

hazards) was the restoration of Popery, should be favourably disposed towards the principles of toleration ?

The indulgence, in truth, was nothing but an expedient for sheltering the Papists from persecution, and was designed to prepare the way for an entire repeal of the penal laws with respect to that obnoxious party: in other words, the King suddenly affected a tolerating spirit merely in order that he might afterwards more effectually serve the designs of persecution. Sooner than the Papists should be persecuted, he was willing that the nonconformists should for a while go free; and in order to secure his own party from oppression, he was ready to extend protection to others. Thus in the mysterious counsels of that Providence, which, when it would give rest to the church of Christ, can compel even her worst enemies to do her service, bigotry, in this instance, toiled in the work of toleration, and the "same fountain," for once, "sent forth waters both bitter and sweet." But the nonconformists were, in fact, no more indebted for this indulgence to the superstitious James, than their ancestors were, for the blessings of the Reformation, to the licentious Henry. Both monarchs were the reluctant instruments of good.

The sagacious Prince of Orange showed that he fully saw through the motives of James, in the interview with which Howe was favoured previous to his departure from Utrecht. On that occasion the prince told him that his brethren ought to be very sparing of their " congratulatory addresses ; " that it was their duty to offer the most strenuous resistance to the designs of the court as to the abolition of the penal laws and tests; and implored him to urge on his party the necessity of circumspection. Though some few of the nonconformists, deceived by the King's seeming lenity, indulged in a strain of gratitude which would have soon abated, had they known how very small their obligations were ; and though some of the high church faction (secretly favourable to the King's designs) sent up addresses, conceived in a style of the most fulsome flattery ; it is but justice to say, that the bulk of both the great Protestant parties saw through the disguise of royal hypocrisy, and reasonably distrusted a revolution of sentiments and policy so suspiciously sudden.

Nothing can be more noble than the conduct of the nonconformists on more than one occasion in which the country has been menaced with danger from the designs of Popery.* With a magnanimity which entitles them to the veneration of posterity, they have repeatedly shown their willingness to remain under an undeserved stigma rather than allow a dangerous freedom to the enemies of their country, and to secure the liberty of the nation at the expense of their own.† In the present instance, under the guidance of Howe, and some few others of equal influence and reputation, they maintained their ancient character for integrity. In our day, indeed, a readiness in one party of religionists to sacrifice their own interests, in order to perpetuate penal laws against another, would be justly thought a most gratuitous display of bigotry. But at that crisis, when the dangers from Popery were so obvious and so imminent; when the throne was filled by a bigot, resolutely bent on restoring that party to power, the conduct of the nonconformists deserves the praise of the purest patriotism.

When the court, more fully disclosing its designs, endeavoured to get the nonconformists to sanction the " dispensing power " as applied to the Papists, the bulk of them (amongst whom Howe was foremost) sturdily refused. The spirit with which they were animated, was strikingly exemplified at a meeting, (of which Calamy has preserved an account,) held at Howe's own house. This meeting, it appears, was called for the purpose of " considering the advisableness of drawing up a writing to signify their concurrence with the King, as to the ends of his declaration." While discussing this question, " two persons came from court, and told them that the King was waiting in his closet, and would not stir from thence till he had received an account of their proceedings." On this, one of the party intimated, " that he thought it but reasonable that they should comply with his majesty's request; " to which another instantly replied, that " if the King expected

* As on this, and the yet more memorable occasion of 1673, when the " Test Act " was passed.

† See this strongly stated in Howe's " Case of the Protestant Dissenters," on a subsequent page.

that they should join in approving such a conduct as would give liberty to the Papists, he for one would rather that his majesty should resume their own." Howe, in summing up, told the persons who had come from court, that these were the sentiments of the meeting generally, and instructed them to convey the same to his majesty.

Calamy confesses, that some few of the ministers, who were afterwards "closeted with the King," and "who received some particular favours, might be drawn too far into the snare;" but he adds, "that they were very few; that as soon as their conduct became known, their influence with their party was visibly lessened; that the far greater number stood out; and that Howe, particularly, when the King discoursed with him in private, told his majesty 'that he was a minister of the gospel; that it was his province to preach, and endeavour to do good to the souls of men; but as for meddling with state affairs, he was neither inclined nor called to it, and must beg to be excused.'"

About this time a circumstance occurred which showed the purity and disinterestedness which habitually actuated Howe's public conduct. The King, in pursuance of his designs, insisted that the clergy should read his Declaration of Indulgence, in their respective churches, throughout the kingdom. Some of the bishops, consulting together, came to the conclusion, that to comply with this demand, would be to sanction the "dispensing power." They therefore requested his majesty to excuse them. The petition, in which they preferred this request, was declared a libel; and, for presenting it, its authors were committed to the Tower.

At this important crisis, Howe received an invitation from Dr. Sherlock, then Master of the Temple, to dine with him. Accepting the invitation, Howe found two or three other clergymen assembled to meet him. After dinner, the conversation naturally turned on the imminent danger with which the Church was threatened. In the midst of it, the Doctor abruptly asked Howe, "what he thought the nonconformists would do, should the preferments of the Church become vacant, and a proposal be made that those vacancies be filled up out of the ranks of the seceders?" Howe was so taken by surprise, that at first he knew not what to answer. The Doctor then proceeded to give more full expression to his apprehensions. He declared, "that the bishops would as certainly be cast, as they were at that time imprisoned in the Tower: that the rest of the clergy who had so generally refused reading the King's declaration, would be treated in the same manner: that it was not to be imagined that their places should be suffered to remain vacant: that no way could be thought of for filling them up, except from among the nonconformists; and who knows," he concluded, "but Mr. Howe may be offered the place of Master of the Temple?" He added, "that he was of course anxious to know how the nonconformists would act under such circumstances; and that he believed none could satisfy him on that point better than his present visitor." Thus appealed to, Howe replied, that the "issue of the present perplexed state of affairs was altogether uncertain; that it was improbable that Dr. Sherlock's fears should ever be realized; that if they should, he could not venture to answer for the conduct of the nonconformists as a body, as they were split into different parties, and as those parties were actuated by different principles; that he could answer only for *himself;* that so far as he was concerned, he did not hesitate to say, that should such an improbable case occur as that which the Doctor had supposed, he should not feel himself warranted in declining altogether an opportunity of more public usefulness, should it be offered on such terms as he could conscientiously accept; but *that as for any emolument accruing from such a situation,* he should have nothing to do with it, except as the channel to convey it to the legal proprietor." This reply threw the Doctor into ecstasies; he rose from his seat, and, embracing his visitor, told him "how rejoiced he was to find him that ingenuous, honest man he had always supposed him to be." Howe, in relating this curious occurrence to a dignitary of the Church, to whom Sherlock was well known, particularly mentioned his perplexity at being thus abruptly called to give an opinion on a case so extraordinary; a case which had never even entered his imagination.

"Sir," replied the gentleman to whom Howe told the story, "you must give me leave to say, that if you had studied the case for seven years together, you could not have said anything which had been more to the purpose, or more to Dr. Sherlock's satisfaction."

The Revolution, in the following year, happily dissipated the terrors which had overhung the nation during the reign of the Second James, and terminated a dynasty which had been equally the curse and the disgrace of the nation.

Shortly after the Prince of Orange had arrived at St. James's palace, a deputation of the nonconformist ministers waited on him. Being introduced by the Lords Devonshire, Wharton, and Wiltshire, Howe delivered an address, in the name of his brethren, the purport of which was as follows :—

"That they professed their grateful sense of his highness's hazardous and heroical expedition, which the favour of Heaven had made so surprisingly prosperous.

"That they esteemed it a common felicity, that the worthy patriots of the nobility and gentry of this kingdom had unanimously concurred unto his highness's design, by whose most prudent advice the administration of public affairs was devolved in this difficult conjuncture, into hands which the nation and the world knew to be apt for the greatest undertakings, and so suitable to the present exigence of our case.

"That they promised the utmost endeavours which in their stations they were capable of affording, for promoting the excellent and most desirable ends for which his highness had declared.

"That they added their continual and fervent prayers to the Almighty for the preservation of his highness's person, and the success of his future endeavours for the defence and propagation of the Protestant interest throughout the Christian world.

"That they should all most willingly have chosen that for the season of paying this duty to his highness when the Lord Bishop and the clergy of London attended his highness for the same purpose, (which some of them did, and which his lordship was pleased condescendingly to make mention of to his highness,) had their notice of that intended application been so early as to make their more general attendance possible to them at that time.

" And that, therefore, though they did now appear in a distinct company, they did it not on a distinct account, but on that only which was common to them and to all Protestants.

" That there were some of eminent note, whom age or present infirmities hindered from coming with them ; yet they concurred in the same grateful sense of our common deliverance."

The prince, in answer, assured them, " that he came on purpose to defend the Protestant religion, and that it was his own religion, in which he was born and bred ; the religion of his country and of his ancestors : and that he was resolved, by the grace of God, always to adhere to it, and to do his utmost endeavours for the defence of it, and the promoting a firm union among Protestants."

In the year (1688) Howe published nothing except three discourses—one, " Directing what we are to do, after a strict inquiry whether or no we truly love God ; "* and two, preached at Thurlow, in Suffolk, " On yielding ourselves to God."†

In 1689, he addressed the following letter in behalf of the French Protestants, to a certain personage, " whom," Calamy says, " he must leave the reader to guess at ; " adding, that " he himself could do no more." Happily, the mystery is of little consequence,

" *Sir*,

    " But that I am learning as much as I can to count nothing strange among the occurrences of the present time, I should be greatly surprised to find that divers French Protestant ministers, fled hither for their consciences and religion, who have latitude enough to conform to the rites of the Church of England, do accuse others of their brethren, who are fled hither on the same account, but have not that latitude, as schismatics, only for practising according to the principles and usages of their own church, which at home were common to them both ; and, as schismatics, judge them unworthy of any relief here. Their common enemy never yet passed so severe

---

* On John v. 42.   † On Rom. vi. 13.

a judgment on any of them, that they should be famished. This is put into the hands of the appellants from this sentence, unto your more equal judgment. And it needs do no more than thus briefly to represent their case, and me,

"Most honoured Sir,

"Your most obliged,

"And most humble Servant,

"JOHN HOWE.

"*Walbrook, April 5, 1689.*"

At the commencement of 1689, Parliament was engaged in discussing bills for "comprehension" and "indulgence." Not a few of the high church party, in contravention of the solemn pledges which had been given to the nonconformists, were still anxious for the perpetuation of persecution under a somewhat milder form.

At this critical period, Howe drew up the following paper, in which the claims of his party to relief are argued in a most cogent and eloquent manner:—

The Case of the Protestant Dissenters Represented and Argued.

"They are under one common obligation with the rest of mankind, by the universal law of nature, to worship God in assemblies.

"Men of all sorts of religions, that have ever obtained in the world, Jews, Pagans, Mahometans, Christians, have in their practice acknowledged this obligation. Nor can it be understood how such a practice should be so universal, otherwise than from the dictate and impression of the universal law.

"Whereas the religion professed in England is that of reformed Christianity, some things are annexed to the allowed public worship, which are acknowledged to be no parts thereof, nor in themselves necessary, but which the Dissenters judge to be in some part sinful.

"They cannot, therefore, with good conscience towards God, attend wholly and solely upon the public worship which the laws do appoint.

"The same laws do strictly forbid their assembling to worship God otherwise.

"Which is in effect the same thing as if they who made,

or shall continue such laws, should plainly say, ' If you will not consent with us in our superadded rites and modes against your consciences, you shall not worship God; or if you will not accept of our additions to the Christian religion, you shall not be Christians;' and manifestly tends to reduce to paganism a great part of a Christian nation.

"They have been wont, therefore, to meet, however, in distinct assemblies, and to worship God in a way which their consciences could approve; and have many years continued so to do, otherwise than as they have been hindered by violence.

"It is therefore, upon the whole, fit to inquire,

"*Qu.* 1. Whether they are to be blamed for their holding distinct meetings for the worship of God?

"For answer to this, it cannot be expected that all the controversies should be here determined, which have been agitated about the lawfulness of each of those things which have been added to the Christian religion and worship by the present constitution of the Church of England.

"But supposing there were none of them simply unlawful, while yet the misinformed minds of the Dissenters could not judge them lawful, though they have made it much their business to inquire and search; being urged also by severe sufferings, which through a long tract of time they have undergone, not to refuse any means that might tend to their satisfaction; they could have nothing else left them to do than to meet and worship distinctly as they have.

"For they could not but esteem the obligation of the universal, natural, Divine law, by which they were bound solemnly to worship God, less questionable than that of a law which was only positive, topical, and human, requiring such and such additaments to their worship, and prohibiting their worship without them.

"The Church of England, (as that part affects to be called,) distinguished from the rest by those additionals to Christian religion, (pretended to be indifferent, and so confessed unnecessary,) hath not only sought to engross to itself the ordinances of Divine worship, but all civil power. So that the privileges that belong either to Christian or human society are enclosed, and made peculiar to such as are distinguished by things that in themselves can signify nothing to the making of persons either better Christians, or better men.

"*Qu.* 2. Whether the laws enjoining such additions to our

religion as the exclusive terms of Christian worship and communion, ought to have been made, when it is acknowledged on all hands, the things to be added were before not necessary; and when it is known a great number judge them sinful, and must thereby be restrained from worshipping the true and living God?

"*Ans.* The question, to any of common sense, answers itself. For it is not put concerning such as dissent from any part of the substance of worship which God hath commanded, but concerning such additions as he never commanded. And there are sufficient tests to distinguish such Dissenters from those that deny any substantial part of religion, or assert anything contrary thereto. Wherefore, to forbid such to worship that God that made them, because they cannot receive your devised additions, is to exclude that which is necessary, for the mere want of that which is unnecessary.

"And where is that man that will adventure to stand forth, and avow the hindering of such persons from paying their homage to the God that made them, if we thus expostulate the matter on God's behalf and their own? Will you cut off from God his right in the creatures he hath made? Will you cut off from them the means of their salvation upon these terms? What reply can the matter admit?

"It is commonly alleged that great deference is to be paid to the laws, and that we ought to have forborne our assemblies, till the public authority recalled the laws against them; and we will say the same thing, when it is well proved, that they who made such laws, made the world too.

"And by whose authority were such laws made? Is there any that is not from God? and hath God given any man authority to make laws against himself, and to deprive him of his just rights from his own creatures?

"Nor, if the matter be well searched into, could there be so much as a pretence of authority derived for such purposes from the people, whom every one now acknowledges the first receptacle of derived governing power. God can, it is true, lay indisputable obligations, by his known laws, upon every conscience of man, about religion or anything else. And such as represent any people, can, according to the constitution of the government, make laws for them, about the things they intrust them with: but if the people of England be asked, man by man, will they say they did intrust to their representatives their religion and their consciences, to do with them what they please? When it is your own turn to be represented by others, is this part of the trust you commit? What Dr. Sherlock worthily says concerning a bishop, he might (and particularly after doth) say concerning every other man, 'He can be no more represented in a council, than at the day of judgment: every man's soul and conscience must be in his own keeping, and can be represented by no man.'*

"It ought to be considered that Christianity, wherein it superadds to the law of nature, is all matter of revelation. And it is well known, that even among pagans, in the settling rites and institutes of religion,† revelation was pretended at least, upon an implied principle, that in such matters human power could not oblige the people's consciences.

"We must be excused, therefore, if we have in our practice expressed less reverence for laws made by no authority received either from God or man.

"We are therefore injuriously reflected on, when it is imputed to us that we have, by the use of our liberty, acknowledged an illegal dispensing power. We have done no other thing herein, than we did when no dispensation was given or pretended, in conscience of duty to him that gave us our breath; nor did therefore practise otherwise, because we thought those laws dispensed with, but because we thought them not laws. Whereupon little need remains of inquiring further.

"*Qu.* 3. Whether such laws should be continued? Against which, besides what may be collected from that which hath been said, it is to be considered, that what is most principally grievous to us, was enacted by that parliament, that, as we have too much reason to believe, suffered itself to be dealt with to enslave the nation, in other respects as well as this; and which (to his immortal honour) the noble Earl of Danby procured to be dissolved, as the first step towards our national deliverance.

"And let the tenor be considered of that horrid law, by which our Magna Charta was torn in pieces; the worst and most infamous of mankind, at our own expense, hired to accuse us; multitudes of perjuries committed, convictions made without a jury, and without any hearing of the persons accused; penalties inflicted, goods rifled, estates seized and embezzled,

---

* "Vindication of some Protestant Principles," etc., p. 52.
† "As by Numa, from his Egeria. And their priests, to whom the regulation of such matters was left, were generally believed to be inspired."

houses broken up, families disturbed, often at unseasonable hours of the night, without any cause, or shadow of a cause, if only a malicious villain would pretend to suspect a meeting there! No law in any other case like this! As if to worship God without those additions, which were confessed unnecessary, were a greater crime than theft, felony, murder, or treason! Is it for our reputation to posterity, that the memory of such law should be continued?

"And are we not yet awakened, and our eyes opened enough to see, that the making and execution of the laws, by which we have suffered so deeply for many by-past years, was only that Protestants might destroy Protestants, and the easier work be made for the introduction of Popery, that was to destroy the residue?

"Nor can any malice deny, or ignorance of observing Englishmen overlook, this plain matter of fact. After the dissolution of that before-mentioned parliament, Dissenters were much caressed, and endeavoured to be drawn into a subserviency to the court designs, especially in the election of after-parliaments. Notwithstanding which, they everywhere so entirely and unanimously fell in with the sober part of the nation, in the choice of such persons for the three parliaments that next succeeded, (two held at Westminster, and that at Oxford,) as it was known would, and who did, most generously assert the liberties of the nation, and the Protestant religion. Which alone (and not our mere dissent from the Church of England in matters of religion, wherein Charles II. was sufficiently known to be a prince of great indifferency) drew upon us, soon after the dissolution of the last of those parliaments, that dreadful storm of persecution, that destroyed not a small number of lives in gaol, and ruined multitudes of families.

"Let English freemen remember, what they cannot but know, that it was for our firm adherence to the civil interests of the nation, (not for our different modes of religion from the legal way, though the laws gave that advantage against us, which they did not against others,) that we endured the calamities of so many years.

"When by the late King some relaxation was given us, what arts and insinuations have been used with us, to draw us into a concurrence to designs tending to the prejudice of the nation! And with how little effect upon the generality of us, it must be great ignorance not to know, and great injustice to deny.

"But he that knoweth all things, knoweth that though, in

such circumstances, there was no opportunity for our receiving
public and authorized promises, when we were all under the
eye of watchful jealousy; yet as great assurances as were
possible were given us, by some that we hope will now remember it, of a future established security from our former pressures.
We were told over and over, when the excellent Heer Fagel's
letter came to be privately communicated from hand to hand,
how easily better things would be had for us, than that encour-
aged Papists to expect, if ever that happy change should be
brought about, which none have now beheld with greater joy
than we.

"We are loth to injure those who have made us hope for
better, by admitting a suspicion that we shall now be disappointed and deceived, (as we have formerly been, and we
know by whom,) or that we shall suffer from them a *religious
slavery*, for whose sakes we have suffered so grievous things,
rather than do the least thing that might tend to the bringing
upon them a *civil slavery*.

"We cannot but expect from Englishmen that they be just
and true.   We hope not to be the only instances whereby the
Anglica fides and the *Punica* shall be thought all one.

"But if we, who have constantly desired, and, as we have
had opportunity, endeavoured the saving of the nation, must
however be ruined, not to greaten (one hair) the wealth and
dignity of it, but only to gratify the humour of them who
would yet destroy it; we, who are competently inured to
sufferings, shall, through God's mercy, be again enabled to
endure : but he that sits in the heavens will in his own time
judge our cause, and we will wait his pleasure ; and, we hope,
suffer all that can be inflicted, rather than betray the cause of
reformed Christianity in the world.

"But our affairs are in the hands of men of worth and honour,
who apprehend how little grateful a name they should leave to
posterity, or obtain now with good men of any persuasion, if,
under a pretence of kindness to us, they should now repeat the
arts of ill men, in an ill time.   Great minds will think it
beneath them to sport themselves with their own cunning, in
deceiving other men ; which were really in the present case
too thin not to be seen through, and may be the easy attainment of any man, that hath enough of opportunity, and
integrity little enough for such purposes.   And it is as much
too gross to endeavour to abuse the authority of a nation, by
going about to make that stoop to so mean a thing, as to make

a show of intending what they resolve to their utmost shall never be.

"But some may think, by concessions to us, the Church of England will be ruined, and a great advantage given to the bringing in of Popery.

"To which we say, the generality of the Dissenters differ from the Church of England, in no substantials of doctrine and worship, no, nor of government, provided it be so managed as to attain its true acknowledged end: the favouring of us, therefore, will as much ruin the Church, as its enlargement and additional strength will signify to its ruin.

"And doth not the world know, that wherein we differ from them, we differ from the Papists too? and that for the most part, wherein they differ from us, they seem to agree with them?

"We acknowledge their strong, brave, and prosperous opposition to Popery: but they have opposed it by the things wherein they agree with us. Their differences from us are no more a fence against Popery, than an enclosure of straw is against a flame of fire.

"But it is wont to be said, we agree not among ourselves, and know not what we would have.

"And do all that go under the name of the Church of England agree among themselves? We can show more considerable disagreements among them, than any can between the most of us and a considerable part of them. They all agree, it is true, in conformity; and we all agree in nonconformity. And is not this merely accidental to Christianity and Protestantism? and herein is it not well known that the far greater part of reformed Christendom do more agree with us?

"An arbitrary line of uniformity, in some little accidents, severs a small part of the Christian world from all the rest. How unreasonably is it expected that therefore all the rest must in everything else agree among themselves! Suppose any imaginary line to cut off a little segment from any part of the terrestrial globe; it is as justly expected that all the rest should be of one mind. If one part of England be tailors, they might as well expect that all the people besides should agree to be of one profession.

"Perhaps some imagine it dishonourable to such as have gone before them in the same ecclesiastical stations and dignities, if now anything should be altered, which their judgment did before approve and think fit.

"But we hope that temptation will not prove invincible, namely, of so excessive a modesty as to be afraid of seeming wiser, or better natured, or of a more Christian temper, than their predecessors.

"But the most of us do agree not only with one another, but, in the great things above mentioned, with the Church of England too : and, in short, that the reproach may cease for ever with those that count it one, they will find with us, when they please to try, a very extensive agreement on the terms of King Charles II.'s declaration about ecclesiastical affairs, in 1660.

"*Qu.* 4. Whether it be reasonable to exclude all, that in everything conform not to the Church of England, from any part or share of the civil power?

"*Ans.* The difference or nonconformity of many is so minute, that it would be as reasonable to exclude all whose hair is not of this or that colour. And what if we should make a determination, by the decision this way or that of any other disputed question, that may be of as small concernment to religion? suppose it be that of eating blood, for the decision whereof one way, there is more pretence from God's word, than for any point of the disputed conformity : would it not be a wise constitution, 'that whosoever thinks it lawful to eat black-pudding shall be capable of no office?' etc.

"But we tremble to think of the exclusive sacramental test, brought down as low as to the keeper of an ale-house. Are all fit to approach the sacred table, whom the fear of ruin or hope of gain may bring thither? We cannot but often remember, with horror, what happened three or four years ago. A man that led an ill life, but frequented the church, was observed not to come to the sacrament, and pressed by the officers to come; he yet declined, knowing himself unfit : at length, being threatened and terrified, he came; but said to some present at the time of the solemn action, that he came only to avoid being undone, and took them to witness that what he there received, he took only as common bread and wine, not daring to receive them as the body and blood of Christ. It is amazing, that among Christians, so venerable an institution should be prostituted to the serving of so mean purposes, and so foreign to its true end! and that doing it after the manner of the Church of England must be the qualification! as if England were another Christendom; or it were a greater thing to conform in every punctilio to the rules of this church, than of Christ himself!

"But we would fain know whose is that holy table? is it the table of this or that party, or the Lord's table? If the Lord's, are not persons to be admitted or excluded upon his terms? Never can there be union or peace in the Christian world till we take down our arbitrary enclosures, and content ourselves with those which our common Lord hath set. If he falls under a curse that alters a man's landmark, to alter God's is not likely to infer a blessing.

"The matter is clear as the light of the sun, that as many persons of excellent worth, sobriety, and godliness, are entirely in the communion of the Church of England, so there are too many of a worse character, that are of it too; and divers prudent, pious, and sober-minded persons that are not of it. Let common reason be consulted. in .this case. Suppose the tables turned, and that the rule were to be made the contrary way, namely, that to do this thing, but not by any means after the manner of the Church of England, were to be the qualification : and now suppose one of meaner endowments, as a man and a Christian, do what is required, and not in the way of the Church of England ; and another, that is of much better, does the same thing in that way ; were it suitable to prudence or justice, that because it is done after the way of the Church of England, a fitter man should. be reckoned unqualified ? and one of less value be taken for qualified, because he does it a different way? Then is all that solid weight of wisdom, diligence, sobriety, and goodness, to be weighed down by a feather.

"It must surely be thought the prudence of any government, to comprehend. as many useful persons as it can, and no more to deprive itself of the service of such, for anything less considerable than those qualifications are by which they are useful, than a man would tear off from himself the limbs of his body, for a spot on the skin.

"And really if, in our circumstances, we thus narrow our interest, all the rest of the world will say, that they who would destroy us do yet find a way to be our instructors, and our common enemies do teach us our politics.

"The names of Mr. Hales, of Eton College, and of a later most renowned bishop of the Church of England, who asserted this principle, that 'if things be imposed under the notion of indifferent, which many think sinful, and a schism follow thereupon, the imposers are the schismatics,' will be great in England, as long as their writings shall live, and good sense can be understood in them."

At length, May 24, 1689, the Act of Toleration received the royal assent, and diffused content and gladness throughout the nation.

That this event should lead to some violent ebullitions of party spirit, was to be anticipated. There were not wanting bigots who grudged their fellow-subjects the enjoyment of their new-born liberty; and who, after having so long gratified their malignant passions, were impatient at being compelled to restrain them. It was as unwelcome as a fast would be to a man who had been accustomed to the free indulgence of appetite.*

Neither was it to be wondered at, if there were some amongst the nonconformists, who, in the first flush of their triumph, indulged in an unwise and unseemly spirit of jubilation. It is superfluous to remark that Howe was not of the number: the novel circumstances in which he was now placed, only served to exhibit his excellence under another and most pleasing aspect. He had borne persecution with fortitude; he now enjoyed victory with moderation. The triumph of his principles and his party could not tempt his noble spirit to any display of mean and malignant exultation. On the contrary, he exerted himself to the utmost to heal the wounds which had festered so long, and to prevent the perpetuation of useless animosity. Of this, the following paper, which will never be perused by any candid reader without the warmest admiration, affords irrefragable evidence.

"HUMBLE REQUESTS BOTH TO CONFORMISTS AND DISSENTERS, TOUCHING THEIR TEMPER AND BEHAVIOUR TOWARD EACH OTHER, UPON THE LATELY PASSED INDULGENCE.

"1. That we do not over-magnify our differences, or count them greater than they really are. I speak now of the proper differences which the rule itself makes, to which the one sort conforms, and the other conforms not. Remember that there

---

* Dr. South owned, that "he did not like it." Still stronger expressions were used at a subsequent period, by the celebrated Sacheverell and his party. One of the articles of impeachment against him was, "that he had suggested nd maintained, that the toleration granted by law was unreasonable, and the allowance of it unwarrantable."

are differences on both parts, among themselves, incomparably greater than these, by which the one sort differs from the other. There are differences in doctrinal sentiments that are much greater. How inconceivably greater is the difference between good men and bad! between being a lover of the blessed God, the Lord of heaven and earth, and an enemy! a real subject of Christ, and of the devil! Have we not reason to apprehend there are of both these on each side? Let us take heed of having our minds tinctured with a wrong notion of this matter, as if this Indulgence divided England into two Christendoms, or distinguished rather between Christians and Mahometans, as some men's Cyclopic fancies have an unlucky art to represent things; creating ordinary men and things into monsters and prodigious shapes at their own pleasure. It has been a usual saying on both sides, that they were (in comparison) but little things we differed about, or circumstantial things. Let us not unsay it, or suffer a habit of mind to slide into us, that consists not with it. Though we must not go against a judgment of conscience in the least thing, yet let us not confound the true differences of things; but what are really lesser things, let them go for such.

"2. Let us hereupon carefully abstain from judging each other's state God-ward upon these differences: for hereby we shall both contradict our common rule and ourselves. When men make conscience of small and doubtful things on the one hand and the other, about which they differ, blessed God! how little conscience is made of the plainest and most important rule, not to judge one another for such differences! Rom. xiv. 3, 13. Why, of all the parts of that holy book, is this chapter only thought no part of God's word? or this precept, so variously enforced in this chapter, and so awfully in a preceding verse, 'But why dost thou judge thy brother? or why dost thou set at nought thy brother? We shall all stand before the judgment-seat of Christ. For it is written, As I live, saith the Lord, every knee shall bow to me, and every tongue shall confess to me!' Is it a light matter to usurp the throne of Christ, the judgment-seat of God? Yet how common has it been to say, such a one conforms, he hath nothing of God in him! such a one conforms not; it is not conscience, but humour! God forgive both. Had they blotted Rom. xiv. out of their Bibles? It is plain by the whole series of discourse, that it is the judging of men's states, and that by such small matters of difference, that is the thing here forbidden. Some few things contained in this chapter, as, 'to receive one another,' (as Christians, or such whom God receives,) notwithstanding remaining doubts about small matters, and not determining such doubted things in bar to the doubter ; and not 'to lay stumbling-blocks in each other's way,' not to do the doubted thing with a mind still unsatisfied, not to censure either him that does or forbears ; not admitting a hard thought of him, or less favourable, than that what such a one does, 'he does to the Lord, and what the other forbears, he forbears to the Lord ;'—these few things, I say, put in practice, had taken away all differences (that we are now considering), or the inconvenience of them, long ago. And we shall still need them as much as ever.

"3. Let us not value ourselves upon being of this or that side of the severing line. It is Jewish, yea, pharisaical, to be conceited, and boast ourselves upon externals, and small matters, especially if arbitrarily taken up ; and is itself an argument of a light mind, and incomprehensive of true worth. Though I cannot sincerely be of this or that way, but I must think myself in the right, and others in the wrong that differ from me, yet I ought to consider, this is but a small minute thing, a point compared with the vast orb of knowables, and of things needful, and that ought to be known. Perhaps divers that differ from me are men of greater and more comprehensive minds, and have been more employed about greater matters : and many, in things of more importance, have much more of valuable and useful knowledge than I. Yea, and since these are not matters of salvation we differ about, so that any on either side dare considerately say, He cannot be saved that is not in these respects of my mind and way ; he may have more of sanctifying savoury knowledge, more of solid goodness, more of grace and real sanctity, than I ; the course of his thoughts and studies having been by converse and other accidents led more off from these things, and perhaps by a good principle been more deeply engaged about higher matters : for no man's mind is able equally to consider all things fit to be considered ; and greater things are of themselves more apt to beget holy and good impressions upon our spirits, than the minuter and more circumstantial things, though relating to religion, can be.

"4. Let us not despise one another for our differing in these lesser matters. This is too common, and most natural to that temper that offends against the foregoing caution. Little-spirited creatures valuing themselves for small matters, must consequently have them in contempt that want what they count their own only excellency. He that hath nothing wherein he places worth belonging to him, besides a flaunting peruke and a laced suit, must at all adventures think very meanly of one in a plain garb. Where we are taught not to judge, we are forbidden to despise or set at nought one another upon these little differences.

"5. Nor let us wonder that we differ. Unto this we are too apt, that is, to think it strange, (especially upon some arguing of the difference,) that such a man should conform, or such a one not conform. There is some fault in this, but which proceeds from more faulty causes. Pride, too often, and an opinion that we understand so well, that a wrong is done us if our judgment be not made a standard and measure to another man's. And again, ignorance of human nature, or inconsiderateness rather, how mysterious it is, and how little can be known of it; how secret and latent little springs there are that move this engine to our own mind this way or that; and what bars (which perhaps he discerns not himself) may obstruct and shut up towards us another man's. Have we not frequent instances in other common cases, how difficult it is to speak to another man's understanding? Speech is too penurious, not expressive enough. Frequently, between men of sense, much more time is taken up in explaining each other's notions, than in proving or disproving them. Nature and our present state have in some respects left us open to God only, and made us inaccessible to one another. Why then should it be strange to me, that I cannot convey my thought into another's mind? It is unchristian to censure, as before, and say, such a one has not my conscience, therefore he has no conscience at all; and it is also unreasonable and rude to say, such a one sees not with my eyes, therefore he is stark blind. Besides, the real obscurity of the matter is not enough considered. I am very confident an impartial and competent judge, upon the view of books, later and more ancient, upon such subjects, would say, there are few metaphysical questions disputed with more subtlety, than the controversies about conformity and nonconformity. Blessed be God that things necessary to the salvation of souls, and that are of true necessity even to the peace and order of the Christian church, are in comparison so very plain.

"Moreover, there is, besides understanding and judgment, and diverse from that heavenly gift which in the Scriptures is called grace, such a thing as gust and relish belonging to the mind of man, and, I doubt not, to all men, if they observe themselves; and this is as unaccountable and as various as the relishes and disgusts of sense. This they only wonder at, that either understand not themselves, or will consider nobody but themselves. To bring it down to the present case. As to those parts of worship which are of most frequent use in our assemblies, (whether conforming or nonconforming,) prayer, and preaching, and hearing God's word, our differences about them cannot but in part arise from the diversity of this principle, both on the one hand and the other. One sort do more savour prayer by a foreknown form; another, that which hath more of surprise, by a grateful variety of unexpected expressions. And it can neither be universally said, it is a better judgment, or more grace, that determines men the one way or the other; but somewhat in the temper of their minds, distinct from both, which I know not how better to express, than by mental taste, the acts whereof (as the objects are suitable or unsuitable) are relishing or disrelishing, liking or disliking: and this hath no more of mystery in it, than that there is such a thing belonging to our natures as complacency or displacency in reference to the objects of the mind. And this, in the kind of it, is as common to men as human nature; but as much diversified in individuals, as men's other inclinations are, that are most fixed, and least apt to admit of change. Now, in the mentioned case, men cannot be universally determined, either way, by their having better judgment; for no sober man can be so little modest as not to acknowledge, that there are some of each sentiment that are less judicious than some that are of the contrary sentiment in this thing. And to say that to be more determined this way or that, is the certain sign or effect of a greater measure of grace and sanctity, were a great violation both of modesty and charity. I have not met with any that have appeared to live in more entire communion with God, in higher admiration of him, in a pleasanter sense of his love, or in a more joyful expectation of eternal life, than some that have been wont with great delight publicly to worship God in the use of our Common Prayer; and others I have known as highly excelling in the same respects, that could by no means relish it, but have always counted it insipid and nauseous. The like may be said of relishing or disrelishing sermons preached in a digested set of words, or with a more flowing freedom of speech. It were endless and odious to vie either better judgments, or more pious inclinations, that should universally determine men either the one way or the other in these matters. And we are no more to wonder at these peculiarities in the temper of men's minds, than at their different tastes of meats and drinks; much less to fall out with them, that their minds and notions are not just formed as ours are: for we should remember, they no more differ from us than we do from them; and if we think we have the clearer light, it is like they also think they have clearer. And it is in vain to say, Who shall be judge? for every man will at length judge of his own notions for himself, and cannot help it: for no man's judgment (or relish of things, which influences his judgment, though he know it not) is at the command of his will; and much less of another man's. And, therefore,

"6. Let us not be offended mutually with one another, for our different choice of this or that way, wherein we find most of real advantage and edification. Our greatest concern in this world, and which is common to us all, is the bettering of our spirits, and preparing them for a better world. Let no man be displeased, (especially of those who agree in all the substantials of the same holy religion,) that another uses the same liberty, in choosing the way most conducing in his experience to his great end, that he himself also uses, expecting to do it without another man's offence.

"7. But above all, let us, with sincere minds, more earnestly endeavour the promoting the interest of religion itself, of true reformed Christianity, than of this or that party. Let us long to see the religion of Christians become simple, primitive, agreeable to its lovely original state, and again itself: and each in our own stations contribute thereto all that we are able, labouring that the internal principle of it may live and flourish in our own souls, and be to our utmost diffused and spread unto other men's. And for its externals, as the ducture of our rule will guide us, so gradually bend towards one common course, that there may at length cease to be any divided parties at all.

"In the meantime, while there are, let it be remembered that the difference lies among Christians and Protestants, not between such and pagans. Let us therefore carry it accordingly towards each other; and consider our assemblies are all Christian and Protestant assemblies, differing in their administrations, for the most part, not in the things prayed for or deprecated, or taught, but in certain modes of expression;

and differing really, and in the substance of things, less by mere conformity or nonconformity to the public rule of the law, than many of them that are under it do from one another, and than divers that are not under it. For instance, go into one congregation that is a conforming one, and you have the public prayers read in the desk, and afterwards a form of prayer perhaps used by the preacher in the pulpit, of his own composure, before he begins his sermon. Go into another congregation, and prayer is performed without either sort of form; and perhaps the difference in this is not so great. It may be the conformist uses no preconceived form of his own, and the nonconformist may. Both instruct the people out of the same holy book of God's word. But now suppose one of the former sort reads the public prayers gravely, with the appearance of great reverence, fervency, and pious devotion; and one of the latter sort that uses them not, does, however, pray for the same things with judgment and with like gravity and affection, and they both instruct their hearers fitly and profitably; nothing is more evident than that the worship in these two assemblies doth much less considerably differ to a pious and judicious mind, than if in the latter the prayers were also read, but carelessly, sleepily, or scenically, flauntingly, and with manifest irreverence, and the sermon like the rest; or than if, in the former, all the performance were inept, rude, or very offensively drowsy or sluggish.

"Now, let us show ourselves men, and manly Christians, not swayed by trifles and little things, as children by this or that dress or mode, or form of our religion, which may perhaps please some the more for its real indecency : but know, that if, while we continue picquering about forms, the life be lost, and we come to bear the character of that church, 'Thou hast a name that thou livest, and art dead,' we may, ere long, (after all the wonders God hath wrought for us,) expect to hear of our candlestick's being removed, and that our sun shall go down at noonday.

"The true serious spirit and power of religion and god-liness will act no man against his conscience, or his rule understood, but will oblige him in all acts of worship (as well as of his whole conversation) to keep close to gospel pre-scription, so far as he can discern it. And that, he will find, requires that, in subordination to the Divine glory, he seriously design the working out the salvation of his own soul, and take that course in order thereto, put himself under such a ministry, and such a way of using God's ordinances, as he finds most profitable and conducing to that great end, and that doth his soul most real good. If you are religious, or of this or that mode or way of religion, to serve a carnal design for yourself or your party, not to save your soul, you commit the most detestable sacrilege, and alienate the most sacred thing in the world, religion, from its true end; which will not only lose that end, but infer a heavy vengeance. Yea, and it is too possible to transgress dangerously, by preferring that which is less, (though never so confidently thought to be Divine,) before that which is greater, or separately from its true end. You greatly prevaricate, if you are more zealously intent to promote independency than Christianity, presbytery than Christianity, prelacy than Christianity, as any of these are the interest of a party, and not considered in subserviency to the Christian interest, nor designed for promoting the edification and salvation of your own soul. But that being your design, living religion will keep your eye upon your end, and make you steady and constantly true to that, and to your rule, without which you can never hope to reach your end.

"Now hereupon such as conform to the public Establishment, and they that dissent from it, may differ from each other upon a twofold account: either, 1, as judging the contrary way to be simply unlawful; or, 2, as judging it to be only less edifying. It is not the business of this paper to discuss who herein judge aright, and who wrong; but supposing their judgment to remain as it is, (which they themselves, however, should examine; and, if it be wrong, rectify:) I shall say somewhat to each of these cases.

" To the former, while your judgment continues as it is, it is true you cannot join in worship with the contrary minded: but nothing forbids, but you can be kind, conversable, courteous towards them; and your common Christian profession (besides the rules of humanity) obliges you so to be; yea, and even to converse with them, as occasion invites, more intimately as Christians, the visible marks of serious Christianity appearing in them.

" To the latter sort, it is acknowledged, you cannot constantly join in worship with those of the contrary way, because you ought ordinarily to worship God in that way which you judge to be best, and most agreeable to the Divine rule; (though you are not obliged utterly to abandon any for its imperfections or corruptions, that is not corrupt in the very essentials ;) and you ought most frequently to attend on that which you find to be most edifying to your own soul; as that should be your more ordinary diet that best agrees with you. That way, therefore, you must most constantly adhere to, which is most grateful and savoury to you; because you cannot so much edify by what you less relish. But your judgment and latitude will well allow you sometimes to frequent the assemblies with which you hold not constant communion. And if it will allow, it will also direct you thereto for a valuable end; as that you may signify, you ordinarily decline them not as no Christians, or their worship as no worship, but as more defective, or less edifying; and that you may maintain love, and both express and beget a disposition to nearer union. And if our rulers shall judge such intercourses conducing to so desirable an end, they may, perhaps, in due time think it reasonable to put things into that state, that ministers of both sorts may be capable of inviting one another occasionally to the brotherly offices of mutual assistance in each other's congregations. For which, and all things that tend to make us a happy people, we must wait upon him in whose hands their hearts are."

But such, for a time, was the state of public feeling, that even appeals like these exerted only a very partial influence. The waters had not yet subsided, and Howe sent forth the dove of peace in vain; it found no rest for the sole of its foot. His efforts, however, brought their own reward; if he could not allay the animosities of others, he himself was calm. From the ark of a quiet and untroubled spirit, he looked forth serenely on the tempestuous waters, and mourned over the ravages he could not prevent.

In the year 1690, Howe published a funeral sermon for Esther, the wife of Dr. Henry Sampson,* (physician,) who was a member of his church. The lady died on a *Sunday*, after a

---

* Dr. Sampson is noticed by Calamy in his "Ejected Ministers." He was educated for the Church, and preached for a considerable time, but was never ordained. He afterwards studied physic at the universities of Padua and Leyden. Having a strong taste for history and antiquities, he became intimate with Ralph Thoresby, the topographer of Leeds; from whose diary, recently published, I have extracted a few particulars respecting Howe in the next chapter.

lingering illness of *eighteen* years; a circumstance which suggested to Howe the following appropriate text for the funeral sermon:—"Ought not this woman, being a daughter of Abraham, whom Satan hath bound, lo, these eighteen years, to be loosed from this bond on the sabbath day?"*

* Luke xiii. 16.

CHAPTER X.

FROM 1690 TO 1703.

EVENTS were now at hand, destined to try the truly Christian principles and temper of Howe most severely. Relieved from the fear of persecution, the nonconformists began to quarrel among themselves. Pressure from without had hitherto kept them together; and its removal was the signal for internal disunion. The first symptoms of dissension betrayed themselves shortly after the publication of the "Heads of Agreement," * (as they were most infelicitously called,) by the "United Ministers." The object of those resolutions was to effect a formal coalition between the Presbyterians and Congregationalists. As these parties had already many points of union, and were bound together by community of interest and of feeling as well as by entire agreement in doctrine, any stricter union than as yet subsisted would have been more wisely left to the influence of time, and the silent and spontaneous operation of Christian charity. As it was, the project terminated, as might have been foreseen, only in exciting jealousies that might not otherwise have existed, and awakening prejudices that might have slumbered for ever.†

---

* Published in 1691.

† The "Heads of Agreement" will be found in Calamy's Abridgment of Baxter's Life. Howe himself took an important part in preparing them.

These disputes, however, were of little consequence, compared with those which were occasioned by the reprinting of Dr. Crisp's works;* which, from certain circumstances connected with their publication, led to a fierce agitation of the whole Antinomian controversy. Never were the words of the wise man more completely verified. It was, indeed, a "little spark" which first kindled the flames of this fearful conflagration.

The circumstances were as follow :—The works of Dr. Crisp were republished by his son. Having enriched the precious farrago by some discourses from his father's MSS., never before printed, the editor must needs solicit the *signatures* of several of the most deservedly popular ministers in the metropolis to an attestation, that they believed the sermons in question to be the genuine productions of Dr. Crisp! A sinister purpose is, I think, evident on the very face of the transaction. One cannot but regard it as a mean artifice for securing an additional popularity to the sermons, by leading the public to conclude, either that this attestation to the *genuineness* of the sermons implied an approval of their *contents,* (as was really inferred in a great many cases,) or, at least, that the attesting parties must deem the sermons of considerable value, since they had thought it worth while gravely to subscribe a belief in their authenticity. That such a conclusion was most natural, who can deny ? What but this, it might plausibly be asked, could induce them to give such a testimony ? What conceivable reason was there for such a step, had they thought the sermons worthless ? Why should they, in that case, take the trouble to tell the world that the sermons might be relied on as the veritable productions of Dr. Crisp ? Thus what was, in fact, merely an act of easy good-nature to the importunate and, perhaps, needy publisher, would be construed, and *was* construed, into a sanction of sentiments which most of the subscribing parties abhorred.

That it was a trick, I am led to believe for the following

---

reasons.   First, what imaginable reason could the editor have
for supposing that the world would, without the shadow of a
cause, doubt his affirmation as to the genuineness of the sermons in question, or suspect that he had palmed on the public,
as Dr. Crisp's productions, what were not his?   Was there
anything incredible in the representation that his father had
left some MSS. behind him?   Or, when MSS. are published
under such circumstances, is it customary to seek attestations
to their genuineness before the world has already hinted some
suspicion of fraud?   Does an honest man think it worth while
to anticipate slander, or to declare himself innocent before any
one has breathed a suspicion of guilt?   These reasons, if there
were no others, would be sufficient to show that the younger
Crisp's pretended motives could not have been the real ones.

But, secondly, could the works of Dr. Crisp—inimitably
ridiculous in sentiment, vulgar in conception and style—need
any other attestation to their genuineness than their own
intrinsic absurdity?   Would they not authenticate themselves
all the world over?   If, indeed, the posthumous sermons had
indicated any diversity in point of style or sentiment from
those published in his lifetime; if they had manifested either
sobriety of mind or elegance of diction, there would have been
some reason for demanding attestations: and, in truth, under
such circumstances, scarcely any amount of testimony would
have been sufficient.   But as long as their genuineness was
sustained by the same internal evidence which authenticated
his former writings, such testimonies were quite superfluous.
Dr. Crisp had a patent for nonsense and vulgarity, which
defied successful imitation.

Upon the supposition that this eager solicitation of signatures was, as I believe, a trick, it must be confessed that it
was a trick exactly suited to the genius of Antinomianism;
perfectly worthy of the mean, treacherous, dishonest spirit,
which such a system cannot fail to inspire.

I grieve to say, that amongst those who fell into the ambush, was John Howe.   It is the only instance, so far as I
know, in which his characteristic prudence signally failed him.

The impression which the signatures in question produced,

was such as might be expected. It was in vain that Howe protested against the absurdity of confounding a simple attestation to the *genuineness* of a document with a belief in the *truth* of its contents. Simple and obvious as the distinction was, the explanation, to many, was far from satisfactory. The stupid could not see it, and the prejudiced would not.

Amongst others who expressed their surprise at this incautious proceeding, was Richard Baxter. In his earlier and more vigorous days, this great man, whose zeal had engaged him, at one time or other, in combating almost every form of error, had particularly signalized himself by his efforts to expose the enormous follies of Antinomianism. It is not surprising, therefore, that he should have been disposed to regard with peculiar jealousy and suspicion anything, however trivial, which seemed to favour its progress. Even if this special stimulus had been wanting, it is by no means improbable that he would have exulted, old as he was, in the opportunity of once more brandishing his redoubtable quill in an honourable cause. He had been all his life long a sort of knight-errant in controversy, and relinquished with reluctance his career of adventure. Repose was irksome: he looked with a lingering eye on the trophies of his younger days, and on the idle weapons which were now rusting on the wall. He resembled an old war-horse, who still starts at the sound of a trumpet; or, rather, some pugnacious cudgel-player, who, as soon as he comes within the grateful sound of a broil, feels irresistibly impelled to take part in it. In this case, however, he had something more than his innate pugnacity of disposition to stimulate him.

With his usual promptitude, he drew up a paper on the subject. It was just ready for publication, when Howe, hearing of it, hastened to him, and conjured him to suppress it; promising, in order to show that his testimony to the genuineness of Crisp's sermons implied no approbation of the doctrines they advocated, to prefix his name to the forthcoming refutation of those doctrines which John Flavel was preparing for the press, under the title of "A Blow at the Root; or, the Causes and Cures of Mental Errors." Baxter reluctantly acquiesced; Howe fulfilled his promise; and all but the most obstinate were satisfied.

The controversy, however, proceeded. The press teemed with pamphlets on both sides, till party spirit became inflamed to a pitch of bitterness altogether unprecedented. But as it is not necessary for the illustration of Howe's life and character, to pursue the history of the controversy any farther, I gladly drop a veil over these excesses of party.

As Howe's sentiments on the controverted points had been already fully and frequently expressed in his previous writings, he would not in all probability have engaged in these disputes, even if they had been carried on in a less rancorous spirit. As it was, a ship in a tempest would have been about as pleasant to a philosopher, as such a scene of tumultuous and passionate controversy to a spirit like that of John Howe.* He contented himself, therefore, with an earnest attempt to soften the ferocity of party spirit, and to reclaim the disputants to a recollection of what was due to truth, to themselves, and to one another.†

It was partly with this view that he published his sublime discourses, entitled, "The Carnality of Religious Contention." ‡ He makes no special reference, however, to the controversy then agitated; but confines himself to the exposition of principles of universal application.

These discourses were originally preached at the Merchants'

---

* During a considerable part of the autumn of the year 1692, Howe was out of town on a visit in the north; probably at the seat of Lord Wharton, in Yorkshire. It was at this time he visited Thoresby, from whose diary I extract the following notice of him:—

"Sept. 10.—Afternoon, had a letter recommendatory from Lord Wharton, for the eminent Mr. Howe, of London; whose excellent company, with the Rev. Mr. Todd's, I enjoyed rest of day; and, evening, his assistance in family duty.

"12th.—Morning, enjoyed Mr. Howe's assistance in family prayer, then accompanied him to Pontefract. Lord, preserve him from the danger of his journey, and convey him safe to his own habitation, that he may be continued as a blessing to this nation."

In July of this year, Howe preached a funeral sermon for the Rev. John Kempster, who was ejected from Brixham, Devon. He died in London.

† In 1692, appeared a paper, entitled "The Agreement in Doctrine among the Dissenting Ministers in London." To this Howe's name was attached. It did little or nothing towards appeasing the wrath of the contending parties.

‡ The text is, "Walk in the Spirit, and ye shall not fulfil the lusts of the flesh."

Lecture, in Broad-street, 1693. They are distinguished in almost equal degree by the exquisite spirit of charity which pervades them, and the profoundly philosophical character of the principles they unfold. Of the preface to these discourses, Mr. Spademan, Howe's coadjutor, thus speaks: * "It breathes so heavenly a charity and concern for the truly Christian interest, that a very eminent divine of the Established Church did profess a willingness to lay down his own life, if such a state of things as is there described might obtain among Christians." The most striking part of the first sermon is that in which he shows that it is very possible this spirit may exist in its worst forms, even where it is least likely to be suspected,—in the hearts of those who advocate the *truth*. The second sermon (which is worthy of universal perusal in this age of party strife) presents us with a masterly delineation of the various modes in which this spirit may display itself.

"It displays itself," he tells us, "when Christians, who are very far agreed in the most important things, make little of the things wherein they are agreed, though ever so great, in comparison of the much less things wherein they differ;" "when there is too much aptness to lay greater stress than is needful upon some unscriptural words, in delivering Scripture doctrine;" "when we consider with too little indulgence one another's mistakes and misapplications in the use even of Scripture words, placing them (as some may do) upon things to which they do not properly belong, when yet they agree about the things themselves;" "when there is an agreement about the main and principal things that the Scripture revelation contains and carries in it, but there is not that agreement about their mutual respects and references unto one another;" "when we are over-intent to mould and square gospel truths and doctrines by human measures and models, and too earnestly strive to make them correspond;" "when there is a discernible proneness to oppose the great things of the gospel to one another, and to exalt or magnify one above or against an-

---

* In Howe's Funeral Sermon.

other;" "when any do with great zeal contend for this or that opinion or notion as very sacred and highly spiritual, with no other design than that under that pretence they may indulge their own carnal inclination with the greater liberty;" "when, in maintaining any doctrine of the gospel in opposition to others, we industriously set ourselves to pervert their meaning, and impute things to them that they never say; or if we charge their opinions whom we oppose with consequences which they disclaim;" "when disputes arise at length to wrath, to angry strife, yea, and even to fixed enmity;" "when any adventure to judge of the consciences and states of them whom they oppose, or from whom they differ;" "when we over-magnify our own understandings, and assume too much to ourselves;" and, finally, "in an affectation and desire of having such disputes still kept afoot, and the contests continued, without either limit or rational design."

But the tempest of passion ran so high, that the voice of reason was lost in it. In 1694, Mr. Daniel Williams* was excluded from the Tuesday's Lecture at Pinners' Hall, which led to the establishment of a new one on Thursday, at Salters' Hall, where Howe, Bates, and Alsop, joined their expelled brother. Howe's first sermon at this new Lecture is said to have been deeply affecting. The text was, "And there is none that calleth upon thy name, that stirreth up himself to take hold of thee: for thou hast hid thy face from us, and hast consumed us because of our iniquities." †

An account of the final rupture which terminated in the establishment of the new Lecture, is given in an interesting letter of Howe to his early and beloved friend, Mr. Spilsbury, dated in the spring of the following year. It appears that he had previously written on the subject, but the communication does not seem to have come to hand.

It is clear, from this letter, that the spirit of the more intemperate among those who remained at Pinners' Hall, soon alienated the affections of the more moderate, especially of the venerable and truly excellent Matthew Mead.

---

* Afterwards Dr. Williams, the founder of the library in Redcross-street.
† Isaiah lxiv. 7.

" London, April 20, 95.

" My dear Brother,

" You strangely forget yourself, when you say I gave you no account of the Pinners' Hall business, of which I sent you a large narrative when the business was recent; which, if it miscarried, tell me so, and I promise you I will never do the like again: for it is a very discouraging thing, when it is so hard a matter to get time to write such long letters, to have them lost by the way; or it is not better, if, when they are received, they are taken pro non scriptis. God knows how I strove against that division. Almost all my friends that called me to bear a part in that lecture, perceiving the violence of the other party, agreed to remove to a much more convenient place; and they were, so far as I can learn, the greatest part of the ancient subscribers, who were grave, sober citizens. They invited Mr. Mead as well as me. If he would not go, I could not help that. His acquaintance lay more among the other, as mine did with these. He and they all know the many meetings we have had to prevent the breach—he and I with divers of them on both sides. And they (who are now of Pinners' Hall) ran against his advice and mine, when they had desired us to meet purposely to advise them. · He hath been since as weary of them as others, as he hath owned to me. They avowed it for a principle, before we parted, they would lay any of us aside at their pleasure, without giving a reason; and were told thereupon, we would lay down without giving them a reason, though I think that itself was a sufficient reason. They know, too, how often, since the Lecture was broken into two—and it appeared now there were two congregations, which no one place could receive—I have urged, both publicly and privately, that the same lecturers might alternate in both places, which would take away all appearance of disunion, and who they were only that opposed it. Upon these terms I had preached with them still; but I will not be tied to them, nor any party, so as to abandon all others. My frequent insisting, in sermons among them, when I saw whither things tended, that these were tokens of what was coming, (just as thou writest,) will be thought on, it may be, hereafter, though then it was not. Above all, that which determined me was, that when I solemnly proposed to them, in a sermon, the keeping a fast, before they went on to that fatal rupture—and it was as solemnly promised by the chief of them, there should be no step further made without a fast—it should be declined afterwards. Hereupon I told them, in my last sermon there, I should be afraid of confining myself to such as were afraid of fasting and prayer in so important a case, (repeating their own good resolution to that purpose,) and began my course in the other place with a fast, to lament what we could not prevent. These things will be recollected another day.

"In the meantime, there never was greater intimacy or endearedness between Mr. Mead and me than now. Last week he desired me only, without any other, to join with him in keeping a fast at his house, about some private affairs of his own, which we did. I was to have preached at his place to-morrow, after my own work at home; but present indisposition prevents me as to both. We have, however, agreed to exchange sometimes: but this cannot last long. The things that threaten us make haste. Only let us be found among the mourners in Zion: comforts will come, in this or the better world. I just now heard from Mr. Porter out of Sussex, who inquires after thee.

"In the Lord, farewell:
"To thee and thine,   ·
"From me and mine,
"With most entire and
undecaying affection,
"J. H."

Simultaneously with these unseemly disputes, occurred others, scarcely less so, on the Trinitarian controversy,—principally, however, amongst writers in the Establishment. Amongst others who had recently published on the subject, were Wallis, Sherlock, South, and Cudworth. A tract having appeared, professing to be a review of the several theories maintained by these writers, Howe was induced to compose his celebrated piece, entitled, "A Calm and Sober Inquiry." This was followed, the same year, by a "Postscript," containing certain letters to Dr. Wallis; to which, in reply to some animadversions that had been made on the "Inquiry," he afterwards added some further remarks.

In the year 1694, as appears from the following letters, published in this work for the first time, from the MSS. in the library at Woburn Abbey, Howe paid a visit to the Duke·

of Bedford. The following letter is addressed to his Grace's chaplain, and apologizes, for not having visited Woburn Abbey again, according to promise.

TO THE REV. MR. THORNTON.

" Love-lane,* Aldermanbury,
" London, Aug. 16, 94.

" *Worthy Sir,*

"When I lately waited on my Lord Duke, it not a little troubled me that my narrow limits of time allowed me not to comply with his Grace's desire of passing one Lord's day at Woburn Abbey; which I told him (having then been some weeks already absent from the congregation under my care) I might better do after I had been some time at home. I did, therefore, in pursuance of that intention, begin my journey Tuesday last; but by that time I had rid to Highgate, so violent a rain fell, that I was forced to take up for several hours; and upon its holding up a little, went on as far as Barnet, in continual rain; for that intermission wherein I set forward afresh proved very short. And (that I may freely accuse myself to you) I was so great a coward, that, not having of late been used to ride in wet weather, fearing ill consequences, I durst adventure no further; but yesterday morning, not seeing any hope of better weather, I returned home. You know better than I (with the tender of my humble duty) to make an apology for me to his Grace, as handsomely as the matter will admit. My turn's now come on at our monthly Lecture, which, by our ordinary rule, is not wont to be transferred, and will tie me here some weeks : for in each month two alternate, each preaching twice in the month : and afterwards, I doubt the journey is not to be attempted on horseback. Nor do I know another way as yet. Perhaps I may obtain the indulgence to have it judged in my case—though the thing attempted was not great—*voluisse sat est.* I lately met in the street (which you may please, with the tender of my humblest services, to let my Lady Russell know) Mrs. Howland, in her coach, which she suddenly caused to be stopped, and told me that, being shortly to take a journey to Canmers in Essex,

---

* In what year Howe removed to Love-lane I know not. All the subsequent letters, except two, are dated from thence : those are dated from St. John-street.

she desired to see me at Streatham before she went,—where, waiting on her, after some discourse, I having intimated to her, that probably I might ere long see Woburn Abbey, she desired me to say some things to my Lady Russell, which I shall not write, unless my Lady command it; and give direction to whom, (for I know her ladyship is not to be put upon using her own eyes in reading letters;*) yet, so far I can apprehend, it is rather decency than the nature of the thing I have to say, that makes me so reserved for the present.†

"I kiss the hands of your noble charge; and am,
"Sir,
"Your very respectful,
"Humble Servant,
"JOHN HOWE.

"My Lord Duke's intended favour of venison (though I have little reason to expect it) is now like to find me at home the next week.

"Give my respects to Mr. Bingley.

"*For the Rev. Mr. Thornton,*
"*Chaplain to his Grace the Duke of Bedford,*
"*At Woburn Abbey, Bedfordshire.*"

---

* Lady Russell was at this time nearly blind.

† I have little doubt that this has some reference to the proposed marriage between Wriothesley, son of Lady Rachel Russell, and Elizabeth, daughter and co-heiress of John Howland, of Streatham, with whom he received a princely fortune. The marriage took place in the following year, 1695; and, in consequence of it, he was created Baron Howland, of Streatham, in the county of Surrey.

We have already had one other instance of Howe's being employed in negotiations of this kind. We may mention a third. He had some years before been commissioned by the wealthy merchant, Sir Josiah Child, to propose a marriage between this very son of Lady Russell, and Sir Josiah's grand-daughter, the Lady Henrietta Somerset. This proposal Lady Russell declined; on which the merchant, evidently somewhat piqued, wrote to Howe as follows:—"I received your favour of the 22nd inst., and your letter of the 28th. The answer intimated in your first was so cold, that I concluded the noble lady either understood not the considerableness of the proposal, or had predetermined the disposal of her son some other way, and did expect to hear no more of it: the rather I thought so, from that expression in your letter, that the young lord was in the course of his education,—which I never knew to be a bar to parents discoursing of the matching of their children, which are born to extraordinary great fortunes; and that being the case of the noble young lord, as well as of my grand-daughter, made me the forwarder, without her mother's privacy, to write that letter to you, that so great a fortune, as God's providence has cast upon her, might fall into the best and most pious noble family I know—for such I esteem my Lord Bedford's to be."

Notwithstanding Howe's doubts, the promised venison arrived in a few days. His correspondent having dated the letter which accompanied it a day too late, he makes a playful allusion to this circumstance, at the commencement of his reply :—"The venison," he says, "is incomparably good;" which is the nearest approach to anything like an expression of animal gratification that is to be found in any writings of John Howe. Doubtless, however, he found, like less abstracted mortals, that physical enjoyment was not altogether to be despised.

The note does not contain much; yet it is amusing, as containing one or two of the little touches, which show us that human nature, in its familiar moods, is always the same, and that the gravest of our race have eaten, and drunk, and jested, and laughed, like their less sedate fellows.

" Love-lane, Aldermanbury,
" Aug. 21, 94.

" The venison is arrived with greater expedition than if it had come upon its own swift legs. For by the date of your letter, the 21st, it is here as soon as it could be sent away from Woburn Park. *Hâc raptim.* It is indeed incomparably good. I am mightily pleased to think, my most humble thanks to his Grace, will by such a hand as yours be tendered with that becoming decency, that would have been wanting, had the part of a grateful orator been to be immediately performed by,

" Sir,
" Your very respectful, humble Servant,
" JOHN HOWE."

In this year he addressed the following letter of condolence to a lady, whose name is unknown, on the loss of a daughter.

" Dear and honoured Madam,

" Did you think, two or three months ago, such a trial was so near ? Such sad futurities God, in mercy to us, hides from us, that we may not afflict ourselves before he afflicts us; and that when he intends we should suffer that particular affliction but once, namely, when it comes, we may not impose so hardly upon ourselves, as to suffer it a thousand times over before it comes. ' Sufficient for the day,' &c. If he should have made us all prophets, in reference to all the events of our time, we should bring all the evils of every future day into every former day; as if the evil of the day were not enough for the day.

"But though he gives us not certain predictions of such evils, lest he should torment us, he gives forewarnings, lest he should surprise us. He hath told us we must all once die, and not when; that life is a vapour; that all flesh is grass; that the beauty or glory of it is but as the flower of grass; withering things! He hath asserted his own dominion over lives, and over the spirits of all flesh, as the God of them, to lodge and dislodge them, where and as he pleases. And who are we, that we should grudge him that dominion; or so much as wish we could have wrested that part of his empire out of his hands? But when he afflicts, it is good to consider what it is for. It comes not ' out of the dust,' though it may reduce us or ours thither. And if our utmost search cannot find out a particular cause, (wherein we should take heed of being too indulgent and partial to ourselves, but should beg that what we know not he would teach us,) yet we should, however, more earnestly endeavour to improve the affliction to the general end, which we may be sure he aims at; to withdraw our minds from this present world and state of things; to take heed of being peremptory in laying any designs that must be measured by time, and be subject to the uncertainties of it; to determine nothing but with that reserve, ' If God will, we shall do this, or that,' James iv. 15; to have our minds engulfed and swallowed up, not of the stream of time, but of the ocean of eternity; to be easily taken off from any purpose, the scene whereof must be laid on this earth or lower world; to have our hearts more entirely and more strongly set upon God, so as to be able to say, ' Whom have I in heaven or earth besides thee?' that the true end may be gain, though such a comfort be lost, and the particular offending cause cannot be found.

"We may err, in thinking some such particular offence must be fastened upon. If it clearly can, it ought; if not, it is better forbear judging than misjudge. Possibly, chastening for a particular sin may not be God's design: it is not always. We may be sure it never is his principal design, in taking away one relative from another. He made all things (principally) for himself; he made us but secondarily for one another. If his principal design in making such a creature was not to please me, his principal design in taking it away was not to displease or afflict me. He hath his own greater and higher end concerning his own creature, to glorify himself upon it, and by it, in a greater world than this. Many afflictions are for trial; and that in such a case is an awful thought.

"The jealous God hath me now under trial, how I can bear, how I can submit, how I can reverence his hand, how I can behave myself towards him when he afflicts; whether I will venture to contend with him, or be sullen and morose towards him, because he hath bereaved me of a child I delighted in; whether I better loved him or my child. The trial may be manifold; of my faith, of my patience, of my fear of him, of my love to him; and, I may add, it may be intended for a trial of gratitude, and a mighty trial that is. We are required in everything to give thanks. And Job did it, and said, 'Blessed be the name of the Lord,' when with all his substance he took away all his children at once; 'The Lord hath given, the Lord hath taken.' The injunction, 'In every thing give thanks,' signifies there is in everything some matter of praise. I know not so immediately what was in this case; but if there was what I have heard, great indications of early piety, if there were grounds to hope there were a work of regeneration wrought, there is infinitely more matter of thanksgiving than complaint. What had the life of a child been worth without this? when better never to have been born! It is a far greater thing if he have taken her as his own child, than if he had left her to you, only as yours. If you have faith to look into the unseen world, and behold her taken into the society of angels, and of the spirits of just men made perfect, how much more hath God done for her and you, than if he had left her to your care and provision in this wretched world! We are told there is joy in heaven for the conversion of a sinner: much more for the glorification of a convert! That joy ought to swallow up in very great part your sorrow. The good Lord frame your spirit suitably to these things, in whom I am

"Your truly respectful Servant,
"(Very sensible of your case,)
"J. HOWE.

"*Love-lane, Aldermanbury,*
   "*London, Sept. 29, 1694.*"

In December, 1694, Howe's congregation removed to a new

chapel, in Silver-street. The place in which they had hitherto worshipped belonged to the Haberdashers' Company. Howe's colleague at this period was Mr. Thomas Reynolds.*

In 1695, he published the Funeral Sermon for Queen Mary. It is entitled, " Heaven a State of Perfection," and is dedicated to Lady Russell.

Thoresby was in town this year, and heard Howe. He has thus noted the circumstance in his diary. " May 19, Dio Dom. Heard the famous Mr. Howe, both morning and afternoon, who preached incomparably."

In this year, within eight months of one another, died Howe's old patron and his lady, the Viscount and Viscountess Massarene. Their daughter Mary, as stated on a preceding page, had married Sir Charles Hoghton, of Hoghton Tower, in the county of Lancaster. With them and their family Howe maintained a most endeared intimacy until his death. On the decease of her parents, he sent Lady Hoghton the following letter of condolence.

" *Most honoured, dear Madam,*

    " When I heard of your former great loss, I was confined by distemper to my bed : and I received information of the other, when I was going a great journey to accompany my wife and daughter to the Bath, from whence they are not returned as yet, and I came home from my journeyings but last week. I have not in the meantime forgot your ladyship's affliction, nor been without the apprehension how tender a sense your loss of two such parents must be accompanied with. Nor should I now mention it, did I not apprehend it may yet be reflected on to better purpose, than only to renew your sorrow. And that it may, I pray you, let it be remembered in the first place, with serious gratitude, (for we are required in everything to give thanks,) that God continued to you the comfort of such relations so long, and for the many mercies he made them instrumental of to you, in your tender years ; that he vouchsafed to you the blessing of so excellent an education by their means ; that you were thereby brought to know him and his Christ ; that by their care you were so

---

* Calamy's Life and Times, vol. i., p. 339.

comfortably settled in the world, and in a station wherein he hath given you the opportunity of being so serviceable in building up a family for him, and of contributing to the planting and propagating religion in it; and that you see so much of a blessing from heaven upon the plantation. Your part is that of a mother, and you have had a great example before your eyes. *That* may still live (and I doubt not will) in your mind and heart, while the person that gave it still lives in a higher region, whither, following such steps, you also will be translated in the fittest season.

"I pray for the welfare, in all valuable respects, of your ladyship, and all yours; being, in great sincerity, your ladyship's

"Most respectful,
"And most faithful, humble Servant,
"J. Howe.

"*Love-lane, Aldermanbury, London,*
"*Sept. 5, 1695.*"

I find no further trace of Howe till 1697, when he wrote a letter to Mr. Spademan, who was then residing at Rotterdam, but who was soon to become his colleague. The contemplated connexion between them forms, in all probability, the main subject of the letter; at the same time, I confess, the allusions in it are for the most part unintelligible to me. I found the document among the MSS. in the Ayscough catalogue, British Museum. It is given below.*

---

* To Mr. Spademan.

"*Dear Sir,*

"You very well know, and I desire to consider, that to mutter, or even more inwardly to repine, at that providence which overrules all our affairs, especially when they are involved with the concernments of many others besides, is both undutiful and vain; injures the sovereign Ruler, and doth ourselves no good. My last to you was by the gentleman of whom I had writ to you before. But I presume he may still be in the fleet that hath lain windbound some weeks at Harwich. The truth is, before he went hence, he was in [doubt] whether to go with that or the packet-boat, but his friends have advised him to the former course, as safer, and possibly, if the wind proved direct, (considering the land journey to Harwich,) more expeditious: but being actually [close,] and the wind continuing long adverse, I thought, he, being before indifferent, might have left the fleet to go with the packet that sails often with a less favourable wind than fleets use to set forth with. But I apprehend the continual expectation of a change of wind would withhold him. And *my* expectation of the same change hath withheld me too from writing by the packet ever since: still supposing what I writ by him would be sooner with

On the day of thanksgiving for the restoration of peace, December 2, 1697, Howe preached a sermon, which was published in the ensuing year. It was dedicated to Lord Haversham.

In the beginning of 1698, he addressed the two following letters to his venerable friend, Mr. Spilsbury, which closed their long and delightful intimacy.

"*My dear Brother,*

"How hard a matter is it to keep up converse at this rate! when all that is pleasant and gainful in it lies on one side only. I read thy lines with fruit and delight; but have nothing to return of any value. And if a conscience is to be exercised in this sort of traffic, or indeed but a tolerable ingenuity, it cannot but occasion some regret, to barter away things of no worth for good commodities. If I tell thee I live, what doth that signify? when life itself is so little worth, how despicable is the notice of it! If I tell thee I love thee, thou knowest it before as to the *quod sit;* but for the *quid sit,* no words can express it; therefore the offer at it is vain. When, when shall we meet above? That will make us pure good company, when dulness and sluggishness are shaken off and gone, and we shall be all spirit and life. Yet we shall be doing our Lord some service here, or that he will accept as such, if we be sincere. Thou wilt be visited by a worthy person ere long, that is gone first to Kidderminster, and means, after he hath seen the son, to come to the father.

"Cordial salutations from me and mine, to thee and thine. Farewell in our dear Lord: and still remember,

"Thy entirely affectionate,
"J. HOWE.

"*St. John-street, Jan.* 25, 1698."

"May I once more hope to salute my dear brother in this world? Whether I shall or not, I must leave to Him to whom

---

you. I saw what your last said to Mr. Gunston. When either his, or mine by Mr. Wallis, or this, reaches your hands, you will be delivered from your [amazement,] which the wind (continuing long so constantly opposite) hath, I hope, in good measure, expelled already. Patient expectation of the issue, with prayers and hopes of a good one, is the [duty] of you and

" Your affectionate Brother and Servant,
"J. H.

"*London, April* 6, 1697."

greater, and all things, must be left. Thou mayest have taken thy flight before *this* reach thee; but the soul and spirit from whence it comes *may* in due time, through the infinite riches of freest grace, and the atoning blood of that sacrifice which once for all was offered up. 'We come to the general assembly and to the spirits of just men made perfect,' but as we come to 'Jesus the Mediator' of the new testament, and to the blood of sprinkling.' 'By his own blood he is entered into the holy of holies, as the forerunner, and for us.' Upon such terms may sinful unprofitable servants hope to enter, and be received under the notion of faithful, and as those that are graciously counted such, into the joy of their Lord. Thou art ready to enter, and wilt shortly be adoring before the throne: oh, with what complacency, receiving the end of thy faith, having fought the good fight of it! And must thy poor brethren left behind, sigh and groan still? amidst their drowsy hearers, and too drowsy fruitless labours? But I envy thee not; and those that are dearest and nearest to thee owe thee so much as to rejoice in thy joy, while they cannot as yet in their own. Thou art upon my heart, if God saw it good, to live and die with thee. This day se'nnight thy worthy brother B. and my brother F. dined with me, when thou wast most affectionately remembered; but art no day forgotten, by thy sincere lover, and of all thine, hoping and aiming (though faintly) to be thy follower.

"J. HOWE.

"*March* 18, 1698."

"If there be joy in heaven for a converted sinner, shall there not for a glorified saint, and the leader and teacher of many such; some that are in glory, and others that shortly shall be? Oh, the triumph at thy abundant entrance!"

Mr. Spilsbury died the 10th of July following.

In this year Howe addressed the following striking letter of consolation to Sir Charles and Lady Hoghton, on the loss of that hopeful and beloved son, on whose untimely death he composed his sublime discourse on "The Redeemer's Dominion over the Invisible World."

"*Most worthily honoured Sir, with my dearest and most honoured Lady,*

"It would be incomparably more grievous to me at

this time to write to you, if I were under a necessity of writing nothing but what were mournful and sad. The same thing, if we turn it round, will be found to have a double aspect. That dispensation that represents you deprived of an earthly son, speaks you the parents of a glorified child, more highly dignified than it was possible he could have been on earth. This post brings you greater news than if it had informed you, your son is created emperor of Germany, or king of France or Spain. Let us speak and think of things as we believe, and profess to believe. Indeed, if our apprehensions of their state in the unseen world, who were true lovers of God, have nothing of solace and pleasure in them, it is mere useless empty profession they are all to be resolved into, and not faith.

"My heart bleeds for you, and with you both, but it can do you no good to tell you so. I believe your lovely son unfeignedly loved God; and then read the rest, 1 Cor. ii. 9; James i. 10, 12. Of how great use might he have been in this world! But, are those glorious creatures above, to whom he is now joined, inactive or unemployed? And are not their employments more noble and •sublime, according to the more enlarged capacity of their faculties, and the higher dignity of their state? He was born to very considerable things as your heir; but 'he was begotten again to a more glorious inheritance, and the lively hope of it.' They that were about him, before it was possible. for me to see him, told me he was insensible, as he was before I heard of his illness; but at my coming to him, he knew me at first sight, and seemed to have the use of his understanding for nothing but religion. He then spake not one misplaced word; said, he doubted not God was his Father, and that his present affliction was from the hand of that Father, not of an enemy. He desired me to pray with him, and seemed understandingly and affectionately to concur. This was on the Lord's day, and the next was the day of his glorious translation, near noon, before I could reach him a second time.

" Mr. C—— came to me presently after, to advise with me about disposal of the body; who could give no advice but in the general, to have it prepared for interment in a way that might be decent, and not profusely expensive; not doubting but that there might be more particular direction from yourself, before actual interment, sent to Mr. C——, &c., who is willing to take the care upon him of seeing instructions fulfilled.

" The Lord support you both, and abundantly bless the rest of yours.

"I am, most honoured Sir and Madam,
"Your most affectionately sympathising
"Servant in Christ our Lord,
"JOHN HOWE.

"*St. John-street, London,*
"*Jan.* 14, 1698."

In this year he printed a funeral sermon for his old college friend, the Rev. Richard Adams; and also a discourse preached before the "Societies for Reformation of Manners."

The following year, 1699, must have been to Howe a most melancholy one, and must have drawn largely on his strength and spirits. Within a few months he lost two of his oldest and most endeared friends, the Rev. Matthew Mead, and the Rev. Dr. Bates. He preached the funeral sermons for both, and these were afterwards printed.

About this time his friend Thoresby, having long practised what was called "Occasional Conformity," (on which, some remarks will be found in the following pages,) went over entirely to the Church of England. He had been a member of the Presbyterian church, under the care of Dr. Manlove, of Leeds. The editor of Thoresby's Journal says, "Mr. John Howe, a very eminent nonconformist minister, wrote on the subject to Mr. Boyse, of Dublin, who happened to be at Leeds at the time, a letter which seems to have been intended for Thoresby's perusal." This letter I have recovered. I found it among the MSS. in the Ayscough catalogue. It is as follows.

TO THE REV. MR. BOYSE, AT MR. THOS. FENTON'S, IN LEEDS.

"*Worthy Sir,*
"The K went away the night before yours came to my hand, which is too short, but a full answer to all the first part of your letter. I have thought Dr. M[anlove]'s removes to have been twice too hasty. I shall be glad, for the sake of so considerable a place as Leeds, if a supply can be got satisfactory and seasonable, that no prejudice accrue by the change. It hath been said here, it hath so much disgusted Mr. R.

Thoresby, that he inclines totally to withdraw to the Church; and that to justify his inclination, if not intentions to that purpose, he hath in some late discourses seemed to lay great stress upon that trivial sophism, rather than argument, that, *if occasional communion* (that is, with the Church of England) *was lawful, constant* [communion] *was a duty.* This I am not to take notice of to him. But if you have time to discourse with him, and shall, or have heard anything to the purpose from him, it were well, if he were closely dealt with, before your leaving that town. He hath seemed to have a great reverence for Mr. Baxter, who, I believe, gave as full assent to this proposition as to most, 'That occasional communion with the Church of England was lawful;' and to this, 'That our distinct communions in our present circumstances were necessary.' I neither have [call] nor time (Saturday evening) to discuss this matter. The [above] excellent author hath said enough to prove this; [and to keep] a man of Mr. T.'s understanding from being imposed upon by so transparent a fallacy. If theirs or any church be put to it to show their authority for making other terms of church-communion than Christ hath made, and then to make *theirs* the sole communion within such and such districts, our practice (till they have proved that talk) may with great satisfaction be continued long enough. * * * * * And if such a [cause,] to which so great a part of God's heritage in England have borne witness, by about forty years' suffering, and to which God hath borne witness by the great [success] and blessing he hath given to them in their tabernacles, (when in this way they have endeadeavoured to keep [alive a sense of religion] in a time when hell was endeavouring the total extirpation and extinction of it,) shall be deserted and given up by a man of Mr. T.'s abilities, upon such a trifle of an argument,—it will stand without him; but I should be sorry that he should lose the things he hath wrought, so as not to obtain that full reward I wish him. If you have time, you will need none of these suggestions from,

" Your affectionate Brother,

" H. I.

" Other matters must be left till your desired return.
" *January 3, 99.*"*

---

* Under this is written by another hand; "Alias J. H., namely, Mr. John Howe; the noted N. C. minister, at London; a learned, pious, and excellent man, though I suppose not infallible in this argument."

The above letter forms no unsuitable introduction to the account it is needful to give of the unpleasant controversy in which Howe was involved, in 1701-2, respecting "Occasional Conformity." As the principles on which he defended that practice (whatever may be thought of the *extent* to which he applied them) are precisely the same with those which are employed to advocate catholic intercommunion among Christians of all denominations,—a subject which is deservedly attracting the attention of many of the excellent of all parties, —I shall make no apology for treating the matter at some length.

From the very commencement of the great schism of 1662, many of the more moderate nonconformists, both lay and clerical, had practised "occasional communion" with the Church of England; partly, because it was the *establishment*, under some modification of which they would have been willing to "conform,"* although they could not approve of the present constitution; and partly (in the case of Howe it was the principal reason,) for the purpose of recognising the essential unity of Christians of every name, and expressing sympathy with the church universal. The same principle of course implied a willingness on his part to hold occasional communion with any other body of Christians, with whom such communion was not, in his estimation, *sinful.* The question, then, must evidently be determined by the *nature* of the objections on which the person seceding justified his secession; in other words, by the state of the individual conscience. If a man thought the very rites and ceremonies, in which he would be called to join in any such communion, either sinful in themselves, or sinful from the circumstances attending the performance of them, there can be no doubt that in *him,* "occasional conformity" would be altogether unjustifiable. If, on the other hand, he did *not* think this; but justified his secession on the ground, that it is every man's duty ordinarily to adopt that system of worship which in his conscience he

---

* It must be remembered that the bulk of the early nonconformists did not object to the *principle* of establishments.

believes to be most in harmony with the New Testament, and best calculated to promote his own spiritual benefit, it is obvious that such a man might consistently adopt the practice in question; since he would not suppose the mere act of communion with the Church of England, sinful, but merely that the system of worship adopted in another community possessed greater advantages. Supposing Howe sincere in declaring such to be his sentiments,—of which there has never, so far as I know, been the shadow of a doubt,—then the best way of testing the soundness of the principles by which he justified the practice, is to throw the argument into a general form, putting the Church of England, or any other community, entirely out of the question.

The advocate of the practice would reason thus :—He would say, that of differing forms and modes of worship, every man is bound, as a general rule, to adhere to that which he believes most in accordance with the nature and design of the gospel, and best adapted to promote his spiritual welfare; but that such reasons do *not* bind him invariably to abstain from communion with any other body of Christians with whom, in his estimation, such communion can be practised without sin; that is, whose system he does not deem unlawful, but simply not so advantageous as his own; that with all such parties he is fully warranted to hold occasional communion, (either on stated occasions, or as circumstances may afford convenient opportunity,) for the purpose of practically recognising the essential unity of the universal church, and his own sense both of the infinite importance of those points in which all Christians agree, and the comparative insignificance of those in which they differ; this being a much more noble end than any which could be subserved by invariable communion only with his own party.*

Different persons may of course judge differently as to what is not absolutely unlawful in the modes of worship adopted by

---

* To illustrate this ; who would deny that a Congregationalist might safely practise occasional worship or communion with a body of Presbyterians or Wesleyan Methodists, although he would, for the reasons already mentioned, statedly prefer the modes of worship adopted by his own body ?

other religious communities than their own. This question, as I have said, must be determined, after all, by a reference to the conscience of the individual. Many of Howe's contemporaries, for instance, could not have held communion with the Church of England; yet *he* might safely do it.

Into the discussion of the limits within which the above principles should be applied, I do not enter. The general correctness of the principles themselves is all that I at present maintain.

To affirm, as was often done, that he who could go thus far, ought to go farther, and that if occasional conformity was lawful, constant conformity was lawful also, or, as it was sometimes argued, even a duty: in other words, to affirm that what an individual might, for special reasons, sometimes do, that he ought for general reasons to do always,—is to forget the very grounds on which the man is supposed to secede; namely, because he is in duty bound to adopt as his ordinary system of religious worship, not that in which he *might* join without positive sin, but that which he deems most scriptural and most profitable.*   Besides, in the case of Howe, as well as of every other *minister*, was there no difference between an *occasional* compliance with certain rites and ceremonies, which he did not think unlawful, and his acquiescence in the oaths and subscriptions required by the Act of Uniformity; his *ex-animo* assent and consent to everything contained in the Thirty-nine Articles, and the Book of Common Prayer? Would not entire conformity, moreover, have demanded (what in his case would have been worse than all the rest) a renunciation of that liberty of universal communion which was far dearer to him than the ties of party, and the adoption of that exclusive system, against which this, his condemned practice of occasional conformity, was mainly designed as a testimony?

But it is time to proceed to a brief narrative of the controversy on this subject, in which Howe became involved. Amongst

---

* To recur to the illustration of the preceding note;—what would be thought of the man who should argue that a Congregationalist, who occasionally, and for special reasons, held communion with Wesleyan Methodists, was *bound* to adopt their system of ecclesiastical polity and discipline?

other persons who, on the principles above explained, practised
" occasional conformity," was Sir Thomas Abney, a member of
Howe's congregation. In 1701, he became Lord Mayor of
London, and some persons began to suspect that he practised
occasional conformity, simply as a qualification for civil office.
It is proper to add, for the purpose of doing full justice to
Howe's conduct, that Sir Thomas had formed his opinions on
this subject long before it was probable that he would be
called on to comply with the law which made it imperative on
every person holding any civil office to partake of the Lord's
supper as administered in the Church of England. Amongst
others who were scandalized at his conduct, was Daniel De Foe,
who published an anonymous pamphlet, entitled, " Inquiry
into the Occasional Conformity of Dissenters."   The preface
is addressed to Howe, who is required, either to vindicate the
practice, or to condemn it.   Howe showed some reluctance to
enter into the controversy with his anonymous antagonist;
but at length overcame his scruples, and put forth a small
pamphlet, entitled, " Some Considerations of a Preface to an
' Inquiry concerning the Occasional Conformity of Dissenters.' "
In the introduction he justifies *his own* consistency by an appeal
to his known moderation of sentiment on the subject of the
controversies between the Church and the nonconformists; and
quotes largely from the letter which he had prefixed to his
" Delighting in God," and which had been published more
than twenty years before. He there declares, " That he for
a long time had had an habitual aversion in his own mind,
from perplexing himself, or disturbing others, by being concerned in agitating the controversies that have been on foot
about the circumstantials of religion; that he had contented
himself, by the best means he could be furnished with, and the
best use God enabled him to make of them, so far to form and
settle his own judgment, as was necessary to his own practice;
that he had faithfully followed his judgment, and abstained in
the meantime from censuring others, who took a different way
from him; that he was sensible every one must give account
of himself to God : and that it is a great consolation to such as
sincerely fear God, that if with upright minds they principally

study to approve themselves to him, and, if they mistake, do only err for fearing of erring, he will not with severity animadvert upon the infirmity of a weak and merely misguided judgment." He then proceeds to an able and closely reasoned defence of the practice on the principles I have already explained.* Howe declared at the close of this pamphlet, that no reply of his adversary should provoke him to resume his pen. De Foe, whose habits of controversy were inveterate, of course replied; and here the matter ended.

But though Howe published nothing farther in his life-time on this subject, a letter was found among his papers, addressed to a noble lord, and drawn up with much ability. I here subjoin it.

---

* Walter Wilson, Esq., the learned and laborious author of the "History of Dissenting Churches," and the "Life of De Foe," after quoting, in the latter work, (vol. ii., pp. 37, 38,) part of the above citation from Calamy, says, "Notwithstanding the *liberality* of these sentiments, they were beside the question;" as though they were the *main arguments* on which Howe insisted. This remark would lead one to suppose, (what I confess from his habits of accurate research would be improbable,) that the writer had not *read* the tract of Howe in question; or, at least, that he had not read it for some time.

If, however, it be true, that the propriety of this practice as respected the Church of England, must, after all, be decided by the nature of the objections on which the seceder grounds his dissent, that is, by the state of the individual conscience; the above remarks are *not* "beside the question," but most strictly to the purpose.

Mr. Wilson observes, that in "his controversy with De Foe, Howe gained no credit." I confess myself unable to perceive that he *lost* any. That his pamphlet is written with more severity than is his wont is most true. But it must also be confessed that he had considerable provocation. Thus De Foe had entitled his pamphlet, "An Inquiry into the Practice of Occasional Conformity, *in Cases of Preferment;*" evidently intending to insinuate (for such a title would have been absurd unless this had been his intention) that the conduct of Sir Thomas Abney had been prompted by the basest and most sinister motives; although if he did not know, he might easily have ascertained, that it had been the practice of Sir Thomas for many years before it was necessary as a qualification for civil office. If in his pamphlet he merely intended to refer to known cases (if any there were) in which individuals *had* adopted the practice he condemns from the love of "preferment," there was no necessity to appeal to Howe on the subject; nor indeed to discuss it at all; for such cases none would defend.

In the same spirit, he had prefixed to his title-page the words, "If the Lord be God, follow him; but if Baal,——:" evidently implying that it was not possible there should exist a condition of conscience in which the practice of occasional conformity was compatible with sincerity. These unworthy artifices of the pamphleteer, Howe severely exposes; as well as the illogical assumption, on which De Foe's argument evidently rests; namely, that all the nonconformists seceded from the Church on the same grounds, and that each adopted to the full every objection of the rest. This was notoriously untrue.

" A Letter to a Person of Honour, partly representing the Rise of Occasional Conformity, and partly the Sense of the present Nonconformists, about their yet continuing Differences from the Established Church.

" *My Lord,*

"It is well known to such as have understood the state of religion in this kingdom, since the beginning of the Reformation, that there have been very different sentiments about the degrees of that reformation itself. Some have judged the Church with us so insufficiently reformed, as to want as yet the very being of a true Christian church; and wherewith they, therefore, thought it unlawful to have any communion at all. Of whom many thereupon, in the several successive reigns, withdrew themselves into foreign parts, for the enjoyment of the liberty of such worship as they judged more agreeable to the word of God.

"There have been also no inconsiderable numbers, in former and later times, that, though not entirely satisfied with our reformation, were less severe in their judgment concerning the constitution and practice of the Established Church; that is, did not judge its reformation so defective, that they might not communicate at all with it, nor so complete but that they ought to covet a communion more strictly agreeable to the Holy Scripture; and, accordingly, apprehended themselves to lie under a two-fold obligation of conscience in reference hereto.

"1. Not, by any means, totally to cut themselves off on the one hand from the communion of the Established Church, in which they found greater and more momentous things to be approved of, and embraced with great reverence and complacency, (namely, all the true noble essentials of Christian religion—not subverted, as among the Romanists, by any contrary doctrines or practices,) than could be pretended to remain the matter of their disapprobation and dislike.

"2. Nor, on the other hand, to decline other communion, which to the judgment of their conscience appeared, in some considerable circumstances, more agreeable to the Christian rule, and, to their experience, more conducing to their spiritual advantage and edification.

"Which latter judgment of theirs (whether itself justifiable or no, we are not now considering) hath been with many so fixed and inflexible, that, in several successive reigns, great numbers of such persons, who, we had no reason to apprehend, had any thought totally to abandon the Established Church, yet thought themselves obliged, besides, to seek and procure opportunities for such other communions, even with extreme peril, not only to their estates and liberties, but to their very lives themselves.

"They could not, therefore, but think both these sorts of communions lawful, namely, whereto they might adjoin, but not confine themselves.

"And though to that former sort of communion, there hath, for many years by-past, been superadded the accidental consideration of a place or office attainable hereby, no man can allow himself to think, that what he before counted lawful, is by this supervening consideration become unlawful—especially if the office were such as was in no manner of way to be an emolument, but rather an occasion of greater expense to the undertaker of it; that is, only enabled him to serve God, the government, and his country, being regularly called hereto, in the condition of a justice of peace, or otherwise. In which capacity, it is notorious that divers persons, of eminent note, of this persuasion, (and some in higher stations,) have, within the space of forty years past, and upwards, been serviceable to the public in divers parts of the nation.

"It is not, indeed, to be thought, that the judgment and practice of such men can be throughout approved by our reverend fathers and brethren of the Established Church, as neither can we pretend it to be so universally by ourselves. But we are remote from any the least suspicion, that persons of so excellent worth and Christian temper, as now preside over the Established Church, can suffer themselves to judge or censure men of this sentiment, as being for this single reason men of hypocritical and insincere minds; but that they will rather think it possible their understandings may be imposed upon, so as this may be the judgment, in the whole, of a sincere though misinformed conscience.

"For when they apprehend this church, having all the essential parts of Christian religion, has not, by adding some much disputed things, that are not pretended to be any parts thereof, (but that are become as necessary to communion with it as any the most essential part,) thereby unchurched itself, but that they may hold communion with it; yet they do not see that they ought to appropriate their communion to it, so as to refuse all other communion, where the same essentials of Christian religion are to be found, without those additions which really belong not to it; they are apt to think such sentiments of theirs not to be altogether destitute of some plausible ground.

"However, among those that are not entirely in every punctilio of this church, it hath not any so firm friends, or that are so nearly united in judgment and affection with it, as men of this sentiment.

"We, for our parts, (who, because in some things we conform not, are called nonconformists, whereas no man conforms in everything,) are not allowed to be counted members of this church, by those that take denominations, not from the intimate essentials of things, (as sameness of doctrine, and the institutions of Christian worship,) but from loose and very separable accidents: yet, thanks be to God, we are not so stupid as not to apprehend we are under stricter and much more sacred obligations than can be carried under the sound of a name, to adhere to those our reverend fathers and brethren of the Established Church, who are most united among themselves, in duty to God and our Redeemer, in loyalty to our sovereign, and in fidelity to the Protestant religion, as with whom in this dubious state of things we are to run all hazards, and to live and die together. Whether they can have the same assurance, both from interest and inclination of mind, concerning all that are of the same external denomination with themselves, they need not us to advise with.

"We have our yet depending lesser differences, about which we have (notwithstanding whatsoever provocation) been generally and for the most part silent; and see not, in reference to them, what can further remain, than that we, for our part, do consider that all minds are not turned the same way; that such from whom we dissent, no further differ from us than we do from them; and we are, therefore, no more to wonder at them than ourselves.

"And we cannot disallow ourselves to hope, that our reverend fathers and brethren will conceive of us as humbly dissenting from them, without diminution of that great reverence which their real worth claims from us, and without arrogating anything unduly to ourselves on that account. For though we cannot avoid thinking we are in the right, in those particular things wherein we differ, yet, at the same time, we know ourselves to be far excelled by them in much greater and more important things.

"My honoured Lord,

"Your lordship's most obedient, humble Servant,

"J. H."

Hitherto the consciences of the nonconformists had been always considered too *strict;* their enemies finding that "occasional conformity" would enable those who could conscientiously practise it, to qualify for a civil office, and thus evade the law, now determined that they were too *lax;* and therefore introduced the bill against occasional conformity;* which provided that, unless a man maintained constant communion with the establishment, he should be utterly incapacitated for holding any civil office. Had this measure become law, the exclusive system would have been complete: but, after having passed the House of Commons, it was rejected, by a decisive majority, in the Lords. While the matter was pending, Howe exposed the absurdity of the bill, by an ingenious hypothetical case, which will be found below.†

While the Bill against occasional conformity was still under

---

* 1702.

† A CASE.

" Two sorts of Christian assemblies are wont to meet, severally, for the worship of God, which both hold all the same articles of doctrine taught by Christ or his apostles; and use the same institutions of worship appointed by them: only they differ in this, that the one sort use also some rites, not so appointed, which the other use not.

" Two gentlemen, Sir T—— and Sir J——, are of equal estates: but Sir T—— lives not so regularly, more seldom comes to the worship of God in any Christian assembly; yet, when he doth, resorts only to one of the former sort.

" Sir J—— is a sober, virtuous person, of approved piety, prudence, justice, fortitude, and who publicly worships God, sometimes in the one sort of assembly, and sometimes in the other.

" The question is not, whether some lewd and vicious persons may not frequent both sorts of assemblies; nor whether some sober and pious persons may not frequent those of the former sort only.

" But whether Sir J—— ought to be rendered incapable of serving the government (to which he hath constantly expressed himself well affected) in any station, civil or military, for this single reason, because he sometimes worships God in assemblies of the latter sort; (whether it be his infelicity, ill humour, or mistake, whereof yet he is not convinced;) while Sir T—— (who is as little convinced of his ill life) is left capable? At least, if the one be incapable, should not both ?

" But if the question be determined the other way, monstrous ! How will that determination of an English parliament stand in the annals of future time? How will wiser posterity blush they had such progenitors ! For can it be supposed a nation will be always drunk? Or if ever it be sober, will it not be amazed there ever was a time, when a few ceremonies, of which the best thing that ever was said was that they were indifferent, have enough in them to outweigh all religion, all morality, all intellectual endowments, natural or acquired, which may happen in some instances to be on the wrong side, (as it must now be reckoned,) when, on the other, is the height of profaneness, and scorn at religion; the depth of debauchery and brutality, with half a wit, hanging between sense and nonsense: only to cast the balance the more creditable way,

discussion, the following characteristic incident occurred. As Howe was one day walking in St. James's Park, a noble lord, to whom he was well known, sent his footman to say that he desired to speak with him. When he came up, his lordship saluted him with much cordiality, and told him that he was glad to see him. He then entered into conversation on the obnoxious "Bill," which he assured Howe "he had opposed to the utmost." Gradually getting warm upon the subject, he so far forgot his company as to say, "Damn these wretches, for they are mad, and will bring us all into confusion." Howe calmly replied, "My Lord, it is a great satisfaction to us, who in all affairs of this nature desire to look upwards, that there is a God that governs the world, to whom we can leave the issues and events of things: and we are satisfied and may thereupon be easy, that he will not fail, in due time, of making a suitable retribution to all, according to their present carriage. And this great Ruler of the world, my Lord, has among other things also declared, he will make a difference between him that *sweareth*, and him that *feareth an oath.*" His lordship was struck with Howe's reply, and after a pause said, "Sir, I thank you for your freedom; I understand your meaning, I shall endeavour to make a good use of it." Howe adroitly answered, "My Lord, I have a great deal more reason to thank your lordship, for saving me the most difficult part of a discourse, which is the *application.*"

In 1702, Howe published the second part of his great work, "The Living Temple." It is dedicated to William Lord

---

there is the skill to make a leg, to dance to a fiddle, nimbly to change gestures, and give a loud response, which contain the answer for the villanies of an impure life!

"If those little pieces of church-modishness have so much in them of real value, in all these are they not well enough paid by the whole Church revenues of England, without stigmatizing everybody that so much admires them not?

"And while divers of real worth live upon charity, some with difficulty getting, others (educated to modesty) with greater difficulty begging their bread!

"But do those who are not contented to engross all the legal emoluments, think there is no God in heaven, that knows their large promises, at the beginning of this revolution, of great abatements in their Church constitution; when now, without abating one hair, they must have all conform to it in every punctilio, or be (as much as in them is) made infamous, and the scorn of the nation?"

Pagett, Baron of Beaudesert, in the county of Stafford.* In this year, he also published a funeral sermon for the Rev. Peter Vink.

In 1702 and 1703, Howe seems to have been in a very shattered state of health, but had lost nothing of, his vigour of mind. On the 5th of November of the latter year, he preached a striking sermon, which was afterwards published, from the words, "Who hath delivered us from the power of darkness, and hath translated us into the kingdom of his dear Son."

I shall conclude this chapter with an exquisite letter of condolence " on the loss of an excellent wife." It is preserved in Calamy's Life; but it bears no date, nor can it now be ascertained to whom it was addressed. The close is surpassingly beautiful.

TO A FRIEND, ON THE LOSS OF AN EXCELLENT WIFE.

" L seriously lament your new affliction, whereof I lately had the surprising account. And I should be the more concerned for it, if I did not consider it hath befallen one who can with judgment estimate and suffer it. He hath enough to relieve him against the ungrateful events which our present state is liable to, who is serious in the belief of God's universal government over this world, and that there is another. The former of these is a principle much abused by some; which no more proves it false than the gospel, out of which some have the mischievous skill to extract a deadly savour. It is our great privilege, for which we ought to be thankful, that by such arguments whereby we can most certainly demonstrate to ourselves that there is a God, we can as certainly prove that he is not an Epicurean God; unto which imaginary idol only that could belong, 'to be disturbed by being concerned about human affairs.' But if he knew the true nature of God better, who came forth from him into our world, on purpose to make him known, we are sufficiently assured, not a hair can fall from our head without him, much less so considerable a part of ourselves.

" This is not the state wherein things are to be unexcep-

---

tionably well. But we have cause, as things are, to acknowledge and adore the wisdom and goodness of Providence, that
the wickedness of the world hath not in so many thousand
years quite confounded families, and all human society, long
ago : but that as wise counsel did first settle the institution of
those lesser societies, God hath from age to age renewed the
impression of that part among others of the law of nature, by
which men are prompted as by instinct to preserve them ; besides the positive precept he hath given, setting out to each
relative the duty whereby order is to be preserved in them.
And when we know his government extends so low, how
gladly ought we to submit ourselves to it, and allow him to
determine how long we should enjoy such relatives, as well as
that there should be any such. For we know that they were
appointed but for this temporary estate, not for that wherein
we are to be as the angels of God in heaven, where each one
hath a subordinate self-sufficiency, and needs not the meet
helps which the exigency of this state makes so useful. And
therefore the reason, as well as the authority of such precepts,
is most entirely to be subscribed to, that because the time is
short, they that have wives be as though they had none ; they
that rejoice, (in having them,) as if they rejoiced not ; they
that weep, (in losing them,) as though they wept not. So our
affections will correspond to the objects which are of the same
make ; for the fashion of this world passeth away. And it
were a gloomy thought to consider all as passing and vanishing, if we did not seriously believe, that it vanishes to make
way for another, that shall never vanish, and that shall shortly
enter in its perfect glory, and fill up the whole stage. Scaf-
folds are taken down when the eternal building is finished."

CHAPTER XI.

HOWE'S LAST ILLNESS—STATE OF MIND—DEATH—EXTRACT FROM HIS
WILL—HIS PERSON—ANALYSIS OF HIS CHARACTER.

AT the close of 1704, it was obvious to his friends that Howe
was fast approaching the term of all his toils and sufferings.
His constitution had long been crumbling under a complication
of maladies; and no new and violent form of disease was
necessary to complete the work of destruction. "The earthly
house of his tabernacle" was already tottering.

His decline was so slow, that, feeble as he was, he did not
entirely relinquish his public duties till a very short time before
his death. The peculiar circumstances under which these his
last services were performed, rendered them in the highest
degree solemn and imposing. His now intensely vivid per-
ceptions of Divine truth, and of approaching glory, imparted
such preternatural vigour to his mind, that he sometimes
seemed completely to triumph over all the infirmities of nature.
Once, in particular, at the communion, he was rapt into such
an ecstasy of joy and peace, that both himself and his audience
thought he would have died under the strength of his emotions.
It seemed as though, in that entranced and earnest gaze on the
already opening glories of the heavenly world, the struggling
spirit would have broken the feeble tie which was all that
bound it to earth and time.

In the spring of 1705, and only a very few weeks before his
death, he sent to the press the last thing he ever published;
and nothing surely, under his present circumstances, could
have been more appropriate. It was entitled, "On Patience

in Expectation of Future Blessedness;" a virtue, alas! which few find it difficult to practise. The generality of Christians bear the sentence of prolonged exclusion from heaven with most exemplary endurance. With Howe the case was different; like the apostle, " he desired to depart, and to be with Christ." He was weary of a world of sorrow and of sin, and longed to be at home and at rest.

His death, gradual in its approach, and long foreseen, was such as might be expected from the character of his mind, and the calm tenor of his life. He was a total stranger to the raptures into which some have been transported in that hour, and equally so to those alternations of light and darkness, of hope and dread, which now raise the soul to the very gate of heaven, and now fill it with despair. He was full of joy and hope; but it was joy and hope serene and unfaltering. This, of all the states of mind in which the Christian can meet the dying hour, is surely the most enviable; the most satisfactory to himself, and the most impressive to spectators. Such deep, solemn tranquillity of soul at such a moment, is the surest evidence of the reality of religious character, and best illustrates the power of religious truth. It can in no degree be attributed to a fictitious source; to the illusions of a perturbed imagination, or to that morbid excitement which disease will now and then impart to the intellect, and which resembles the delirious splendour which it can sometimes kindle in the eye.

Howe continued to receive the visits of his friends after he was confined to his chamber; and, as they frequently declared, he addressed them more like one who was already an inhabitant of the heavenly world, than as " a man of like passions with themselves;" rather as a messenger from the skies, than as one who was just departing on his journey thither: so stedfast, so assured was his hope, so full of tranquil certainty. To him, indeed, the scenes he was about to visit could hardly be said to be in a " strange land." They had become familiarized by the vivid exercise of that faith which penetrates the invisible and eternal world. Those visions of faith seemed now brighter than ever. Like the Jewish legislator, he died on Mount Nebo, with the glittering scenes of the "better country" spread out beneath his feet.

Amongst others who came to see him a short time before his death, was Richard Cromwell, now, like himself, far advanced in years. He came to pay his old friend and servant a visit of respect and of affectionate farewell. The interview, if we may judge either from the character of the men, or the brief account which Calamy has given us of it, must have been peculiarly affecting. He tells us, "There was a great deal of serious discourse between them; tears were freely shed on both sides; and the parting was very solemn, as I have been informed by one that was present on the occasion."

That Howe was among the few who needed "*patience* in the expectation of future blessedness," is shown in the following incident. He once told his wife, that "though he thought he loved her as well as it was fit for one creature to love another; yet if it were put to his choice, whether to die that moment, or to live that night, and the living that night would secure the continuance of his life for seven years to come, he would choose to die that moment."

One morning, finding himself much better than could have been expected after the severe sufferings of the preceding evening, he became remarkably cheerful. One of his attendants noticed it; upon which he made the characteristic reply, that "he was for feeling that he was *alive*, though most willing to die and lay the clog of mortality aside."

In those "considerations, and communings" with himself, which he committed to paper just before he left Antrim, and which have been already laid before the reader, he tells us that he dreaded "sharp pains more than death." This was exemplified in his last illness. His son, Dr. George Howe, a physician, having, without apprising him of his intention, lanced his father's leg (part of which was already gangrened), Howe asked "what he was doing;" saying at the same time, "I am not afraid of *dying*, but I am afraid of pain."

It appears from a passage in Matthew Henry's MS. diary, that such an amendment took place shortly before his dissolution, that, though his death had been long expected, hopes were again entertained of his recovery. On Thursday, March the 29th, those hopes were finally abandoned ; and the following Monday, April 2, 1705, he expired without a struggle.

He was buried in the parish church of All Hallows, Bread-street ; and his funeral sermon was preached on the following Sabbath, by his beloved friend and coadjutor, Mr. John Spademan. The text was, " But continue thou in the things which thou hast learned, and hast been assured of, *knowing of whom thou hast learned them.*" *

I proceed to give a brief description of his person, and an analysis of his character.

Howe's external appearance was such as served to exhibit to the greatest advantage his rare intellectual and moral endowments. His stature was lofty, his aspect commanding, and his manner an impressive union of ease and dignity. His countenance—the expression of which is at once so sublime and so lovely, so full both of majesty of thought and purity of feeling—is best understood by the portrait. It is (to use the language of Gregory Nyssen in reference to Basil) βλέμμα τῷ τόνῳ τῆς ψυχῆό ἐντεινςμενον, " a countenance attuned to harmony with the mind."

What Howe said of Bates (in the celebrated funeral sermon) might be said with still greater truth of himself; that he was " wrought ' *luto meliore,*' of better, or more accurately figured and finer-turned clay." Calamy, who knew him well, tells us

---

* The commencement of his *will* (which has been preserved by Calamy, and, as he truly remarks, is a noble confession of his faith) is as follows :—

"I, John Howe, minister of the gospel of Christ, in serious consideration (though, through God's mercy, in present health) of my frail and mortal state, and cheerfully waiting (blessed be God) for a seasonable unfeared dissolution of this my earthly tabernacle, and translation of the inhabitant spirit into the merciful hands of the great God, Creator, Lord of heaven and earth, whom I have taken to be my God, in and with his only begotten Son, Jesus Christ, who is also over all, GOD blessed for ever, and my dear and glorious Redeemer and LORD ; with and by the Holy Spirit of grace, my light, life, and joy ; relying entirely and alone upon the free and rich mercy of the Father, vouchsafed on the account of the most invaluable sacrifice and perfect righteousness of the Son, applied unto me, according to the gospel covenant, by the Spirit, for the pardon of the many seriously repented sins of a very faulty fruitless life, and the acceptance of my person, with my sincere though weak desires and endeavours to do him service in this world, especially as my calling wherewith he graciously honoured me, did more particularly require, in promoting the welfare and salvation of the precious souls of men."

that, "as to his person, he was very tall and exceeding graceful.   He had a good presence, and a piercing, but pleasant eye;
*and there was that in his looks and carriage, that discovered
that he had something within that was uncommonly great, and
tended to excite veneration.*"

If it were asked, what was the *characteristic* peculiarity of
Howe, we should probably not err in replying, that it consisted
in the complete absence of all *ordinary* peculiarities; in that
exquisite harmony of all the faculties, which is the rarest and
yet the noblest perfection of our nature; the harmony of a
mind, all whose powers are capacious, yet none out of proportion to the rest.

The *tendencies* of Howe's mind, it is true, were all of the
noblest kind; to the abstract and subtle in the department of
reason; to the lofty and sublime in that of imagination; and
to the pure and elevated in that of sentiment: but all this,
though sufficient to invest his whole character with peculiar
majesty, did not prevent (as too often happens with exalted
genius) the development of the inferior faculties, or unfit him
for a graceful and punctual discharge of the practical duties of
life.   The only perceptible difference in this point, between
him and others, was, that he sustained the ordinary relations of
life with unusual dignity.

Most of those characters which have won the admiration of
mankind, have been marked by a peculiar *individuality*, resulting from the disproportionate, and, in some cases, enormous
development of some master-faculty.   In Bacon, it is true, we
are dazzled by a constellation of almost all intellectual excellencies; yet even in him, the philosophic temperament was so
prevailingly strong, as to throw into comparative shade his
other vast endowments; endowments which, if they can be
considered secondary at all, are so only in him.   In Edwards
we see the utmost logical acuteness; in Barrow, wonderful
comprehensiveness; in Jeremy Taylor, the utmost opulence of
imagination; in Milton, its utmost sublimity.   In all these, and
many other minds, the glare of some overpowering faculty
makes the rest shine with feeble light, and, in some cases,

nearly quenches them altogether. But from the calm firmament of Howe's mind shine forth all the various faculties of the soul, each with its allotted tribute of light, and with a serene and solemn lustre. "One star," it is true, "differeth from another star in glory;" but none extinguish or eclipse the rest.

That disproportionate development of some particular faculty, which almost uniformly distinguishes great genius, is in general, we must admit, far more desirable, in a world like this, than a more harmonious adjustment of all its powers. By the mingling of the several elements of mental strength in different proportions, that endless variety, which is so characteristic of all the works of God, is kept up in the world of intellect; just as the ten thousand phenomena of the physical world all flow from the infinitely diversified inter-action of a few elementary principles.

None can doubt that, for a world like ours, such a conformation of mind is the most *useful* that can be imagined. Since all progress depends upon a minute division of labour; since we must be contented with less than absolute excellence, even when the whole powers of the mind are concentrated on a single point, and unremittingly exerted there; and since all can be happy only by each pursuing a different path to happiness; how necessary was it that every facility should be afforded for determining men's minds to different objects! This is effectually done by the prominence generally given to some one faculty. No sooner is the mind exposed to the various influences of active life, than this faculty, like the senses, finds an appropriate sphere of action provided for it.

If it be so rare to meet with a mind originally characterized by that harmonious adjustment of all its powers, which we have described as the peculiar excellence of John Howe; still more rare is it to meet with such a mind, when time has laid his touch upon it. Some disturbing forces almost inevitably destroy the equilibrium; the influence of circumstances determines its tastes and habits exclusively to some particular pursuits.

But though an unequal distribution of the mental faculties is necessary in a world like ours, and ordained for the wisest purposes, it is not in itself a perfection. It is true that such an exaggeration (if I may so speak) of some mental feature is more likely to attract the attention of mankind. This, however, is owing to the limitation of our faculties. Men, in general, are incapable of appreciating the more complicated forms of mental beauty. While the most unpractised ear, possessing any susceptibility for music at all, can enjoy some simple melody, how much knowledge, taste, and sensibility does it require, thoroughly to appreciate the complicated excellence of the compositions of a Handel or a Mozart,—

> " To untwist all the chains that tie
> The hidden soul of harmony ! "

To this strange passion for mutilated beauty, the world abundantly ministers, since, in the loveliest scenes of nature, as well as the least imperfect specimens of intellect, we discern only a few of the scattered elements of beauty and of excellence ; some of the lineaments are sure to be wanting.

But, to a superior being, capable of admiring the higher and more complicated forms of intellectual beauty, the overshadowing greatness of some particular faculty probably appears an imperfection; he may look upon it just as *we* look upon the remarkable exaggeration of some feature of the face—as a real deformity. The perfection of *animal* existence consists in the acuteness of all the senses, not in the unusual perfection of one to balance the defects of another. It is no adequate compensation to the deaf, that in general the eyesight of such is unusually penetrating. As man sustains such various relations both to God, to himself, and to the universe, that conformation of mind is the most perfect, which enables him to bring all his faculties into play upon their appropriate objects, with equal power and flexibility.

If it be so rare to meet with an individual whose mental faculties are thus admirably adjusted, the probabilities are greatly multiplied against our meeting them conjoined with the far higher qualities of religious and moral excellence. Who does not sigh over the frailties which, as they recur to the mind, cast their dark shadows over the otherwise bright disk of Bacon; and trouble, "as with a dim eclipse," the feelings of pure delight with which we were hailing and rejoicing in his beams? And even when no deep stain rests upon the character, how rarely has genius been adequately alive to the more elevated species of moral greatness! How often has it lived for nothing better than selfish knowledge, or a still more selfish reputation! How seldom has it consecrated its endowments, with a *distinct feeling* that this was its highest honour, to the glory of God and to the welfare of man! Yet, every now and then, just to illustrate the power of God, to show how his grace can ennoble our nature, to shame prostituted genius, to " adorn the doctrine" of Christ by proving that the most perfect specimens of humanity can count it their highest glory to do homage to the gospel, there appears, upon our world, some mind in which the various elements of excellence harmoniously meet, and are wrought into an exquisite form of beauty and of grandeur: a mind which, enjoying the happiest conformation of the mental and moral powers of which our imperfect and depraved nature is capable, and favoured with all the advantages of finished cultivation and a long and various discipline, is early subjected to the transforming and purifying power of Divine grace, beneath whose expansive and benigu influences it is seen, even while on earth, almost " putting off its mortality," and visibly ripening for the paradise of God. Such a mind was that of Howe.

His intellect was one of the few which conjoined in almost equal measure the highest attributes of the philosophical character; it was equally comprehensive and acute, possessed both of great range and great subtlety. These qualities cannot fail to strike any reader of his more elaborate works.

In his "Living Temple," in which he pursues Atheism through all the tortuous windings of its dark and subtle sophistry; in his " Treatise on the Divine Prescience," in which he has penetrated as far, perhaps, as ever was given to man, into that dusky region which skirts the confines both of the Calvinistic and Arminian systems; in his " Letters on the Trinity," a subject on which it is one of the highest achievements of a merely mortal mind not to fail, and to fail disgracefully,—

the generality of those who have presumptuously attempted to lift the veil from that great mystery, having been scathed and blasted by the ineffable vision,—in all these works, as well as in many of his sermons, any one capable of appreciating John Howe, will concede to him metaphysical acumen, little, if at all, inferior to that of Locke; a power of continuous and patient abstraction, and of searching, subtle analysis, which leaves no part of a subject unexplored. Indeed, he sometimes almost seems to accumulate difficulties, especially in the first part of his discourses, for the mere pleasure of demolishing them.

The *judgment* of Howe was such as might be expected from such qualities of intellect; and rendered yet more sound, by the fact that his noble qualities of intellect were conjoined with a moral temperament most enviably equable and serene.

In confirmation of the above remarks, it is sufficient to mention the following facts :—

His writings display a remarkable exemption from theological paradox and extravagance of all kinds. *There is hardly a sentiment in the many volumes which he has left behind him, which one would wish to blot out.*

They display in an equal degree an abstinence from what is the chief *source* of theological paradox, (especially to a bold and excursive mind,) unhallowed and presumptuous speculation.

His work on the "Trinity," the only publication in which there is even an approach to this audacious style of speculation, displays such a deep sense of the inexplicable mystery and awful grandeur of the subject, so much modesty and caution, such uncommon sobriety of mind, as effectually to shield him from the charge of dogmatism or presumption. Indeed, he seems to have written in the same cautious spirit which afterwards dictated the immortal "Analogy" of Butler. His principal aim appears to be, to show the too confident Unitarian, as that of the other was to show the too confident Deist, "that it is not so a clear thing" (to use the quaint language of Butler) "that there is nothing in it;" and that though (when the question is removed from the authoritative ground of Scripture) the orthodox cannot pretend to *demonstrate* that the doctrine of the Trinity is true, the heterodox would find it equally impossible to prove it to be false.

To refrain from pushing speculation too far, especially when such self-control is conjoined with that originality and inventive power of genius, which would seem to promise success, (if success be possible at all,) is in itself an indication of the highest style of mind. It is the prerogative of great genius, and of that alone, to know its limits; to understand what Locke calls "the length of its line," and to feel that there are numberless "depths in the ocean which it cannot fathom." Such men, by a sort of instinct, seem to discern the limitations which the Supreme himself has put upon the human mind, and which shut it in as between walls of adamant; and seeing this, they cease to exhaust their energies (bestowed for *practically* useful purposes) in vainly beating against the bars of their prison.

In his acute analysis of Robert Hall's mind, Mr. Foster mentions this same reverential silence on the subject of mysteries, as characteristic of that great man. While he acquiesces in the wisdom of such silence, he seems, with the love of speculation inseparable from a highly original and inventive mind, almost to regret "that Mr. Hall did not allow himself in some degree of exception." Mr. Foster's observations on this subject form one of the most beautiful parts of that noble piece of criticism.

Of the difference between first and second rate minds, in this point, there is an amusing instance in Boswell's "Life of Johnson." I do not recollect to have ever seen the passage cited to that end, and yet it is, in truth, the most exquisite specimen of *Boswellism* in the book. Speaking of the sensitiveness, or rather horror, with which Johnson avoided the discussion of the subject of predestination, Boswell says, "He avoided the question which has excruciated philosophers and divines beyond any other. . . . . He was confined by a chain, which early imagination and long habit made him think massy and strong, *but which, had he ventured to try, he could have snapt asunder.*" Boswell was incapable of seeing what

Johnson saw plainly enough, the insurmountable difficulties of the question. Johnson evidently possessed, in a high degree, the peculiarity of mind which I have attributed to Howe. No one can read his celebrated "Review of Soame Jenyns on the Origin of Evil," without being convinced of it. He could demolish with ease the flimsy hypotheses which others have constructed to solve that great mystery, but was too discreet to construct one of his own.

This very uncommon sobriety of judgment (manifested through life, and in every relation) is the more extraordinary, when we consider the *times* in which Howe lived, and the scenes in which he moved. He was one of Cromwell's chaplains, be it remembered. He lived in a period of unparalleled excitement, and with those upon whom that excitement acted most strongly; a time in which comparatively few quite escaped the contagion of fanaticism.

Some obliquities of judgment, or some rash speculation, or an enthusiastic mode of interpreting public events and the designs of Providence, or (where there was none of these) some extravagancies of manner, showed, almost everywhere, how the temper of the times had destroyed the equipoise even of the best-regulated minds. The lightest barque can keep its way in calm weather; but it must demand very uncommon ballast to steady the vessel in times like those of the civil wars and the Commonwealth. The majestic mind of Howe rode out the storm.

Another proof of the judgment of Howe, as well as of that harmony of mind of which I have so often spoken, was his exemption from those *eccentricities*, as they are called, which are so often associated with exalted genius, and which generally display themselves, either in a contempt for *little things*, —which are often of sufficient importance, however, to affect seriously the convenience of others,—or in some ludicrous peculiarities of appearance or manner. These are sometimes the effect of sincere negligence; and, perhaps, quite as frequently of affectation. To be forgiven,—in consideration of the nobler qualities which they may obscure, but assuredly cannot enhance,—is the utmost that ought to be demanded for them. Yet, strange to say, they are often the objects of admiring wonder, and even of sedulous imitation, to the fools who imagine, that because genius is often eccentric, eccentricities will establish a claim to genius. Now such eccentricities are, at best, infirmities, and not excellences; and in proportion as a mind is more perfect, in that proportion will it avoid them: it will not only think nothing beneath its attention which ought to be attended to, but be capable of adapting itself to the various demands of life, whether great or little, with Protean facility.

The *imagination* of Howe was such as might be expected from that harmonious and mutually subservient adjustment of all the faculties of his mind, which I have represented as his prime excellence. It was powerful and active, but not disproportionately so; lights up the page with a sober lustre, but never dazzles the reader; never seduces him into a forgetfulness of the argument. As regards the measure of its exercise, it is always under strict discipline. It is *used*, not *abused*; employed, as the imagination ought to be employed, to illustrate truth, not to overlay and encumber it with superfluous ornament. But the uncommon novelty, as well as beauty and grandeur of many of his illustrations, show, that of the two, Howe rather restrained than tasked its energies. That it was generally employed within such just limits,—not in excess, yet sufficiently,—is principally to be attributed to his being always engrossed with his subject. This absorption of mind is sure to stimulate the imagination enough to make it supply spontaneously those illustrations which will render a writer's meaning either more clear or more impressive, but leaves little leisure to search for curious or elaborate ornament, and this is just the position which the imagination ought to occupy.

The *character* of his imagination was in strict keeping with the general complexion of his mind. It was sublime rather than beautiful. Indeed, there are not a few passages in his writings, which would almost sustain comparison with some of the finest passages of Milton's prose works. It is true that the imagination of Howe does not possess the opulence and vastness of Milton's; but it is also true that such qualities would have disturbed that balance of all the mental faculties which distinguished Howe, and which required that his reason and his judgment should be as superior in vigour and accuracy to those of Milton, as the imagination of the latter was superior to that of the former.

Nor is it simply in the character of the imagination that these two great minds resembled one another; they resembled one another in elevation generally. There is, however, this remarkable difference between them. Howe's sublimity is uniformly that of *sentiment*, never that of *passion*; he is always calm and self-possessed. In consequence, we never see in him those bursts of impassioned feeling, with which the sublimest exercises of Milton's imagination are sometimes accompanied; that δεινότης, as the Greeks were wont to term it, which is perpetually flashing out in his prose writings. The heavenly placidity, the habitual repose of Howe's mind, were quite incompatible with such a display of the combined energies of intellect and passion; his spirit was "sphered" in too lofty and serene a region for it. The clouds and tempests in which the mighty spirit of Milton careered during the troubled period of his political life, rolled far beneath Howe. Still, in the loftiness of his conceptions, as well as *occasionally* in the majestic rhythm, the stately and dignified march of his sentences, the critical reader will detect no inconsiderable resemblance to Milton. I could illustrate my meaning by many noble passages from his "Living Temple;" but I shall content myself by referring to the celebrated description of the "human soul in ruins;" in which he pours forth his sublime, but melancholy musings, amidst the still magnificent remains of that once glorious dwelling of Deity.

Few men, however, possessed of so fine an imagination, have exhibited it to so little advantage. I do not speak merely of the mean and unseemly *attire* in which he has often clothed his noble conceptions: to this I shall advert presently. I now refer to the incongruities of *thought*, which so often impair the beauty of his finest illustrations,—to his broken metaphors, and his trivial allusions. Seldom has there been a criticism more just than that of Robert Hall—that "there was in Howe an innate inaptitude for discerning minute graces and proprieties." It is true that we sometimes meet with an image, not only surpassingly sublime and beautiful, but nobly sustained throughout. This, however, is comparatively rare. Such are his defects of taste, that his writings present us with few, if any passages *of considerable length*, that are not sadly enfeebled by the want of keeping and harmony.

These faults are aggravated by the extreme poverty of his diction, and ruggedness of his style. Such limited powers of expression, indeed, have seldom, if ever, been associated with so much opulence and grandeur of intellect. He not only dispenses with every elegance, but often degrades the noblest thoughts by the meanest phraseology.

The defects of which I am now speaking—I mean of diction and of style—affect, of course, not merely the exercises of his *imagination*, but those of his intellect generally. It may be said of all his conceptions, that they seldom have justice done them. The soil of his mind was abundantly fertile, and poured forth its productions with all the wealth and spontaneity of nature, but with all her negligence and wildness too. Slight indeed are the traces of cultivation. He constantly writes with the air of a man who has much to say, but is nearly indifferent as to how it is said. His thoughts and illustrations, generally, are clothed in attire so coarse and mean, that, if a certain innate grandeur and majesty did not proclaim their origin, we should never suspect them to belong to the rank and family of genius.

The toils of revision, on which elaborate excellence always depends, were generally neglected by the writers of that day; but Howe, it must be confessed, must have been far more negligent than were some of his contemporaries.

But though his power, generally, is greatly impaired by his gross deficiencies of taste and expression, it is his imagination which suffers most from them. This, indeed, must always be the case, as the imagination, more than any other mental faculty, depends for producing its due effect on the graces of language. A poverty of expression, a ruggedness of style, which might be borne in pure argument, may almost ruin the effect of poetical illustration.

With respect to *diction*, Howe's defects may be attributed in great part, no doubt, to negligence, but, I think, in still greater measure, to his very limited command of language. Thus, though we may often find solitary expressions singularly beautiful and original, he never sustains this excellence of diction beyond a minute or two. He almost immediately falls back into his ordinary baldness of phraseology.

If we pass from his diction to the *structure* of his composition, we find faults equally glaring. He is almost universally rugged and unmusical; full of involution, parenthesis, and awkward transposition. What was said of his diction may be said of his style. Though we occasionally meet with sentences full of majesty and rhythm, they scarcely ever extend beyond a short paragraph. His excellencies seem happy accidents; his faults and negligences are systematic and habitual.

As though the above defects of style were not sufficient, he has adopted a mode of *punctuation* as absurd as can possibly be conceived, and for which, so far as I at this moment can recollect, he had no adequate apology in the fashions of the age. He actually often comes to a full stop in the very career of his sentences, and fairly *throws* the luckless reader who is not acquainted with this vice of the author. In numberless instances, he has divided one complete sentence into not less than three or four periods. It is a great pity that the editors, even the modern editors, of Howe's writings have, in a great many cases, followed but too faithfully this eccentric system of punctuation. A complete revision, in this respect, would have rendered his writings abundantly more perspicuous, and tended greatly to abate that disgust which often besets the reader who for the first time sits down to their perusal.

On the whole, it may be said that very few writers have been less indebted for their reputation to language or style, than John Howe; if, indeed, we might not rather say, that his deficiencies in these respects have seriously lessened and impaired it; and that he has attained his present eminence not only without the aid, but in spite of the want, of such auxiliaries.

In these respects Howe presents a striking contrast to another of his great contemporaries: I mean Bates. I cannot but think that excellent man is mainly (I am far from saying wholly) indebted for his considerable reputation to the studied prettinesses of his style and diction. These, I regret to say, often appear so artificial, that the reader cannot help suspecting he is *trying* to sparkle. He is perpetually displaying the rings on his fingers. At the same time, it must be confessed, that his style is distinguished by great elegance and polish, when compared with that of Howe, or even of his contemporaries generally.

Unless the modern reader be fairly forewarned of the defects of style and manner which characterize not only the writings of John Howe, but those of many of his great contemporaries, he will be likely to turn away from them with disgust; and even if he be so forewarned, must expect to relish them only after repeated perusal. He must learn to look at what is sublime and beautiful in thought itself, abstracted from the forms of elegance and beauty in which he has often seen them embodied. Many have been so little accustomed to this effort of mind, have been so long habituated to look on the metal only after it has passed through the refining fires of the furnace, that they cannot admire the veins of precious ore which enrich the pages of our author.

And even those who do peruse his writings are liable, for want of such an attempt to rectify their judgment, to underrate most grossly his intellectual greatness. They understand him, it is true; but half the grandeur and beauty of his conceptions is lost upon them.*

---

* There seems something so paradoxical in the view here presented, not indeed of the inferiority of Howe's powers as a writer to his powers as a thinker, (for that must be obvious to every intelligent reader,) but in the *degree* in which it is here alleged to exist, that some might be disposed to demur to the strong language I have used. It certainly does seem strange, that one to whom such opulence and splendour of imagination are ascribed, should have wielded the great instrument of language with so little power, flexibility, and grace. I feel inclined, therefore, to fortify my own criticisms, by citing, though not for this reason only, the judgment of one who, in the little circle in which he was known —now, alas! growing every day less and less—was justly regarded as no slight authority. I allude to my beloved friend, J. M. Mackenzie, M.A., whose sudden death, encountered so heroically in the wreck of the Pegasus, off the coast of

That Howe was not totally destitute of *wit*, sufficiently appears from some instances of it recorded in the present volume, as well as from a few passages in his writings. It deserves to be considered, however, as the least conspicuous feature in his intellectual character.

Northumberland, nearly twenty years ago, excited a thrill of sympathy and admiration throughout the kingdom. His talents were of the most varied and brilliant order, and his knowledge more accurate and extensive than I almost ever saw in any one man. His versatility was such, that it enabled him to master almost everything to which he chose to apply himself; and his prodigious memory, which I never saw equalled, except in the case of the late lamented Lord Macaulay, and not surpassed even in him, enabled him to retain all he acquired. To knowledge, extensive and profound, of classical literature, he added an equally extensive and profound acquaintance with every department of our own. His critical judgment and acumen were such as to entitle any opinion of his to much weight. Among some fragmentary shorthand notes of his on a few of our English preachers, which lately fell into my hands, I find the following remarks on John Howe, in which he expresses, as strongly as I have done, the singular contrast between Howe's noble intellectual endowments and their inadequate exhibition in his works. I have pleasure in citing these remarks, not only for their own sake, but as it gives me the opportunity of thus honouring the memory of one who well deserves not to be forgotten.

"John Howe is, indeed, *clarum et venerabile nomen*, and his substantial excellence both of character and genius is of the very highest order. His intellect was in a most uncommon degree sound, penetrating, and comprehensive; his imagination was really magnificent; he had wit and learning in abundance; his theology was profoundly evangelical, and his piety as seraphic, perhaps, as that of any saint since the days of the apostles. All these qualities, of which I have given anything but an exaggerated description, tended to fit him for extraordinary effectiveness as a preacher; *but*, so far as the intellectual powers are concerned, success in preaching depends quite as much, perhaps more, upon what Sir James Mackintosh calls the *secondary* faculties of the mind, as upon the *primary*. And in these Howe was singularly deficient. He thought distinctly and methodically; but he wrote without any of that easy and perspicuous order for which the best French preachers are remarkable. He indulged to excess, like most of his age, in divisions and subdivisions; and even his sentences are generally as ill-constructed as total carelessness can make them. His diction is frequently poor, harsh, and clumsy, in a high degree; so that nothing but the transcendent vigour of his thoughts and sublimity of his imagination redeem his writings from being positively repulsive. A few exceptions to this last remark occur throughout his works, in which by some accidental felicity, the idea seems to have clothed itself in exquisitely beautiful language. The chief faults of his *sermons* are comprised in those already noticed; to which I must add, that he not unfrequently indulges in speculative discussions much too abstruse to be generally edifying to a promiscuous congregation. Still, the intrinsic merits of his mind and character were such, that he was a very acceptable preacher in his own day; and those who attentively study his works, will find them rich beyond description, in sound sense, conclusive reasoning, deep sentiment, just exposition of Scripture, pathetic appeals to conscience, and imagery of a most sublime kind. He was one of the many writers of his day who studied Plato and the Alexandrian school with, perhaps, too fond a partiality; but very many of his most beautiful illustrations are either drawn direct from these writers or strongly tinctured by their phraseology."

The severe rebukes which occasionally, and after much provocation, he could administer to extreme malignity and folly, would serve to show that he could have employed sarcasm with considerable effect; and that the almost perfect freedom from everything of the kind by which his controversial writings are so honourably distinguished from those of his age in general, is to be attributed, not to a want of *power*, but to the absence of *will.*

Calamy tells us, that in ordinary conversation he was "many times very pleasant and facetious." One or two instances of his "pleasantry," in addition to those which have been mentioned in the course of the narrative, will not be unacceptable to the reader. They afford, at the same time, fine illustrations of his judicious mode of administering reproof.

One day, when he was dining in company with persons of note, a gentleman at table thought proper to expatiate at great length on the merits of Charles I. Howe, observing that he frequently indulged in profane oaths, quietly remarked, "That in his enumeration of the excellencies of the prince he had undertaken to panegyrize, he had totally omitted *one*, which had been universally and justly ascribed to him." The gentleman was delighted to find Mr. Howe a witness in favour of the prince he had so much praised, and "was quite impatient to know what was the excellence which had escaped him." Howe suffered him to press for the information a little, and then told him, that "Charles was never known to utter an oath in his common conversation." It is pleasing to add, that the gentleman bore the reproof well, and promised to abandon the habit for the future.

At another time, as he was walking along the street, he came up to two persons of rank, who were engaged in a very angry dispute with one another. As he passed them, he heard them "damn" each other in a most vehement manner. On this, Howe taking off his hat, and bowing to them with great courtesy, said, "I pray God *save* you both." They were so struck with this salutation, that they forgot their anger, and joined in thanking him.

As a *preacher*, whether we judge from the discourses he has left behind him, or from the testimony of his contemporaries, Howe must have possessed very considerable powers. Still, the impression he produced is to be attributed, I apprehend, *principally*, to the intrinsic excellence of his matter, (equally valuable whether presented in books or sermons,) and to the earnestness, solemnity, and majesty of his manner.

The distinguishing characteristics of his genius were certainly not such as promise great oratorical excellence. Considered in this point of view, his principal defects are obvious. He was evidently too philosophical; too fond of metaphysical discussion, of refinement and subtlety. Often must his audience have been wearied out by the long trains of reasoning, and the abstruse speculations, in which he took so much delight. That this was the case, we may safely conclude from the fact, that, (though, for obvious reasons, such a disquisitory style is far more tolerable in a treatise than in a sermon,) even his readers often have cause to complain of the above peculiarities.

These peculiarities have, most undoubtedly, rendered some of the finest pieces of Howe less popular than they would have been, and, so far, less useful. The reader is apt to be wearied with so much preliminary skirmishing. Calamy tells us, that the same peculiarity marked his usual style of preaching; the first part of his sermons generally displaying great depth and reach of thought. They usually closed, however, in a strain level to the comprehension of the meanest, and with an earnestness and pathos in the application calculated to produce the deepest impression. Mr. Foster has remarked, that the very same peculiarities often distinguish Mr. Hall's sermons; nor is this the only point in which Howe and Hall resembled one another.

I have heard of a good woman who, having read some of Howe's pieces, showed her displeasure at the above-mentioned defects of method, by saying, that *"he was so long laying the cloth, that she always despaired of the dinner."*

From the mere faults which had their origin in the barbarous taste and uncouth fashions of the age, Howe was for the most part free. No one can charge him with an ostentatious display.

of his learning, or with an idle and pedantic introduction of scraps of Greek and Latin. Neither does he often indulge in the quaint conceits or the coarse and ridiculous allusions, which in that age were so general. The sobriety of his mind, and his strong sense of propriety, equally concurred to preserve him from such follies as these.

In one fault of the age, however, (as Robert Hall justly remarks,) he far outwent many of his most extravagant contemporaries—I mean, in minute and frivolous subdivision. We have sometimes *heads,* arranged rank and file, four or five deep.

It is astonishing that such a man as Howe, or indeed, that men every way inferior to him, should not have perceived the utterly unphilosophical character of all such divisions. To affix numbers to the few leading topics of a discourse, (and these must of necessity be few,) is all very well. It serves to indicate the great line of thought on which the speaker intends to march, and thus to assist the memory of the hearer. But if that division becomes intricate—if it consists of several *sets* of figures,—a more successful expedient for thoroughly and hopelessly bewildering the mind can hardly be devised.

If any would wish to see the full extent to which Howe carried this fault, they may look into the "Scheme" (a very accurate one) which his publishers prefixed to the first edition of the "Delighting in God." By the time the student has thoroughly digested that, he will find little difficulty, I apprehend, in mastering any theorem in the first six books of Euclid.

Though Howe's genius was not peculiarly adapted for oratory, the talents he did possess were diligently and successfully cultivated. The ministry of the gospel was not only his duty, but his delight; and he spared no efforts which might enable him to discharge it with success. Calamy tells us, " his ministerial qualifications were singular. He could preach offhand with as great exactness, as many others upon the closest study. He delivered his sermons without notes, though he did not impose that method upon others." I may remark, that all contemporaneous accounts represent his preaching as deeply impressive.

As a *controvertist*, the extracts from his reply to Stillingfleet, and other writings, already laid before the reader, show what his *spirit* was, better than any attempt of mine could do. Not only is his temper amiable, not only does he abstain from all sarcasm and invective; but he is equally distinguished by his candour and fairness—qualities which resulted scarcely less from the severely logical character of his understanding than from the operation of Christian principles. To him, victory was nothing; truth, everything. Thus, we never detect him in any mean subterfuge or shuffling evasion. His adversaries' arguments he strenuously endeavours not only to understand, but to exhibit in a fair and honest light. Indeed, if we except Locke and Jonathan Edwards, I do not think a more upright or single-minded controvertist is to be found.

As a *theologian*, the soundness of his judgment has already been adverted to, when speaking of certain intellectual peculiarities. So sober, so rational, and so comprehensive are his views of revealed truth, that, if it were right to take any mere mortal as a guide, it would be difficult to name one who would so seldom lead us astray. Not that his theological writings are devoid of originality; far from it; but it is the originality of a soundly philosophical mind, which never needs take refuge in dazzling paradox, or in mere novelty and extravagance of conception. *His* originality is shown, rather in presenting known truths under new and striking aspects—in pointing out the mutual connexion and harmony between them—or in ascending by analogical reasoning (often of an exceedingly felicitous character) from admitted truths, to sober and warranted conjecture respecting such as are uncertain. He is especially happy in pointing out the relations which the several parts of the Divine economy of the gospel bear to one another; their harmony as a system; and the *manner* in which, considered as a piece of complex moral machinery, they conspire to effect the great object to which they are subservient,—an entire moral transformation of the spirit of man.

In such disquisitions as these, he often turns to a good use his extensive acquaintance with ancient philosophy; especially the sublime speculations of his great favourite, Plato. Not that such speculations at all depraved his views of Christianity : they have, it is true, *tinctured* his habits of thought and expression, but they have done nothing more. The system he expounds is Christianity—simple Christianity still. When he availed himself of ancient philosophy, (to use the striking language of Spademan in his funeral sermon,) " he took care to wash the vessel, that it might be receptive of Divine communications."

But though Howe is quite at home in the profoundest speculations of theology, he seldom long loses sight of the elementary principles of the gospel. On these he best loves to expatiate, and to these he perpetually returns. Even in those pieces which were intended more particularly for the initiated—for those who had already crossed the threshold of the temple, he never fails to remind them of the terms on which they first sought and found admittance, and to inculcate, as the indispensable condition of all progress in the Divine life, an habitual recollection of the cardinal doctrines of the gospel. 'I scarcely know any discourse of his, however circumscribed the topic of which it treats, or however special the occasion which produced it, which does not contain a full, clear, distinct recognition of those fundamental principles on which rests the whole superstructure of evangelical truth.

It is necessary only to observe further, the singularly *practical* character of all Howe's theology. Even the most abstruse speculations, he manages somehow or other to imbue with this quality.* It is evident, indeed, that he habitually considered the knowledge of religious truth as totally worthless, if not subservient to holiness and virtue. " He did not look upon religion," says Calamy, with a felicity very unusual with him, " as a system of opinions or a set of forms, so much as *a Divine discipline*, to reform the heart and life." But on this topic I have already touched in the Introductory Chapter.

I have already had occasion to remark, that Howe possessed, in an unusual degree, the talents appropriated to active life. His genius was as eminently *practical* as it was *contemplative*.

---

* See, particularly, the first part of his " Living Temple."

It is here that many of the greatest minds have totally failed, either from some incurable defect in the mental conformation, or from long and exclusive devotion to abstract pursuits. There is either an excessive refinement of intellect, which produces an inaptitude for the less exact reasonings of practical life; or a sensitiveness of taste, which shrinks from contact with the vulgar; or a timidity and bashfulness, which recoil from the arduous conflict with human selfishness; or an impetuosity of character, which will consult no prejudices and brook no control. Thus unfitted for the world, and soon disgusted with it, they sigh for the luxuries of a studious solitude.

Howe well knew what it was to relish them too; the *tendencies* of his mind were towards the most elevated pleasures of intellect. His countenance proclaims it: and doubtless it was often with feelings which nothing but a paramount sense of duty enabled him to conquer, that he tore himself away from a life of delightful contemplation or of retired usefulness, to mingle with a turbulent and a selfish world. Yet when he did so, he was fitted for his task. Of prudence, he himself used to say, that "he was so far from doubting whether it was a virtue, that he counted imprudence to be a great vice and immorality." Of the consummate ability with which he must have conducted himself, no other proof is needed than the statement of the following facts;—that he was often employed in the most delicate affairs by Cromwell, yet without incurring either blame or suspicion, without displaying vanity or coveting power, without abandoning his trust or compromising his principles; well pleased to be employed, when his efforts might be useful, still better pleased not to be employed at all;—that, though exposed to the scrutinizing eyes of a baffled party, and not always agreeing with his own, (and when *not* agreeing, boldly saying so,) he left not a rivet of his armour open to the shafts either of malice or of envy;—that though sometimes imperatively urged to reprove even the most powerful and the most honoured, such was the weight of his character, such the esteem of his wisdom, and such the mingled dignity and prudence of his manners, that he could awe Cromwell into silence, and move Tillotson to tears;—and lastly, that he never made an enemy, and never lost a friend.

Let it be recollected that all this was unaccompanied by the slightest compromise of principle. This alone shows a rare assemblage of peculiar excellencies. His prudence was ever conjoined with integrity, the "wisdom of the serpent with the harmlessness of the dove."

When we consider this rare union of qualities, the rectitude which no sinister influence could warp, and the calm prudence which ever governed his actions, we need not wonder at what Calamy tells us, that Howe was often consulted in the most perplexing cases of *casuistry*. He was truly qualified to be a "*ductor dubitantium*."

When we turn from the province of intellect to that of sentiment and passion, we still find the same singular harmony and proportion. It was not with Howe as with many great men. Neither love of abstract science, nor unusual solidity of judgment, was incompatible with the warmest sensibility. This was as vivid as his intellect was strong. Both deficiency and excess of feeling, though not in equal degree destructive to repose of mind, imply an equal departure from the perfection of our nature. Howe was characterized by neither; his mind dwelt remote both from that tropical region of the passions, in which the soul is alternately scorched by heat and wrapped in tempests, and from that frigid zone, in which the sun of intellect may shine brightly, indeed, but like that of winter— with a cold and powerless gleam, and over regions of perpetual snow. In a word, the sensibilities of Howe were such as they ought to be, and what humanity need never be ashamed of; and *where* they ought to be, under the dominion of reason, itself purified by religion. Hear the just and beautiful language in which he himself denounces the absurd philosophy of those who pretend that the perfection of our nature consists in the extinction of the passions. The passage closes with an image of surpassing magnificence.

It is "right that we endeavour for a calm indifferency and dispassionate temper of mind towards the various objects and affairs that belong to this present life. There are very narrow limits already set, by the nature of the things themselves, to all the real objects and value that such things have in them ; and it is the part of wisdom and justice to set the proportionable bounds to all the thoughts, cares, and passions, we will suffer to stir in our minds in reference to them. Nothing is a more evident acknowledged character of a fool, than upon every slight occasion to be in a transport. To be much taken with empty things betokens an empty spirit. It is a part of manly fortitude to have a soul so fenced against foreign impressions, as little to be moved with things that have little in them : to keep our passions under a strict and steady command, that they be easily retractable and taught to obey; not to move till severe reason have audited the matter, and pronounced the occasion just and valuable: *in which case, the same manly temper will not refuse to admit a proportionable stamp and impress from the occurring object. For it is equally a prevarication from true manhood, to be moved with everything and with nothing : the former would speak a man's spirit a feather, the latter a stone. A total apathy and insensibleness of external occurrents hath been the aim of some, but never the attainment of the highest pretenders. And if it had, yet ought it not to have been their boast ; as, upon sober thoughts, it cannot be reckoned a perfection. But it should be endeavoured, that the passions, which are not to be rooted up (because they are of nature's planting) be yet so discreetly checked and depressed, that they grow not to that enormous tallness as to overtop a man's intellectual power, and cast a dark shadow over his soul."*

Of the manner in which he exemplified these just and beautiful sentiments, we have abundant proof in many impressive incidents of his life, and in the general strain of his writings.

It is a delightful spectacle to see great genius (dignified and elevated by extensive attainments) capable of unbending itself; of exhibiting all the charities of life ; and vindicating its connexion with our common nature by a vivid exercise of those sympathies which are as endearing as they are universal. Such traits are the more pleasing from the contrast in which they stand to qualities of a more lofty character. Discovered in such men as Howe, they impress us with the same kind of emotion which travellers tell us they have felt when they have suddenly come upon some sheltered spot of fertility and gentle beauty, blooming amidst the grandeur and sublimity of Alpine solitudes. Those who thus conjoin the lofty and the amiable, humbly imitate him who softens ineffable majesty with ineffable condescension; and that Great Example, in whom dwelt not only "all the fulness of the Godhead," but all the fulness of humanity.

It is true, that the expression of *feeling* is, in Howe, tempered by that severe judgment and that habitual dignity, which so eminently distinguished him. He is never, by any possibility, transported into extravagance or enthusiasm—if, by the last word, be meant what it is so frequently employed to denote—a manifestation of feeling disproportioned to the occasion. This self-control, however, renders indulgence of feeling (when it does occur) the more impressive, because we may be sure both that it is genuine, and that the importance of the occasion demands it. If the surface of Howe's mind was ordinarily unruffled, it was only an indication that the channel of its feelings was the deeper. That he was susceptible of the strongest feeling, and could express it with the deepest pathos, is proved by some exquisite letters of consolation which he has left behind him—more especially that to Lady Russell, shortly after the execution of her noble husband; —by innumerable passages of the most touching expostulation scattered through his works;—and by that deep and most heavenly compassion with which he often pours out his soul over the miseries of fallen and guilty man.

The letter to Lady Russell (which was not only private but anonymous, and therefore never intended to be known as his) is worthy of universal perusal. It was prompted by reports that the noble lady to whom it was addressed was in danger "of being swallowed up by over-much sorrow." Excessive grief had already begun upon her that petrifactive process which sometimes completely seals up the fountain of the affections and sensibilities. Even the consolations of religion, it was said, had partially lost their influence upon her. "She had gone to the sepulchre to weep there," and, like her of whom these words were written, she was in danger of forgetting "him who is the Resurrection and the Life."

With what gentleness, with what paternal tenderness, does Howe chide her excessive sorrow, while his accents, so to speak, seem to falter beneath the weight of his own emotions! What a spirit of purest, deepest sympathy, animates the consolatory truths which he so beautifully touches! How infinitely removed is his manner from the formality of professional condolence! And with what affecting pathos does he assure her, at the close, that he scarcely ever bent the knee "at the mercy-seat" without remembering her sorrows there!

But it is in the profoundly pathetic expostulations with which he often mourns and chides the madness and the guilt of men, that his soul reveals the depths of its sensibilities. Like Paul, he tells them, *even weeping*, that they are the enemies of the cross of Christ. Nothing can exceed the mingled dignity and tenderness which often distinguished his appeals: and hard must be that heart, which is not somewhat overawed by a majesty of manner so peculiar and impressive, and softened by a compassion so disinterested and so pure.

Illustrations of the above remarks, the reader will find in many portions of the "Living Temple," and in the "Redeemer's Tears, wept over Lost Souls;" in the latter incomparable treatise, particularly, Howe seems to have caught much of the spirit which animated his Divine Master on that sad occasion to which the discourse in question refers.

Allied to the excellence of which I have just spoken, and, indeed, only a further manifestation of the same spirit, is that enlarged and compassionate charity towards the infirmities and frailties of mankind,* of which some of the most excellent men have often possessed least. Ever in extremes, our nature is sure to distort, in some way or other, the features even of the divinest excellence. Thus, holiness itself is too apt to put on a harshness of tone, a coldness of mien, which, though it

---

* See this exquisitely exemplified in his beautiful sermon, on "Charity towards other Men's Sins."

covers guilt with shame, covers it also with despair, and compels it to feel, not only "how awful goodness is," but—how unattractive. In general, this is likely to be seen in men who have somewhat of that loftiness and purity of character which distinguished John Howe. Yet, in conformity with that wonderful principle of amalgamation, which combined in him qualities almost incongruous, his writings teem with the brightest displays of an opposite spirit; in him, goodness inspires as much love as veneration; he allures as well as awes; as he pleads for the majesty of truth, guilt not only stands abashed, but melted and softened by the unexpected exhibition of sympathy with its wretchedness. This should be a trait much coveted by every Christian minister; it is an imitation of Him whose immaculate purity did not prevent him from compassionating our sorrows; and who, "though without sin, can be touched with the feeling of our infirmities."

Of the exemplary manner in which he filled the various *domestic* and *social* relations of life, it is amply sufficient to point to the indications of enthusiastic love and veneration, with which almost every notice of him that has come down to us, however incidental, is full.

His humility, his modesty, his unambitious temper, cannot be better illustrated than by his conduct in public life. Great as his practical talents were, he never coveted the influence and the fame which would have been the certain reward of their energetic exercise. If honours came, they came unsought; and even then were endured rather than enjoyed. Well as he filled a public station, he felt that there was one which he not only could fill better, but which was infinitely more in harmony with the make of his mind and the habits of his life. It is evident from the whole tenour of his history, as well as from the air of sincerity which characterizes him, when touching on such subjects, that it was matter of sincere regret when he was called forth from the calm retreat of devotion and study, to fill a more public station. It is true, he complied; he complied cheerfully, because it was a duty; but only as a duty. He resembled the angelic messengers, so often mentioned in Scripture, who, when they visited earth upon the missions of heavenly benevolence, tarried as short a time as possible on our dark and troubled orb, and after fulfilling their commission, sped back again to the dwellings of serenity and love. How touching was the importunity with which he implored Cromwell not to separate him from his flock! How did he deprecate promotion, as earnestly as others would have sought it! And how sincere was the delight with which the pastor, once more free, returned to his early and humble labours! the same simple-minded man as before,—a man (rare excellence!) unchanged by prosperity.

Not that Howe,—for he was still true to what I have so often represented as the *ruling principle* of his character, and recoiled from every extreme, even when it was but an exaggeration of an acknowledged excellence,—not that Howe had any sympathy with that proud humility, which affects to consider the dignities and honours of earth as absolutely worthless. He did not, like the ascetic, undervalue them; he merely valued them at their proper price. He thought them of little worth, it is true; because he was perpetually contrasting them with what was of infinitely greater value. He was too sincerely engaged in the contemplation of the incorruptible and eternal, not to feel, when he turned to earth, that her brightest scenes shone only with a faded and tarnished lustre. There is one passage on this subject, so remarkably beautiful and touching, in his "Vanity of Man as Mortal," that I cannot resist the temptation to transcribe it.

"Thus also ought we to look upon secular honours and dignity; neither to make them the matter of our admiration, affectation, or envy. We are not to behold them with a libidinous eye, or let our hearts thirst after them; not to value ourselves the more for them, if they be our lot, nor let our eye be dazzled with admiration or distorted with envy, when we behold them the ornaments of others. We are not to express that contempt of them, which may make a breach on civility, or disturb the order and policy of the communities whereto we belong. Though this be none of our own country, and we are still to reckon ourselves but as pilgrims and strangers while we are here; yet it becomes not strangers to be insolent or rude in their behaviour, where they sojourn, how much soever greater value they may justly have of their own country. We should pay to secular greatness a due respect, without idolatry, and neither despise nor adore it ; considering, at once, the requisiteness of such a thing in the present state, and the excelling glory of the other : as, though in prudence and good manners we would abstain from provoking affronts towards an American sachem or sagamore, if we did travel or converse in their country, yet we could have no great veneration for them, having beheld the royal pomp and grandeur of our own prince ; especially he who was himself a courtier and favourite to his much more glorious sovereign, whom he is shortly to attend at home, could have no great temptation to sue for offices and honours, or bear a very profound intrinsic homage to so mean and unexpressive an image of regality."

It now only remains that I speak of the *piety* of John Howe. It was this which attuned the whole of that intellectual and moral harmony, of which I have been speaking. We have seen that he was gifted with the most various talents by nature, and these, too, in singular perfection ; and that they were improved by very finished cultivation, and a diversified discipline ; but it was religion that presided over all, determined each faculty to its appropriate objects, and regulated the measure of its exercise. It permitted none of them, if I may use such an expression, to break the ranks, but led them on in a stately and solemn march in the progress towards perfection.

None can study the writings, or, what is better still, the life of this truly great man, without feeling that his piety was of the very highest order ; that religion was his element ; that in communion with the supreme good, in a diligent preparation for a nobler state of being, in the contemplation of the future and the unseen,—he really found the highest pleasures of his existence ; that he had attained as complete an ascendency over sensual and animal nature, and as lofty an elevation above the world, as was ever vouchsafed to poor humanity. This, indeed, is the secret of that unclouded serenity, that repose of mind, which characterized his life.

His piety partook of the harmony which reigned throughout his character. It was remarkably free from the exaggerations

into which even some of the best of men have been betrayed.
He displays none of the *affectation* of contempt for the present
world, which is compatible with the utmost worldliness; nor
aims at a preternatural elevation of soul, which would imply
something more than human. In a word, he had nothing
either of the anchorite or ascetic in his composition. He
neither thought that earth was worth nothing, because heaven
was worth infinitely more, nor that religion could only be
founded on the ruins of humanity.

It may be said, indeed, that to be free from the extravagances of the hermitage and the cell is no uncommon merit.
But the *spirit* in which these extravagances originate is not
restricted to any particular communion; it is almost as universal as human nature; and it is a more rare thing than such
an objector would perhaps imagine, to find a piety, like that
of Howe, quite free from these and similar extravagances.

Some perhaps would demur to the statement that the religion of Howe was quite free from every tinge of enthusiasm;
and they would point, in justification of their doubt, to the
remarkable passages which were found inscribed on the blank
leaf of his study Bible. On these passages I shall offer a
single observation, merely remarking at present, that they
commence with expressions which indicate a soundness and
sobriety of religious sentiment, very inconsistent with the
character of an enthusiast. The passages are as follows :—

"Dec. 26, 89. Quum diu apud me seriò recogitarem, præter
certum et indubium assensum rebus fidei adhibendum, *neces-
sarium insuper esse vivificum quendam earundem gustum et
saporem, ut majori cum vi et efficacia in ipsissima cordis penetra-
lia sese insererent; ibidemque altius infixæ, vitam eo potentius
regerent; neque aliter de bono Deum versus statu conclusum iri,
sive sanum judicium posse ratum haberi*; cumque pro concione,
2 Cor. i. 12, fusiùs tractâssem, hoc ipso mane ex hujus modi
somnio dulcissimo, primò evigilavi: mirum scilicet à superno
Divinæ Majestatis solio, cœlestium radiorum profluvium in
apertum meum hiansque pectus, iufusum esse videbatur.

"Sœpiùs ab illo insigni die, memorabile illud pignus Divini
favoris, grato animo recolui, atque dulcedinem ejusdem iterum
atque iterum degustavi.

"Quæ autem Octob. 22, 1704, id genus mirandâ Dei mei benignitate, et suavissimâ Spiritûs Sancti operatione percepi, omnium verborum quæ mihi suppetit copiam, plane superant! Perquam jucundam cordis emollitionem expertus sum, fusis præ gaudio lachrymis, quod amor Dei per corda diffunderetur, mihique speciatim donato in hunc finem Spiritu suo. Rom. v. 5." *

Some may perhaps ask the curious question,—was the dream mentioned in the first paragraph naturally suggested by a holy and happy state of mind, (in this respect, following a well-known law of dreams,) or was it designed as a special disclosure of the Divine love and favour? If either of these suppositions could be established, they would reject the other. But the fact is, that these suppositions do not exclude one another. That there may have been nothing supernatural in any of the circumstances of the dream itself—that they may be all referred to the intervention of ordinary second causes—that there was no disturbance or suspension of the regular order of nature, may be admitted; and yet it will not follow from such admission, that the Divine Being did not *intend* this dream to be a special manifestation of his regard; unless it be first admitted, that he never will employ any combina-

---

* I subjoin Mr. Spademan's translation :—

"Dec. 26, 89. After that I had long, seriously, and repeatedly thought with myself, that besides a full and undoubted assent to the objects of faith, a vivifying, *savoury taste and relish of them was also necessary, that with stronger force and more powerful energy, they might penetrate into the most inward centre of my heart, and there being most deeply fixed and rooted, govern my life : and that there could be no other sure ground whereon to conclude and pass a sound judgment, on my good estate God-ward ;* and after I had in my course of preaching been largely insisting on 2 Cor. i. 12, ' This is my rejoicing, the testimony of a good conscience,' etc. ; this very morning I awoke out of a most ravishing and delightful dream, that a wonderful and copious stream of celestial rays, from the lofty throne of the Divine Majesty, did seem to dart into my open and expanded breast. I have often since with great complacency reflected on that very signal pledge of special Divine favour vouchsafed to me on that noted memorable day ; and have, with repeated fresh pleasure, tasted the delights thereof. But what of the same kind I sensibly felt through the admirable bounty of my God, and the most pleasant comforting influence of the Holy Spirit, on Oct. 22, 1704, far surpassed the most expressive words my thoughts can suggest. I then experienced an inexpressibly pleasant melting of heart, tears gushing out of mine eyes, for joy that God should shed abroad his love abundantly through the hearts of men, and that for this very purpose mine own should be so signally possessed of and by his blessed Spirit. Rom. v. 5."

tions of ordinary causes to conspire in such a result—an admission, by the way, which would go far to banish the doctrine of a providence altogether.

The devotion of Howe was one of the loveliest parts of his character. It was deep, habitual, and intense; it was not founded on a partial or distorted view of the Divine character, but was just the impression likely to be produced, by a harmonious perception of the various relations in which man stands to God under the gospel economy.

That the piety of Howe was as habitual as it was deep, that he applied it to every event of life, those most beautiful and affecting reflections, which he penned when deliberating at Antrim, whether he should remove to London or not, are a striking proof.

He, who could thus make every duty a matter of conscience, and lay bare his bosom to the searching inspection of the Spirit of God, could not fail to make rapid progress in the attainment of every species of excellence: since to obey implicitly the will of God is to act, in each case, from the noblest and the most exalted motives.

To recapitulate;—Howe seems to have been a combination of very various and, in some respects, almost heterogeneous excellencies, any one of which may have been seen in a greater degree somewhere or other, but have seldom been concentred in such perfection in one person. To the acutest powers of argument, and the finest talents for speculation, he conjoined a discriminating judgment, and shed around all, the light of a powerful and sublime imagination. He possessed talents which equally fitted him for a contemplative or an active life; and though the tendencies of his mind would have led him to the former as a matter of choice, he was capable of performing the most arduous services in the latter, when a matter of duty. To the most enlarged acquaintance with abstract science, he united a knowledge, not less profound, of human nature. In all transactions with the world, he exhibited a rare combination of prudence and integrity. In that most delicate task, the reproof of others, he was inflexibly faithful, yet always kind; and while he remembered what was due to the majesty of truth, never forgot what was also due to the claims of charity. He was frank, yet not rash; and cautious, yet free from suspicion. In his deportment, he knew how to conciliate elevation of character with the gentlest condescension, and the acutest sensibility. Dignified, but not austere, he was "grave without moroseness, and cheerful without levity." While he subjected all the inferior principles of his nature to the severe control of reason, itself enlightened by the Spirit of God, he was not so absurd as to attempt their annihilation; nor did the loftiest attainments of intellect interfere with the varied display of all human charities.

Above all, these qualities were crowned, or rather sustained and nurtured, by a deep, ardent, habitual, all-pervading spirit of piety; a piety which united burning zeal with the coolest judgment; the most intense desire for the glory of God, with ceaseless efforts for the welfare of man; the loftiest exercises of a deeply meditative and devotional spirit, with the sedulous cultivation of the homeliest graces; that rarest of all combinations—the closest communion with the future and the eternal, with a conscientious and busy discharge of all the duties of to-day. Such was John Howe: the rude elements of this various excellence were, indeed, bestowed at his birth; but it was the *power of the gospel of Christ*, and that alone, which developed and expanded them; which directed them to the noblest objects; which controlled, purified, and exalted them. As his reception of the gospel was an illustrious tribute paid to its truth, so his character and life were an emphatic exhibition of its power. That he had his faults, we are certain; for he was *man:* while all the excellencies he possessed, he would have been the first to attribute solely to the influence of the Spirit of God. That these were many, we may judge from the language of Spademan, his friend and coadjutor,—language already quoted, and worthy of being quoted again,—that "it seemed as though he was intended to be an inviting example of universal goodness."

CHAPTER XII.

ANALYSIS OF HOWE'S WRITINGS.

INTRODUCTORY REMARKS—HIS POSTHUMOUS WORKS—THE LIVING TEMPLE—THE TREATISE ON DELIGHTING IN GOD—THE BLESSEDNESS OF THE RIGHTEOUS—THE VANITY OF MAN AS MORTAL—THE TRACTATE ON THE DIVINE PRESCIENCE—THE CALM AND SOBER INQUIRY INTO THE POSSIBILITY OF A TRINITY IN THE GODHEAD—THE REDEEMER'S DOMINION OVER THE INVISIBLE WORLD—HOWE'S FUNERAL SERMONS, AND OTHER OCCASIONAL DISCOURSES.

IT is my intention, in the following remarks on Howe's writings, to confine myself to those pieces which he himself prepared for the press, and for which alone, therefore, he is responsible. These are contained in the two folio volumes of Calamy's edition.

Of his *posthumous writings*, as they are often called, a great part are not his writings in any proper sense. They are merely notes of some of his sermons, taken by some of his hearers who wrote shorthand, and published after his death. Those notes are, I acknowledge, in some respects valuable. They contain, here and there, thoughts worthy of the lips from which they fell. At the same time, it is obvious that the continuity of thought, which so greatly distinguished Howe, is often lost, the transitions from one topic to another are often exceedingly abrupt, and sometimes very different topics are confounded together. These are defects which will always be inseparable from such an inadequate method of preserving the discourses of a public speaker.

Though, therefore, the notes in question are of value, they are not to be placed on a level with the writings which Howe himself prepared for publication; and it would be unjust to make him answerable for them. This would hardly be fair, indeed, had they been faithful transcripts of the discourses in

T

question—since they were merely ordinary pulpit exercises, and not composed with the remotest idea of publication. Nor had any of his "posthumous works" been prepared by him for the press.

Almost all Howe's controversial pieces, (being so closely connected with his own history, and that of his times,) have already been the subject of remark. These are, his "Letter to a Person of Quality," in reply to Stillingfleet; his sermon on "Union among Protestants;" his two discourses on the "Carnality of Religious Contention;" and his tract on "Occasional Conformity."

The remaining works will be considered, not in the order of their publication, but according to their magnitude or importance. The circumstances under which they were severally composed have already been mentioned, and will not be alluded to in this portion of the volume.

Neither shall I make any remarks on peculiarities of style or manner—these points having been fully discussed, in considering Howe's character as an *author*.

The work which, in accordance with the principle of arrangement laid down, first demands our attention, is the "Living Temple." It is by far the largest, most important, and most elaborate, of all the author's publications. It was published originally in two parts, and at dates differing by an interval of nearly thirty years. The first appeared in 1676, the year after his return from Ireland—the second, in 1702.

The whole work professes to be "a designed improvement of that notion, that a good man is the Temple of God;" and forms, in fact, a system of theology,—an exposition of all the great principles of religion, both natural and revealed.

As the idea of a "Temple" obviously presupposes an object of worship, and the willingness of the Deity to hold intercourse with his worshippers, the author devotes the first part to an elaborate demonstration of the "existence and perfections" of God, and of his "conversableness with men."

It was certainly the ablest work on the atheistical and deistical controversies which had yet appeared.

The crisis at which the first part of the "Living Temple"

was written, was a most important one. It was but too evident that the controversial genius of the age was about to take an entirely new direction. The spirit of sceptical speculation was rapidly advancing. It continued to advance, till, at length, it boldly questioned all the fundamental principles both of ethics and theology.

Hitherto there had not been the remotest cause for apprehension from such a source. The danger, for at least many years after the Reformation, was rather of an opposite nature. Men so recently, and, in thousands of instances, so partially emancipated from a system of the most abject superstition, were far more likely to believe too much than too little, far more inclined to credulity than scepticism. If a faint whisper of infidelity was now and then heard, it was little heeded; the less so, that sceptics were compelled, out of deference to public opinion, and (to our shame be it spoken) from a dread of public punishment, either to conceal their doctrines in a learned tongue, or to disguise them, (an expedient which the apostles of sceptical schools have employed with singular adroitness from the remotest times,) in language which would not shock popular belief; to teach pantheism, like Spinosa, in the specious language of devotion; or deism, like Tindal, by representing "Christianity" to be "as old as the creation." Up to the middle of the seventeenth century, not a single English writer of any eminence had openly avowed a disbelief in Christianity, except Lord Herbert, of Cherbury, brother to that simple-minded and excellent man, George Herbert, the poet.

It was in reply to Lord Herbert, as well as to some other more obscure and less able writers, that Baxter composed his voluminous work on the Christian evidences.

When Howe published the first part of his "Living Temple," a very obvious change had taken place in the aspect of those controversies which respected the fundamental principles of theology. By this time, Hobbes and others had published their daring and presumptuous speculations.

To the rapid changes which had taken place in the aspect of the controversies in question, Howe alludes in the first chapter of his "Living Temple." The passage is one of uncommon force and beauty, and contains the following striking and characteristic observations on the probable connexion between the progress of scepticism and the rancour of religious contentions; and on the best mode of defending religion,—that of practically exhibiting it in its purity and glory :—

"Since matters are brought to that exigency and hazard, that it seems less necessary to contend about this or that mode of religion, as whether there ought to be any at all; what was said of a former age could never better agree to any than our own, that 'none was ever more fruitful of religions, and barren of religion or true piety.' It concerns us to consider whether the fertility of these many doth not as well cause, as accompany, a barrenness in this one.

      *   *   *   *   *   *   *

"Who fears to insult over an empty, dispirited, dead religion? which alive and shining in its native glory (as that Temple doth which is compacted of 'lively stones' united to the 'living corner stone') bears with it a magnificence and state that would check a profane look, and dazzle the presumptuous eye that durst venture to glance at it obliquely or with disrespect.

"The temple of the living God, manifestly animated by his vital presence, would not only dismay opposition, but command veneration also, and be its own both ornament and defence. Nor can it be destitute of that presence if we ourselves render it not inhospitable, and make not its proper inhabitant become a stranger at home."

In his attempt to demonstrate the existence and perfections of God, he does not restrict himself, as Clarke* has professed to do, or as Paley † has really done, to any one species of argument. Provided it be in his judgment sound, and can be rendered intelligible, he is content to avail himself of any argument, from whatsoever source derived; to prove one part of his propositions by one train of reasoning, and another by another. As to whether his arguments are uniform and homo-

---

* In his (so called) à *priori* demonstration.
† In his 'Natural Theology.'

geneous throughout,—a point about which Clarke is so curiously solicitous,—Howe is totally careless. He justly thought that the momentous character of the cause he advocated, as much required that he should not neglect any sound argument, as that he should reject every argument that was not sound ; that the magnitude and importance of the object justified him in pursuing it *"velis et remis."*

The first chapter is wholly introductory. In the second, he argues both " the existence of God and his conversableness with man," from "the general consent" of mankind. This consent, in accordance with the prevailing philosophy of the day, he appears to attribute to "innate ideas." The doctrine of *such* innate ideas, as it was the object of Locke to refute, (if any one, indeed, ever really held it) may well be rejected; but the argument for any truth, founded on *the universal belief* of mankind, remains precisely the same in force, whether we reject *that* doctrine or not. It is the universality of the belief which constitutes the argument, not the manner in which that universality may be supposed to be produced. Whether we admit, with the advocates of a better " doctrine of innate ideas," that such and such truths are congenital with the mind, and are involved with the very elements of its being; or simply say, that they infallibly commend themselves as true, to reason, as soon as reason is fully developed ; that is, that the human mind is so *constituted* that, as its faculties unfold, it will inevitably arrive at such and such conclusions,— the argument from *universal belief* is in either case just the same.

That the all but universal prevalence of a belief in a Deity —a belief which has prevailed throughout all ages and nations, and amidst every conceivable variety of prejudice, education, and civil polity; above all, which has been most generally cherished and most firmly held by the most enlightened communities of mankind, and if absent in any, absent only in tribes little raised above the brutes,—is a strong presumptive argument against the atheistic theory, must surely be acknowledged by any candid atheist, if, indeed, any such person is to be found. It is an instance, as Whately, in his Rhetoric, justly observes, of the argument from " progressive approach."

After having briefly but powerfully touched on this topic, our author proceeds to a more formal proof of the existence of God, whom he defines to be "an eternal, uncaused, independent, and necessary Being, that hath action, power, life, wisdom, goodness, and whatsoever other supposable excellency, in the highest perfection, originally in and of itself."

Before proceeding to insist on those arguments which appear to him most satisfactory, he gives his reason for declining to employ the methods of Descartes and others, alluded to in Cudworth's "Intellectual System," (as well as in Henry More's "Enchiridion Metaphysicum"); that is, of proving the existence of God from the very conception of him as an absolutely Perfect Being. This argument Howe, with characteristic judgment, rejects; not, as he affirms, that he thinks it might not, "in spite of cavil, be managed with demonstrative evidence," but "because some most pertinaciously insist, that it is, at bottom, a mere sophism:" he therefore, "without detracting anything from the force of it, prefers to go another way, as plainer and less liable to exception, though more circuitous."

I not only think Howe was right in rejecting such a species of argument, as likely to be absolutely unintelligible to the mass of readers, and of doubtful significance even to the most acute and the best instructed, but I must confess I cannot see its "demonstrative evidence" at all.*

It has often been supposed that what is called Clarke's *à priori* "demonstration" is based on a single principle, and is homogeneous and concatenated throughout.† Such a notion is not unnaturally suggested by the author's declaration,— "that he has confined himself to one only method or *continued* thread of argument, which he has endeavoured should be as near to mathematical as the nature of such a discourse would allow;"‡ or, as he yet more boldly expresses it in the

---

* The reasons I have stated elsewhere. Essay on Descartes.—*Ed. Review*, Jan. 1852.

† Dugald Stewart speaks on this subject as though the whole of the "demonstration" was but an elaborate exposition of *one* logically connected argument.

‡ Preface.

introduction, "one clear and plain series of propositions, necessarily connected, and following one from another." Such a representation, however,—though Clarke, who was a most honest controvertist, must have believed it in some sense true,—will hardly be received by those who will carefully analyse the piece for themselves. To such, his performance will plainly appear to be made up of *three distinct* trains of argumentation, two of them strictly *à posteriori*; and the other, the argument from the conceptions of infinite space and duration. This last is introduced in the "third proposition." But even this argument is not—what the whole demonstration has so often been styled—properly *à priori*. Indeed, no argument on such a subject can have any claim to such a title. To reason *à priori*, in the ordinary sense of those words, is to reason from the *cause* to the *effect*. Now, supposing the *argumentation* in the present case quite valid, it is plain it is not *à priori*; infinite space and infinite duration not being the cause of the existence of Deity, but only the cause of our knowing the fact. From this argument, I confess, whether called *à priori* or not, I could never derive the slightest satisfaction.

The argument is as follows:—Infinite space and infinite duration are real existences; as such, they are *either* substances or attributes: they cannot be the former; they must be, therefore, the latter. Attributes cannot exist *alone:* there must, therefore, be some substance of which they are properties, and in which they inhere! Here are no less than two or three propositions absolutely taken for granted; and these, too, on a subject on which we are least capable of speculating at all,—infinite space and infinite duration.

When, indeed, we have attained satisfactory proof of the existence of God on other grounds, one can easily conceive that the ideas of immensity and eternity will harmonize with the idea of such a Being; we seem instinctively to feel that he must be infinite;—that he fills infinite space and exists through infinite duration. But it is hard to conceive how the ideas of space and duration can form the *medium* of proof that God exists.

And even if it could be logically made out, that infinite space and infinite duration necessarily implied the existence of *some being*, of whom these were attributes, how would they prove the *intellectual* and *moral* perfections of such a being? Yet it is plain, that unless such attributes can be proved of God, Atheism is distinguishable from Theism only in name.

And here it is worthy of remark, that when Clarke proposes to prove the *intelligence* of this infinite First Cause, he openly, and in apparent forgetfulness of his professions "of having adopted but one method, and one continued thread of argument," abandons all the principles on which he had been before reasoning, acknowledging that the intelligent nature of the First Cause cannot well be proved *à priori*; and, therefore, recurring to the usual *à posteriori* argument from the traces of wisdom and design, of which the whole universe is full.

This forms *one* of the two trains of *à posteriori* reasoning, which I have said are to be found in this so-called *à priori* demonstration. The *other* is found in the first two propositions of the work, and is exactly similar to that on which Howe insisted in the second chapter of his "Living Temple," more than thirty years before: I mean the argument for "an eternal, uncaused, independent, and necessarily existent Being," from the admitted fact, that something exists *now*. This is plainly an argument from effects to their cause.

Instead, therefore, of Clarke's piece being what it aspires to be, one continued chain of reasoning, whereof every proposition depends on the preceding proposition, and all on one set of premises, it is in reality (what, indeed, in spite of all affectation of severe logical accuracy, every such work must be) a collection of inferences argued on different grounds, and by different methods. None of the reasoning, it is true, is *à priori* in the strictest sense: not even that which professes to demonstrate the existence of God from the ideas of infinite space and infinite duration; while the rest, as just said, consists of two distinct trains of strictly *à posteriori* reasoning; the one, proving the eternity and self-existence of God, and depending on the postulate, "that every effect must have a cause;" the other, his intelligence and wisdom, and depending on a similar postulate, "that whatever exhibits marks of design, must have had an intelligent author." These portions of the work, if taken separately, and considered as independent trains of reasoning, founded on independent premises, are abundantly clear and satisfactory. But these topics had been already frequently insisted on, and especially by Howe, in the work now under consideration. Whatever value may belong to these trains of reasoning, taken separately, it assuredly cannot be said that Clarke demonstrated the existence and perfections of God "in one continued thread of argument, or in one series of necessarily dependent propositions." It is this unwise claim which defrauds his work of much of the merit to which it would otherwise be entitled.

Clarke seems to have been betrayed into this error by that love of logical subtlety and scientific exactness, which his habits, as a mathematician, could not fail to inspire.*

Howe has fallen into no such error: he has wisely contented himself with proving the different parts of his great proposition, by different premises, and by different methods.—But to resume the exposition of his argument.

The principal part of the *second* chapter is taken up with an elaborate and very able exposition of the *à posteriori* argument for the existence of an "eternal, independent, uncaused, necessarily existent Being," as deduced from the fact that something exists *now*. That argument is simply as follows :—

1st. Since "something" exists *now*,—something must always have existed, unless we admit that at some period or other, "something" sprang out of "nothing."

2nd. Something or other must have existed from all eternity *of itself*, unless we are still prepared to embrace the absurdity above mentioned. This we must do, if we maintain that *all things* that have ever existed have owed their origin to *some-*

---

* Not only is Howe's general method preferable; he also anticipates most of Clarke's argumentation. It is well remarked by Dr. Doddridge, that if everything were abstracted from the "Demonstration," which had been already stated in the "Living Temple," the residue would be little indeed. From this it must not be supposed that Clarke plagiarized, but merely that he was to a great extent anticipated. Clarke, as already said, was not only an acute but an honest disputant.

thing else, since that something else would be of course included.

3rd. This something which has eternally existed of itself, exists necessarily; in other words, is of such a nature that it could not but exist.

4th. For similar reasons, it will never *cease* to exist.

5th. Whatsoever partakes not of this necessary, self-existent nature, must obviously owe its existence to that which does : unless we come back to the former absurdity, that something may spring from nothing.

The reasoning thus far is clear and well sustained, and the first part of the proposition established; that there is an *eternal, uncaused, necessarily existent something*, which is the primary cause of whatsoever is created, successive, and mutable. But then what is the character of this mysterious *something*? Is it a blind unintelligent agent, or is it invested with any intellectual and moral attributes? and if with any, with what? These questions, so far as the above reasoning goes, are left altogether undecided. Instead, therefore, of suspending on the chain a greater weight than it will bear; instead of attempting to educe (as Clarke promises to do, but really does not) the intellectual and moral perfections of Deity "from one clear and plain series of propositions, necessarily connected and following one from another," Howe wisely proceeds to establish the other parts of his proposition on other grounds.

In the third chapter, therefore, in which he affirms *intelligence* of this eternal and uncaused Being, he gives us a long, and, considering the defective philosophy of the age, a very masterly exhibition of the usual *à posteriori* argument, founded on the traces of wisdom displayed in every part of creation.

The force of this argument, as such, depends on the admission, that "whatever exhibits traces of design must have had an intelligent author." As the marks of consummate skill and wisdom displayed in the works of God are so obvious, even on the most superficial survey, and not only attract, but compel observation, it is impossible that God should ever be in this respect "without witness." Accordingly, we find that many of the same facts have been insisted on by all writers who have treated this subject, from Plato and Cicero, down to the authors of the "Bridgewater Treatises." Still, as the argument is perpetually *cumulative*, (for all the discoveries of science are but so many disclosures of the Creator's wisdom,) the degree of impressiveness with which the argument may be exhibited, will always depend, *cæteris paribus*, on the extent and accuracy of scientific knowledge. A writer of the present day, who should possess exactly the qualities which distinguished Paley,—the same perspicacity of mind—the same powers of reasoning—the same command of forcible and homely illustration—the same perspicuity and vigour of style—would possess far greater facilities for composing a work on "Natural Theology" than his predecessor; nor is it impossible that, hereafter, such a work as that of Paley may appear quite antiquated. As the great revolution which took place in the state of physical science during the seventeenth century, had only just commenced at the time Howe wrote, it was not to be expected that the argument should be treated with anything like the copiousness and splendour of illustration which distinguish many modern treatises. His scientific knowledge was comparatively limited, and, of course, by no means free from the prevailing errors of the time. The chapter on this subject, however, is distinguished by great comprehensiveness. In proof of this, it may be observed, that he has made much of the traces of design exhibited in the *constitution* of the human mind—a department which, until lately, has rarely been touched by writers on "Natural Theology." *

The manner, too, in which he states the *nature* of the argument from design, is exceedingly able. It is worthy of remark that, in doing this, he adopts the very same illustration with which Paley introduces his "Natural Theology."

The following sentences (and there is a much more minute application of the illustration in the context) may be read with interest on this account:

---

* Lord Brougham has remarked this in his work on the subject. He has also done much to supply the deficiency.

"That we may also make the case as plain as possible to the most ordinary capacity, we will suppose, for instance, that one who had never seen a watch or anything of that sort, hath now this little engine first offered to his view; can we doubt that he would, upon the mere sight of its figure, structure, and the very curious workmanship which we will suppose appearing in it, presently acknowledge the artificer's hand? But if he were also made to understand the use and purpose for which it serves, and it were distinctly shown him how each thing contributes, and all things in this little fabric concur, to this purpose,—the exact measuring and dividing of time by minutes, hours, and months,—he would certainly both confess and praise the great ingenuity of the first inventor.

* * * * * * *

"But surely such general easy reflections on the frame of the universe, and the order of parts in the bodies of all sorts of living creatures, as the meanest ordinary understanding is capable of, would soon discover incomparably greater evidence of wisdom and design in the contrivance of these, than in that of a watch or clock.

* * * * * * *

"And let them that understand anything of the composition of a human body (or indeed of any living creature) but bethink themselves whether there be not equal contrivance at least appearing in the composure of that admirable fabric, as of any the most admired machine or engine devised and made by human wit and skill. If we pitch on anything of known and common use, as suppose again a clock or watch, which is no sooner seen, than it is acknowledged (as hath been said) the effect of a designing cause, will we not confess as much of the body of a man?"*

---

* It is, perhaps, not very probable that Paley had seen Howe's illustration; if he had, he has abundantly made it his own. But he has been supposed to have *stolen* a like illustration, together with some others from Nieuwentyt, and a vehement, but most absurd charge of plagiarism was brought against him some years ago in one of our journals. I have replied to the charge against Paley elsewhere, and extract a few sentences; for we ought not lightly to let odious imputations of plagiarism rest on illustrious men who have deserved the grateful remembrance of all friends of truth and religion:—

"In fact, it is absurd to charge Paley with plagiarism for having selected matter from other writers; his whole work proceeds on that supposition; it is the manner in which he has employed his materials (in themselves commonplace enough), that stamps his work as original. The facts of science he deals with he did not *discover;* he knew perfectly well that he must be indebted for

This chapter also contains an excellent refutation of the Cartesian doctrine, "that animals are mere machines;" and a long, and, in some parts, rather jocose refutation of the "atomic theory of Epicurus." The humour, it must be confessed, is somewhat unwieldy, and contrasts strangely with the usual gravity of the author. He himself seems not a little surprised that he should have been betrayed into this extraordinary fit of pleasantry, for he closes the argument with an apology for it.

The fourth chapter is an attempt to demonstrate, from the propositions previously established, *the absolute perfection and infinity* "of the eternal and self-existent Cause;" and I confess that, considered in a *purely logical* point of view, certain portions of it are to my mind the most unsatisfactory in the whole work. They are so for the same reasons which render all merely human speculation on the transcendental subjects of the "Infinite" and "Absolute" unsatisfactory. In Howe's day, however, seeming success was more easy than it would be now. Sundry metaphysical axioms would then be accepted, or at least not be denied, which would now be thought pre-

---

every one of them to others. But the same charge of plagiarism might be brought against any formal treatise, either of science or history, for nine-tenths of the substance of it must exist in previous writers. Such charge, if it had any force at all, might much more reasonably be brought against Paley for the use he has made of Derham and Ray; for he is more indebted to these than to the Dutchman. But he who is at the trouble of comparing them with Paley will soon find that though the materials must of necessity be much the same, the interval is wide enough to leave Paley's originality in all that is really claimed for him unquestionable.

"We have no hesitation in saying that if, out of Nieuwentyt's three ill-compacted volumes, Paley had evoked such a work as his 'Natural Theology' by selections, by rejections, by condensation, by re-arrangement, and by diffusing over the whole the vivid lights of his vigorous mind and style, his claims to originality would have suffered as little abatement as that of Shakespeare (on whom a similar charge was once fastened), because in a few of his plays he has condescended to make use of materials of inferior dramatists, and turned, by his magic touch, their lead into gold.

"The truth is, as just said, that the merit of Paley's work is that of having wrought materials, open to everybody, into a beautiful fabric; and to blame him that his materials were got from other quarters, is much as if it were charged upon a great architect that his stone was not of his own quarrying, nor his bricks of his own burning.

"The impress of Paley's very peculiar mind is on this work, as on all the rest, and would alone show that it was no plagiarism, unless all of them be so."—*Encycl. Brit.*, art. *Paley*.

carious or futile. I cannot think that the conclusions (though most true) strictly follow from the premises; or, indeed, that they can be absolutely proved by anything short of revelation. That the great *First Cause* must possess power and knowledge, wisdom and goodness, to the extent displayed in his works; that, even if we were to stay here, these attributes appear to be great beyond all conception; that there is no reason whatever why we should conclude them limited; that it seems more probable that they are *without* limit;—all these points will be most readily conceded; but they do not amount to strict proof that the Author of the universe is absolutely infinite.

Not that this can ever make the slightest difference in *our* relations to him, even if revelation had not decided the point. Whether we can prove God to be absolutely infinite, or not, it is plain that a being who has power and wisdom to the overwhelming extent displayed in the works of creation, would justly demand from his creatures the profoundest adoration and reverence. We are *nothing* relatively to him, and therefore, to use the language of mathematics, he is infinite relatively to us, whether we can demonstrate his *absolute* infinity or not. On this subject Howe has some sublime and eloquent observations in a subsequent chapter.

In the same chapter also he attempts to prove the absolute *unity* of God. I must confess my inability to see that this follows conclusively from the propositions already established; or, indeed, from anything but the book of Revelation. To prove, in absolute strictness of logic, that there is only one necessarily existent Being, passes, I think, the power of the unaided intellect of man. If it be granted that there is one self-existent Being, mere reason would find it difficult to demonstrate that there could not be more than one. It is of no avail to say that all but that ONE who created the universe must have been eternally inactive; it might be plausibly said, first, that more than one such Being might have conspired in the creation of the universe; or, secondly, that since we must suppose all creation to be finite, there was in infinite space scope enough for many separate creations of a plurality of self-existent Beings; or, lastly, that if only one had evinced his power and wisdom by external manifestations, the supposed eternal inactivity of other self-existent Beings is but the condition in which, as far as human reason can conjecture, that One must also have existed when "he inhabited eternity" alone. He, too, as far as we can perceive, must have dwelt in eternal solitude before the work of creation began. If it be said that more than one such Being could not be omnipotent, reason might suggest that it sees not why there should not be more than one Omnipotent in the only sense in which we use the term; that is, possessing power to do all things which do not imply a contradiction,—as, for example, to destroy that which is *necessarily* self-existent: similarly, that it does not see any contradiction in more than one such Being possessing unlimited wisdom and goodness, as well as power. Such a supposition would merely suggest the idea of perfect consentaneousness of purpose and of action; nay, it might perhaps suggest the possibility of some such transcendental truth as that of the Trinity, but would not prove the impossibility of there being more than one self-existent Being. In short, the subject. is beyond the compass of a finite mind, and devoutly as we believe the unity of God from revelation, no philosophical demonstration that we have seen is wholly satisfactory. When Robert Hall, in his "Sermon on Modern Infidelity," dismisses the question by saying, "It is sufficient to observe that the notion of more than one Author of nature is inconsistent with the harmony of design which pervades her works, that it solves no appearance, is supported by no evidence, and subserves no purpose but to embarrass and perplex our conceptions," we have no difficulty at all in acquiescing in his conclusion; but if given as a proof of the absolute unity of God, it must be pronounced unworthy of so logical a mind, and evasive of the real difficulties of the problem. The greater part of theologians, we apprehend, would now concede that for certainty on this subject we must come to revelation.* The sophism, sometimes used, that there can only be one *neces-*

---

* Some able remarks on this subject will be found in the *Quarterly Review* for March, 1826. The utmost that the speculations of antiquity achieved in this direction is there dispassionately stated.

sarily existent Being, because the supposition of one is all that is *necessary* to explain the phenomena of the universe, is, I suppose, likely to impose on no one, who is even moderately on his guard against the ambiguities of language. But though the argumentation of this chapter is not absolutely conclusive, it displays, in every part, conspicuous subtlety and acuteness. If it does not fully convince, it at least shows the hazards of denying the conclusion.

The fifth chapter is one of the most original and best reasoned in the whole work. It demands of the Atheist, whether—if he will reject all the preceding evidence for the existence of God—there are any conceivable methods by which the fact (conceding it be true) could be certified to us? Supposing this question answered in the affirmative, Howe proceeds to examine all the other methods of certifying the great fact, at all conceivable to human reason; and then proves that they would every one be open to stronger objections, and would on the great scale be less convincing, than the evidence which the Atheist has already rejected as insufficient. Thus he compels him to adopt the strange conclusion, that, if there *be* a God, it is, so far as we can conceive, *impossible* that his existence should ever be adequately ascertained to us !

The sixth and last chapter is well worthy of comparison with anything of the kind that has ever appeared. It is in proof of the *second* proposition with which he had set out— "God's conversableness with men." It is principally directed against the system of Epicurus, who, while admitting the existence of gods, was too devout, or rather too polite, to trouble them even to create the world, much more to superintend its concerns. Leaving all this to his fortuitous concourse of atoms, he graciously permitted his deities to enjoy an eternity of happy indolence !

But, though professedly directed against this absurd system, the principal part of Howe's reasoning applies with equal force, and some of it with greater, to those systems of deism, which, admitting the existence of a *Creator* of the universe, excluded him, for very obvious reasons, from all inconvenient share in the administration of its affairs. He made the world, and then abandoned it! These systems were not fully developed in Howe's day, nor, indeed, till the age of Bolingbroke, whose superficial genius was suitably employed in defending such a shallow theory.

The origin of such systems it is not difficult to conjecture. Their authors thus hope to get rid of the logical difficulties which press every modification of the atheistic theory, and, at the same time, to secure that liberty from moral restraints which nothing less than the expulsion of Deity from his throne can insure them. So long as they can secure that, these sovereign arbiters, these *makers* of their Maker, are willing to behave with the most magnanimous generosity! They consent to commute his sentence from death to banishment. They do not absolutely prohibit his existence; they merely forbid him to appear on earth, on the peril of being again resolved into a nonentity! Thus, while affecting to consult the ease of Deity by relieving him of the irksome and sordid cares of universal empire, they are in reality only intent upon their own. Such men are theists in name, and atheists in reality; or, as Cicero well said, "*verbis reliquerunt deos, re sustulerunt.*"

At the conclusion of this chapter, Howe proceeds to assert the omniscience, omnipotence, immensity, and unlimited goodness of the Deity. Some parts of his reasoning on these topics, considered purely as *reasoning*, are vitiated by their dependence on the argumentation of the fourth chapter, that is, on the reception of some of those metaphysical axioms, especially in relation to the infinite, which would not now be so readily conceded. In that chapter, he endeavours to demonstrate, by unaided reason, that GOD is "absolutely perfect and infinite." Assuming that this has been done, he proceeds to prove some of the attributes above-mentioned by a rather summary process: something in this way,—"It has been proved that GOD is absolutely perfect; none can doubt that foreknowledge is a perfection; he therefore has it.—It has been proved that he is infinite; his foreknowledge therefore extends to everything future." These remarks, however, only apply to some portions of the reasoning; very much of it is truly admirable.

The *second* part of his "Living Temple," as already stated, did not make its appearance till 1702; that is, nearly thirty years after the publication of the *first*. During that interval had appeared the "Ethics of Spinosa," a posthumous publication, in which alone, of all his writings, the author has given an undisguised exposition of his opinions. In that work, as is well known, Spinosa affirms that there is but *one* substance throughout the universe, the two great properties of which are, thought and extension; this he represents as God; consequently, every part of the universe partakes, in some mysterious way, of the Divine nature! This system combines in itself all the difficulties of Pantheism and Atheism.

It is obvious that, so far as religion is concerned, "it little matters," to employ the language of Howe, "whether we make *nothing* to be GOD, or *everything*; whether we allow of no GOD to be worshipped, or leave none to worship him." He adds, "Spinosa's attempt to identify and deify all substance, attended with that strange pair of attributes, extension and thought (and an infinite number of others besides), hath a manifest design to throw religion out of the world that way."

Against this system of Spinosa, as well as against that of a French writer, who, in a work professedly written in refutation of the "Posthumous Ethics," had defended the dangerous doctrine of a "necessary self-existing matter," Howe addresses himself in the first two chapters of the "Second Part."

The name of the French writer, Howe intimates, was not unknown to him. But he has kept it secret: "he would not divulge," he tells us, "that which the author seemed desirous to conceal." The title of the work in question is "L'Impie Convaincu." *

The arguments of John Howe on this subject are acute and cogent. If they are not entirely satisfactory, if the reader is disposed to think that the discussion sometimes becomes a *νυκτομαχία*, it is certainly for no want of subtlety in our author; but partly from the suspicion that some of the metaphysical

---

* It is attributed (Fabricius *Script. Vet. et Rec. pro Veritate Relig*. p. 359) to *Aubert de Versé*. Another work on the same subject, with a very similar title ("L'Impiété Convaincue,") was written by Pierre Yvon. (*Ib*. p. 344.)

axioms assumed on either side are by no means *axiomatic*, and lead only to logomachy; and partly from the congenial darkness in which pantheistic speculation naturally enshrouds itself. Controversy here is somewhat like a battle in a subterranean cavern.

Having dismissed these topics in the first two chapters, and given, at the beginning of the third, a brief recapitulation of the "First Part," he proceeds to the ulterior objects he contemplated in the work.

Before he could go further, it was obviously necessary to establish the authority of the book of Revelation. One would have thought that having spent so much time in proving the fundamental truths of *all* religion, he would have insisted with proportionable copiousness on the evidences of Christianity. He contents himself, however, with a very short, though very able summary of the principal arguments on which the truth of revelation rests, referring the reader for more ample satisfaction to Grotius' "De Veritate," Stillingfleet's "Origines Sacræ," and Baxter's "Reasons of the Christian Religion," all of them now superseded by innumerable works of greater power and comprehensiveness.

This leaves him at liberty to enter, without further delay, on his great design in this second part; an exposition of the sublime scheme the gospel reveals for the restitution of the now desolate "Temple" of Deity.

By way of appropriate introduction, he calls us first to contemplate this "Temple in Ruins."

The depravity of man he proves from the testimonies of Scripture, and from the actual and notorious condition of the whole race. He confirms his reasoning by many striking passages from the works of heathen writers: and here his extensive acquaintance with ancient philosophy is displayed to great advantage.

The close of this chapter is undoubtedly the most eloquent portion in the whole work. In the frequently quoted and memorable passage, in which he describes the human soul in ruins, there is not only beauty in the conceptions, and great power of expression, but a mournful rhythm in the sentences, exquisitely adapted to the sentiments, and contrasting strongly with our author's too frequent ruggedness. For example :—

"That he hath withdrawn himself, and left this his temple desolate, we have many sad and plain proofs before us. The stately ruins are visible to every age, and bear in their fronts (yet extant) this doleful inscription : 'HERE GOD ONCE DWELT.' Enough appears of the admirable frame and structure of the soul of man to show the Divine presence did sometime reside in it; more than enough of vicious deformity to proclaim he is *now* retired and gone. The lamps are extinct; the altar overturned : the light and love are now vanished, which did the one shine with so heavenly brightness, the other burn with so pious fervour. . . . Look upon the fragments of that curious sculpture, which once adorned the palace of that great king; the relics of common nations; the lively prints of some undefaced truth ; the fair ideas of things; the yet legible precepts that relate to practice. Behold! with what accuracy the broken pieces show these to have been engraven by the finger of God ; and how they now lie torn and scattered, one in this dark corner, another in that, buried in heaps of dirt and rubbish. There is not now a system, an entire table of coherent truths to be found, or a frame of holiness, but some shivered parcels. And if any, with great toil and labour, apply themselves to draw out here one piece, and there another, and set them together, they serve rather to show how exquisite the Divine workmanship was in the original composition, than for present use to the excellent purposes for which the whole was first designed. . . . You come amidst all this confusion as into the ruined palace of some great prince, in which you see here the fragments of a noble pillar, there the shattered pieces of some curious imagery, and all lying neglected and useless amongst heaps of dirt. He that invites you to take a view of the soul of man gives you but such another prospect, and doth but say to you, 'Behold the desolation ! All things rude and waste.' So that, should there be any pretence to the Divine presence, it might be said : 'If God be here, why is it thus ?' The faded glory, the darkness, the disorder, the impurity, the decayed state in all respects of this temple, too plainly show the great inhabitant is gone. . . ."

Many other passages, however, are almost equally impressive and eloquent; what, for example, can be more beautiful than the following description of that glorious felicity to which man was originally destined and invited?

"It was a most delectable and pleasant state, to be separated to the entertainment of the Divine presence; that, as soon as man could first open his eyes, and behold the light and glory of this new-made world, the great Lord and Author of it should present himself, and say, 'Thou shalt be mine.' How grateful a welcome into being! 'Thee, above all my works, which thou beholdest, I choose out for myself. Thine employment shall be no laborious, painful drudgery; unless it can be painful to receive the large communications of immense goodness, light, life, and love, that shall, of their own accord, be perpetually flowing in upon thee! Whatsoever thou espiest besides, that is even most excellent and pleasant to thy sense, is yet inferior to thee, and insufficient for thy satisfaction and highest delight, and but the faint shadow of that substantial fulness which I myself will be unto thee.'"

The remaining chapters are entirely taken up in the prosecution of his main object—an exposition of the great system of moral restitution which Infinite Wisdom and Benevolence have devised. No reader can fail to be impressed with the clearness, the comprehensiveness, and the self-consistency of Howe's doctrinal views,—the thorough knowledge he seems to possess not only of the peculiarities of the gospel system, taken separately, but of their mutual coherence and harmony, and of the manner in which they severally conspire to the attainment of those sublime purposes for which they were revealed. On such topics as these he loved to expatiate.

The most striking and valuable portions of these chapters are, his description of the Incarnate Messiah; his acute defence of the doctrine of the atonement, in reply to the oft-reiterated charge, that it is inconsistent with equity;* his delineation

---

* In the following passage he forcibly puts the argument that to account for the sufferings of the perfectly holy and innocent Messiah is made abundantly more difficult by denying the Atonement. "The loud clamours wherewith some later contenders have filled the Christian world on this subject make it fitting to say something of it, and the thing itself needs not that we say much. We do *know* that the *innocent* Son of God was crucified; we know it was by God's

of the character of Christ, as the *archetype* of the character to which that of every Christian must ultimately correspond, or the *model-temple*, in harmony with which every other temple of the heart is to be reared; his exposition of the necessity of spiritual influences; of the laws and methods by which they are dispensed; and of the manner in which they conspire with all the moral means and instruments with which Divine Wisdom has been pleased to associate them.

Throughout this noble performance, as well as in all his other writings, Howe abundantly justifies the remark of Calamy, that he did not consider "religion so much a system of doctrines, as a Divine discipline, to reform the heart and life." His practical views of its nature and design are perpetually manifesting, I had almost said, *obtruding* themselves. That, at least, is the word I should have used, if the introduction of such topics could, in such works, have been at any time inappropriate. Even amidst the most purely speculative and disquisitory portions of the "First Part," he is perpetually interspersing important practical reflections, and reminding the reader that speculative truth is of value only as it tends to form the heart to virtue.

He concludes the work with referring his readers to the three sermons on "Self-dedication" and on "Yielding ourselves to God;" which, indeed, though published on very different occasions, and at distant periods, form a sort of continuation of the subject.

The treatise of "Delighting in God," though largely infected with the vices of Howe's style and manner, is one of the most valuable works on practical religion in our language. It is

---

determinate counsel; we know it was for the *sins of men*, which the adversaries, in a laxer and less significant sense, deny not, though it must by no means be understood, say they, as a *punishment* of those sins; we know many of those sinners do finally escape deserved punishment. The truth of these things, in fact, is disputed on neither side. All these, then, are acknowledged reconcilable and consistent with the justice of God. What then is to be inferred? Not that the things are not so; for that they are is acknowledged on all hands. What then? That God is unjust? Will their zeal for the expiation of God's justice admit of this? No: but it is only unjust, ' to count this suffering of his Son a punishment.' That is, it is unjust he should suffer for a valuable and necessary purpose; *not*, that he should suffer needlessly, or for no purpose that might not have been served without it!"

founded on those words of the Psalmist, "Delight thyself also in the Lord, and he shall give thee the desires of thine heart."

Like the "Living Temple," it is divided into two parts. The first explains the *import* of the precept; the second enforces the *practice* of it.

He introduces the work by a clear and forcible statement of the great relations which the Divine Being sustains to the renewed soul of man—as "a Lord to be obeyed, and a Portion to be enjoyed," and of the "sufficiency and communicableness of that good," which, more especially under the latter of these aspects, He cannot but impart. He then enters at large into the nature of that "Divine communication" (in itself accompanied with "delight") which must render God an *object* of delight, and on which, as respects depraved and fallen man, the very susceptibility of such delight depends. This topic he copiously treats under the following heads. The communication implies, he tells us,—I. "An inwardly enlightening revelation of God to the mind." II. "A transforming impression of his image." III. "The manifestation of the Divine love to the soul in particular."

Under the first of these heads, he has some just and philosophical observations on the far greater influence which even the most limited knowledge of religious truth will exert on a devout and pious mind, than the most accurate religious knowledge on the most comprehensive intellect, if destitute of real piety. He shows, that the greater *vividness* of conception, consequent on a moral renovation of heart, will impart a power to truths imperfectly understood, of which the clearest and most capacious understanding, without such Divine preparation, can know nothing.

In this part of the work he has the following striking observations on the difference of vividness between the intellectual apprehension and the moral appreciation of religious truths. "There is a certain acceptableness in some truths (necessary to their being received in the love thereof), which is peculiarly so represented to some as that their apprehension is clear and vivid beyond that of other men; who, however they have a representation of the *same things*, yet have not the *same re-*

presentation." He then illustrates the obstruction which a depraved heart presents to the due apprehension of practical truth, by a magnificent image—in fact, an image identical with that by which Burke illustrates the condition of atheists: yet how feeble is Howe's expression in comparison! "God," says Burke, "never presents himself to their thoughts but to menace and alarm them. They cannot strike the sun out of heaven, but they are able to raise a smouldering smoke that obscures him from their own eyes." The expression in Howe is less worthy of the thought; but we must (as I have said) learn to look at his thoughts abstracted from the graces of language. The passage is as follows : " For a vicious prejudice blinds their eyes ; their corrupt inclinations and rotten hearts send up a malignant, dark, and clammy fog and vapour, and cast so black a cloud upon these bright things, that their tendency and design is not perceived. . . . Against which poisonous cloud God's own glorious revelation directs its beams, dissolves its gross consistency, scatters its darkness. . . ."

Under the second of the above heads, he enters largely on two of his most favourite topics,—the great *transformation* which passes on the spirit of the Christian man, and on the *delight* which that transformation necessarily brings with it. With characteristic rapture he dwells on the extent of this transforming influence ; as diffusive over the whole nature of man ; as affecting all the principles and passions of the soul ; as "rectifying" us in relation to God, to ourselves, and to our fellow-creatures.

Under the third of the above heads, he tells us, that he does not mean any "*enthusiastical assurance ;*" or "such a testification of the love of God to the soul, as excludes any reference to an external revelation, or the exercise of our own enlightened reason and judgment thereupon; or wherein these are of no use, nor have subservience thereto:" but "such a manifestation as is always in accordance with the Divine word, and ordinarily employs that as its instrument." He denies, however, that it can be proved that " God *never* doth immediately testify his own special love to holy souls, without

the intervention of some part of his external word, made use
of as a present instrument to that purpose, or that he always
doth it in the way of methodical reasonings thereupon." His
observations on this subject are exceedingly cautious and
modest, and contain nothing at which sober piety or sound
philosophy can be in the slightest degree justly offended.

The whole of the remarks on the latter part of this head are
full of genuine Christian philosophy. They are far too long
to insert, but are well worthy of the devout and attentive
perusal of every Christian.

Having thus largely insisted on these Divine communications (themselves attended with delight), which are necessary
to render God an object of delight to man, and man susceptible of taking delight in God, he proceeds to explain the
nature of the delight itself. This delight, in a phraseology
not very perspicuous, though the thought itself is beautiful,
and is beautifully illustrated, he divides into " explicit" and
implicit ;" the former he considers as consisting in direct acts
of contemplation, and communion with God ; the latter, as
latently insinuating itself into all the movements of the soul;
accompanying the exercise of all its faculties ; "lying folded
up," as he powerfully expresses it, "in acts and dispositions
which have another more principal design ;" and spreading
and diffusing a gladdening and happy influence over the whole
contexture of the Christian's occupations and enjoyments.

The Second Part, as already said, treats of the *practice* of
the precept enjoined in the text.

In conformity with his explanation of the twofold *nature* of
the delight itself " as explicit and implicit," he tells us, that
he shall treat the *practice and exercise* of delight as " a thing
adherent to the *other* duties of religion, and as a *distinct duty*
of itself."

Under the former of these, he insists at great length on the
following points, that " we are not to rest, or let our practice
terminate, in any religion which is not *naturally and in itself*
delightful ; and are to seek after and improve in that which is."
After laying down some rules for directing our judgment on
the subject, he gives a masterly delineation of various kinds

of *spurious* religion, as indicated by the absence of that great quality of delight which must ever characterize the *true*; and, in a series of very impressive reflections, rebukes the folly of resting in any such systems of religion.

In this part of the treatise occur some observations which remind one of the celebrated passage in which Butler shows that "going over the theory of virtue in one's thoughts, talking well and drawing fine pictures of it, is so far from necessarily or certainly conducing to form a habit of it in him who thus employs himself, that it may harden the mind in a contrary course." Similarly, Howe shows that the "delight" taken in a merely "notional" or speculative apprehension of religious truth is not only most perverse, but full of danger.

"That religion," he says, "is not duly delightful which consists wholly in revolving in one's own mind the notions that belong to religion, without either the experience or the design and expectation of having the heart and conversation formed according to them. So the case is with such as content themselves to yield the principles of religion true, and behold with a notional assent and approbation the connexion and agreement of one thing with another, but do never consider the aim and tendency of the whole. . . .

"When this is never considered, but men do only know, that they may know, and are never concerned further about the great things of God than only to take notice that such things there are offered to their view which carry with them the appearance of truth, but mind them no more than the affairs of Utopia, or the world in the moon; what delight is taken in this knowledge is surely most perverse. There is a pleasure indeed in knowing things, and in apprehending the coherence of one truth with another; but he that shall allow himself to speculate only about things wherein his life is concerned, and shall entertain himself with delight in agitating his mind in certain curious general notions concerning a disease or a crime that threatens him with present death, or what might be a remedy or a defence in such a case, without any thought of applying such things to his own case, or that the case is his own, one may say of such pleasure, "it is mad," or of this delight, "what doth it?" Or he that only surfeits his eye with beholding the food he is to live by, and who in the meantime languishes in the want of appetite, and a sickly loathing of his proper nutriment; surely such a one hath a pleasure that no sober man would think worth the having. And the more any one doth only notionally know in the matters of religion, so as that the temper of his spirit remains altogether unsuitable and opposite to the design and tendency of the things known, the more he hath lying ready to come in judgment against him; and if, therefore, he count the things excellent which he knows, and only pleases himself with his own knowledge of them, it is but a like case as if a man should be much delighted to behold his own condemnation written in a fair and beautiful hand; or, as if one should be pleased with the glittering of that sword which is directed against his own heart, and must be the present instrument of death to him. And so little pleasant is the case of such a person in itself, who thus satisfies his own curiosity with the concernments of eternal life and death, that any serious person would tremble on his behalf at that wherein he takes pleasure, and apprehend just horror in that state of the case whence he draws matter of delight."

The latter part of the treatise, in which he insists on the "practice and exercise of delight, considered as a distinct duty in itself," is wholly hortatory. Much of it is conceived in the noblest spirit of hallowed eloquence; especially the passage in which, while inciting professed Christians to aspire to a more heartfelt and vivid enjoyment in religion, he calls them to contemplate the devout raptures with which the saints of old were wont to kindle, and to contrast with those exhibitions of almost seraphic ardour the cold and languid devotions of the generality of Christians.

Near the close of the work occurs a striking image, which has probably unconsciously suggested a beautiful sentence in one of Archer Butler's sermons. Speaking of the duty of cherishing humility as a condition of the soul's communion with God, Howe says, "His 'light and glory' shine with great lustre in the eyes of such a one, while there is not a nearer imagined lustre to vie therewith; stars are seen at noon by them that descend low into a deep pit." The parallel image in Archer Butler occurs in his "Sermon on the Syro-phœnician Woman." " Men, from deep places, can see the stars at noonday, and from the utter depths of her self-abasement she catches the whole blessed mystery of heaven. Like St. Paul's Christian, 'in having nothing she possesses all things.'"

This work is, beyond most others, even of Howe, disfigured by minute division and subdivision. There is hardly a single page that is not broken up into two or three formal *heads*. This, together with the meagreness of expression and ruggedness of style, renders it almost as repulsive in manner as it is valuable in matter. But the thoughts will well repay the patience expended on a careful perusal.

" The Blessedness of the Righteous," first published in 1668, was ushered into the world by a recommendatory preface from Richard Baxter. Though the work is seriously disfigured by the same fault of intricate arrangement, which detracts so much from the merit of the treatise I have just noticed, it evinces more care in the composition than almost any other of the author's productions. This may perhaps be accounted for by the fact, that it was his first important publication. On this, authors usually bestow more care, since they cannot as yet presume on their reputation.

The treatise is founded on those words of the Psalmist, " As for me, I will behold thy face in righteousness : I shall be satisfied, when I awake, with thy likeness."* Like the "Delighting in God," it appears to be the substance of a series of sermons preached to the people at Great Torrington.

The first chapter is wholly introductory. It opens with some natural reflections on the folly of supposing man created only for the present life. They contain, in fact, the germ of his noble discourse on the " Vanity of Man as Mortal," which, as so closely connected with the subject of the present treatise, was subsequently bound up with it.

The author next enters at some length into the criticism of the text. His close examination of the various readings, and of the different versions, gives a favourable idea of his talents as an expositor of Scripture.

---

* Psalm xvii. 15.

As this treatise is, in fact, a disquisition on heaven, the character of its inhabitants, their preparatives for entering it, and the nature of its occupations and enjoyments; and as the comprehensiveness of Howe's mind would not permit him to leave any topic untouched which ought to be insisted on,—it would perhaps have been quite as well had he abandoned his *text* altogether, and recast the whole discourse in a new form. It would have facilitated a more natural and simple arrangement, and would have prevented the attempt (in which he imitated the frivolous ingenuity of the day) to find everything in the text.

In the second chapter, he proceeds to distribute the principal topics of discourse. These are, the *subject*, the *nature*, and the *season*, of the blessedness to which the text adverts. To the consideration of the first of these this chapter is devoted.

The righteousness which is to qualify for heaven, he, of course, affirms, cannot consist in sinless obedience to the moral law, that being impossible to depraved man. He tells us, " that it can be understood to be nothing but the impress of the gospel upon a man's heart and life; conformity in spirit and practice to the revelation of the will of God in Jesus Christ; a collection of graces exerting themselves in suitable actions and deportment towards God and man." This part of the work contains some admirable observations on the relations in which man stands to the moral law under the economy of the gospel, and the position which that law occupies in the constitution of that economy. He shows that, while the gospel provides an ample remedy for man's violation of the law, or his defective obedience to it, it still considers that law as the rule of his conduct, and aims ultimately at bringing him into complete subjection to it.

In the third chapter, our author enters on the second consideration, the *nature* of this blessedness. This he represents as consisting in "the vision of God's face, in the assimilation to the character of God, and in the satisfaction resulting thence." These "ingredients" he then proposes to consider separately and in conjunction; or the manner in which the first contributes to the second, and both to the third.

In treating of the "vision of God's face," he maintains the probability that there will be some external manifestation of the Divine glory adapted to the refined organization of the glorified body. Such a manifestation, he justly observes, cannot be imagined to belong to the "*being* of God;" but he contends that it may serve as " some umbrage of him, as a man's garments are of the man, which is the allusion of the Psalmist in those words, 'Thou art clothed with majesty and honour; thou coverest thyself with light as with a garment.'"

May we not, from the representations of Scripture, justly conclude, that such an external representation of the Divine glory will be afforded in the person of Him, "in whom dwelleth all the fulness of the Godhead bodily?"

He reasonably maintains, however, that what is principally intended by the "vision of God's face," is the contemplation of his attributes, as seen in all their harmony and beauty; as stamped on all his then perfect works—works possibly studied and inspected, not only with a far more penetrating glance, but on a far vaster scale and under widely different aspects,—and as illustrated by that providence, the perplexities of which, time, or rather eternity, will have unravelled: when the clouds which obscure our vision shall have rolled away, and many of the mysteries which now overhang the universe and all the works and ways of God, shall fill the rapt mind with the profoundest adoration, and dissolve it in ecstasies of delight and wonder.

In this part of the work is introduced a long marginal digression, in which he exposes, with just severity, the absurd and presumptuous speculations of many of the schoolmen respecting the nature and effects of the beatific vision. Such speculations were equally offensive to his reason and to his piety; more especially when translated, (as he tells us they had been,) by some contemporaneous writers out of the uncouth dialect of the schoolmen into a more vulgar tongue, for the benefit of "modern enthusiasts."

In the fourth chapter, he explains the nature of "that assimilation" to the Divine character, and that perfect "satisfaction" of soul, of which the text speaks. The former he describes as a resemblance to God in every species of communicable excellence, whether natural or moral; but more especially moral; the latter, as that perfect repose of soul, which must follow the enjoyment of perfect good,—the fruition of every hope, and the gratification of every desire.

The next six chapters the author devotes to an ample consideration of the *relation* which these "three ingredients of future happiness" hold to one another; or, the manner in which the contemplation of the Divine glory contributes to an assimilation to the Divine character; and both, to the perfect felicity of heaven. These topics,—the practical influence which the contemplation of moral excellence must exert on the habits and dispositions of the soul, and the felicity which such a transformation of character necessarily brings with it,—were particularly grateful to him. Here, therefore, we might expect to find him at home; and he has, in truth, amply justified every expectation that might be formed of him.

In the discussion of the first of these topics, or the manner in which the contemplation of the Divine glory tends to produce a resemblance to the Divine character, he introduces some most philosophical observations on a very favourite topic, —one which he had evidently often and deeply revolved,—the reciprocal action of the understanding and the will.

The happiness of heaven, so far as it will flow from the "vision of the Divine glory," he attributes partly to the *nature of the objects* contemplated,—embracing the whole circle of the Divine perfections; and partly to the *very acts of the mind*, (then performed without sense of weariness,) by which this contemplation will be carried on.

The blessedness of heaven, so far as it results from an "assimilation" to the character of God, he illustrates by showing, 1st. What that resemblance "involves;"—a felicity arising both from the resemblance itself and from the happy consciousness that such resemblance is possessed; and 2nd. By what it "disposes and tends to;" eternal union and communion with God.

The tenth chapter treats of the *season* of this "blessedness." Here he contends with the generality of orthodox divines, and in clear accordance with the whole tenour of Scripture, that the soul *enters* upon its career of immortal felicity at the dissolution of the body, though the consummation of its blessedness is reserved till the resurrection.

He has adduced the principal texts of Scripture which sustain this view, and argues from them with great cogency. He especially urges the words of the apostle when he expresses a wish to "depart and be with Christ" as "far better." "How strangely mistaken and disappointed," says our author, "had the apostle been, had his absence from the body set him further from Christ!" It may be added, that if Paul did not fully believe that to die was to be in conscious communion with Christ, he would surely have preferred to remain in imperfect communion on earth than dwell in unconscious slumber till the resurrection. "But now," says Howe, speaking of the Christian's dying hour, "now is the happy season of the soul's awaking into the heavenly vital light of God; the blessed morning of that long-desired day is now dawned upon it; the cumbersome night-veil is laid aside, and the garments of salvation and immortal glory are now put on. It hath passed through the trouble and darkness of a wearisome night, and now is 'joy arrived with the morning,' as we may be permitted to allude to those words of the Psalmist, though that be not supposed to be the peculiar sense. It is now come into the world of realities, where things appear as they are; no longer as in a dream or vision of the night. The vital quickening beams of Divine light are darting in upon it on every side, and turning it into their own likeness. The shadows of the evening are vanished, and fled away." He adds, "It is the glory of a Christian to live so much above the world, that nothing in it may make him either *fond* of life, or *weary* of it:" a sentiment he frequently expresses in various forms; nowhere more strikingly than in the words, "We ought to be patient of the body, not fond of it." The brevity and point are worthy of an ancient aphorism.

The remaining ten chapters of this noble work are devoted to an extensive "improvement" of the whole subject. Those from xiv. to xvii., but especially the last, are remarkable for that close, earnest urging home of the claims of religion, that faithful probing of the soul, which so often distinguishes the Puritan writers; which chiefly sprang from their being so thoroughly in earnest themselves, and which still renders them, in spite of diffuseness, tediousness, and formal divisions, among the most valuable writers on religious subjects. Even the most careless readers often find their earnestness infectious, and more impressive than the manner of far more polished authors. Seldom have the sophisms by which conscience cheats and juggles with itself been more faithfully exposed than in the seventeenth chapter. But they all contain passages of impressive, and often impassioned, eloquence; and indicate, in every part, the exalted conceptions the author had formed of that blessedness of which he had been treating; the powerful manner in which the contemplation of it had already tended to transform his own nature; the aspirations of soul with which he panted for it, and his earnest desire that others should partake it also.

"The Vanity of Man as Mortal" is closely connected with the subject of the preceding treatise. It is founded on those words of the Psalmist, "Remember how short my time is; wherefore hast thou made all men in vain?" It is a most felicitous and original train of reasoning, the object of which is to prove that, unless we suppose the nature of man immortal, and that this life is but the initiatory scene of his existence, we can imagine no adequate *object* for which the present system of things was projected. He affirms, that if we exclude the idea of a future state, there is nothing in the condition of such a being as man, nothing in an eternal succession of such beings, which can render their creation worthy of the wisdom and goodness of Deity, or, rather, which is not inconsistent with both; since, on such a supposition, a creature would be formed totally unfit for the sphere to which he is limited—filled with desires which cannot be gratified—endowed with faculties which cannot be adequately employed—and capable of forming conceptions of a happiness which he is destined never to realize. He conclusively shows, that none of the forms of merely earthly good (even if we dismiss the consideration of their *transiency*) are at all commensurate with the lofty aspirations and the boundless desires which fill the soul of man. He further shows, that if we suppose *religion* the prime element of good, the *summum bonum* destined for such an ephemeral . creature, this would only increase the difficulty; since the Divine Being would be supposed to have created a being expressly for pleasures which this world can but imperfectly furnish, and for objects which can only be realized by that very immortality from which he is debarred.

On the hypothesis, therefore, that man is merely mortal, there would be an evident and lamentable disproportion between the faculties with which he is endowed, and the sphere he is destined to occupy;—an absurdity of precisely the same kind, though it may not be so glaring, as if the capacities of an angel had been deposited in some ephemeral insect, to perish in the very day which gave them birth! What would this be, but a prodigal waste of the power of God, and a gross reflection on his wisdom and benevolence?

It is evident, therefore, that this hypothesis leaves this lower universe an incomprehensible enigma.

Mysteries there are in the proceedings of Providence, whatever theory be adopted; but in *such* a theory they are not only multiplied and aggravated, they are rendered hopeless. The very possibility of any solution is excluded. In the view of a Christian, death is the period for which the solution of these mysteries is reserved; if there be no future state, it seals them up in eternal darkness.

This species of argument (together with another, on which this discourse does not touch—I mean the necessity of some great day of *retribution*) form perhaps the strongest proofs of the doctrine of a future state which mere human reason can supply.

I have made a brief extract from this noble discourse in the preceding chapter. One or two more will not be unacceptable to the reader. It is thus Howe combats the notion that the acquisition of knowledge can be the adequate end of " man," if " mortal." After showing its limitation and its transiency, he thus insists on the fact that " increase of knowledge is also increase of sorrow," on which he descants in a spirit not unlike that of Pascal, nor unworthy of him.   It is, he says—

"Increase of sorrow, both because the objects of knowledge do but increase the more man knows; do multiply the more upon him, so as to beget a despair of ever knowing so much as he shall know himself to be ignorant of, and a thousand doubts about things he hath more deeply considered, which his more confident, undiscovered ignorance never dreamt of or suspected; and thence an unquietness and irresolution of mind, which they that never drove at any such mark are, more contentedly, unacquainted with;—and also, because that by how much knowledge hath refined a man's soul, so much it is more sensible and perceptive of troublesome impressions from the disorderly state of things in the world : which they that converse only with earth and dirt have not spirits clarified and fine enough to receive.   So that, except a man's knowing more than others were to be referred to another state, the labour of attaining thereto, and other accessory disadvantages, would hardly ever be compensated by the fruit or pleasure of it.   And unless a man would suppose himself made for torment, he would be shrewdly tempted to think a quiet and drowsy ignorance a happier state."

The supposition that *religion* can be the designed end of "man," if *only* "mortal," he rebuts by a most admirable series of arguments, of which we have space only for a fragment.

"To think every time one enters that blessed presence, 'For aught I know, I shall approach it no more; this is possibly my last sight of that pleasant face, my last taste of those enravishing pleasures!'—what bitterness must this infuse into the most delicious sweetness our state could then admit!   And by how much more free, and large, grace should be in its present communications, and by how much any soul should be more experienced in the life of God, and inured to Divine delights, so much the more grievous and afflictive resentments it could not but have of the approaching end of all, and be the more powerfully tempted to say, 'Lord, why was I made in vain?'"

On the spirit in which it becomes one really convinced that

man is not "mortal" to conduct himself in this world of shadows, he descants thus grandly :—

"It can surely no way become one who seeks and expects the 'honour and glory which is conjunct with immortality,' to be fond of the airy titles that poor mortals are wont to please themselves with ; or to make one among the obsequious, servile company of them whose business it is to court a vanishing shadow, and tempt a dignified trifle into the belief it is a deity; to sneak and cringe for a smile from a supercilious brow, and place his heaven in the disdainful favours of him who, it may be, places his own as much in thy homage,—so that it befalls into the supplicant's power to be *his* creator, whose *creature* he affects to be. What eye would not soon spy out the grossness of this absurdity? and what ingenuity would not blush to be guilty of it? Let then the joyful expectants of a blessed immortality pass by the busy throng of this fanciful exchange, and behold it with as little concern as a grave statesman would the sports and ludicrous actions of little children, and with as little inclination of mind as he would have to leave his business and go play with them; bestowing there only the transient glance of a careless or a compassionate eye, and still reserving their intent, steady views for the 'glorious hope set before them.' And with a proportionable unconcernedness should they look on and behold the various alternations of political affairs; no further minding either the constitution or administration of government, than as the interest of the Universal Ruler, the weal and safety of their prince or country, are concerned in them. . . . But that lofty soul that bears about with it the living apprehension of its being made for an everlasting state, so earnestly intends it, that it shall ever be a descent and vouchsafement with it, if it allow itself to take notice what busy mortals are doing in their—as they reckon them—grand negotiations here below; and if there be a suspicion of an aptness or inclination to intermeddle in them to *their* prejudice to whom that part belongs, can heartily say to it, as the philosopher to the jealous tyrant—'We of this academy are not at leisure to mind so mean things; we have somewhat else to do than to talk of you.' He hath still the image before his eye of this world vanishing and passing away; of the other, with the everlasting affairs and concernments of it even now ready to take place and fill up all the stage; and, can represent to himself the vision,—not from a melancholic fancy or crazed brain, but a rational faith, and a sober, well-instructed mind,—of the world dissolving, monarchies and kingdoms breaking up, thrones tumbling, crowns and sceptres lying as neglected things."

Robert Hall, it is well known, was an enthusiastic admirer of this discourse. He was in the habit of frequently preaching a sermon on the same subject, and from the same words, which he was often, but in vain, solicited to publish. On one occasion, he replied to the importunity of a friend, by candidly saying, "that he would find it all in John Howe." After his death, the outline of this beautiful sermon appeared, from the copious and accurate notes of the Rev. Thomas· Grinfield.* Most of the thoughts, though not all, are in Howe's discourse; and the general resemblance throughout is most evident.

It is singular that, though this discourse of Howe's was composed with more haste than almost anything that he ever wrote,† it is perhaps, as a whole, the most eloquent of all his productions.

The treatise on "Divine Prescience," was written at the request of the Hon. Robert Boyle, and appeared, as I have already mentioned, in 1677. It has also been mentioned, that Wood, totally mistaking the great design of the work, represents the author as a "great and strict Arminian." I believe many other persons, far more likely to be skilled in metaphysical theology, have supposed that it is principally taken up with some of the points immediately at issue between the Calvinists and the Arminians; whereas it is, in fact, an attempt to solve a difficulty with which both parties, or at least the moderate of both parties, are equally liable to be pressed; that is, all who admit, on the one hand, the absolute *certainty* of the Divine foreknowledge,—no matter what may be their hypothesis as to the *mode* of that foreknowledge,—and, on the other, the responsibility of man,—no matter in what they make his responsibility to consist. That difficulty is,—to

---

* Hall's Works, vol. vi.

† See an account of the circumstances in which it was produced, in the fifth chapter.

reconcile the *certain foreknowledge* of the Deity with his *wisdom* and *sincerity* in employing exhortations, counsels, and other moral means, to deter men from doing that which he knows they will certainly do, or to induce them to do that which he knows they will as certainly leave undone. With this difficulty, it is manifest, that all who fully admit the two great doctrines above mentioned,—no matter under what modifications, or by what variety of explication they attempt to reconcile them with one another,—are equally liable to be pressed. In this respect, there is no difference between the Arminian and the Calvinist, or between the Libertarian and the Necessarian. The one, while he refrains from forming any hypothesis as to the *mode* of the Divine foreknowledge, admits its absolute certainty; the other, while he contends that the certainty of that foreknowledge depends on the infallible connexion between moral causes and effects, admits the doctrine of human responsibility. In other words, they alike concede those two great doctrines, in which the difficulty Howe professes to discuss, originates, and may alike avail themselves of those profound and ingenious reasonings by which he attempts its solution. None, in fact, are excluded from employing these reasonings, except those who, not being able to account for the certainty of the Divine foreknowledge on the hypothesis of the absolute contingency of human actions, divest the Deity of such an attribute altogether; or those who, being unable to reconcile the absolute foreknowledge of God with the responsibility of man, represents us as the victims of a resistless necessity.

To the first of these classes, such a book as Howe's would be manifestly useless; they do not need it; they have already got rid of the difficulty by a short but terrible process, which leaves Deity shorn of some of his most peculiar glories. Having stolen these Divine regalia, they can afford to dispense with the usual guards upon them. To the second class, the treatise must of course be totally unsatisfactory, since it is manifest that nothing can vindicate the wisdom and sincerity of God in exhorting and warning men to this or that course of conduct, when they are but the impotent slaves of an inexorable destiny. They therefore, when consistent, deny that those warnings and exhortations are intended for all mankind.

If any should be inclined to say, that, according to this representation, Howe's treatise leaves the main difficulties of Calvinism and Arminianism where it found them, this is true; but then he did not pretend (at least in this treatise) to offer anything for their solution. He expressly disclaims any intention of ascending to those questions which would compel him to discuss the *modes* of the Divine foreknowledge, or to reconcile such foreknowledge with human accountability. All that he says on the subject of Divine "predetermination" also, is purely incidental, and solely respects his present inquiry. Further he does not pursue the subject.

All that he denies, and all that it was necessary for him to deny, are these two propositions; 1st, that there is no such attribute of the Divine nature as foreknowledge, and 2nd, that God, " being good and holy," should " irresistibly determine the wills of men to, and punish, the same thing;" " that he should irresistibly determine the will of a man to the hatred of his own most blessed self, and then exact severest punishments for the offence done." He took his stand on that point where both parties were agreed,—in admitting the absolute foreknowledge of God, and the moral accountability of man.

It would have been deeply interesting, it is true, to have had the thoughts of a man so acute, and yet so comprehensive, so speculative, and yet so sober, on the difficult and long perplexed points to which I have above adverted,—if it were not those very qualities, rather, which induce him to abstain from such discussions; but we certainly have no right to expect any such discussions in this little tractate. No one could more fully explain the exact *nature* and *limits* of the question he intended to treat. The very title at once shows that his design is not to reconcile the attributes of the Divine, with any properties of the human, nature,—as, for example, the absolute foreknowledge of God, with any hypothesis respecting the grounds of moral accountability;—but to reconcile the *Divine character with itself*—to show that it is consistent; to prove that the absolute prescience of God is not at war with the wisdom and sincerity of his conduct. The title is, "The Reconcilableness of God's Prescience of the sins of men, with the wisdom and sincerity of his counsels, exhortations, and whatsoever other means he uses to prevent them."

The following is a brief analysis of the contents of this admirable little work.

After having very clearly laid down the limits within which he intends to confine himself, he proceeds to caution us against the two-fold danger, of either attributing absolutely repugnant and contradictory properties to God, or of hastily determining that all are such which we are unable to reconcile with one another. Neither are we to conclude, on a hasty and indolent survey, that they are irreconcilable. The whole of this section is admirable.

Howe next proceeds to affirm, that none of those attributes, the mutual harmony of which he is about to maintain, can be excluded from a just conception of the character of God; that his moral perfections require us to believe his sincerity; and his intellectual perfections, his wisdom and foreknowledge.

Before going further, he deems it right to declare in what sense and to what extent he believes the efficacious influence and determination of the Divine will necessary to the production of human actions. It is necessary, he tells us, "to *all* actions in themselves good and holy; but with reference to *other* actions, he doth only supply men with such a power as whereby they are enabled either to act, or, in many instances, (especially when they attempt anything that is evil,) to suspend such actions." With reference to "all wicked actions," he denies the efficacious, irresistible determination of the Divine will altogether.

As to the *mode* of the Divine foreknowledge, he declines saying anything; the discussion of this topic being foreign to the present subject. He contents himself, therefore, with asserting that the perfection of Deity requires us to suppose that he possesses such an attribute.

He then proceeds to enumerate the principal arguments by which he intends to meet the proposed difficulty. They are as follows.

He maintains that on the supposition that man is account-
able at all; that is, that there are *duties* which he is called to
perform; the Divine foreknowledge, let it be supposed ever so
perfect, cannot annul human obligations,—there being no *contrariety* between them; and, that as God is obliged to insist on
the performance of those duties, his foreknowledge can in no
way exempt him from the necessity of *enjoining* them.

This is in analogy with all our conceptions of government,
and is quite independent of the question of probable obedience
or disobedience. The civil governor is perfectly *certain* that
his laws will be in many cases violated and punishment in-
curred. If he could actually divine the individual culprits,
(as in many cases he may be morally certain of them) it would
make no difference in his conduct; he would still give his
laws a universal promulgation.

Again: Howe contends that as one of the great ends of the
Divine "exhortations and counsels" to mankind is, to vindicate God's own character as sovereign Ruler; to display the
purity of his nature; to impress the universe with the idea of
his inflexible justice and equity; and, it may be, to deter the
loyal inhabitants of innumerable worlds from conceiving,
through his silence, a disregard to his authority, or a diminished dread of disobedience; it was right, on these grounds,
if on no other, that he should address to mankind such
"warnings, counsels, and exhortations" as he has done; quite
irrespectively of the reception they might meet with, and even
upon the supposition that they would prove entirely futile. Now
he argues, as many of these great ends are attained, it cannot
be justly said, that it is inconsistent with the Divine *wisdom*
to urge men to do that which he well knows, in many cases,
they will never do.

He further vindicates the Divine wisdom in issuing such
"commands, exhortations, and counsels," by arguing, that
though many to whom they are addressed will never comply
with them, vast multitudes *will;* that with such design they
are issued; that in order to effect it, such "commands, exhortations, and counsels" were necessarily addressed to all
mankind, there being no possibility of avoiding this, except

by making a distinct revelation of the individuals who would, or who would not, comply with them; an expedient which would have implied the total subversion of the present system of God's moral government.

He then proceeds to vindicate the *sincerity* of the Divine "counsels, exhortations, and commands" to *all* men. He remarks, that there can be no doubt of this, with regard to those who *comply* with them. With regard to those who do not, he argues, that God is, in an intelligible sense, truly *willing* that all men should be saved, and that it would be really grateful to the infinite benevolence of his nature, if they were all to accept the salvation which the gospel provides; but that, though he is *willing* that all should be saved on such terms as the gospel offers, and in a method that harmonizes with the intelligent and moral nature of man, he is *not willing* that they should be saved at any rate or in any method.

Howe's sentiments on this subject may, I suppose, be illustrated in a very familiar manner. A parent is truly willing to reclaim a disobedient child, and to employ many apt methods for this purpose. But there is, at the same time, a point beyond which he will not go. He will not persist in his beneficent intention at all hazards; he will not compromise his own character; he will not expose his authority to the contempt of the rest of his family; he will not procure obedience by concessions, which, though they might succeed probably in a single instance, might fearfully weaken his general authority.—Now what is more common than such a case?—Do we not often really desire to attain a certain object, provided it can be attained only at a certain expense; and yet firmly resolve to forego it, if we find it cannot?

Thus it is, Howe argues, with God: there is a sense in which he really *wills* the salvation of all men; and, in consequence, has *sincerely* provided all those means of moral suasion which are likely to operate on a reasonable creature; but that, when men persist in refusing to yield to these, he resolves to do no more, and leaves them to the consequences of their own obstinacy. This, he contends, is his general conduct; conduct by no means inconsistent with the supposition, that he may employ still "further and more efficacious means" for the recovery of "some." The reasons which limit the employment of those means we know not.

The "Calm and Sober Inquiry concerning the possibility of a Trinity in the Godhead," was occasioned, as the title-page informs us, by some "lately published considerations" on the recent speculations of Wallis, Sherlock, South, and Cudworth, on the same subject.

Many, who too hastily imagined that Howe's design was the same with that of some of the above writers; or that his object was to show the actual constitution of the Trinity, censured—as they justly might, had their opinion been well founded—the boldness of his speculations. But, in fact, he had no such design. His object is simply to prove that the idea of a Trinity involves nothing self-repugnant or contradictory; or, which is the same thing, that the Trinity is not, as Unitarians affirm, an impossibility. In order to illustrate his argument, he subjoins a particular explication of the Trinity, which, while it includes, as he affirms, all that is essential to the unity of Deity, excludes not such varieties in his mode of existence, as are necessary to the supposition of a Trinity. This explication, he does not pretend to say, is the true one: it being sufficient only to show that it involves no contradiction; that it is possible. For since Unitarians are called on to show the impossibility of a Trinity, any explication (no matter whether the true one or not) which includes all that is predicated of the Trinity, and cannot be proved self-repugnant or contradictory, would show their argument to be fallacious. If a Trinity could subsist in such a way, it might, for aught we know, in other ways.

At the same time, he very properly contends, that even if they were to show that his hypothesis did imply a contradiction, its refutation would only prove that particular explication false. The impugners of the doctrine would still be required to *prove* that a Trinity was impossible in *every other* way.

That they are bound to show this impossibility,—to show that the very idea of the Trinity, howsoever explicated, and under all possible modifications, involves a contradiction,—is a consequence, as Howe maintains, of the clearness with which the doctrine is asserted in Scripture. It is plainly taught in many passages ; it is as clearly *implied* in others ; it manifestly harmonizes with the whole tenor and strain of the inspired volume, and with the only interpretation of which a natural, unforced construction of its- language admits. On the other hand, its complete expulsion from the sacred page, requires the most licentious and desperate system of criticism, and leaves the sacred volume, considered as " a revelation " of the few and simple doctrines of Socinianism, a mass of inscrutable perplexities. Under such circumstances, Howe justly argues, that nothing less than the most apparent necessity,—the utter impossibility of the truth of any such doctrine,—could justify us in denying it. No mere *à priori* improbability in the doctrine itself—which, indeed, it is admitted on all hands, is entirely matter of revelation—will suffice : those who deny it, must prove its absolute, total impossibility. So that, in fact, the question is, as to whether we are more likely to be *mistaken* in deciding on the *meaning* of Scripture, or on the *possibility* of a Trinity in the Godhead ?

One would think that, to a modest mind, the mere terms in which the question is propounded would be sufficient to determine it. In the one case, we are called to judge of a matter to which we are fairly competent; in the other, to . decide on a question which none but the Divine intellect could grasp : in the one case, we have only to pronounce on the meaning of a certain document, written in human language, with all the appliances of criticism to aid us ; and, in the other, invited to decide on a problem, the terms of which are *possibilities* and *infinitudes !* If those superior intelligences, whose humility and modesty have kept pace with their knowledge, because every accession to their knowledge has only disclosed to them more of those illimitable regions of mystery which still lie in deep shadow beyond them, could regard the spectacle of human folly with any other feeling than that of benignant compassion, what boundless merriment would it afford them, to hear that the infinitesimal soul of man, lodged in its prison-house of clay, had gravely pronounced on what *can* be, and on what *cannot* be, within the wide realms of possibility ; and, above all, in the constitution of the Infinite and Eternal Mind ! Unitarians, it is true, maintain that they have proved the doctrine of the Trinity an impossibility and contradiction, because it is admitted, that one cannot be three, nor three one ; a brief and summary demonstration. They must excuse us, however, for refusing to listen to this too obvious sophism. What they are called upon to demonstrate is, the impossibility that what is ONE in one sense, should be THREEFOLD in another : that the Divine unity is not compatible with *any* such distinctions in the mode of the Divine subsistence, (though we need not be ashamed to own that we are ignorant what those distinctions are,) on which the doctrine of the Trinity may be rationally defended.

In the introductory paragraphs of the " Calm and Sober Inquiry," Howe states his object with great clearness and force.

After premising, that whatever conceptions we form of God, that of *necessary* existence must be included, he proceeds to offer some admirable and eloquent remarks on those presumptuous speculations with respect to the *simplicity* of the Divine essence, which, originating in the schools, have done so much to perpetuate error on this subject.

He then proceeds to his main object—to unfold his theory of the *possibility* of a Trinity.

I am spared the necessity of attempting an analysis of his reasoning, since he himself has appended to his discourse a series of " summary propositions, more briefly offering to view the substance of what is contained in it." Those which contain the leading principles of his theory are given in the note.*

---

* " We have among the *creatures*, and even *in ourselves*, instances of very *different* natures continuing *distinct*, but so *united* as to be *one* thing ; and it were more easily supposable of *congenerous* natures.

" If such *union with distinction* be impossible in the Godhead, it must not be from any *repugnancy* in the thing itself, since very intimate union, with continuing distinction, is in itself no impossible thing ; but from somewhat *peculiar* to the Divine Being.

" That peculiarity, since it cannot be *unity* (which because it may admit

To the " Calm and Sober Inquiry," Howe appended several letters, signed "Anonymous," originally addressed to Dr. Wallis, and written in 1691. They are all explicatory of some of the points touched in the treatise itself.

The " Calm and Sober Inquiry " involved its author in controversy. He was compelled to publish two pieces in its defence. The first was entitled, " A Letter to a Friend, concerning a Postscript to the Defence of Dr. Sherlock's Notion of the 'Trinity in Unity.' "

The second was entitled, " A View of that part of the late Considerations, addressed to H. H., about the Trinity, which concerns the Sober Inquiry on that subject." These pieces contain only a further exposition and defence of what he had already advanced.

The " Redeemer's Tears wept over Lost Souls," is deservedly ranked amongst the most valuable pieces of practical divinity in the English language. It is founded on Luke xix. 41: " And when he was come near, he beheld the city, and wept over it, saying, If thou hadst known, even thou, at least in this thy day, the things which belong unto thy peace! but now they are hid from thine eyes."

The first part strikingly corroborates the remarks made in a preceding chapter, on Howe's defects of *method*. The introductory paragraphs are, it is true, eminently beautiful: but the division of the text, and the distribution of matter, are exceedingly formal and needlessly minute. The first and second topics of the discourse, moreover, are pursued to a far greater

---

distinctions in one and the same thing, we are not sure it *cannot* be so in the Godhead) must be that *simplicity* commonly wont to be ascribed to the Divine nature.

"Such simplicity as shall exclude that distinction which shall appear necessary in the present case, is not by expressed Scripture anywhere ascribed to God; and therefore must be *rationally* demonstrated of him, if it shall be judged to belong at all to him.   *   *   *   *

"It is not a just consequence,—which is the most plausible one that seems capable of being alleged for such absolute simplicity,—that otherwise there would be a *composition* admitted in the Divine nature, which would import an imperfection inconsistent with Deity. For the several excellencies that concur in it, (howsoever distinguished,) being never *put together*, nor having ever existed apart, but *in eternal necessary union*, though they may make some sort of variety, import no proper composition, and carry with them more apparent perfection, than absolute, omnimodous simplicity can be conceived to do."

length than they need have been. They consist, for the most part, of a long, and, considering the *main* object of the discourse, a most disproportionate exposition of all those great truths and doctrines which the gospel reveals, which " belong to men's peace," and the knowledge of which constitutes "their day." I have always regretted the disproportionate length of this part. Many readers, I fear, have been tempted from this circumstance, to throw the work aside, only half perused.

The concluding portions of the work are in his best style.

The descriptions of the fearfully narrow limits of that *day,* which is to decide our eternal destinies; of the possibility— inferred from the text—that it may be over with men even before the day of life is itself spent; of the obdurate, self-infatuated state of those from whom the Spirit of life and of peace is departed, never to return; of the horror which the bare contemplation of such a state should inspire; are full of terrific sublimity, interspersed with touches of the most sub-duing tenderness.—And how beautifully, after dwelling on these dreadful themes, and inculcating those fearful lessons with which they are pregnant, does he proceed to address those, who suppose that they have already fallen into such a state, and who, oppressed with this horrible imagination, dwell even in this world on the confines of hell! How reviving and con-solatory are the assurances that the very doubts and fears which torment such persons, their very jealousies, and salutary misgivings of heart, are totally inconsistent with the sup-position of their having fallen into a state of which torpor of conscience is the most melancholy and fatal symptom,—thus, converting into hope the very suggestions of despair!

I should think it unpardonable in a volume of this kind if I omitted to point the reader's attention to the close of this discourse. For profound yet simple pathos,—pathos the more affecting because so simple,—for felicitous turns of thought, and even for beauty of expression, it will bear comparison with almost anything in the whole range of hortatory eloquence.

The concluding sentences are as follow :—

" These tears show the remedilessness of thy case, if thou

persist in impenitency and unbelief till the things of thy peace be quite hid from thine eyes. These tears will then be the last issues of even defeated love,—of love that is frustrated of its kind design. Thou mayest perceive in these tears the steady, unalterable laws of heaven, the inflexibleness of the Divine justice, that holds thee in adamantine bonds, and hath sealed thee up, if thou prove incurably obstinate and impenitent, unto perdition; so that even the Redeemer himself, he that is mighty to save, cannot at length save thee, but only weep over thee, drop tears into thy flame, which assuage it not, but, (though they have another design, even to express true compassion,) do yet unavoidably heighten and increase the fervour of it, and will do so to all eternity. He even tells thee, 'Sinner, thou hast despised my blood; thou shalt yet have my tears. THAT would have saved thee; *these* do only lament thee lost!'

"But the tears wept over others as lost and past hope, why should they not yet melt thee, while as yet there is hope in thy case? If thou be effectually melted in thy very soul, and looking to him whom thou hast pierced, dost truly mourn over him, thou mayest assure thyself the prospect his weeping eye had of lost souls did not include thee. His weeping over thee would argue thy case forlorn and hopeless; thy mourning over him will make it safe and happy. That it may be so, consider further, that,—

"They signify how very intent he is to save souls, and how gladly he would save thine, if yet thou wilt accept of mercy while it may be had. For if he weep over them that will not be saved, from the same love that is the spring of these tears would saving mercies proceed to those that are become willing to receive them. And that love that wept over them that were lost, how will it glory in them that are saved! There his love is disappointed and vexed, crossed in his gracious intendment; but here, having compassed it, 'how will he joy over thee with singing, and rest in his love!' And thou also, instead of being involved in a like ruin with the unreconciled sinners of the old Jerusalem, shalt be enrolled among the glorious citizens of the new, and triumph together with them in eternal glory."

To this "discourse" is added an appendix on two points involved in the discussion of the text; "On the Blasphemy against the Holy Ghost," and "How God is said to will the salvation of those that perish." On the first of these he most judiciously argues, that none have cause to conclude that they are *certainly* involved in such guilt; on the second, he .insists on the same views as are unfolded in his treatise on the "Divine Prescience," and to these I have already adverted.

"The Redeemer's Dominion over the Invisible World," is the last publication which requires any specific notice. The occasion on which the outline of this magnificent discourse * was preached, has been already referred to. As it was one of the last, so it is one of the richest and maturest fruits of our author's genius.

It is founded on those words of the Redeemer, "I have the keys of death and of hell." In a long and very able marginal digression, he shows that the word "hell," is a very erroneous, or, rather, inadequate translation of the original word,—and that it ought to be rendered, in accordance with its etymology and more usual meaning, "the invisible world."

I do not think that any man who has any, even though a faltering and inconstant hope that he is a *Christian*, and that to him death will be but admission into heaven, can peruse this discourse without feeling the dread of dissolution sensibly diminished;—nay, the grave itself rendered in his better moods almost an object of desire and fascination. The descriptions which its author gives of that invisible world to which he leads our contemplation; of its splendour and magnificence; of the felicity it promises and insures; of the plenitude of life which fills it, instead of the solitude and silence, the darkness and desertion, with which our imaginations are so apt to invest it; of that great and beneficent Being, whom it describes as Sovereign Lord of it,—who has already passed into it by the same dreary path,—who is familiarized to us by intimate communion with humanity,—whose own gracious hand unlocks the portals which are to admit us to immortality, and whose voice it is which first

---

* I observe Dean Trench applies a similar epithet to this discourse, which for range, elevation, and nobleness of thought, well deserves to be so characterized: "Howe's grand sermon on the Redeemer's Dominion over the Invisible World."—Trench, on the "Authorized Version of the New Testament," p. 21.

welcomes the spirit to its resting place;—are absolutely ravishing. On these themes, Howe seems to descant with a sort of privileged familiarity; as of a spirit to whom the scenery of heaven had been already unfolded. Yet, glowing as his descriptions are, they contain nothing to which a sober and chastened judgment can take exception; nothing at variance with the reserve which the comparative silence of Scripture, on all such topics, should impose on our speculations.

A few brief extracts we must find space for.

On the ultimate purpose of the gospel, its enfranchisement of man from the *dominion* of sin, (and to suppose less would be to imagine man "redeemed," without "any redemption,") he has the following striking observations :—

"Had it been otherwise, so firm and indissoluble is the connection between our duty and our felicity, that the Sovereign Ruler had been eternally injured, and we not advantaged. Were we to have been set free from the preceptive obligation of God's holy law, and most of all from that most fundamental precept, 'Thou shalt love the Lord thy God with all thine heart, soul, might, and mind,'—had this been redemption, which supposes only what is evil and hurtful, as that we are to be redeemed from—this were a strange sort of self-repugnant redemption, not from sin and misery, but from our duty and felicity. This were so to be redeemed as to be still lost, and every way lost; both to God and to ourselves for ever. Redeemed from loving God! what a monstrous thought! .   .   . This had been to legitimate everlasting enmity and rebellion against the blessed God, and to redeem us into an eternal hell of horror and misery to ourselves. This had been to cut off from the Supreme Ruler of the world, for ever, so considerable a limb of his most rightful dominion, and to leave us as miserable as everlasting separation from the fountain of life and blessedness could make us."

So saving us, Christ "would save us to the eternal wrong of him that made us, and so as we should be nothing the better; that is, he should *save* us without *saving* us!"

On the composure with which the Christian should consign himself to the disposal of him "who liveth," but himself once died, and now has the "keys of Hades and of Death," he thus beautifully discourses :—

"Do not regret or dread to pass out of the one world into the other at his call and under his conduct, though through the dark passage of death; remembering the keys are in so great and so kind a hand; and that his good pleasure herein is no more to be distrusted, than to be disputed or withstood. Let it be enough to you, that what you cannot see yourself, he sees for you. You have oft desired your ways, your motions, your removals from place to place, might be directed by him in the world. Have you never said, 'If thou go not with me, carry me not hence?' How safely and fearlessly may you follow him blindfold, or in the dark, any whither; not only from place to place in this world, but from world to world, how lightsome soever the one, and gloomy and dark the other may seem to you! 'Darkness and light are to him alike.' To him Hades is no Hades, nor is the dark way that leads into it to him an untrodden path. Shrink not at the thoughts of this translation, though it be not by escaping death, but even through the jaws of it."

Among the reasons which may determine the Supreme Disposer in the, to us mysterious, removal of "hopeful young persons," in the blossom of their life and the promise of much usefulness; he assigns the following as one: and the expression is as beautiful as the thought is impressive :—

"He will have it known, that though he uses instruments, he needs them not. It is a piece of Divine royalty and magnificence, that when he hath prepared and polished such an utensil, so as to be capable of great service, he can lay it aside without loss. They that are most qualified to be of greatest use in this world, are thereby also the more capable of blessedness in the other. It is owing to his most munificent bounty that he may vouchsafe to reward sincere intentions, as highly as great services. He took David's having it 'in his heart to build him a house,' as kindly as Solomon's building him one; and as much magnifies himself in testifying his acceptance of such as he discharges from his service here at 'the third hour,' as of them whom he engages not in it till 'the eleventh.' . . . Moreover, 'the lustre of that virtue and piety which had provoked nobody, appears only with an amiable look, and leaves behind nothing of such a person, but a fair, unblemished, alluring, and instructive example.'"

On the extent of the "Redeemer's dominion" as Lord of the Hades, the vast invisible world, he says, that it is a matter of "duty in us, and for his just honour, to magnify this his *Prefecture.*"

"But it is no obscure hint that is given of the spaciousness of the heavenly regions, when purposely to represent the Divine immensity, it is said of the unconfined presence of the great God, that even 'heaven, and the heaven of heavens cannot contain him.' How vast scope is given to our thinking minds to conceive heavens above heavens, encircling one another, till we have quite tired our faculty, and yet we know not how far short we are of the utmost verge! And when our Lord is said to have ascended *far* above all heavens, whose arithmetic will suffice to tell how many they are ? whose uranography to describe how far that is. . . . And when we are told of many heavens, above all which our Lord Jesus is said to have ascended, are all those heavens only empty solitudes ? uninhabited glorious deserts ? . . . And they that rest not night or day from such high and glorious employment, have they nothing to do ? or will we say or think it, because we see not how the heavenly potentates lead on their bright legions to present themselves before the throne, to tender their obeisance, or receive commands and dispatches to this or that far remote dynasty ; or, suppose, to such and such a mighty star whereof there are so numberless myriads,—and why should we suppose them not replenished with glorious inhabitants ?—whither they fly as quick as thought, with joyful speed, under the all-seeing eye ? . . . But, alas! in all this we can but 'darken counsel by words without knowledge.' We cannot pretend to *knowledge* in these things; yet if from Scripture intimations and the concurrent reason of things, we only make suppositions of what *may be,* not conclusions of what *is,*—let our thoughts ascend as much higher as they can, I see not why they should fall lower than all this."

There are a few minor pieces of Howe, of which my space will not permit me to give an analysis; but I may just enumerate some of those which are most characteristic of his genius, and most worthy of the reader's perusal. Among these I would specify his sermons on "Thoughtfulness for the Morrow;" "Of Charity in reference to other Men's Sins;" and "On Man's Creation in a Holy but Mutable State." Several also of the "Funeral Sermons" fully sustain his reputation. They, of course, possess very different degrees of merit; but there is hardly one which is not worthy of attentive perusal. Those for Queen Mary, Dr. Bates, and Mr. Fairclough, are noble productions, and will suffer little by comparison with any other compositions of the same kind.

It may be added that the funeral discourses of Howe have one feature which distinguishes them very favourably from most compositions of the same kind. They are full of vivid and novel thoughts in the *application*. Consolation is not expressed in commonplaces of ordinary condolence; nor counsels and warnings, in the platitudes usually suggested by funeral solemnities. The conclusion is in general full of turns of thought which strike at once by their combined truth and novelty, and is almost cheerful with animating hopes drawn from the deepest experience that Christ had indeed vanquished Death, and "brought Life and Immortality to light." This feature distinguishes not only those two more memorable sermons (or rather treatises) entitled "The Vanity of Man as Mortal," and "The Redeemer's Dominion over the Invisible World," but the funeral discourses generally; and on this account they are worthy of attentive study by every preacher. I am tempted to give a few brief specimens. The following striking sentences close the sermon of his friend, the Rev. Mr. Fairclough :—

"Yea, and it may incline us to have somewhat the kinder thoughts of this our meaner native element, and less to regret that our earthly part should dissolve and incorporate with it, to think what rich treasure, what shrines of a lately-inhabiting Deity (now become sacred dust) it hath from time to time received, and transmuted into itself. How voluminously have some written of ' Roma Subterranea;' of the tombs of martyrs, and other excellent persons, as many of them were, collected in one little spot of this earth!   And if there were as particular an account of the more refined part of the subterraneous London, much more of all places where just and holy men have dropt and deposed their earthly tabernacles, how would our earth appear ennobled, and even hallowed, by such continual accessions to it, in all times and ages!   What a glorious host will arise and spring up, even out of one London!   Is not the grave now a less gloomy thing?   Who would grudge to lie obscurely a while among them with whom we expect to rise and ascend so gloriously?"

In the following passage of the funeral sermon for Mrs. Baxter he has the following original thoughts on the duty of familiarizing ourselves with the idea of dissolution:—

"Yea, and we should endeavour to make the thoughts more familiar to ourselves, of spiritual beings in the general, for we are to serve and converse with him in a glorious community of such creatures; 'an innumerable company of angels, the general assembly and church of the firstborn, and the spirits of just men made perfect,' in a region where an earthly body, remaining such, can have no place.   Why do we make the thoughts of a spirit, out of a body, so strange to ourselves? We meet with hundreds of spirits in bodies, and moving bodies to and fro, in the streets every day, and are not startled at it. Is a body so much nearer akin to us than a spirit, that we must have so mean a thing to come between, to mediate and reconcile us to it?   Why are we afraid of what we are so nearly allied unto?   Can we not endure to see or think of a man *at liberty*, (suppose it were a friend or brother,) if we ourselves were *in prison?*   The more easy you make the apprehension to yourselves of a disembodied spirit that is *free*,—I mean, of any terrestrial body,—the better we shall relish the thoughts of him who is the head of that glorious society you are to be gathered unto; 'for the Lord is that Spirit,' the eminent, almighty, and all-governing Spirit, to be ever beheld, too, in his glorified body, as an eternal monument of his undertaking for us, and an assuring endearment of his relation to us."

In the sermon on Mrs. Esther Sampson, he thus reproves that selfish sorrow which repines at the Divine arrest when laid on those dear to us, and which, come when it may, is always counted too early. Howe strikingly represents the unreasonableness of it by showing its contrariety to all the Christian's professed hopes and aims, and by reminding us that if all had their wish in this matter, heaven must remain an unpeopled region, the great designs of redemption unachieved, and Christ occupy his throne in solitude.

"It is little considered how opposite such a temper of spirit, as commonly appears in us, is to the very design of all Christianity. For doth not the whole of Christianity terminate upon eternity, and upon another state and world? Now do but consider the inconsistencies that are to be found in this case between the carriage and temper of many that profess Christianity and their very profession itself. They acknowledge, they own, that the design of Christ's appearing here in this world, and of his dying upon the cross, was to 'bring us to God,' to 'bring the many sons to glory.' They grant that this is not to be done all at once, not all in a day, but it is to be done by degrees. Here he takes up one, and there another, leaving others still to transmit religion, and to continue it on to the end of time. So far they agree with our common Lord, and seem to approve the Divine determinations in all these steps of his procedure. But yet, for all this, if they might have their own will, Christ should not have one to ascend to him of those for whom he died and himself ascended, to open heaven for them and to prepare a place for their reception, as their forerunner, there. I say not one to ascend after him; for they take up with a general approving of this design of his. 'Very well,' say they, 'it is fitly ordered, his method is wise, and just, and kind, and let him take them that belong to him when he thinks fit, only let him excuse my family; let him take whom he will, only let him touch no relation of mine, not my husband, wife, child, brother, sister; take whom he will, but let all mine alone. I agree to all he shall do well enough, only let him allow me my exception.' But if every one be of this temper and resolution for themselves and theirs, according to this tendency and course of things he shall have none at all to ascend, none 'to bring with him' when he returns. Those that are dead in Jesus he is to bring with him. No, he should be solitary and unattended for all them. They and all their relations would be immortal upon earth. How ill doth this agree and accord with the Christian scheme and model of things!"*

The concluding sentences of this sermon, in which he declares he would rather die alone than amidst the clamorous sorrows of relatives who "despair of futurity," are most characteristic.

"In short, it were desirable, if God see good, to die amidst the pleasant friends and relatives who were not ill pleased that we lived,—that living and dying breath might mingle and ascend together in prayers and praises to the blessed Lord of heaven and earth, the God of our lives,—if then we would part with consent, a rational and a joyful consent. Otherwise, to die with ceremony, to die amongst the fashionable bemoanings and lamentations, as if we despaired of futurity, one would say, with humble submission to the Divine pleasure, 'Lord, let me rather die alone, in perfect solitude, in some unfrequented wood, or on the top of some far remote mountain, where none might interrupt the solemn transactions between thy glorious blessed self, and my joyfully departing self-resigning soul!' But in all this we must refer ourselves to God's holy pleasure, who will dispose of us, living and dying, in the best, the wisest, and the kindest way."

---

* "If," he says, in another place, speaking of those to whom we doubt not "death is gain"—"If God be pleased, and his happy creature pleased, who are. we that we should be displeased?"

APPENDIX.

No. I.

A few particulars respecting Howe's family and descendants :—

It has been mentioned in Chap. II. that Howe's father was educated by Francis Higginson, of Leicester. An account of Higginson may be found in Brooke's "Lives of the Puritans," vol. i. p. 372.

Higginson went to New England in 1629, with about two hundred passengers and planters: some settled at Nehumtak, afterwards Salem; some at Massachusetts bay.

Whether Howe's father possessed the living of Loughborough, or was merely curate, is a point that cannot be ascertained. Calamy says that he was appointed by Laud, minister of the parish of Loughborough. The living was then in the gift of Lady Bromley.

There is no authenticated list of the rectors of Loughborough. In a book of miscellanies collated and written by the late clerk from various parish records, is a list of rectors in which the name of Howe does not appear. The list states "John Brown, 1597,—buried 1622-3. John Brown, 1623,—buried Oct. 7, 1642."

In the register of our author's baptism (given below) the father is mentioned as Mr. John How, *preacher*.

Probably he never was inducted into the living as rector, but was appointed by Laud to preach in the room of the above John Brown, who might, for some reason, be silenced for a time.

The following is the register of the baptism of two of his children, that of his son John, the subject of these memoirs, and of a daughter; whether he had any other children I know not.

"July, 1628, Ann How, daughter of Mr. John How, preacher, baptd. x day."

"May, 1630, John How, sonne of Mr. John How, bapt. xx day."

In both entries the final *e* is left out of the father's name. Indeed, Howe himself spelt his name sometimes with and sometimes without it, except in the latter part of his life, when he always spelt it "Howe." Marvell, in his tract against Danson, always calls him How.

The volume from which the register is taken is a very curious one, and perhaps as old as any in the kingdom. It extends from 1538 to 1651.

A paragraph at the commencement intimates that it was begun and kept "according to the command of our Sovereign Lord King Henry the 8th."

The volume is parchment, much discoloured in various places, and written throughout in antiquated but very legible hands.

Mr. Howe's marriage with Katherine, daughter of his intimate friend the Rev. George Hughes, of Plymouth, took place March 1st, 1654. Several of his children were born in London during his residence at Whitehall, but of the exact dates of their respective births no information has been obtained.

His eldest son, George, studied medicine; received the diploma of M.D., and afterwards practised in London with considerable reputation and success. He married Lætitia Foley, probably daughter of Thos. Foley, Esq., of Whitley Court, in the county of Worcester, who is honourably mentioned in Baxter's Life. He died in March, about 1710, leaving two sons, John (the elder) and Philip, who both died before 1729, without issue male. He was buried in the same vault with his father, in Allhallows Church, Bread-street.

Mr. Howe's *second* son was named James; he studied the law; was of the Middle Temple, and was in due time called to the bar. He married Mary, daughter of Samuel Saunders, Esq., of Little Ireton and Caldwell, in the county of Derby, eldest son of Col. Thomas Saunders, a military officer of some celebrity on the Parliament side during the Civil Wars. He practised his profession with so much success, that it appears he acquired considerable property. He died April 12, 1714, leaving three sons, John, Samuel, and James. John, his eldest son and heir, was of Hanslop, in the county of Buckingham. He attained the age of 21, about 1729, and married the Hon. Caroline Howe, daughter of the Rt. Hon. Scroop Lord Viscount Howe. In 1754 he is described as of Burrow Green, in the county of Surrey. He died in Sept. 1769.

Mr. Howe's *third* son was named John. No particulars are

known concerning him. Whom he married does not appear, nor when he died; but he left two sons, John and James.

Another son, named Obadiah, was born at Torrington, 1661, and baptized at the church, April 21st, in that year. He probably died in childhood or youth.

A daughter, named Philippa, was born towards the end of 1664, and baptized at Torrington Church, January 4, 1665. She was afterwards married to Mr. Matthew Collett, who held some situation in the Bank of England. When she died does not appear, but she left two sons, John, the elder, and Matthew: the latter was dead in 1754.

When Mr. Howe's wife Katherine (who was the mother of the two last, and, I have no doubt, of all the children mentioned above) died, there is now no means of ascertaining; but that he married again is beyond question. The date of Mrs. Howe's death, given below, proves this; and that she must have been many years younger than Howe. James Howe, the second son, makes mention, in his Will, of his *own* mother. Who was Howe's second wife is not certain.

Mr. Howe's widow, as I learn from a letter printed in the "Diary and Correspondence of Dr. Doddridge," died at Bath, toward the end of February, 1743, at a very advanced age.*

No. II.

The following is Calamy's account of the treatment of John Howe's father by Archbishop Laud :—

" As to the father of our Mr. Howe, he was settled in the parish of Loughborough by Archbishop Laud, and afterwards thrust out by the same hand, on the account of his siding with the Puritans, contrary to the expectation of his promoter. He was one of those who could not be satisfied to give in to that nice and punctilious conformity, upon which that prelate laid so great a stress; and therefore it was not thought fit to suffer him to continue in the exercise of his ministry in that populous town. Great was the rigour that was at that time used in the ecclesiastical courts, by which as several were driven into America, and others into Holland and other foreign parts, so was this worthy person, from whom Mr. John Howe immediately descended, driven into Ireland, whither he took this his son, (then very young) along with him. While they continued in that country, that execrable rebellion broke out, in which so many thousands of the poor Protestants, who were altogether unprovided, were so miserably

---

* " Mrs. How widow of the great and pious Mr. How, died here last week; a good woman and full of years, being near ninety."—Letter to Mrs. Doddridge, dated Bath, March 2nd, 1743.

butchered, and a great number of flourishing families ruined and undone by the enraged papists, whose very tenderest mercies were found to be cruelty.

"Both father and son were at that time exposed to very threatening danger, the place to which they had retired being for several weeks together besieged and assaulted by the rebels, though without success. A very special Providence did upon this occasion guard that life, which was afterwards made so serviceable to great and considerable purposes. Being driven from thence by the war, which continued for some years, the father returned back to his native country, and settled in the County Palatine of Lancaster; and there it was that our Mr. Howe went through the first rudiments of learning, and was trained up in the knowledge of the tongues, though I have not been able to get any certain information who were his particular instructors, nor any further notices relating to his infancy and childhood."—Calamy's *Life of Howe*, pp. 6, 7. These last points are in part determined by the following article of the Appendix.

No. III.

The following is the extract from the register at Cambridge, alluded to at p. 14. "A°. Domi. 1647. Mai. 19°. Johannes Howe, filius Johannis p'.sbyteri, natus Loughborough, in agro Leicestrensi, Literis v. institutus Winwick a M^{ro}. Gorse, Anno Ætatis decimo septimo admissus est sizator sub M^{ro}. Field, spondente pro eo M^{ro}. Ball. Solvit Collegio 5".."

No. IV.—p. 31.

Here several pages of the former edition, containing remarks on Cromwell's character, have been omitted, not only as irrelevant, but as conveying a harsher judgment than subsequent study, and, I hope, a larger charity, will allow me to express. At the same time, I confess that the problem of the Protector's religious character still seems to me, as to multitudes more, as insoluble as ever. When twenty-five years ago, I published the first edition, I was not insensible, and still less am I now, of the many illustrious qualities which adorned this extraordinary man; it was admitted that he was no "mere fanatic," still less, a vulgar "hypocrite;" it was admitted, as his apologists assert, that he did not "employ his power for the gratification of malignant passions;" that "his character will more than sustain comparison with that of any other usurper;" that if "the gratification of his ambition seemed to be his first object, he seems to have been really desirous to render his ambition subservient, as far as possible, to the glory and welfare of his country;" and that "his conduct often indicates traits of magnanimity, clemency, and moderation, which gild no other pages in the dark annals of usurpation." All this I still believe; but whether it be possible to reconcile his career from 1647 to his death, his acts of violence and dissimulation—the acts by which he gathered into his single hand the entire liberties of his country, and made and unmade constitutions at his pleasure,—with a *then* active religion, I confess very doubtful. We are happily not called on to form any absolute judgment in the matter, and should certainly abstain from any uncharitable and presumptuous judgment on his final state. He may have been sincerely religious in his early life, and before temptation so severely taxed him, and he may have recovered from his lapse before he died; for even behind "the curtains of a death-bed," as Cowper says, with no less charity than beauty, "there is often a work going on, of which doctor and nurse know nothing."

While it is assuredly difficult to reconcile many parts of Cromwell's conduct with the conscious integrity of a Christian, many facts seem to forbid a harsh judgment. On the whole, the entire phenomena seem best accounted for by supposing—what experience shows to be only too common in less illustrious men—a mind warped from rectitude, and a conscience partially silenced, before the influences of ambition and worldly prosperity. It may be said that it is a narrow and vulgar way to judge the actions of such a man as Cromwell by the ordinary standard of moral obligation, and that political necessities must have their own ethics. I am sure that it is still more narrow and vulgar to concede to great genius, merely because it is such, an indulgence which we refuse to concede to ordinary men. This is, in fact, that mere idolatry of power and intellect which too often condones to the successful great the crimes for which it would hang other people; and which robs history and biography of their most instructive lessons. In general, censure ought to be more severe in the case of great minds; for superior intelligence must increase, not diminish, responsibility. But, at all events, in considering whether a man has consistently acted the Christian, or been warped from his integrity, we are not at liberty to employ any of the tortuous apologetics which have been so usually at the service of splendid successes.

"The genius of Christianity," to adopt expressions in the former edition, "pays no deference to mere greatness; it prescribes exactly the same rules of conduct to all; no power can terrify, no splendour can dazzle it; with sublime indifference to all that bewilders and perverts the judgment of this world's too compliant moralists, it considers guilt on the throne precisely in the same light with guilt on the scaffold." It "refuses to set off the practice of certain virtues, be they ever so imposing and splendid, against the commission of great crimes;" it is not disposed "to palliate such crimes by alleging that, considering the circumstances, they were not so frequent or so enormous as they might have been;" or "to plead any, even the most pressing exigencies, as an apology for violations of the eternal laws of truth and rectitude. . . . Now the apologists of Cromwell sometimes forget this. They admit he was ambitious; but then his power was generally exerted for the benefit of his country. He did often dissemble, but dissimulation was better than cruelty. If sometimes arbitrary and tyrannical, we are told not to forget the necessities of his situation, and are re-minded that when he *was* cruel and unjust, it was only when he could not afford to be upright and humane; that he did not employ his power for the gratification of the malignant passions, and, unlike most other usurpers, was an economist of injustice and cruelty."

All this has been frankly admitted; but it does not touch the merits of the case in the one point now under consideration—the question of the *religious* character of Cromwell during the more dubious parts of his career. It seems to me more candid, and more accordant with probability, to say that whatever his real character *before* that vision of the " weird sisters " which evoked his ambition, or *after* the approach of death had shown the shadowy nature of *all* ambition, his conduct in the interval can only be accounted for by supposing that this "warld had got an ower strang grip o' his heart," and dazzled and often blinded his conscience and his better judgment.

No. V.

The following is an outline of the sermon preached before Crom-well, "On a Particular Faith in Prayer;" referred to in p. 61.

The Notes from which Calamy copied were so brief, and the MS. in some parts so illegible, that he has in some places attempted to supply the sense by conjecture. His own remarks he has placed between brackets.

James v. 15, the former part. "And the prayer of faith shall save the sick; and the Lord shall raise him up."

It is to be inquired how this is to be understood and applied.

I. How to be understood. Where in the general we must know, it is not to be looked upon as an universal maxim, admitting of no restriction or limitation; for then prayer might make a man immortal, if in every case wherein life were in hazard any could be procured to employ their faith in prayer on his behalf.

Unless we should say, that wherever the·desired effect follows not, the faith was wanting, which ought to have been exercised in the case. To say that every prayer that has faith in it shall save the sick, is false: but that every prayer that has this special faith in it, shall save the sick, is true.

That therefore we may speak the more distinctly, we must understand,

I. That there was somewhat in this matter *extraordinary*, and appropriate to that time.

II. Somewhat *ordinary*, and common to all times. We are to distinguish the one and the other.

I. There was somewhat *extraordinary* in this matter, and appropriate to that time: and that both as to the faith to be exercised, and the *effect* thereupon.

1. As to the *faith* to be exercised. *The prayer of faith shall save the sick;* that is, in those days, when the state of things did to the Divine Wisdom make it necessary that frequent miracles should be wrought for the confirmation of Christianity, faith was necessary to be exerted in prayer, that should, according to tenour of the promise made in those times, engage omnipotency, in reference to the thing prayed for: the promise then was, " Whatsoever ye pray, believing, ye shall receive; or it shall be done."

2. As to the *Effect*, that also was supernatural.

Ques. But it may be said, What! universally? What work might the disciples have made in that case!

Ans. The Divine power did go forth in two ways.

1st. In working the faith to be exercised: And,

2nd. In effecting the thing. So that the matter was always in God's own hand. The Spirit of God could be the Author of no vain or imprudent faith, or of any thing consequent upon it.

This faith of miracles was such a fiducial recumbence on the Divine power in reference to this or that particular work, as whereby that was by his rule engaged to go forth, *in saving the sick.* This and common faith differ, in respect to the end and the nature of the influence.—Not *holy*, but *physical*.

II. There was here also somewhat that was *ordinary*. The instance of Elias is mentioned, who, v. 17, 18, it is said, " was a man subject to like passions as we are, and yet he prayed earnestly that it might not rain; and it rained not on the earth by the space of three years and six months. And he prayed again, and the heaven gave rain, and the earth brought forth her fruit." There is somewhat from that extraordinary case to be learnt for common use, namely, that what the promise says to us now, we ought as confidently to believe, as they then, what it said to them.

Therefore take some propositions, concerning the nature and operation of the faith to be exercised in such a case, and the way wherein prayer ought to be managed and guided, so as that it may be expected to have influence in reference thereto.

1. Prayer is a great and indispensable duty. [There is here some reference in the manuscript: but after the utmost search I know not what to make of it.]

2. That therefore we must conclude, whatsoever tends to render it an impertinence, must either be false or misapplied. For it is most plainly a great part of our duty, and it could not consist either with the wisdom or truth of God to have enjoined us such a duty, and have put energy incessant into the nature of it in vain. We must therefore resolve what is doubtful by what is plain. It is more plain that prayer is duty, and more known than what changes the nature of God can admit.

3. The argument of God's unchangeableness would conclude as well against the usefulness of any other duty, that never so directly concerns our salvation.

4. Prayer is to be considered, not only as a means to obtain from God what we would have, but as a becoming homage of an intelligent creature.

5. Whatsoever unchangeableness we can suppose in the nature of God, [here there is something added in the manuscript I can make nothing of, and then it follows,] and is unreasonable he should lose his right by his perfection.

6. Yet also it is to be considered as a means to obtain good things Job xxi. 15, [by which I suppose it was intended to be intimated, that it would be very wicked language in any, to offer to say with those whom Job speaks of in the text cited, "What is the Almighty, that we should serve him? and what profit shall we have if we pray unto him?"]

7. We are not to think prayer, though never so qualified, hath any proper efficacy, to move God this way or that: not so much as instrumental.

8. It is only a condition upon which it seems good to God to put forth His power.

9. It is a condition that hath not always equally certain connexion with the thing we pray for, or other than the promise hath made.

10. The promises of God are, or must be, understood proportionably to the nature of the thing promised: which may be either of such a nature as, etc. [Here the sense is incomplete. I suppose that which may be meant, is, that the things which God has promised, may either admit or exclude a change. And then it is added] make men immortal. [That is, I suppose, as to this present life. And then the manuscript goes on.] Things of a variable goodness cannot be the matter of an universal absolute promise, miracles, etc.

11. Prayer may yet be the prayer of faith that God will do what is best. We should not make light of this more valuable object of faith. Suppose two children; which is the most privileged. [This, I apprehend, refers to the case of Esau and Jacob, so often taken notice of in Scripture.]

12. If God will do the thing, prayer in reference to it is not vain. For perhaps he hath wisely and rightly determined that he will not do it but upon trust of his being acknowledged. This is a great piece of his sovereignty; his dominion and power over lives. "I kill, and make alive;" q.d., God of every life Universal Cause.

13. It is very absurd to think, it were vain to pray unless we were certain. It contradicts the nature of prayer. For that supposes the thing in power of them to whom we pray, and implies a referring it to their pleasure.

14. It must be submitted to him to judge what is most honourable for himself. It argues base thoughts of the invisible world, to think, etc., [that is, I suppose, to think we should be able to keep people from thence at our pleasure.]

15. What if he had said, Pray not, [I take this to be designed for an intimation, that had intercourse between an all-sufficient God and us, by prayer, been prohibited, we should have been left in a very helpless and hopeless, miserable and destitute condition.]

No. VI.

The following letter of Howe's I found amongst the MSS. in the Ayscough Catalogue, British Museum. As it has no date, and as the circumstances and the parties alluded to are quite unknown, I thought it better to insert it in the Appendix than in the body of the work.

"*For the Rev. Mr. Thomas Whitaker, at Leeds, Yorkshire.*

"WORTHY SIR,

"I deferred writing back to yours, having, before I received it, made it my request to friends at Newcastle, that they would return me copies of what I wrote thither, or my own again; whereof the haste wherein I wrote allowed me not to transcribe any. I hoped they would have granted that request, which had made my writing back to you easier, and, perhaps, clearer. I wish you could obtain from them a sight of what I wrote, whereby you would collect what I can now but summarily tell you, that I am very sure I did write nothing tending to animate Mr. B^r. to the course of dividing or disturbing that church of Christ: which he was only invited and (by the common Christian rule) obliged to prove.

"It being acknowledged to me, by some who are now grieved at his spirit and conduct, that they had pressed him to be ordained, [I said] I knew not to what office in the church they could mean he should be ordained, to which the power of dispensing the seals of the covenant belonged not: that even constant feeding of the flock by office was pastoral work: that I knew no reason why the name of co-pastor should be scrupled, whereof the Christian church (even primitive, as well as of later time) afforded frequent instances: that yet we were too apt to amuse ourselves and one another about names, when about the things they most truly signify it was less possible to disagree: that yet the *word co-pastors* could by no means always signify *equal* pastors: that though the office was the same, and could not be unequal to itself, yet in the acts and exercise of that office, there might be, and, in some cases, ought to be great *inequality*. That in this case, as much as any, there ought to be inequality, when the peace, satisfaction, and consequent edification of the church depended thereon: that some yielding to Mr. B^r. was better than a rupture: but yet, if his terms were grossly unreasonable, or opposite to the more general [sense] of the church, and he were more for a breach than [healing], I reckoned such an affectation of * * * * did so slur his character, and was so disagreeable to a gospel minister, that I could not advise they should close with him on any terms; and that his absence was much more desirable. I pray God direct and heal you.

"Dear Sir,
"Your very respectful Brother in Christ,
"John Howe."

I have also copied from the MSS. in Dr. Williams's Library, a long and very tedious letter, the whole of which, for the following reasons, I do not think it worth while to insert. Baxter, it is well known, wrote a recommendatory preface to the " Blessedness of the Righteous." Before he allowed it to appear, he wrote to Howe for a more full explication of his views on certain points connected with the economy of grace, on which he had touched in the first part of his work. As the sentiments which Howe's reply contains may be found in the work itself, (indeed, he proposes that they should be appended to the preface, from which they were probably transposed into the body of the work in subsequent editions,) and as the letter itself was written in great haste, and is in Howe's worst style, I shall suppress by far the greater part of it; merely inserting the few paragraphs which tend to throw any light on his personal history, or on his connexion with Baxter at this period.

"Most dear and Reverend Sir,

"It is a renewed argument of your very condescending spirit, that you yet detain so kind a remembrance of one, who am conscious to myself never to have deserved any place in your friendship. Nor could you have expressed that undeserved friendly respect by any more acceptable or endearing medium, than in the endeavour of your late letter, that I may not in anything wrong the truth or the church of God; which I am the more concerned to be tender of, by how much I am less capable of doing unto either any real or considerable service. I did, indeed, some months since, intimate to my friend, Mr. Fairclough, then in the city, (and by whom I treated with Mr. Thompson,) my hope, that if he desired it, for the better sale of my book, you might be procured to recommend the subject and design of it: and promised upon that supposition to write to you for that purpose. But having since received a letter from Mr. Thompson, wherein he said nothing of it, I had laid aside these thoughts, judging the affectation of such a testimony, on my account, onght rather to be checked and suppressed than complied with. Since I now find he hath applied himself to you, and that you are pleased to discover an inclination to that charitable office, I shall accept it from you with gratitude, hoping it may induce some to the reading of it with the better preconceived opinion, and so with more advantage.

"Your letter finds me in a journey, whence I cannot very speedily return to my study, or have the opportunity of viewing what I wrote in the passage you refer to. I remember not my words, but am sure those of Mr. Gilbert, (though if he be the same, that wrote the animadversions on Dr. Owen's '*Diatribe de Justif: Dei vindicate:*' I esteem him a man of much worth,) that no sins of the regenerate *incur* the *guilt* of eternal punishment, and that Christ died *only* to prevent that guilt, not to pardon it actually, is very alien to my settled formed judgment.

* * * * * * *

"This is a hasty account of my thoughts in this matter, as indeed that was in my book; for I wrote them upon former apprehensions having heretofore read '*Grot. de Satisf.*,' with most of what you have published on any such subject, and divers others, but not for ten years before; and had scarce any such book at hand, nor had the opportunity of consulting any such at that time.

"If there be any difference in my apprehensions from yours, I conceive it is very little momentous, and that the enclosed paper subjoined to my preface, may serve to clear my meaning. I tender you my affectionate thanks for this friendly advertisement, and your further offered assistance for promoting the success of that poor labour of, Sir,

"Your obliged, though very unworthy fellow Servant

In the work of Christ,

"JOHN HOWE.

"Plymouth, June 2, 1668."

No. VII.

The following unpublished letter of Howe, written in reply to some question of "Church order," propounded to him by a meeting of ministers in the North of England, has been forwarded to me by the Rev. James Turner, of Knutsford, who copied it from a book in the possession of a gentleman in that town. The preamble to the letter is not without interest, as illustrating in some measure the proceedings of the Nonconformist "synods" of those times.

"The first meeting of ministers was in March, 1690-1, at Macclesfield. Dr. Eaton began with prayer, afterwards the case relating to the gesture to be used by the minister in the administration of the Lord's Supper was debated, there being present, Mr. Sam. Angier, Dr. Eaton, Eliezer Birch, Thos. Kinaston, Jno. Byrom, —Stringer, Thos. Irlam, Jn. Sidebottom, G. Jones. Mr. Angier concluded, and another meeting was appointed to be at Lawrence Downs's, April ye 14, 1691.

"Then the case above-mentioned being before undetermined, was reassumed, and Mr. Howe's letter, in the name of the London ministers relating to that affair, read and approved of, and recommended to the congregation at Macclesfield, as expedient to settle the matter, a copy of which here followeth:—

"'SIR,

"'A case was propounded this day among divers ministers which I was (privately) told was yours, viz., that some of your society scrupled to receive the Lord's Supper, otherwise than as having the elements delivered immediately to them by your own hand.

"'Two things in reference hereto agreed unanimously—

"'1. That they might very lawfully and fittly passe from hand to hand, which the rule forbids not; and (if we may judge by parity of reason) seems rather to favour; and herein the constant practice of the Church of Scotland hath long concurred, and still doth.

"'2. However, that it being a matter of indifferency, you ought to offend none herein, nor impose a thing not determined expressly by rule as a condition of Church communion, and therefore to let such as desire it from your own hand be placed near you (successively if not altogether, as it is the manner in Holland to fill the table successively). This may be done with you if one table will not receive at once all that are unsatisfied to receive otherwise: That so none may be deprived of so needful a privilege needlessly, either through their own weakness or the want of that indulgence thereto which their case may require, and in this advice the brethren that were consulted formerly of both persuasions, Presbyterial and Congregational, (though now there is no such distinction with us,) were most unanimous, and it was left to be communicated to you by

"'Your affectionate Brother
"'and fellow Servant,

"'London, April 6, 1691.'" "'JOHN HOWE.

"Afterwards the agreement of the London ministers was read over, and ordered to be read again the next meeting."

The following brief letters, hitherto unpublished, have been procured from the Bodleian Library, through the courtesy of the Librarian, Mr. H. O. Coxe. The allusions in them are not very intelligible.

"SIR,

"I have sent you inclosed the receipt you desired, and have no more (in so much haste) to add, but to desire you to tender my most humble duty and service to my honoured Lord and the excellent Lady Russell, and represent me to the worthy gentlemen as their humble servant, not omitting my hearty salutations to Mr. Bingley, with my other friends, whom I gave so much trouble to of late, among whom you had no little share, as you ought and have, of the cordial thanks of,

"Worthy Sir,
"Your obliged affectionate Servant,

"London, May 26, '84." "J. HOWE.
    (No address.)

"Reverend and worthy Sir,

"I hope you were going on some other account that way, when you called at my house; otherwise, you had not balked both the days on which I have often told you I am never absent (unless on some very extraordinary account), Thursday and Saturday. *Hæc per jocum.* But to be serious. The person I recommended for Preston will not be the man. As for Mr. Lorain, if you can procure my Lord Stamford's recommendation of him to the Mayor of Preston (into whose hands with some other, Sir Charles Hoghton hath devolved the power of electing), it is likely to signify much. But herein no mention must be made of Sir Charles, nor of

"Your affectionate humble Servant,

"Feb. 23, 1708.   "John Howe.

"If my Lord of Stamford will be prevailed with, my Lord Duke's own name will carry a great weight, if his Grace think fit to add it."

(Endorsed) "For the Rev. Mr. Thornton, Chaplain to his Grace the Duke of Bedford, Bedford House, in the Strand."

No. VIII.

Dedications and Prefaces of Howe not contained in any edition of his Works.

Preface to the Funeral Sermon for the Rev. Henry Newcome,
of Manchester, by John Chorlton.

"To the Christian Reader, especially such as lived under the excellent Mr. Newcome's most fruitful ministry.

"Two things come under present consideration—the following discourse, and the occasion of it. There is nothing to make the former unacceptable, but the latter. You have, here, a most sublime portion of Scripture very aptly explained, and usefully applied, so as to minister light and warmth to them that read. That only in the whole which is grievous is, that we are told worthy Mr. Newcome is dead! This is a gloomy theme, and is only capable of a more lightsome, pleasant aspect, from the brightness of the firmament, and the lustre of the stars, into which so wise and powerful preachers of the glorious gospel are at length transformed, as this discourse excellently shows. In the meantime, this is a loss which few can estimate, though they that suffer it are very many. It may be truly said of such a man, as unknown, and yet well known. They that knew him best, could know but a small part of his true and great worth, and might always apprehend, when they knew most of him, there was still much more that they knew not; his most sincere and inartificial humility, still drawing a veil over his other excellencies, which it hid and adorned at once; so as the appetite of knowing more, must always meet with a check, and an incitation at the same time. There was in him a large stock of solid learning and knowledge, always ready for use; for ostentation, never. Conscience the most strict, and steady to itself, and the remotest from censoriousness of other men. Eloquence without any labour of his own, not imitable by the greatest labour of another. Oh, the strange way he had of insinuating and winding himself into his hearers' bosoms! I have sometimes heard him when the only thing to be regretted was, that the sermon must so soon be at an end. Conversation, so facetious and instructive together, that they who enjoyed it, if they were capable of improving it, could scarce tell whether they went away from him more edified or delighted. He was a burning and a shining light. O Manchester, Manchester! that ancient, famed seat of religion and profession, may Capernaum's doom never be thine! May thy Heyrick, Hollingworth, Newcome, and thy neighbours, Angier, Harrison, and divers more, never be witnesses against thee! They are dead! 'And all flesh is grass, and the word of the Lord endureth for ever,' even that word of the gospel which hath by them been presented to you. It never dies. And may it still abide with you, and in you. O labour to hold forth the word of life, that such as have laboured among you, 'may rejoice in the day of Christ, that they have not run in vain, nor laboured in vain.' Let it appear you are the 'epistles of Christ ministered by them, to be known and read of all men;' so what there appeared of Christ in them will, as in another edition, be seen in you. And thus will the memory of this your last deceased pastor be best preserved among you, when you shall every one discern Mr. Newcome still, in each other's savoury speech, pleasant and composed looks, becoming behaviour, and regular well-ordered conversation. This will make the love of him live still in your hearts, which will no doubt appear, and be exercised towards any of his, you have yet surviving among you, to whom you may show kindness for his sake. Thus you may let the world know your love to him did not die with him, nor was buried in his grave. You will by real proofs testify your value of him whose circumstances at last gave real proof that he sought not yours, but you. I pray God a double portion of Elijah's spirit may rest upon your remaining Elisha.

"And am
"Yours in our common Lord,
"J. Howe."

It has been stated in the narrative, that after Howe had signed the unwise attestation to the *genuineness* of Dr. Crisp's posthumous sermons, he promised Baxter that he would append his name to a recommendatory preface to Flavel's "Blow at the Root; or, the Causes and Cure of Mental Errors." This he did accordingly, in conjunction with six other gentlemen who had signed the attestation to Dr. Crisp's Sermons. His own name stands first. I have little doubt that he drew up the "Preface." I have no doubt, also, that he drew up the "Paper" on the same subject, which he tells us was "printed soon after the publication of Dr. Crisp's works;" and from which the writer of the Preface has largely cited. The internal evidence—the peculiarities of the style—and the *spirit* which pervades these compositions—all favour the supposition that Howe was the author. Still, as I cannot be *certain* of the fact, and as the Preface with the above extracts is somewhat lengthy, I have thought it better to omit it.

I shall close the volume with the following

DEDICATION PREFIXED TO THE THIRD VOLUME OF
DR. MANTON'S WORKS:

"To the High and Mighty Prince William, by the Grace of God King of
England, France, and Ireland, etc.

"MAY IT PLEASE YOUR MAJESTY,

" This relic of the worthy deceased author was long since intended, when
you were at a greater distance, to be sent abroad under the patronage of your
great name. His own name indeed hath long been, and still continues, so
bright and fragrant in England, that your Majesty's condescending goodness
will count it no indignity to yours, to impart some of its more diffused beams
and odours to it. However, if what there was of presumption in that first intention can be pardoned, no reason can be apprehended of altering it upon your
nearer and most happy approach unto us.

" The kind design and blessed effect whereof (compared with the scope and
design of this excellent work) do much the more urgently invite to it. For as
you come to us with the compassionate design of a deliverer and the wonderful
blessing of Heaven hath rendered you also a victor and a successful deliverer;
the design of this book is to represent that faith, which is the peculiar and
most appropriate principle of what is (like your own) the most glorious of all
victories. You have overcome, not by the power of your arms, but by the
sound of your name, and by your goodness and kindness, which so effectually
first conquered minds, as to leave you no opportunity of using the other more
harsh and rugged means of conquest. Yea, and your success is owing to a
greater name than yours; our case, and the truth of the thing, allow and
oblige us in a low and humble subordination to apply those sacred words,
'Blessed is he that cometh to us in the name of the Lord.' The power of
which glorious name is wont to be exerted according as a trust is placed in it.
We acknowledge and adore a most conspicuous Divine presence with you in this
undertaking of yours, which is not otherwise to be engaged than by that faith,
of which the apostle and this author do here treat. This faith, we are elsewhere
told, overcomes this world; and are told here in what way,—by representing
another, with the invisible Lord of both worlds; being the substance of what
we hope for, and the evidence of what we see not, and whereby we see him who
is invisible. This world is not otherwise to be conquered than as it is an enemy;
it is an enemy by the vanities, lusts, and impurities of it. That faith which
foresees the end of this world; which beholds it as a vanishing thing, passing
away with all the lust of it; which looks through all time, and contemplates
all the affairs and events of this temporary state, as under the conduct and
management of an all-wise and almighty invisible Ruler; which penetrates
into eternity, and discovers another world and state of things which shall be
unchangeable and of everlasting permanency, and therein beholds the same
invisible glorious Lord, as a most gracious and bountiful rewarder of such as
serve and obey him with sincere fidelity in this state of trial and temptation
here on earth; such a faith, cannot but be victorious over the lusts, vanities,
impurities, and sensualities of this present evil world. Such a faith working
by love to God, and good men, and all mankind, and being thereupon fruitful
in the good works of piety, sobriety, righteousness, and charity, will be the
great reformer of the world, conquer its malignity, reduce its disorders, and
infer an universal harmony and peace.

" Even among us, the noblest part of your Majesty's conquest is yet behind.
It cannot but have been observed, that for many years by-past, a design hath
been industriously driven, that we might be made papists, to make us slaves;
and for the enslaving us, to debauch us, and plunge us into all manner of sensuality; from a true apprehension, that brute and slave are nearest akin, and that

there is a sort of men so vile and abject, (as the ingenious expression of a great man among the Romans once was) *quos non decet esse nisi servos*, to whom liberty were an indecency; and who should be treated unbecomingly, if they were not made slaves; that we should be fit to serve the lusts and humours of any other man, when once we become servile to our own. And next, that the religion might easily be wrested away from us, which was become so weak and impotent as not to be able to govern us : and that if humanity were eradicated, the principles and privileges that belong to our nature torn from us, easy work would be made with our Christianity and religion. What hath been effected among us by so laboured a design, through a long tract of time, is before you as the matter of your remaining victory; which as on our part it will be the more difficult, where the pernicious humour is inveterate; so your Majesty's part herein will be most easy, your great example being, under the supreme power, the mover, the potent engine which is to effect the hoped redress; and your more principal contribution hereunto consisting but in being yourself, in express-ing the virtue, prudence, goodness, and piety, which God hath wrought in your temper. The design of saying this is not flattery, but excitation. Give me leave to lay before your Majesty somewhat that occurs in a book written twenty-seven years ago, not by way of prophecy, but probable conjecture of the way wherein a blessed state of things in these parts of the world is likely to be brought about.

" 'God will stir up some happy king or governor in some country of Chris-tendom, endued with wisdom and consideration, who shall discern the true nature of godliness and Christianity, and the necessity and excellency of serious religion, and shall place his honour and felicity in pleasing God and doing good, and attaining everlasting happiness ; and shall subject all worldly respects unto these high and glorious ends ; shall know that godliness and justice have the most precious name on earth, and prepare for the most glorious reward in heaven,' etc.

" With how great hopes and joy must it fill every upright heart, daily (as they do) to behold in your Majesty and in your Royal Consort (whom a Divine hand hath so happily placed with you on the same throne) the same lively characters of this exemplified idea ! It cannot but inspire us with such pleasant thoughts, that winter is well-nigh gone, and the time of singing of birds approaches ; the night is far spent, and the day is at hand, a bright and glorious morning triumphs over the darkness of a foul tempestuous night ; the sober serious age now commences, when sensuality, falsehood, cruelty, oppres-sion, the contempt of God and religion, are going out of fashion ; to be a noted debauchee, of a vicious life and dishonest mind, capable of being swayed to serve ill purposes without hesitation, will no longer be thought a man's praise or a qualification for trusts. It shall be no disreputable thing to profess the fear of God, and the belief of a life to come. A scenical unserious religion, a spurious adulterated Christianity, made up of doctrines repugnant to the sacred oracles, to sound reason, and even to common sense, with idolatrous and lu-dicrous formalities, and which hate the light, shall vanish before it. There shall be no more strife about unnecessary circumstances ; grave decencies in the worship of God, that shall be self-recommending and command a veneration in every conscience, shall take place. There shall be no contention amongst Christians, but who shall most honour God and our Redeemer, do most good in the world, and most entirely love, and effectually befriend and serve one another ; which are all things most connatural to that vivid, realizing, victorious faith here treated of.

" Nor are other victories alien to it over the armed powers of God's visible enemies in the world, such as he may yet call your Majesty with glorious suc-cess to encounter in his name, and for the sake of it. In some following verses of this chapter (wherein the line of the apostle's discourse went beyond that of this worthy author's life) this is represented as the powerful instrument which

those great heroes employed in their high achievements of ' subduing kingdoms, working righteousness, (or executing God's just revenges upon his unyielding enemies) obtaining promises, stopping the mouths of lions, quenching
the violence of fire, escaping the edge of the sword, whereby out of weakness
they were made strong, waxed valiant in fight, turned to flight the armies of the
aliens ;'—by this *faith*, they in the prophet's lofty style,[1] as it were 'bathed
their sword in heaven,' gave it a celestial tincture, made it resistless and penetrating.   This is the true way, wherein (according to the divinest philosophy)
the spirit of a man may draw into consent with itself the universal almighty
Spirit.   And if the glorious Lord of Hosts shall assign to your Majesty a
farther part in the employments of this noble kind, may he gird you with
might unto the battle ; may your bow abide in strength, and the arms of ' your
hands be made strong by the hands of the mighty God of Jacob,' even by the
God of your fathers, who shall help you, and by the Almighty who shall bless
you ; and may he most abundantly bless you ' with blessings of heaven above,
blessings of the deep that lyeth under, blessings of the breasts and of the
womb.'   May he cover your head in fight, and crown it with victory and glory,
and grant you to know, by use and trial, the power of that faith, in all its operations, which unites God with man, and can render, in a true and sober sense,
and to all his own purposes, a human arm omnipotent.   Which is the serious
prayer of,

" Your Majesty's most devoted
" And most humble Servant and Subject,
" JOHN HOWE."

---

* Isa. xxxiv. 5.

THE END.

Butler & Tanner, The Selwood Printing Works, Frome, and London.

A NEW EDITION

OF THE

WORKS OF JOHN HOWE,

Printed on fine paper in Demy 8vo.

THIS Edition includes the *Life* by Mr. HENRY ROGERS, revised by the Author. The same gentleman, who was long impressed with the conviction that the uncouthness of many parts of Howe's writings might be at least considerably diminished, and his pages made more *readable*, by a careful revision of the punctuation (which was very faulty in the early editions, and has much fluctuated in the later), consented to attempt its revision throughout, and, in order to secure a correct text, compared the printer's proofs with editions of the several works published in Howe's lifetime. Beyond the changes of punctuation, however, and the adoption of modern forms of orthography, etc., no alterations whatever have been made; one of the objects of the Editor being to insure the utmost possible accuracy in the text. A preface to the first volume of the " Works," by Mr. Rogers, more fully explains the nature and extent of the improvements attempted in this Edition.

It is not probable that the Society would have engaged in an undertaking of this magnitude had there been, when they entered upon it, any immediate prospect of its being prosecuted by private enterprise. But the failure of one laudable attempt (owing to causes which had nothing to do with any doubts of the expediency of the object itself) made it very uncertain whether any new effort would be made; and there being a strong desire in many to see the works

A A

of JOHN HOWE in a form and type worthy of him, the Society thought they would be conferring a boon on the religious public generally, but especially on Christian ministers of every name, by preparing the present Edition for the press. They may add, that it is at a price which, considering the paper, style of printing, etc., every reader will admit to be very cheap.

The Society have contented themselves with printing only those works which Howe himself published, and prepared for the press, *i.e.* all that is contained in Calamy's two folio volumes. Whether they shall afterwards extend the issue to what are generally called Howe's "posthumous works"—which are exceedingly unequal, most of them inferior in value, and some of them mere reports of his Sermons published many years after his death—will depend entirely on whether the public shall express a desire to have them. If that should be the case, the present issue, which is confined to six volumes (exclusive of the Life), may be extended.

Each volume consists of from 460 to 510 pages on the average, price 5s.

BIBLICAL WORKS

PUBLISHED BY

THE RELIGIOUS TRACT SOCIETY.

Heaven taken by Storm ; or, The holy violence the Christian is to put forth in the pursuit after Glory. By Rev. THOMAS WATSON. A.D. 1699. 18mo. 1*s.* boards ; 1*s.* 6*d.* half-bound.

The History of Redemption. By PRESIDENT EDWARDS. A.D. 1739. New edition. 2*s.* 6*d.* cloth boards ; 3*s.* 6*d.* half-bound.

Human Nature in its Fourfold State. By the Rev. T. BOSTON. A.D. 1720. 18mo. 2*s.* 6*d.* cloth boards ; 3*s.* 6*d.* half-bound.

The Crook in the Lot. By the Rev. T. BOSTON. A.D. 1753. 1*s.* cloth boards ; 1*s.* 6*d.* half-bound.

On Indwelling Sin in Believers. By Rev. JOHN OWEN. A.D. 1691. 18mo. 1*s.* 6*d.* cloth boards ; 2*s.* half-bound.

Discourses on the Glory of Christ, in His Person, Offices, and Grace. By Rev. JOHN OWEN. A.D. 1691. 18mo. 1*s.* 4*d.* cloth boards ; 1*s.* 6*d.* half-bound.

Mistakes in Religion Exposed. By Rev. H. VENN. A.D. 1774. 32mo. 1*s.* cloth boards ; 1*s.* 4*d.* half-bound ; 3*s.* morocco.

The Mortification of Sin in Believers. By Rev. JOHN OWEN. A.D. 1691. 18mo. 1*s.* cloth boards ; 1*s.* 6*d.* half-bound.

The Power and Grace of Christ. By PHILIP DODDRIDGE, D.D. 18mo. 1*s.* 6*d.* cloth boards ; 2*s.* half-boards.

A Practical View of Christianity. By WILLIAM WILBER-FORCE. 18mo. 1*s.* 6*d.* cloth boards.

On the Religious Affections. By PRESIDENT EDWARDS. A.D. 1739. 18mo. 2*s.* cloth boards ; 3*s.* half-bound.

The Rock of Ages ; or, Scripture Testimony to the One Eternal Godhead of the Father, and of the Son, and of the Holy Ghost. By the Rev. E. H. BICKERSTETH, M.A. Crown 8vo. 4*s.* cloth boards.

The Spirit of Life ; or, Scripture Testimony to the Divine Person and Work of the Holy Spirit. By the Rev. E. H. BICKERSTETH, M.A. Crown 8vo. 4*s.* cloth boards.

The Saint's Everlasting Rest. By RICHARD BAXTER. A.D. 1650. 18mo. 1*s.* 6*d.* cloth boards ; 2*s.* 6*d.* half-bound.

Christ set forth in His Death, Resurrection, etc. By THOMAS GOODWIN. A.D. 1679. 1*s.* 6*d.* cloth boards ; 2*s.* 6*d.* half-bound.

The Outpouring of the Holy Spirit. By JOHN HOWE. 1*s.* 6*d.* cloth boards.

The Divine Glory of Christ. By Dr. C. J. BROWN, of Edinburgh. New edition. Crown 8vo. 2*s.* cloth boards.

The Soul's Life ; its Commencement, Progress, and Maturity. By the Rev. Canon GARBETT, M.A. Crown 8vo. 4*s.* 6*d.* cloth boards.

God's Word Written: the Doctrine of the Inspiration of the Holy Scriptures Explained and Enforced. By the Rev. Canon GARBETT. Crown 8vo. 4s. 6d. cloth boards.

The Plant of Grace. By the Rev. C. STANFORD. 16mo. 8d. cloth.

The Throne of Grace. By ROBERT TRAILL. A.D. 1696. 18mo. 1s. 6d. cloth boards; 2s. 6d. half-bound.

The Way of Life. By CHARLES HODGE, D.D., Professor in the Theological Seminary, Princeton. 18mo. 1s. 6d. cloth boards; 2s. 6d. half-bound.

DIVINITY—PRACTICAL AND EXPERIMENTAL.

Experiences of the Inner Life. Lessons from its Duties, Joys, and Conflicts. By the Rev. Canon GARBETT. A Sequel to " The Soul's Life." Crown 8vo. 3s. 6d. cloth boards.

Religion in Daily Life. By the Rev. Canon GARBETT, M.A. Fcap. 8vo. 2s. 6d. cloth boards; 6s. morocco.

Before the Cross. A Book of Devout Meditation. By the Right Rev. J. H. TITCOMB, D.D., Bishop of Rangoon. Crown 8vo. 2s. 6d. cloth boards, red edges.

Working for Jesus; or, Individual Effort for the Salvation of Precious Souls. By J. A. R. DICKSON. 16mo. 8d. cloth boards.

The Golden Diary of Heart Converse with Jesus in the Book of Psalms. Arranged for every Sunday in the Year. By ALFRED EDERSHEIM, D.D., author of " The Temple and its Services," " The Bible History," etc. New and revised edition. 4s. cloth gilt.

The Home at Bethany: its Joys, its Sorrows, and its Divine Guest. By the Rev. J. CULROSS, M.A., D.D. Crown 8vo. 2s. 6d. cloth boards.

The Christian Voyage. By the Rev. T. CAMPBELL FINLAYSON. Crown 8vo. 2s. cloth boards.

Acceptable Words. Collected and arranged by S. M. L. Fcap. 8vo. 2s. 6d. cloth boards.

THE WISDOM OF OUR FATHERS.

EACH VOLUME CONTAINS A MEMOIR.

Bound in glazed cloth, red edges, 15s. the set. Either volume may be had separately, 2s. 6d.

1. **Selections from Archbishop Leighton.**
2. **Selections from Lord Bacon.**
3. **Selections from Thomas Fuller.**
4. **Selections from Isaac Barrow.**
5. **Selections from Robert South.**
6. **Selections from Stephen Charnock.**